HEIR TO THE SHADOWS

The Black Jewels Trilogy
Book II

ANNE BISHOP

RoC

A ROC BOOK

ROC
Published by New American Library, a division of
Penguin Group (USA) Inc., 375 Hudson Street,
New York, New York 10014, USA
Penguin Group (Canada), 90 Eglinton Avenue East, Suite 700, Toronto,
Ontario M4P 2Y3, Canada (a division of Pearson Penguin Canada Inc.)
Penguin Books Ltd., 80 Strand, London WC2R 0RL, England
Penguin Ireland, 25 St. Stephen's Green, Dublin 2,
Ireland (a division of Penguin Books Ltd.)
Penguin Group (Australia), 250 Camberwell Road, Camberwell, Victoria 3124,
Australia (a division of Pearson Australia Group Pty. Ltd.)
Penguin Books India Pvt. Ltd., 11 Community Centre, Panchsheel Park,
New Delhi - 110 017, India
Penguin Group (NZ), 67 Apollo Drive, Rosedale, North Shore 0632,
New Zealand (a division of Pearson New Zealand Ltd.)
Penguin Books (South Africa) (Pty.) Ltd., 24 Sturdee Avenue,
Rosebank, Johannesburg 2196, South Africa

Penguin Books Ltd., Registered Offices:
80 Strand, London WC2R 0RL, England

First published by Roc, an imprint of New American Library,
a division of Penguin Group (USA) Inc.

First Printing, April 1999
30 29 28 27 26 25 24 23 22

Copyright © Anne Bishop, 1999
All rights reserved

ROC REGISTERED TRADEMARK—MARCA REGISTRADA

Printed in the United States of America

PUBLISHER'S NOTE
This is a work of fiction. Names, characters, places, and incidents either are
the product of the author's imagination or are used fictitiously, and any resem-
blance to actual persons, living or dead, business establishments, events, or
locales is entirely coincidental.

The publisher does not have any control over and does not assume any
responsibility for author or third-party Web sites or their content.

Praise for the novels of Anne Bishop

Heir to the Shadows

"A wonderful story . . . amply peopled with
interesting and nearly always dangerous characters."
—*Romance Reader*

"Bishop seems to delight in turning fantasy
conventions on their heads . . . still darkly opulent,
often exotic."
—*Locus*

Daughter of the Blood

"Anne Bishop has scored a hit with *Daughter of the
Blood*. Her poignant storytelling skills are
surpassed only by her . . . deft characterization. A
talented author."
—*Affaire de Coeur*

"Vividly painted . . . dramatic, erotic, hope-filled. A
promising debut."
—Lynn Flewelling, author of *Stalking Darkness*

"A fabulous new talent . . . a uniquely realized
fantasy filled with vibrant colors and rich textures.
A wonderful new voice, Ms. Bishop holds us
spellbound from the very first page."
—*Romantic Times* (4½ stars)

"Lavishly sensual . . . a richly detailed world based
on a reversal of standard genre clichés."
—*Library Journal*

"Mystical, sensual, glittering with dark magic, Anne
Bishop's debut novel brings a strong new voice to
the fantasy field."
—Terri Windling, coeditor of
The Year's Best Fantasy and Horror

continued

Queen of the Darkness

"As engaging, as strongly characterized, and as fully conceived as its predecessors . . . a perfect—and very moving—conclusion."   —SF Site

"A storyteller of stunning intensity, Ms. Bishop has a knack for appealing but complex characterization realized in a richly drawn, imaginative ambience."
                    —*Romantic Times*

"A powerful finale for this fascinating, uniquely dark trilogy."   —*Locus*

The Invisible Ring

"Entertaining otherworlds fantasy adventure. Fresh and interesting."   —*Science Fiction Chronicles*

"A weird, but highly diverting and oddly heartwarming mix."   —*Locus*

"A formidable talent, Ms. Bishop weaves another intense, emotional tale that sparkles with powerful and imaginative magic."   —*Romantic Times*

"Plenty of adventure; romance . . . ; dazzling wizardly pyrotechnics . . . and [a] unique and fascinating hierarchical magic system. . . . [T]he author's overall sublime skill . . . [blends] the darkly macabre with spine-tingling emotional intensity, mesmerizing magic, lush sensuality, and exciting action, all set in a thoroughly detailed, invented world of cultures in conflict. . . . [*The Invisible Ring*] and its predecessors are genuine gems of fantasy much to be prized."
                    —Rambles

for
Nadine Fallacaro
a sister of the heart

ACKNOWLEDGMENTS

Thanks to Blair Boone for patiently answering my questions about hunting and weapons. Hopefully the information remained somewhat accurate after I tampered with it. A cheer for Karen Borgenicht, Nancy Alden, Linda Bovino, and the rest of the gang at weight-training class. And a special thanks to the other sisters of the heart: Lorna Czarnota, Merri Lee Debany, Annemarie Jason, and Pat York.

JEWELS

White

Yellow

Tiger Eye

Rose

Summer-sky

Purple Dusk

Opal*

Green

Sapphire

Red

Gray

Ebon-gray

Black

*Opal is the dividing line between lighter and darker Jewels because it can be either.

When making the Offering to the Darkness, a person can descend a maximum of three ranks from his/her Birthright Jewel.

Example: Birthright White could descend to Rose.

AUTHOR'S NOTE

The "Sc" in the names Scelt, Sceval, and Sceron is pronounced "Sh."

BLOOD HIERARCHY/CASTES

Males:

landen—non-Blood of any race

Blood male—a general term for all males of the Blood; also refers to any Blood male who doesn't wear Jewels

Warlord—a Jeweled male equal in status to a witch

Prince—a Jeweled male equal in status to a Priestess or a Healer

Warlord Prince—a dangerous, extremely aggressive Jeweled male; in status, slightly lower than a Queen

Females:

landen—non-Blood of any race

Blood female—a general term for all females of the Blood; mostly refers to any Blood female who doesn't wear Jewels

witch—a Blood female who wears Jewels but isn't one of the other hierarchical levels; also refers to any Jeweled female

Healer—a witch who heals physical wounds and illnesses; equal in status to a Priestess and a Prince

Priestess—a witch who cares for altars, Sanctuaries, and Dark Altars; witnesses handfasts and marriages; performs offerings; equal in status to a Healer and a Prince

Black Widow—a witch who heals the mind; weaves the tangled webs of dreams and visions; is trained in illusions and poisons

Queen—a witch who rules the Blood; is considered to be the land's heart and the Blood's moral center; as such, she is the focal point of their society

PROLOGUE

Kaeleer

The Dark Council reconvened.

Andulvar Yaslana, the demon-dead Eyrien Warlord Prince, folded his dark wings and assessed the other Council members, not liking what he saw. Except for the Tribunal, who had to attend, only two-thirds of the members were required at each session to listen to petitions or pass judgment when disputes occurred between the Blood in Kaeleer that couldn't be settled by the Territory Queens. Tonight every chair was filled, except the one beside Andulvar.

But the chair's occupant was also there, standing patiently in the petitioner's circle, waiting for the Council's answer. He was a brown-skinned, golden-eyed man, with thick black hair that was silvered at the temples. Seeing him leaning on the elegant, silver-headed cane, one might simply have said he was a handsome Blood male at the end of his prime. His long, black-tinted nails and the Black-Jeweled ring on his right hand said otherwise.

First Tribune quietly cleared his throat. "Prince Saetan Daemon SaDiablo, you stand before the Council requesting guardianship of the child Jaenelle Angelline. You did not, as is customary in a Blood dispute, provide us with the information needed to contact the girl's family so that they could come here and speak on their own behalf."

"They don't want the child," was the quiet reply. "I do."

"We have only your word on that, High Lord."

Fools, Andulvar thought, watching the barely perceptible rise and fall of Saetan's chest.

First Tribune continued. "The most troubling aspect of this petition is that you're a Guardian, one of the living dead, and yet you want us to place the welfare of a living child into your hands."

"Not just any child, Tribune. *This* child."

First Tribune shifted uneasily in his chair. His eyes swept over the tiered seats on both sides of the large room. "Because of the . . . unusual . . . circumstances, the decision will have to be unanimous. Do you understand?"

"I understand, Tribune. I understand very well."

First Tribune cleared his throat again. "A vote will now be taken on the petition of Saetan Daemon SaDiablo for the guardianship of the child Jaenelle Angelline. Those opposed?"

A number of hands went up, and Andulvar shuddered at the peculiar, glazed look in Saetan's eyes.

After the hands were counted, no one spoke, no one moved.

"Take the vote again," Saetan said too softly.

When First Tribune didn't respond, Second Tribune touched his arm. Within seconds, there was nothing in First Tribune's chair but a pile of ash and a black silk robe.

Mother Night, Andulvar thought as he watched body after opposing body crumble. *Mother Night.*

"Take the vote again," Saetan said too gently.

It was unanimous.

Second Tribune rubbed her hand over her heart. "Prince Saetan Daemon SaDiablo, the Council hereby grants you all paternal—"

"Parental. All *parental* rights."

"—all parental rights to the child Jaenelle Angelline, from this hour until she reaches her majority in her twentieth year."

As soon as Saetan bowed to the Tribunal and began the long walk down the room, Andulvar left his seat and opened the large double doors at the far end of the Council chamber. He sighed with relief when Saetan, leaning heavily on his silver-headed cane, slowly walked past him.

It wasn't over, Andulvar thought as he closed the doors and followed Saetan. The Council would be more subtle next time in opposing the High Lord, but there *would* be a next time.

When they finally stepped out into the fresh night air, Andulvar turned to his longtime friend. "Well, she's yours now."

Saetan lifted his face to the night sky and closed his golden eyes. "Yes, she's mine."

PART 1

CHAPTER
ONE

1 / Terreille

Surrounded by guards, Lucivar Yaslana, the half-breed Eyrien Warlord Prince, walked into the courtyard, fully expecting to hear the order for his execution. There was no other reason for a salt mine slave to be brought to this courtyard, and Zuultah, the Queen of Pruul, had good reason to want him dead. Prythian, the High Priestess of Askavi, still wanted him alive, still hoped to turn him to stud. But Prythian wasn't standing in the courtyard with Zuultah.

Dorothea SaDiablo, the High Priestess of Hayll, was.

Lucivar spread his dark, membranous wings to their full span, taking advantage of Pruul's desert air to let them dry.

Lady Zuultah glanced at her Master of the Guard. A moment later, the Master's whip whistled through the air, and the lash cut deep into Lucivar's back.

Lucivar hissed through his clenched teeth and folded his wings.

"Any other acts of defiance will earn you fifty strokes," Zuultah snapped. Then she turned to confer with Dorothea SaDiablo.

What was the game? Lucivar wondered. What had brought Dorothea out of her lair in Hayll? And who was the angry Green-Jeweled Prince who stood apart from the women, clutching a folded square of cloth?

Cautiously sending out a psychic probe, Lucivar caught all the emotional scents. From Zuultah, there was excitement and the usual underlying viciousness. From Dorothea, a sense of urgency and fear. Beneath the unknown Prince's anger was grief and guilt.

Dorothea's fear was the most interesting because it meant that Daemon Sadi had not been recaptured yet.

A cruel, satisfied smile curled Lucivar's lips.

Seeing the smile, the Green-Jeweled Prince became hostile. "We're wasting time," he said sharply, taking a step toward Lucivar.

Dorothea spun around. "Prince Alexander, these things must be do—"

Philip Alexander opened the cloth, holding two corners as he spread his arms wide.

Lucivar stared at the stained sheet. So much blood. Too much blood. Blood was the living river—and the psychic thread. If he sent out a psychic probe and touched that stain . . .

Something deep within him stilled and became brittle.

Lucivar forced himself to meet Philip Alexander's hostile stare.

"A week ago, Daemon Sadi abducted my twelve-year-old niece and took her to Cassandra's Altar, where he raped and then butchered her." Philip flicked his wrists, causing the sheet to undulate.

Lucivar swallowed hard to keep his stomach down. He slowly shook his head. "He couldn't have raped her," he said, more to himself than to Philip. "He can't. . . . He's never been able to perform that way."

"Maybe it wasn't bloody enough for him before," Philip snapped. "This is Jaenelle's blood, and Sadi was recognized by the Warlords who tried to rescue her."

Lucivar turned reluctantly toward Dorothea. "Are you sure?"

"It came to my attention—unfortunately, too late—that Sadi had taken an unnatural interest in the child." Dorothea lifted her shoulders in an elegant little shrug. "Perhaps he took offense when she tried to fend off his attentions. You know as well as I do that he's capable of anything when enraged."

"You found the body?"

Dorothea hesitated. "No. That's all the Warlords found." She pointed at the sheet. "But don't take my word for it. See if even you can stomach what's locked in that blood."

Lucivar took a deep breath. The bitch was lying. She *had* to be lying. Because, sweet Darkness, if she wasn't . . .

Daemon *had* been offered his freedom in exchange for killing Jaenelle. He had refused the offer—or so he had said. But what if he *hadn't* refused?

A moment after he opened his mind and touched the bloodstained sheet, he was on his knees, spewing up the meager breakfast he'd had an hour before, shaking as something deep within him shattered.

Damn Sadi. Damn the bastard's soul to the bowels of Hell. She was a *child*! What could she have done to deserve this? She was Witch, the living myth. She was the Queen they'd dreamed of serving. She was his spitting little Cat. *Damn you, Sadi!*

The guards hauled Lucivar to his feet.

"Where is he?" Philip Alexander demanded.

Lucivar closed his gold eyes so that he wouldn't have to see that sheet. He had never felt this weary, this beaten. Not as a half-breed boy in the Eyrien hunting camps, not in the countless courts he'd served in over the centuries since, not even here in Pruul as one of Zuultah's slaves.

"Where is he?" Philip demanded again.

Lucivar opened his eyes. "How in the name of Hell should I know?"

"When the Warlords lost the trail, Sadi was heading southeast—toward Pruul. It's well-known—"

"He wouldn't come here." That shattered something deep within him began to burn. "He wouldn't dare come here."

Dorothea SaDiablo stepped toward him. "Why not? You've helped each other in the past. There's no reason—"

"There *is* a reason," Lucivar said savagely. "If I ever see that cold-blooded bastard again, I'll rip his heart out!"

Dorothea stepped back, shaken. Zuultah watched him warily.

Philip Alexander slowly lowered his arms. "He's been declared rogue. There's a price on his head. When he's found—"

"He'll be suitably punished," Dorothea broke in.

"He'll be executed!" Philip replied heatedly.

There was a moment of heavy silence.

"Prince Alexander," Dorothea purred, "even someone from Chaillot should know that, among the Blood, there is no law against murder. If you didn't have sense enough to prevent an emotionally disturbed child from toying with a Warlord Prince of Sadi's temperament . . ." She shrugged delicately. "Perhaps the child got what she deserved."

Philip paled. "She was a good girl," he said, but his voice trembled with a whisper of doubt.

"Yes," Dorothea purred. "A good girl. So good your family had to send her away every few months to be . . . reeducated."

Emotionally disturbed child. The words were a bellows, stoking the fire within Lucivar to ice-cold rage. Emotionally disturbed child. *Stay away from me, Bastard. You'd better stay away. Because if I have the chance, I'll carve you into pieces.*

At some point, Zuultah, Dorothea, and Philip had withdrawn to continue their discussion in the cooler recesses of Zuultah's house. Lucivar didn't notice. He was barely aware of being led into the salt mines, barely aware of the pick in his hands, barely aware of the pain as his sweat ran into the new lash wound on his back.

All he saw was the bloodstained sheet.

Lucivar swung the pick.

Liar.

He didn't see the wall, didn't see the salt. He saw Daemon's golden-brown chest, saw the heart beating beneath the skin.

Silky . . . court-trained . . . *liar!*

2 / Hell

Andulvar settled one hip on a corner of the large, black-wood desk.

Saetan glanced up from the letter he was composing. "I thought you were going back to your eyrie."

"Changed my mind." Andulvar's gaze wandered around

the private study, finally stopping at the portrait of Cassandra, the Black-Jeweled Queen who had walked the Realms more than 50,000 years ago. Five years ago, Saetan had discovered that Cassandra had faked the final death and had become a Guardian in order to wait for the next Witch.

And look what had happened to the next Witch, Andulvar thought bleakly. Jaenelle Angelline was a powerful, extraordinary child, but still as vulnerable as any other child. All that power hadn't kept her from being overwhelmed by family secrets he and Saetan could only guess at, and by Dorothea's and Hekatah's vicious schemes to eliminate the one rival who could have ended their stranglehold on the Realm of Terreille. He was certain they had been behind the brutality that had made Jaenelle's spirit flee from her body.

Too late to prevent the violation, a friend had taken Jaenelle away from her destroyers and brought her to Cassandra's Altar. There, Daemon Sadi, with Saetan's help, had been able to bring the girl out of the psychic abyss long enough to convince her to heal the physical wounds. But when the Chaillot Warlords arrived to "rescue" her, she panicked and fled back into the abyss.

Her body was slowly healing, but only the Darkness knew where her spirit was—or if she would ever come back.

Pushing aside those thoughts, Andulvar looked at Saetan, took a deep breath, and puffed his cheeks as he let it out. "Your letter of resignation from the Dark Council?"

"I should have resigned a long time ago."

"You had always insisted that it was good to have a few of the demon-dead serving in the Council because they had experience but no personal interest in the decisions."

"Well, my interest in the Council's decisions is very personal now, isn't it?" After signing his name with his customary flourish, Saetan slipped the letter into an envelope and sealed it with black wax. "Deliver that for me, will you?"

Andulvar reluctantly took the envelope. "What if the Dark Council decides to search for her family?"

Saetan leaned back in his chair. "There hasn't been a

Dark Council in Terreille since the last war between the Realms. There's no reason for Kaeleer's Council to look beyond the Shadow Realm."

"If they check the registers at Ebon Askavi, they'll find out she wasn't originally from Kaeleer."

"As the Keep's librarian, Geoffrey has already agreed not to find any useful entries that might lead anyone back to Chaillot. Besides, Jaenelle was never listed in the registers—and won't be until there's a reason to include an entry for her."

"You'll be staying at the Keep?"

"Yes."

"For how long?"

Saetan hesitated. "For as long as it takes." When Andulvar made no move to leave, he asked, "Is there something else?"

Andulvar stared at the neat masculine script on the front of the envelope. "There's a demon in the receiving room upstairs who has asked for an audience with you. He says it's important."

Saetan pushed his chair away from the desk and reached for his cane. "They all say that—when they're brave enough to come at all. Who is he?"

"I've never seen him before," Andulvar said. Then he added reluctantly, "He's new to the Dark Realm, and he's from Hayll."

Saetan limped around the desk. "Then what does he want with me? I've had nothing to do with Hayll for seventeen hundred years."

"He wouldn't say why he wants to see you." Andulvar paused. "I don't like him."

"Naturally," Saetan replied dryly. "He's Hayllian."

Andulvar shook his head. "It's more than that. He feels tainted."

Saetan became very still. "In that case, let's talk to our Hayllian Brother," he said with malevolent gentleness.

Andulvar couldn't suppress the shudder that ran through him. Fortunately, Saetan had already turned toward the door and hadn't noticed. They'd been friends for thousands of years, had served together, laughed together, grieved together. He didn't want the man hurt because, at times, even a friend feared the High Lord of Hell.

But as Saetan opened the door and looked at him, Andulvar saw the flicker of anger in his eyes that acknowledged the shudder. Then the High Lord left the study to deal with the fool who was waiting for him.

The recently demon-dead Hayllian Warlord stood in the middle of the receiving room, his hands clasped behind his back. He was dressed all in black, including a black silk scarf wrapped around his throat.

"High Lord," he said, making a respectful bow.

"Don't you know even the basic courtesies when approaching an unknown Warlord Prince?" Saetan asked mildly.

"High Lord?" the man stammered.

"A man doesn't hide his hands unless he's concealing a weapon," Andulvar said, coming into the room. He spread his dark wings, completely blocking the door.

Fury flashed over the Warlord's face and was gone. He extended his arms out in front of him. "My hands are quite useless."

Saetan glanced at the black-gloved hands. The right one was curled into a claw. There was one finger missing on the left. "Your name?"

The Warlord hesitated a moment too long. "Greer, High Lord."

Even the man's name somehow fouled the air. No, not just the man, although it would take a few weeks for the rotting-meat stink to fade. Something else. Saetan's gaze drifted to the black silk scarf. His nostrils flared as he caught a scent he remembered too well. So. Hekatah still favored that particular perfume.

"What do you want, Lord Greer?" Saetan asked, already certain he knew why Hekatah would send someone to see him. With effort, he hid the icy rage that burned within him.

Greer stared at the floor. "I . . . I was wondering if you had any news about the young witch."

The room felt so deliciously cold, so sweetly dark. One thought, one flick of his mind, one brief touch of the Black

Jewels' strength and there wouldn't be enough left of that Warlord to be even a whisper in the Darkness.

"I rule Hell, Greer," Saetan said too softly. "Why should I care about a Hayllian witch, young or otherwise?"

"She wasn't from Hayll." Greer hesitated. "I had understood you were a friend of hers."

Saetan raised one eyebrow. "I?"

Greer licked his lips. The words rushed out. "I was assigned to the Hayllian embassy in Beldon Mor, the capital of Chaillot, and had the privilege of meeting Jaenelle. When the trouble started, I betrayed the High Priestess of Hayll's trust by helping Daemon Sadi get the girl to safety." His left hand fumbled with the scarf around his neck and finally pulled it away. "This was my reward."

Lying bastard, Saetan thought. If he didn't have his own use for this walking piece of carrion, he would have ripped through Greer's mind and found out what part the man had *really* played in this.

"I knew the girl," Saetan snarled as he walked toward the door.

Greer took a step forward. "Knew her? Is she . . ."

Saetan spun around. "She walks among the *cildru dyathe*!"

Greer bowed his head. "May the Darkness be merciful."

"Get out." Saetan stepped aside, not wanting to be fouled by any contact with the man.

Andulvar folded his wings and escorted Greer from the Hall. He returned a few minutes later, looking worried. Saetan stared at him, no longer caring that the rage and hatred showed in his eyes.

Andulvar settled into an Eyrien fighting stance, his feet apart to balance his weight, his wings slightly spread. "You know that statement will spread through Hell faster than the scent of fresh blood."

Saetan gripped the cane with both hands. "I don't give a damn who else he tells as long as that bastard tells the bitch who sent him."

"He said that? He really said that?"

Slumped in the only chair in the room, Greer nodded wearily.

Hekatah, the self-proclaimed High Priestess of Hell, twirled around the room, her long black hair flying out behind her as she spun.

This was even better than simply destroying the child. Now, with her torn mind and torn, dead body, the girl would be an invisible knife in Saetan's ribs, always twisting and twisting, a constant reminder that he wasn't the only power to contend with.

Hekatah stopped spinning, tipped her head back, and flung her arms up in triumph. "She walks among the *cildru dyathe!*" Sinking gracefully to the floor, she leaned against an arm of Greer's chair and gently stroked his cheek. "And you, my sweet, were responsible for that. She's of no use to him now."

"The girl is no longer useful to you either, Priestess."

Hekatah pouted coquettishly, her gold eyes glittering with malice. "No longer useful for my original plans, but she'll be an excellent weapon against that gutter son of a whore."

Seeing Greer's blank expression, Hekatah rose to her feet, slapping the dust from her gown as she *tsked* in irritation. "Your body is dead, not your mind. Do try to think, Greer darling. Who else was interested in the child?"

Greer sat up and slowly smiled. "Daemon Sadi."

"Daemon Sadi," Hekatah agreed smugly. "How pleased do you think he'll be when he finds out his little darling is so very, very dead? And who, with a little help, do you think he'll blame for her departure from the living? Think of the fun pitting the son against the father. And if they destroy each other"—Hekatah opened her arms wide— "Hell will fragment once more, and the ones who were always too frightened to defy him will rally around me. With the strength of the demon-dead behind us, Terreille will finally kneel to me as *the* High Priestess, as it would have done all those many, many centuries ago if that bastard hadn't always thwarted my ambition."

She looked around the small, almost-empty room in distaste. "Once he's gone, I'll reside again in the splendor that's my due. And you, my faithful darling, will serve at my side.

"Come," she said, guiding him into another small room. "I realize the body's death is a shock . . ."

Greer stared at the boy and girl cowering in a pile of straw.

"We're demons, Greer," Hekatah said, stroking his arm. "We need fresh, hot blood. With it, we can keep our dead flesh strong. And although some pleasures of the flesh are no longer possible, there are compensations."

Hekatah leaned against him, her lips close to his ear. "Landen children. A Blood child is better but more difficult to come by. But dining on a landen child also has compensations."

Greer was breathing fast, as if he needed air.

"A pretty little girl, don't you think, Greer? At your first psychic touch, her mind will burn to hot ash, but primitive emotions will remain . . . long enough . . . and fear is a delicious dinner."

3 / Terreille

You are my instrument.

Daemon Sadi shifted restlessly on the small bed that had been set up in one of the storage rooms beneath Deje's Red Moon house.

. . . *you are my instrument* . . . riding the Winds to Cassandra's Altar . . . Surreal already there, crying . . . Cassandra there, angry . . . so much blood . . . his hands covered with Jaenelle's blood . . . descending into the abyss . . . falling, screaming . . . a child who wasn't a child . . . a narrow bed with straps to tie down hands and feet . . . a sumptuous bed with silk sheets . . . the Dark Altar's cold stone . . . black candles . . . scented candles . . . a child screaming . . . his tongue licking a tiny spiral horn . . . his body pinning hers to cold stone while she fought and screamed . . . begging her to forgive him . . . but what had he done? . . . a golden mane . . . his fingers tickling a fawn tail . . . a narrow bed with silk sheets . . . a sumptuous bed with straps . . . *forgive me, forgive me* . . . his body pinning her down . . . what had he done? . . .

Cassandra's anger cutting him . . . was she safe? . . . was she well? . . . a sumptuous stone bed . . . silk sheets with straps . . . a child screaming . . . so much blood . . . *you are my instrument . . . forgive me, forgive me* . . . WHAT HAD HE DONE?

Surreal sagged against the wall and listened to Daemon's muffled sobs. Who would have suspected that the Sadist could be so vulnerable? She and Deje knew enough basic healing Craft to heal his body, but neither of them knew how to fix the mental and emotional wounds. Instead of becoming stronger, he was becoming more fragile, vulnerable.

For the first few days after she had brought him here, he had kept asking what had happened. But she could tell him only what she knew.

With the help of the demon-dead girl, Rose, she had entered Briarwood, killed the Warlord who had raped Jaenelle, and then had taken Jaenelle to the Sanctuary called Cassandra's Altar. Daemon had joined her at the Sanctuary. Cassandra was there, too. Daemon had ordered them out of the Altar room in order to have privacy to try to bring Jaenelle's Self back to her body. Surreal had used that time to set traps for Briarwood's "rescue party." When the males arrived, she had held them off for as long as she could. By the time she'd retreated to the Altar room, Cassandra and Jaenelle were gone and Daemon could barely stand. She and Daemon had ridden the Winds back to Beldon Mor and had spent the last three weeks hiding in Deje's Red Moon house.

That's all she could tell him. It wasn't what he needed to hear. She couldn't tell him he had saved Jaenelle. She couldn't tell him the girl was safe and well. And it seemed like the more he struggled to remember, the more fragmented the memories became. But he still had the strength of the Black Jewels, still had the ability to unleash all of that dark power. If he lost his tenuous hold on sanity . . .

Surreal turned at the sound of a stealthy footfall on the stairs at the end of the dim passageway. The sobs behind the closed door stopped.

Moving swiftly, silently, Surreal cornered the woman at the bottom of the stairs. "What do you want, Deje?"

The dishes on the tray Deje was carrying rattled as the woman's body shook. "I—I thought—" She lifted the tray in explanation. "Sandwiches. Some tea. I—"

Surreal frowned. Why was Deje staring at her breasts? It wasn't the look of an efficient matron sizing up one of the girls. And why was Deje shaking like that?

Surreal looked down. Her clenched hand was holding her favorite stiletto, its tip resting against the Gray Jewel that hung on its gold chain above the swell of her breasts. She hadn't been aware of calling in the stiletto or of calling in the Gray. She had been annoyed with the intrusion, but . . .

Surreal vanished the stiletto, pulled her shirt together to hide the Jewel, and took the tray from Deje. "Sorry. I'm a bit edgy."

"The Gray," Deje whispered. "You wear the Gray."

Surreal tensed. "Not when I'm working in a Red Moon house."

Deje didn't seem to hear. "I didn't know you were that strong."

Surreal shifted the tray's weight to her left hand and casually let her right hand drop to her side, her fingers curled around the stiletto's comforting weight. If it had to be done, it would be fast and clean. Deje deserved that much.

She watched Deje's face while the woman mentally rearranged the bits of information she knew about the whore named Surreal, who was also an assassin. When Deje finally looked at her, there was respect and dark satisfaction in the woman's eyes.

Then Deje looked at the tray and frowned. "Best use a warming spell on that tea or it won't be fit to drink."

"I'll take care of it," Surreal said.

Deje started back up the stairs.

"Deje," Surreal said quietly. "I do pay my debts."

Deje gave her a sharp smile and nodded at the tray. "You try to get some food into him. He's got to get his strength back."

Surreal waited until the door at the top of the stairs

clicked shut before returning to the storage room that held, perhaps now more than ever, the most dangerous Warlord Prince in the Realm.

Late that evening, Surreal opened the storage room's door without knocking and pulled up short. "What in the name of Hell are you doing?"

Daemon glanced up at her before tying his other shoe. "I'm getting dressed." His deep, cultured voice had a rougher edge than usual.

"Are you mad?" Surreal bit her lip, regretting the word.

"Perhaps." Daemon fastened his ruby cuff links to his white silk shirt. "I have to find out what happened, Surreal. I have to find *her*."

Exasperated, Surreal scraped her fingers through her hair. "You can't leave in the middle of the night. Besides, it's bitter cold out."

"The middle of the night is the best time, don't you think?" Daemon replied too calmly, shrugging into his black jacket.

"No, I don't. At least wait until dawn."

"I'm Hayllian. This is Chaillot. I'd be a bit too conspicuous in daylight." Daemon looked around the empty little room, lifted his shoulders in a dismissive shrug, took a comb from his coat pocket, and pulled it through his thick black hair. When he was done, he slipped his elegant, long-nailed hands into his trouser pockets and raised an eyebrow as if asking, Well?

Surreal studied the tall, trim but muscular body in its perfectly tailored black suit. Sadi's golden-brown skin was gray-tinged from exhaustion, his face looked haggard, and the skin around his golden eyes was puffy. But even now he was still more beautiful than a man had a right to be.

"You look like shit," she snapped.

Daemon flinched, as if her anger had cut him. Then he tried to smile. "Don't try to turn my head with compliments, Surreal."

Surreal clenched her hands. The only thing to throw at him was the tray with the tea and sandwiches on it. Seeing

the clean cup and the untouched food ignited her temper.
"You fool, you didn't eat anything!"

"Lower your voice unless you want everyone to know
I'm here."

Surreal paced back and forth, snarling every curse she
could remember.

"Don't cry, Surreal."

His arms were around her, and beneath her cheek was
cool silk.

"I'm not crying," she snapped, gulping back a sob.

She felt rather than heard his chuckle. "My mistake."
His lips brushed her hair before he stepped away from her.

Surreal sniffed loudly, wiped her eyes on her sleeve, and
pushed her hair from her face. "You're not strong enough
yet, Daemon."

"I'm not going to get any better until I find her," Daemon said quietly.

"Do you know how to open the Gates?" she asked.
Those thirteen places of power linked the Realms of Terreille, Kaeleer, and Hell.

"No. But I'll find someone who does know." Daemon
took a deep breath. "Listen, Surreal, and listen well. There
are very few people in the entire Realm of Terreille who
can connect you in any way with me. I've made the effort
to make sure of that. So unless you stand on the roof and
announce it, no one in Beldon Mor will have a reason to
look in your direction. Keep your head down. Keep a rein
on that temper of yours. You've done more than enough.
Don't get yourself in any deeper—because I won't be
around to help you out of it."

Surreal swallowed hard. "Daemon . . . you've been declared rogue. There's a price on your head."

"Not unexpected after I broke the Ring of Obedience."

Surreal hesitated. "Are you sure Cassandra took Jaenelle
to one of the other Realms?"

"Yes, I'm sure of that much," he said softly, bleakly.

"So you're going to find a Priestess who knows how to
open the Gates and follow them."

"Yes. But I have one stop to make first."

"This isn't a good time for social calls," Surreal said tartly.

"This isn't exactly a social call. Dorothea can't use you against me because she doesn't know about you. But she knows about him, and she's used him before. I'm not going to give her the chance. Besides, for all his arrogance and temper, he's a damn good Warlord Prince."

Weary, Surreal leaned against the wall. "What are you going to do?"

Daemon hesitated. "I'm going to get Lucivar out of Pruul."

4 / Kaeleer

Saetan appeared on the small landing web carved into the stone floor of one of the Keep's many outer courtyards. As he stepped off the web, he looked up.

Unless one knew what to look for, one only saw the black mountain called Ebon Askavi, only felt the weight of all that dark stone. But Ebon Askavi was also the Keep, the Sanctuary of Witch, the repository of the Blood's long, long history. A place well and fiercely guarded. The perfect place for a secret.

Damn Hekatah, he thought bitterly as he slowly crossed the courtyard, leaning heavily on his cane. *Damn her and her schemes for power. Greedy, malicious bitch.* He'd stayed his hand in the past because he felt he owed her something for bearing his first two sons. But that debt had been paid. More than paid. This time, he would sacrifice his honor, his self-respect, and anything else he had to if that was the price he had to pay to stop her.

"Saetan."

Geoffrey, the Keep's historian/librarian, stepped from the shadow of the doorway. As always, he was neatly dressed in a slim black tunic and trousers and bare of any ornamentation except his Red Jewel ring. As always, his black hair was carefully combed back, drawing a person's eyes to the prominent widow's peak. But his black eyes looked like small lumps of coal instead of highly polished stone.

As Saetan walked toward him, the vertical line between Geoffrey's black eyebrows deepened. "Come to the library and have a glass of yarbarah with me," Geoffrey said.

Saetan shook his head. "Later perhaps."

Geoffrey's eyebrows pulled down farther, echoing his widow's peak. "Anger has no place in a sickroom. Especially now. Especially yours."

The two Guardians studied each other. Saetan looked away first.

Once they were settled into comfortable chairs and Geoffrey had poured a warmed glass of the blood wine for each of them, Saetan forced himself to look at the large blackwood table that dominated the room. It was usually piled with history, Craft, and reference books Geoffrey had pulled from the stacks—books the two men had searched for touchstones to understand Jaenelle's casual but stunning remarks and her sometimes quirky but awesome abilities. Now it was empty. And the emptiness hurt.

"Have you no hope, Geoffrey?" Saetan asked quietly.

"What?" Geoffrey glanced at the table, then looked away. "I needed . . . occupation. Sitting there, each book was a reminder, and . . ."

"I understand." Saetan drained his glass and reached for his cane.

Geoffrey walked with him to the door. As Saetan went into the corridor, he felt a light, hesitant touch and turned back.

"Saetan . . . do you still hope?"

Saetan considered the question for a long moment before giving the only answer he could give. "I have to."

Cassandra closed her book, rolled her shoulders wearily, and scrubbed her face with her hands. "There's no change. She hasn't risen out of the abyss—or wherever it is she's fallen. And the longer she remains beyond the reach of another mind, the less chance we have of ever getting her back."

Saetan studied the woman with dusty-red hair and tired emerald eyes. Long, long ago when Cassandra had been Witch, the Black-Jeweled Queen, he had been her Consort and had loved her. And she, in her own way, had cared for him—until he made the Offering to the Darkness and walked away wearing Black Jewels. After that, it was more a trading of skills—his in the bed for hers in the Black Widow's Craft—until she faked her own death and became a Guardian. She had played her deathbed scene so well, and his faith in her as a Queen had been so solid, it had never occurred to him that she had done it to end her reign as Witch—and to get away from him.

Now they were united again.

But as he put his arms around her, offering her comfort, he felt that inner withdrawal, that suppressed shudder of fear. She never forgot he walked dark roads that even she dared not travel, never forgot that the Dark Realm had called him High Lord while he still had been fully alive.

Saetan kissed Cassandra's forehead and stepped away. "Get some rest," he said gently. "I'll sit with her."

Cassandra looked at him, glanced at the bed, and shook her head. "Not even you can make the reach, Saetan."

Saetan looked at the pale, fragile girl lying in a sea of black silk sheets. "I know."

As Cassandra closed the door behind her, he wondered if, despite the terrible cost, she derived some small satisfaction from that fact.

He shook his head to clear his mind, pulled the chair closer to the bed, and sighed. He wished the room weren't so impersonal. He wished there were paintings to break up the long walls of polished black stone. He wished there was a young girl's clutter scattered on the blackwood furniture. He wished for so much.

But these rooms had been finished shortly before that nightmare at Cassandra's Altar. Jaenelle hadn't had the chance to imprint them with her psychic scent and make them her own. Even the small treasures she'd left here hadn't been lived with enough, handled enough to make them truly hers. There was no familiar anchor here for her to reach for as she tried to climb out of the abyss that was part of the Darkness.

Except him.

Resting one arm on the bed, Saetan leaned over and

gently brushed the lank golden hair away from the too-thin face. Her body *was* healing, but slowly, because there was no one inside to help it mend. Jaenelle, his young Queen, the daughter of his soul, was lost in the Darkness—or in the inner landscape called the Twisted Kingdom. Beyond his reach.

But not, he hoped, beyond his love.

With his hand resting on her head, Saetan closed his eyes and made the inner descent to the level of the Black Jewels. Slowly, carefully, he continued downward until he could go no further. Then he released his words into the abyss, as he had done for the past three weeks.

You're safe, witch-child. Come back. You're safe.

5 / Terreille

A hand caressed his arm, gently squeezed his shoulder.

Lucivar's temper flared at being pulled from the little sleep his pain-filled body permitted him each night. The chains that tethered his wrists and ankles to the wall weren't long enough for him to lie down and stretch out, so he slept crouched, his buttocks braced against the wall to ease the strain in his legs, his head resting on his crossed forearms, his wings loosely folded around his body.

Long nails whispered over his skin. The hand squeezed his shoulder a little harder. "Lucivar," a deep voice whispered, husky with frustration and weariness. "Wake up, Prick."

Lucivar raised his head. The moonlight coming through the cell's window slit wasn't much to see by, but it was enough. He looked at the man bending over him and, for just a moment, was glad to see his half brother. Then he bared his teeth in a feral smile. "Hello, Bastard."

Daemon released Lucivar's shoulder and stepped back, wary. "I've come to get you out of here."

Lucivar slowly rose to his feet, snarling softly at the noise the chains made. "The Sadist showing consideration? I'm touched." He lunged at Daemon, but the leg irons hobbled his stride, and Daemon glided away, just out of reach.

"Not a very enthusiastic greeting, brother," Daemon said softly.

"Did you really expect a greeting at all, *brother*?" Lucivar spat.

Daemon ran his fingers through his hair and sighed. "You know why I couldn't do anything to help you before now."

"Yes, I know why," Lucivar replied, his deep voice changing to a lethal croon. "Just as I know why you came here now."

Daemon turned away, his face hidden in the shadows.

"Do you really think setting me free will make up for it, Bastard? Do you really think I'll ever forgive you?"

"You have to forgive me," Daemon whispered. Then he shuddered.

Lucivar narrowed his gold eyes. There was an unexpected fragility in Daemon's psychic scent. At another time, it would have worried him. Now he saw it as a weapon. "You shouldn't have come here, Bastard. I swore I'd kill you if you accepted that offer, and I will."

Daemon turned to face him. "What offer?"

"Maybe trade is a better word. Your freedom for Jaenelle's life."

"I didn't accept that offer!"

Lucivar's hands closed into fists. "Then you killed her for the fun of it? Or didn't you realize she was dying under you until it was too late?"

They stared at each other.

"What are you talking about?" Daemon asked quietly.

"Cassandra's Altar," Lucivar answered just as quietly while his rage swelled, threatening to break his self-control. "You got careless this time. You left the sheet—and all that blood."

Swaying, Daemon stared at his hands. "So much blood," he whispered. "My hands were covered with it."

Tears stung Lucivar's eyes. "Why, Daemon? What did she do to deserve being hurt like that?" His voice rose. He couldn't stop it. "She was the Queen we had dreamed of serving. We had waited for her for so long. *You butchering whore, why did you have to kill her?*"

Daemon's eyes filled with a dangerous warning. "She's not dead."

Lucivar held his breath, wanting to believe. "Then where is she?"

Daemon hesitated, looked confused. "I don't know. I'm not sure."

Pain tore through Lucivar as fiercely as it had after he had probed the dried blood on the sheet. "You're not sure," he sneered. "You. The Sadist. Not sure where you buried the kill? Try a better lie."

"She's not dead!" Daemon roared.

There was a shout nearby, followed by the sound of running feet.

Daemon raised his right hand. The Black Jewel flashed. Outside the stables where the slaves were quartered, someone let out an agonized shriek. And then there was silence.

Knowing it wouldn't take that long for the guards to find enough courage to enter the stables, Lucivar bared his teeth and pushed to find a crippling weak spot. "Did you just throw her down and take her? Or did you seduce her, lie to her, tell her you loved her?"

"I *do* love her." Daemon's eyes held a shadow of doubt, a hint of fear. "I had to lie. She wouldn't listen to me. I had to lie."

"And then you seduced her to get close enough for the kill."

Daemon exploded into motion. He paced the small cell, fiercely shaking his head. "No," he said through gritted teeth. "No, no, *no!*" He spun around, grabbed Lucivar's shoulders, and shoved him against the wall. "Who told you she was dead? WHO?"

Lucivar snapped his arms up, breaking Daemon's grip. "Dorothea."

Pain flashed over Daemon's face. He stepped back. "Since when do you listen to Dorothea?" he asked bitterly. "Since when do you believe that lying bitch?"

"I don't."

"Then why—"

"Words lie. Blood doesn't." Lucivar waited for Daemon

to absorb the implication. "You left the sheet, Bastard," he said savagely. "All that blood. All that pain."

"Stop," Daemon whispered, his voice shaking. "Lucivar, please. You don't understand. She was already hurt, already in pain, and I—"

"Seduced her, lied to her, raped a twelve-year-old girl."

"No!"

"Did you enjoy it, Bastard?"

"I didn't—"

"Did you enjoy touching her?"

"Lucivar, please—"

"DID YOU?"

"YES!"

With a howl of rage, Lucivar threw himself at Daemon with enough force to snap the chains—but not fast enough. He crashed to the floor, scraping the skin from his palms and knees. It took a minute for him to get his breath back. It took another minute for him to understand why he was shivering. He stared at the thick layer of ice that covered the cell's stone walls. Then he slowly got to his feet, swaying on shaking legs, feeling a bitterness so deep it lacerated his soul.

Daemon stood nearby, his hands in his trouser pockets, his face an expressionless mask, his golden eyes slightly glazed and sleepy.

"I hate you," Lucivar whispered hoarsely.

"At the moment, *brother*, the feeling is very mutual," Daemon said too calmly, too gently. "I'm going to find her, Lucivar. I'm going to find her just to prove she isn't dead. And after I find her, I'm going to come back and tear out your lying tongue."

Daemon disappeared. The front of the cell exploded.

Lucivar dropped to the floor, his wings tight to his body, his arms protecting his head while pebbles and sand rained down on him.

There were more shouts now. More running feet.

Lucivar sprang to his feet as the guards poured through the opening. He bared his teeth and snarled, his gold eyes shining with rage. The guards took one look at him and backed out of the cell. For the rest of the night, they blocked the opening but didn't try to enter.

Lucivar watched them, his breath whistling through clenched teeth.

He could have fought his way past the guards and followed Daemon. If Zuultah had tried to stop him by sending a bolt of pain through the Ring of Obedience around his organ, Daemon would have unleashed his strength against her. No matter how bitterly they fought with each other, he and Daemon were always united against an outside enemy.

He could have followed and forced the battle that would have destroyed one or both of them. Instead he remained in the cell.

He had sworn that he would kill Daemon, and he would. But he couldn't quite bring himself to destroy his brother. Not yet.

CHAPTER TWO

1 / Terreille

The knocking sounded forceful, urgent.

Dorothea SaDiablo hid her shaking hands in the folds of her nightgown and positioned herself in the middle of her bedroom, her back to the single candle-light that dimly lit the room.

She had been searching for Daemon Sadi for seven months now. In the hard light of day, with her court all around her, she could almost convince herself that he wouldn't come to Hayll, that he would stay in whatever hole he'd found to hide in. But at night, she was certain she would open a door or turn a corner and find him waiting. He would spin out the pain beyond even her imagining, and then he would kill her. The insult underneath that violence was that he wouldn't destroy her for all the things she'd done to him, he would destroy her because of that child.

That damned child. Hekatah's obsession, the High Lord's reappearance, Greer's death, her son Kartane's mysterious illness, Daemon's fury, Lucivar's sudden hatred for his half brother—all of it came back to that girl.

The doorknob turned. The door opened an inch.

"Priestess?" a male voice called softly.

Giddy relief was swiftly replaced by anger. "Come in," she snapped.

Lord Valrik, Dorothea's Master of the Guard, entered the room and bowed. "Forgive the intrusion at this hour,

Priestess, but I felt you should know about this immediately." He snapped his fingers, and two guards entered, holding a man roughly by the arms.

Dorothea stared at the young Hayllian Blood male cowering between the guards. Little more than a boy really. And pretty. Just the way she liked them. Too much the way she liked them.

She took a step toward the youth, pleased at the fear in his glazed eyes. "You don't serve in my court," she purred. "Why are you here?"

"I was sent, Priestess. I was t-told to please you."

Dorothea studied him. The words sounded flat, forced. Not his words at all. There were some kinds of compulsion spells that could force a person into performing a specific set of tasks, even against his will.

She took another step toward him. "Who sent you?"

"He didn't tell me his—"

Before he could finish, Dorothea called in a dagger and drove it into his chest. Her attack was so fast and so vicious, the guards were pulled down with the youth. Then she unleashed the strength of her Red Jewel against his pitifully inadequate inner barriers and burned out his mind, leaving no one, leaving nothing to come back and haunt her.

"Take that to the woodlands beyond the city for whatever wants the carrion," she said through clenched teeth.

The guards grabbed the body and hurried out, Valrik following them.

Dorothea paced, clenching and unclenching her hands. Damn, damn, damn! She should have probed the youth's mind before destroying him so completely, should have found out for certain who had sent him. But this had to be Sadi's work! That bastard was toying with her, trying to wear down her vigilance, trying to catch her off guard.

She hid her face in her shaking hands.

Sadi was out there. Somewhere. Until he was dead. . . . *No!* Not dead. There would be *no* hope of controlling him then, and once he was demon-dead, he would surely join forces with the High Lord. And she had never forgotten the threat Saetan had made, his voice rising out of a swirling nightmare: when Daemon Sadi died, Hayll would die.

Finally exhausted, Dorothea returned to her bed. She hesitated a moment, then extinguished the candle-light completely. There was more safety in full darkness—if there was any safety at all.

Dorothea threw back her cloak's hood and took a deep breath before entering the small sitting room in the old Sanctuary. Hekatah was already sitting before the unlit hearth, her hood pulled up to hide her face. An empty ravenglass goblet sat on the table in front of her.

Dorothea called in a silver flask and set it beside the goblet.

Hekatah let out an annoyed sniff at the size of the flask, but pointed one finger at it. The flask opened and lifted from the table. Its hot, red contents poured into the goblet, which then glided through the air to Hekatah's waiting hand. She drank deeply.

Dorothea clenched her hands and waited. Finally out of patience, she snapped, "Sadi is still on the loose."

"And each day will hone his temper a little more," Hekatah said in that girlish voice that always seemed at odds with her vicious nature.

"Exactly."

Hekatah sighed like a sated woman. "That's good."

"Good?" Dorothea exploded from the chair. "You don't know him!"

"But I do know his father."

Dorothea shuddered.

Hekatah set the empty goblet on the table. "Calm yourself, Sister. I'm weaving a delicious web for Daemon Sadi, a web he won't escape from because he won't want to escape."

Dorothea went back to her chair. "Then he can be Ringed again."

Hekatah laughed softly, maliciously. "Oh, no, he'd be useless to us Ringed. But don't worry. He'll be hunting bigger prey than you." She wagged a finger at Dorothea. "I've been very busy on your behalf."

Dorothea pressed her lips together, refusing to take the bait.

Hekatah waited a minute. "He'll be going after the High Lord."

Dorothea stared. "Why?"

"To avenge the girl."

"But Greer is the one who destroyed her!"

"Sadi doesn't know that," Hekatah said. "By the time I'm done telling him the sad tale of *why* this happened to the girl, the only thing he'll want to do is tear out Saetan's heart. Naturally the High Lord will protest such action."

Dorothea sat back. It had been months since she'd felt this good. "What do you need from me?"

"A troop of guards to help me spring a trap."

"Then I'd better choose males who are expendable."

"Don't concern yourself about the guards. Sadi won't be any threat to them." Hekatah stood up, an unspoken dismissal.

When they were outside, Hekatah said coolly, "You've said nothing about my gift, Sister."

"Your gift?"

"The boy. I'd thought to keep him for myself, but you were entitled to some compensation for losing Greer. He's a most attentive servant."

"You know what to do?" Hekatah said, handing two vials to Greer.

"Yes, Priestess. But are you sure he'll go there?"

Hekatah caressed Greer's cheek. "For whatever reason, Sadi has gone to every Dark Altar, working his way east. He'll go there. It's the only Gate left before the one located near the ruins of SaDiablo Hall." She tapped her fingers against her lips and frowned. "The old Priestess there may be a problem. However, her assistant is a practical girl—a trait one finds in abundance among the less-gifted Blood. You'll be able to deal with her."

"And the old Priestess?"

Hekatah shrugged delicately. "A meal shouldn't be wasted."

Greer smiled, bowed over the hand she held out to him, and left.

Humming, Hekatah performed the first movements of a

court dance. For seven months Daemon Sadi had slipped through her traps, and his retaliation every time he was driven away from a Gate had made even her most loyal servants in the Dark Realm afraid to strike at him. For seven months she had failed. But so had he.

There were very few Priestesses left in Terreille who knew how to open the Gates. Those who hadn't gone into hiding after her first warning had been eliminated.

It had cost her some of her strongest demons, but she'd made sure Sadi never had time to figure out for himself how to light the black candles in the correct sequence to open a Gate. Of course, if he had gone straight to Ebon Askavi, his search would have ended months ago. But she had spent century upon century turning a natural awe of the place into a subtle terror—which wasn't difficult since the one time she had been inside the Keep the place had terrified *her*. Now, *no one* in Terreille would willingly go there to ask for help or sanctuary unless he was desperate enough to risk anything—and most of the time, not even then.

So Sadi, with no safe place to go and no one he could trust, would continue hiding, searching, running. When he finally got to the Gate where she would be waiting, the strain of the past months would make him all the more susceptible to what she'd planned.

"Rule Hell while you can, you gutter son of a whore," she said as she hugged herself. "This time I have the perfect weapon."

2 / Hell

Saetan opened the door of his private study and froze as the Harpy standing in the corridor drew back the bowstring and aimed her arrow at his heart.

"A rather blunt way of requesting an audience, isn't it, Titian?" he asked dryly.

"None of my weapons are blunt, High Lord," the Harpy snarled.

Saetan studied her for a moment before stepping back

into the room. "Come in and say what you've come to say." Leaning heavily on his cane, he limped to the black-wood desk, settled himself on one corner, and waited.

Titian came in slowly, her anger swirling like a winter storm. She stood at the other end of the room, facing him, fearless in her fury, a demon-dead Black Widow Queen of the Dea al Mon. Once more the bowstring was drawn back, the arrow aimed at Saetan's heart.

His patience, already frayed from the unrelenting months, snapped. "Put that thing down before I do something we'll both regret."

Titian didn't waver. "Haven't you already done something you regret, High Lord? Or are you so filled with the pus of jealousy you have no room for regret?"

The walls of the Hall rumbled. "Titian," he said too softly, "I won't warn you again."

Reluctantly, Titian vanished the bow and arrow.

Saetan crossed his arms. "Actually, your forbearance surprises me, Lady. I expected to have this conversation long before now."

Titian hissed. "Then it's true? She walks among the *cildru dyathe*?"

Saetan watched the tension building in her. "And if it is?"

Titian looked at him for one awful moment, then threw back her head and keened.

Saetan stared at her, shaken. He had known the rumor would drift through Hell. He had expected that Titian, like Char, the leader of the *cildru dyathe*, would seek him out. He had expected their fury. Their fury he could face. Their hatred he could accept. But not this.

"Titian," he said, his voice unsteady. "Titian, come here."

Titian continued to keen.

Saetan limped over to her. She didn't seem to notice when he took her in his arms and held her tightly against him. He stroked her long silver hair, and murmured words of sorrow in the Old Tongue.

"Titian," he said gently when the keening faded to a

whimper, "I'm truly sorry for the pain I've caused you, but it couldn't be helped."

Titian buried her fist in his belly and sent him sprawling.

"You're sorry," she snarled as she stormed around the room. "Well, so am I. I'm sorry it was only my fist and not a knife just then. You deserve to be gutted for this! Jealous old man. *Beast!* Couldn't you let her enjoy an innocent romance without tearing her apart out of spite?"

Finally able to catch his breath, Saetan propped himself up on one elbow. "Witch doesn't become *cildru dyathe*, Titian," he said coldly. "Witch doesn't become one of the demon-dead. So tell me which you prefer: that I say she walks among the *cildru dyathe*, or that I leave a vulnerable young girl open to further enemy attacks?"

Titian stopped, an arrested look in her large blue eyes. She leaned over Saetan, searching his face. "Witch can't become demon-dead?"

"No. But you and Char are the only others in Hell who know that."

"I suppose," she said slowly, "that the most convincing way to fool an enemy would be to fool a friend." She considered this for a moment more and offered him a hand up. She retrieved his cane and looked him in the eye. "A Harpy is a Harpy because of the way she died. That made it easy to believe the rumors."

That was more of an apology than he'd thought to get from Titian.

Saetan took the cane from her, grateful for the support. "I'll tell you the same thing I told Char," he said. "If you're still a friend and want to help, there is something you can do."

"What is that, High Lord?"

"Stay angry."

A fire kindled in Titian's eyes. A smile brushed her lips and was gone. "An arrow that just misses would be highly convincing."

Saetan raised one eyebrow and clucked his tongue. "A Dea al Mon witch missing a target?"

Titian shrugged. "Even the Dea al Mon don't always succeed."

"Just in case you miss missing, try not to aim for anything terribly vital," Saetan said dryly.

Titian blinked. The smile brushed her lips again. "There's only one part of a male's anatomy a Harpy aims for, High Lord. How terribly vital do you consider it?"

"Go," Saetan said.

Titian bowed and left.

Saetan stared at the study door for a moment before limping to a chair. He sank into it with a sigh, stretching out his legs. A minute later he left the study, making his way through the corridors to the upper rooms in the Hall, hoping Mephis or Andulvar would be around.

He wanted company. Male company.

Having Titian for a friend didn't make a man feel comfortable.

3 / Terreille

In the moonlight, the lawn was a ghostly silver rippled by the wind. Throughout the hot midsummer's day, storm clouds had been piling up on the horizon, and thunder had rumbled in the distance.

Surreal buttoned her jacket and hugged herself for warmth. The air had turned cold. An hour from now the storm would break over Beldon Mor. But she would be back at Deje's Red Moon house by then, the guest of honor at her quiet retirement dinner.

After that night at Cassandra's Altar, she had discovered that she no longer had the stomach for playing the bed, not even when it would have made a kill easier. She wouldn't starve if she gave up whoring. Lord Marcus, Sadi's man of business, also handled her investments and handled them well. Besides, she'd always preferred being an assassin to being a whore.

Surreal shook her head. She could think about that later.

Moving silently through the small shrub garden that backed the lawn, she reached the large tree with the branch that was perfect for a swing. Something hung from that branch, but it wasn't a child's toy.

Surreal looked up, trying to feel the ghostly presence, trying to see the transparent shape.

"You won't find her," a girl's voice said. "Marjane is gone."

Surreal spun around and stared at the girl with the slit throat and bloody dress. She'd met Rose seven months ago when Jaenelle had shown her Briarwood's awful secret. The next night, she and Rose had gotten Jaenelle out of Briarwood, but too late to stop the vicious rape.

"What happened to her?" Surreal said, glancing toward the tree. A silly thing to ask about a girl long dead.

Rose shrugged. "She faded. All the old ghosts have finally returned to the Darkness." She studied Surreal. "Why are you here?"

Surreal took a deep breath. "I came to say good-bye. I'm leaving Chaillot in the morning—and I'm not coming back."

Rose thought about this. "If you hold my hand, maybe you'll be able to see Dannie. I don't know how Jaenelle always saw the ghosts. Even after I became a demon, I couldn't see the oldest ones unless she was here. She said that was because this was one of the living Realms."

Surreal took Rose's hand. They walked toward the vegetable garden.

"Is Jaenelle all right?" Rose asked hesitantly.

Surreal pushed her windblown hair from her face. "I don't know. She was hurt very badly. A witch at Cassandra's Altar took her away to a safe place. She might have reached a Healer in time."

They stopped at the carrot patch where two redheaded sisters had been buried in secret, as all these children had been buried. But there were no shapes, no whispery voices. Surreal didn't feel the numb horror she had the first time she'd seen this garden. Now there was grief mingled with the hope that those young girls were finally beyond the memory of what had been done to them.

Dannie was the only one there. Surreal tried hard not to look at the ghostly stump where a leg should have been. Her stomach tightened as she tried even harder not to remember what had been done with that leg.

Burying her pity, Surreal sent out a psychic thread of warmth and friendship toward the ghost-girl.

Dannie smiled.

Even in death the Blood were cruel, Surreal thought as she squeezed Rose's cold hand. How empty, how lonely the years must have been for those who weren't strong enough to become demon-dead but were too strong to return to the Darkness. They remained, chained to their graves, unseen, unheard, uncared for—except by Jaenelle.

What *had* happened to her?

Surreal and Rose finally walked back to the shrub garden. "They should all be gutted," Surreal growled, releasing Rose's hand. She leaned against the tree and stared at the building. Most of the windows were dark, but there were a few dim lights. Calling in her favorite stiletto, she balanced it in her hand and smiled. "Maybe one or two can feed the garden before I go."

"No," Rose said sharply, placing herself in front of Surreal. "You can't touch any of Briarwood's uncles. No one can."

Surreal straightened, a feral expression in her gold-green eyes. "I'm very good at what I do, Rose."

"No," Rose insisted. "When Jaenelle's blood was spilled, it woke the tangled web she created. It's a trap for all the uncles."

Surreal looked at the building, then at Rose. There *had* been rumors of a mysterious illness that was affecting a number of Chaillot's high-ranking members of the council—like Robert Benedict—as well as a few special dignitaries—like Kartane SaDiablo. "This trap will kill them?"

"Eventually," Rose said.

A vicious light filled Surreal's eyes. "What about a cure?"

"Briarwood is the pretty poison. There is no cure for Briarwood."

"Is it painful?"

Rose grinned. " 'To each will come what he gave.' "

Surreal vanished her stiletto. "Then let the bastards scream."

4 / Terreille

In the light of two smoking torches, the young Priestess double-checked the tools she had placed on the Dark Altar. Everything was ready: the four-branched candelabra with its black candles, the small silver cup, and the two vials of dark liquid—one with a white stopper, the other with a red.

When the stranger with the maimed hands had given her the vials, he'd assured her that the antidote would keep her from being affected by the witch's brew that had been designed to subdue a Warlord Prince.

She paced behind the Dark Altar, chewing on her thumbnail. It had sounded so easy, and yet . . .

She froze, not even daring to breathe as she tried to see beyond the wrought-iron gate into the dark corridor. Was something there?

Nothing but a silence within the night's silence, a shadow within the shadows, gliding toward the Altar with a predator's grace.

The Priestess squatted behind the Altar, broke the seal on the white-stoppered vial, and gulped the contents. She vanished the vial and rose. When she looked toward the wrought-iron gate, she clutched her Yellow Jewel as if it might protect her.

He stood on the other side of the Altar, watching her. Despite the rumpled clothing and the disheveled hair, he exuded a cold, carnal power.

The Priestess licked her lips and rubbed her damp hands on her robe. His golden eyes looked sleepy, slightly glazed.

Then he smiled.

She shivered and took a deep breath. "Have you come for advice or assistance?"

"Assistance," he said in a deep, cultured voice. "Have you the training to open the Gate?"

How could a man be so beautiful? she thought as she nodded. "There is a price." Her voice seemed to be swallowed by the shadows.

With his left hand, he drew an envelope out of an inner pocket in his coat and laid it on the Altar. "Will that be sufficient?"

As she reached for it, she glanced at him, her hand frozen above the thick white envelope. There was something in the question, although courteously asked, that warned her it had better be enough.

She forced herself to pick up the envelope and look inside. Then she leaned against the Altar for support. Gold thousand marks. At least ten times what the stranger with the maimed hands had offered.

But she already had an agreement with the stranger, and there would be time to pocket the marks before the guards arrived.

The Priestess carefully placed the envelope on the far corner of the Altar. "Most generous," she said, hoping she sounded unimpressed.

Taking a deep breath, she lifted the silver cup high over her head, then placed it carefully in front of her. She broke the seal on the red-stoppered vial, poured the contents into the cup, and held it out to him. "The journey through a Gate is a difficult undertaking. This will assist you."

He didn't take the cup.

She made an impatient sound and took a sip, trying not to gag on the bitter taste, then held out the cup.

He held it in his left hand, his nostrils flaring at the smell, but didn't drink.

A minute passed. Two.

With an imperceptible shrug, he gulped the contents of the cup.

The Priestess held her breath. How soon before it worked? How soon before the guards came?

His eyes changed. He swayed. Then he leaned across the Altar and looked at her the way a lover looks at his lady. She couldn't take her eyes off his lips. Soft. Sensual. She leaned toward him. One kiss. One sweet kiss.

Just before her lips touched his, his right hand closed around her wrist. "Bitch," he snarled softly.

Startled, she tried to pull away.

As his hand tightened, she stared at the Black-Jeweled ring.

His long nails pierced her skin. Then she felt the sharp

needle prick of the snake tooth beneath his ring-finger nail, felt the venom chill her blood.

She flailed at him with her other hand, trying to reach his face, trying to scream for help as her vision blurred and her lungs refused to fill with needed air.

He broke both her wrists, snapping the bones as he thrust her away from him.

"The venom in my snake tooth doesn't work as quickly as you may think," he said too quietly, too gently. "In the end, you'll be able to scream. You'll tear yourself apart doing it, but you'll scream."

Then he was gone, and there was nothing but a silence within the night's silence, a shadow within the shadows.

By the time the guards arrived, she was screaming.

5 / Terreille

The floor rolled beneath him, teasing legs that already shook from exhaustion and were cramped by the foul witch's brew.

Behind that door was a safe place. As he reached for it, the floor rolled again, knocking his feet out from under him. His shoulder hit the door, cracking the old, rotting wood, and he fell into the room, landing heavily on his side.

"Bitch," he snarled softly.

Gray mist. A shattered crystal chalice. Black candles. Golden hair.

Blood. So much blood.

Words lie. Blood doesn't.

"Shut up, Prick," he rasped.

The floor kept rolling under him. He dug his long nails into the wood, trying to keep his balance, trying to think.

His fever was dangerously high, and he knew he needed food, water, and rest. Right now, he was prey to whoever might think to look for him in this abandoned house where he had spent his earliest years with Tersa, his real mother.

Everything has a price.

If he had given up outside that Sanctuary three days ago, if he had let the Hayllian guards find him, he might not have become so ill from the brew. But he had ruthlessly pushed his body to the point of collapse in order to reach the Gate near the ruins of SaDiablo Hall.

And every time exhaustion crept in, every time his strength of will slipped a little, a gray mist began to cloud his mind, a mist he knew held something very, very terrible. Something he didn't want to see.

You are my instrument.

Words, like flickering black lightning, came out of that mist, threatening to sear his soul.

Words lie. Blood doesn't.

He was less than a mile from the Gate.

"Lucivar," he whispered. But he didn't have the strength to feel angry at his brother's betrayal.

You are my instrument.

"No." He tried to stand up, but he couldn't do it. Still, something in him required defiance. "No. I am not your instrument. I . . . am . . . Daemon . . . Sadi."

He closed his eyes, and the gray mist engulfed him.

With a groan, Daemon rolled onto his back and slowly opened his eyes. Even that was almost too much effort. At first, he wondered if he had gone blind. Then he began to make out dim shapes in the darkness.

Night. It was night.

Breathing slowly, he began to assess the physical damage.

He felt as dry as touchwood, as inflexible as stone. His muscles burned. His belly ached from hunger, and the craving for water was fierce. The fever had broken at some point, but . . .

Something was *wrong*.

Words lie. Blood doesn't.

The words Lucivar had spoken swam round and round, growing larger, growing solid. They crashed against his mind, fragmenting it further.

Daemon screamed.

You are my instrument.

As Saetan's words thundered inside him, there was more pain—and there was fear. Fear that the mist filling his mind might part and show him something terrible.

Daemon.

Holding on fiercely to the memory of Jaenelle saying his name like a soft, sighing caress, Daemon got to his feet. As long as he could remember that, he could hold the other voices at bay.

His legs felt too heavy, but he managed to leave the house and follow the remnants of the drive that would take him to the Hall. Even though every movement was a fiery ache, by the time he reached the Hall, he was almost moving with his usual gliding stride.

But there was still something very wrong. It was hard to hold on to the Warlord Prince called Daemon Sadi, hard to hold on to his sense of self. But he had to hold on for a little while longer. He had to.

Gathering the last of his strength and will, Daemon cautiously approached the small building that held the Dark Altar.

Hekatah prowled the small building that stood in the shadow of the ruins of SaDiablo Hall. She shook her fists in the air, frustrated beyond endurance by the past three days. Even so, every time she circled the Altar, she glanced at the wall behind it, fearful it would turn to mist and Saetan would step through the Gate to challenge her.

But the High Lord was too preoccupied with his own concerns lately to pay attention to her.

Her main problem now was Daemon Sadi.

After drinking the brew she'd made, he *could not* have walked away from that Dark Altar, despite what those idiot guards swore. But if he was actually making his way to this Gate . . . By now the second part of her brew, the part that would make his mind receptive to her carefully rehearsed words, would be at its peak. She had planned to whisper all her poisoned words while she nursed him through the fever and the pain so that, when the fever broke, those words would solidify into a terrible truth he wouldn't be able to escape. Then all that strength, all that rage would become a dagger aimed right at Saetan's heart.

All her carefully made plans were being *ruined* because . . .

Hekatah jerked to a stop.

There was a silence within the night's silence.

She glanced at the unlit torches on the walls and decided against lighting them. There was enough moonlight to see by.

Not wanting to waste her strength on a sight shield, Hekatah slipped into a shadowy corner. Once he entered the Altar room, she would be behind him and could startle him with her presence.

She waited. Just when she was sure she'd been mistaken, he was there, without warning, standing just outside the wrought-iron gate, staring at the Altar. But he didn't enter the room.

Frowning, Hekatah turned her head slightly to look at the Altar. It was just as it should be. The candelabra was tarnished, and the wax from the black candles she'd burned so carefully so they wouldn't look new hung like stalactites from the silver arms.

Fearing that he might actually leave, Hekatah stepped up to the wrought-iron gate. "I've been waiting for you, Prince."

"Have you?" His voice sounded rusty, exhausted.

Perfect.

"Are you the one I should thank for the demons at the other Altars?" he asked.

How could he know she was a demon? Did he know who she was? Suddenly, she didn't feel confident about dealing with this son who was too much like his father, but she shook her head sadly. "No, Prince. There's only one power in Hell that commands demons. I'm here because I had a young friend who was very special to me. A friend, I think, we had in common. That's why I've been waiting for you."

Hell's fire! Couldn't there be *some* expression in his eyes to tell her if she was getting through to him?

"Young is a relative term, don't you think?"

He was *playing* with her! Hekatah gritted her teeth. "A child, Prince. A special child." She forced a pleading note into her voice. "I've waited here at great risk. If the High

Lord finds out I've tried to tell her friends . . ." She glanced at the wall behind the Altar.

Still no reaction from the man on the other side of the gate.

"She walks among the *cildru dyathe*," Hekatah said.

A long silence. "That isn't possible," he finally said. His voice was flat, totally without emotion.

"It's *true*." Was she wrong about him? Was he only trying to escape Dorothea? No. He had cared for the girl. She sighed. "The High Lord is a jealous man, Prince. He doesn't share what he claims for himself—especially if what he claims is a female body. When he discovered the girl's affection for another male, he did nothing to prevent her from being raped. And he could have, Prince. He *could* have. The girl managed to escape afterward. In time, and with help, she would have healed. But the High Lord didn't want her to heal, so, under the pretense of helping her, he used another male to finish what was begun. It destroyed her completely. Her body died, and her mind was torn apart. Now she's a dead, blank-eyed pet he plays with."

Hekatah looked up and wanted to scream with frustration. Had he heard any of it? "He should pay for what he's done," she said shrilly. "If you've courage enough to face him, I can open the Gate for you. Someone who remembers what she could have been should demand payment for what he did."

He looked at her for a long time. Then he turned and walked away.

Swearing, Hekatah began to pace. Why did he say nothing? It was a plausible story. Oh, she knew he'd been accused of the rape, but she also knew it wasn't true. And she wasn't completely convinced that he *had* been at Cassandra's Altar that night. All the males who'd sworn they had seen him had come from Briarwood. They could have said that to keep the Chaillot Queens from looking too closely at *them*. Surely—

A scream shattered the night.

Hekatah jumped, shaken by the awful sound. Bestial, animal, human. None and all. Whatever could make a sound like that . . .

Hekatah quickly lit the black candles and waited impatiently for the wall to change to mist. Just before stepping through the Gate, she realized there was no one here to snuff out the candles and close the entrance to the other Realms. If that thing . . .

Hekatah raised her hand and Red-locked the wrought-iron gate.

Another scream tore the night.

Hekatah bolted through the Gate. She might be a demon, but she didn't want whatever that was to follow her into the Dark Realm.

Words swam round and round, slicing his mind, slicing his soul.

The gray mist parted, showing him a Dark Altar.

Blood. So much blood.

 . . . *he used another male* . . .

The world shattered.

You are my instrument.

His mind shattered.

 . . . *destroyed her completely.*

Screaming in agony, he fled through the mist, through a landscape washed in blood and filled with shattered crystal chalices.

Words lie. Blood doesn't.

He screamed again and tumbled into the shattered inner landscape landens called madness and the Blood called the Twisted Kingdom.

PART 2

CHAPTER
THREE

1 / Kaeleer

Karla, a fifteen-year-old Glacian Queen, jabbed her cousin Morton in the ribs. "Who's that?"

Morton glanced in the direction of Karla's slightly lifted chin, then went back to watching the young Warlords gathering at one end of the banquet hall. "That's Uncle Hobart's new mistress."

Karla studied the young witch through narrowed, ice-blue eyes. "She doesn't look much older than me."

"She isn't," Morton said grimly.

Karla linked arms with her cousin, finding comfort in his nearness.

Glacian society had started to change after the "accident" that had killed her parents and Morton's six years ago. A group of aristo males had immediately formed a male council "for the good of the Territory"—a council led by Hobart, a Yellow-Jeweled Warlord who was a distant relation of her father's.

Every Province Queen, after declining to become a figurehead for the council, had also refused to acknowledge the Queen of a small village that the council finally had chosen to rule the Territory. Their refusal had fractured Glacia, but it had also prevented the male council from becoming too powerful or too effective in carrying out their "adjustments" to Glacian society.

Even so, after six years there was an uneasy feel in the air, a sense of wrongness.

Karla didn't have many friends. She was a sharp-tongued, sharp-tempered Queen whose Birthright Jewel was the Sapphire. She was also a natural Black Widow and a Healer. But, since Lord Hobart was now the head of the family, she spent much of her social time with the daughters of other members of the male council—and what those girls were saying was obscene: respectable witches defer to wiser, more knowledgeable males; Blood males shouldn't have to serve or yield to Queens because they're the stronger gender; the only reason Queens and Black Widows want the power to control males is because they're sexually and emotionally incapable of being real women.

Obscene. And terrifying.

When she was younger, she had wondered why the Province Queens and the Black Widows had settled for a stalemate instead of fighting.

Glacia is locked in a cold, dark winter, the Black Widows had told her. *We must do what we can to remain strong until the spring returns.*

But would they be able to hold out for five more years until she came of age? Would *she*? Her mother's and her aunt's deaths had not been an accident. Someone had eliminated Glacia's strongest Queen and strongest Black Widow, leaving the Territory vulnerable to . . . what?

Jaenelle could have told her, but Jaenelle . . .

Karla clamped down on the bitter anger that had been simmering too close to the surface lately. Forcing her attention away from memories, she studied Hobart's mistress, then jabbed Morton in the ribs again.

"Stop that," he snapped.

Karla ignored him. "Why is she wearing a fur coat indoors?"

"It was Uncle Hobart's consummation prize."

She fingered her short, spiky, white-blond hair. "I've never seen fur like that. It's not white bear."

"I think it's Arcerian cat."

"Arcerian cat?" That couldn't be right. Most Glacians wouldn't hunt in Arceria because the cats were big, fierce predators, and the odds of a hunter not becoming the prey were less than fifty-fifty. Besides, there was something *wrong* with that fur. She could feel it even at this distance. "I'm going to pay my respects."

"Karla." There was no mistaking the warning in Morton's voice.

"Kiss kiss." She gave him a wicked smile and an affectionate squeeze before making her way to the group of women admiring the coat.

It was easy to slip in among them. Some of the women noticed her, but most were intent on the girl's—Karla couldn't bring herself to call her a Sister—hushed gossip.

"—hunters from a faraway place," the girl said.

"I've got a collar made from Arcerian fur, but it's not as luxurious as this," one of the women said enviously.

"These hunters have found a new way of harvesting the fur. Hobie told me after we'd—" She giggled.

"How?"

"It's a secret."

Coaxing murmurs.

Mesmerized by the fur, Karla touched it at the same moment the girl giggled again, and said, "They skin the cat *alive*."

She jerked her hand away, shocked numb. *Alive.*

And some of the power of the one who had lived in that fur was still there. That's what made it so luxurious.

A witch. One of the Blood Jaenelle had called kindred.

Karla swayed. They had butchered a witch.

She shoved her way out of the group of women and stumbled toward the door. A moment later, Morton was beside her, one arm around her waist. "Outside," she gasped. "I think I'm going to be sick."

As soon as they were outside, she gulped the sharp winter air and started to cry.

"Karla," Morton murmured, holding her close.

"She was a witch," Karla sobbed. "She was a witch and they skinned her alive so that little bitch could—"

She felt a shudder go through Morton. Then his arms tightened, as if he could protect her. And he *would* try to protect her, which is why she couldn't tell him about the danger she sensed every time Uncle Hobart looked at her. At sixteen, Morton had just begun his formal court training.

He was the only real family she had left—and the only friend she had left.

The bitter anger boiled over without warning.

"It's been two years!" She pushed at Morton until he released her. "She's been in Kaeleer for two years, and she hasn't come to visit once!" She began pacing furiously.

"People change, Karla," Morton said cautiously. "Friends don't always remain friends."

"Not Jaenelle. Not with me. That malevolent bastard at SaDiablo Hall is keeping her chained somehow. I know it, Morton." She thumped her chest hard enough to make Morton wince. "In here, I know it."

"The Dark Council appointed him her legal guardian—"

Karla turned on him. "Don't talk to me about guardians, Lord Morton," she hissed. "I know all about 'guardians.'"

"Karla," Morton said weakly.

" 'Karla,' " she mimicked bitterly. "It's always 'Karla.' Karla's the one who's out of control. Karla's the one who's becoming emotionally unstable because of her apprenticeship in the Hourglass coven. Karla's the one who's become too excitable, too hostile, too intractable. Karla's the one who's cast aside all those delightful simpering manners that males find appealing."

"Males don't find that—"

"And Karla's the one who will gut the next son of a whoring bitch who tries to shove his hand or anything else between her legs!"

"*What?*"

Karla turned her back to Morton. Hell's fire, Mother Night, and may the Darkness be merciful. She hadn't meant to say that.

"Is that why you cut your hair like that after Uncle Hobart insisted that you come back to the family estate to live? Is that why you burned all your dresses and started wearing my old clothes?" Morton grabbed her arm and swung her around to face him. "Is it?"

Tears filled Karla's eyes. "A broken witch is a complacent witch," she said softly. "Isn't that true, Morton?"

Morton shook his head. "You wear Birthright Sapphire.

There aren't any males in Glacia who wear a Jewel darker than the Green."

"A Blood male can get around a witch's strength if he waits for the right moment and has help."

Morton swore softly, viciously.

"What if that's the reason Jaenelle doesn't come to visit anymore? What if he's done to her what Uncle Hobart wants to do to me?"

Morton stepped away from her. "I'm surprised you even tolerate me being near you."

She could almost see the wounds the truth had left on his heart. There was nothing she could do now about the truth, but there *was* something she could do about the wounds. "You're family."

"I'm *male*."

"You're Morton. The exception to the rule."

Morton hesitated, then opened his arms. "Want a hug?"

Stepping into his arms, Karla held him as fiercely as he held her.

"Listen," he said hoarsely. "Write a letter to the High Lord and ask him if Jaenelle could come for a visit. Ask for a return reply."

"The Old Fart will never let me send a courier to SaDiablo Hall," Karla muttered into his shoulder.

"Uncle Hobart isn't going to know." Morton took a deep breath. "I'll deliver the letter personally and wait for an answer."

Before Morton could offer his handkerchief, Karla stepped back, sniffed, and wiped her face on the shirt she'd taken from his wardrobe. She sniffed again and was done with paltry emotions.

"Karla," Morton said, eyeing her nervously. "You will write a *polite* letter, won't you?"

"I'll be a polite as I can be," Karla assured him.

Morton groaned.

Oh, yes. She would write to the High Lord. And, one way or another, she would get the answer she wanted.

Please. Sweet Darkness, please be my friend again. I miss you. I need you. Drawing on the strength of her Sapphire Jewels, Karla flung one word into the Darkness. *Jaenelle!*

"Karla?" Morton said, touching her arm. "The banquet is about to start. We need to put in an appearance, if only for a little while."

Karla froze, not even daring to breathe. *Jaenelle?*

Seconds passed.

"Karla?" Morton said.

Karla took a deep breath and exhaled her disappointment. She took the arm Morton offered and went back into the banquet hall.

He stayed close to her for the rest of the evening, and she was grateful for his company. But she would have traded his caring and protection in an instant if that faint but so very dark psychic touch she'd imagined had been real.

2 / Kaeleer

When Andulvar Yaslana settled in the chair in front of the blackwood desk in Saetan's public study, Saetan looked up from the letter he'd been staring at for the past half hour. "Read this," he said, handing it to Andulvar.

While Andulvar read the letter, Saetan looked wearily at the stacks of papers on his desk. It had been months since he'd set foot in the Hall, even longer since he'd granted audiences to the Queens who ruled the Provinces and Districts in his Territory. His eldest son, Mephis, had dealt with as much of the official business of Dhemlan as he could, as he had been doing for centuries, but the rest of it . . .

"*Blood-sucking corpse?*" Andulvar sputtered.

Saetan watched with a touch of amusement as Andulvar snarled through the rest of the letter. He hadn't been amused during his first reading, but the signature and the adolescent handwriting had soothed his temper—and added another layer to his sorrow.

Andulvar flung the letter onto the desk. "Who is Karla, and how does she dare write something like this to you?"

"Not only does she dare, but the courier is waiting for a reply."

Andulvar muttered something vicious.

"As for who she is . . ." Saetan called in the file he usually kept locked in his private study beneath the Hall. He leafed through the papers filled with his notes and handed one to Andulvar.

Andulvar's shoulders slumped as he read it. "Damn."

"Yes." Saetan put the paper back in the file and vanished it.

"What are you going to say?"

Saetan leaned back in his chair. "The truth. Or part of it. I've kept the Dark Council at bay for two years, denying their not unreasonable requests to see Jaenelle. I've given no explanation for that denial, letting them think what they chose—and I am aware of what they've chosen to think. But her friends? Until now they've been too young, or perhaps not bold enough, to ask what became of her. Now they're asking." He straightened in his chair and summoned Beale, the Red-Jeweled Warlord who worked as the Hall's butler.

"Bring the courier to me," Saetan said when Beale appeared.

"Shall I go?" Andulvar asked, making no move to leave.

Saetan shrugged, already preoccupied with how to word his reply. There hadn't been much contact between Dhemlan and Glacia in the past few years, but he'd heard enough about Lord Hobart and his ties to Little Terreille to decide on a verbal reply instead of a written one.

Long centuries ago, Little Terreille had been settled by Terreilleans who had been eager for a new life and a new land. Despite that eagerness, the people had never felt comfortable with the races who had been born to the Shadow Realm. So even though Little Terreille was a Territory in Kaeleer, it had looked for companionship and guidance from the Realm of Terreille—and still did, even though most Terreilleans no longer believed Kaeleer existed because access to this Realm had been so limited for so long. Which meant any companionship and guidance coming from Terreille now was coming from Dorothea, one way or another—and that was reason enough for him to feel wary.

Saetan and Andulvar exchanged a quick look when
Beale showed the courier into the room.

Andulvar sent a thought on a Red spear thread. *He's a
bit young for an official courier.*

Silently agreeing with Andulvar's assessment, Saetan
lifted his right hand. A chair floated from its place by the
wall and settled in front of the desk. "Please be seated,
Warlord."

"Thank you, High Lord." The young man had the typical
fair skin, blond hair, and blue eyes of the Glacian people.
Despite his youth, he moved with the kind of assurance
usually found in aristo families and responded with a confidence in Protocol that indicated court training.

Not your typical courier, Saetan thought as he watched
the young man try to control the urge to fidget. *So why are
you here, boyo?*

"My butler must be having a bad day to overlook intro-
ducing you when you entered," Saetan said mildly. He steepled his fingers, his long, black-tinted nails resting against
his chin.

The youth paled a little when he saw the Black-Jeweled
ring. He licked his lips. "My name is Morton, High Lord."

*Now you're not quite so sure that Protocol will protect
you, are you, boyo?* Saetan didn't allow his amusement to
show. If this boy was going to approach a dark-Jeweled
Warlord Prince, it was better he learn the potential dangers. "And you serve?"

"I—I don't exactly serve in a court yet."

Saetan raised one eyebrow. "You serve Lord Hobart?"
he asked, his voice a bit cooler.

"No. He's just the head of the family. Sort of an uncle."

Saetan picked up the letter and handed it to Morton.
"Read this." He sent a thought to Andulvar. *What's the
game? The boy's not experienced enough to—*

"Nooo," Morton moaned. The letter fluttered to the
floor. "She promised me she'd be polite. I told her I'd be
waiting for a reply, and she promised." He flushed, then
paled. "I'll strangle her."

Using Craft, Saetan retrieved the letter. Whatever doubts
he'd had about motive were gone, but he was curious about

why the question was being asked now. "How well do you know Karla?"

"She's my cousin," Morton replied in the aggrieved tone of a ruffled male.

"You have my sympathy," Andulvar said, rustling his dark wings as he shifted in the chair.

"Thank you, sir. Having Karla like you is better than having her not like you, but . . ." Morton shrugged.

"Yes," Saetan said dryly. "I have a friend who has a similar effect on me." He chuckled softly at Morton's look of astonishment. "Boyo, even being me doesn't make a difficult witch any less difficult."

Especially a Dea al Mon Harpy, Andulvar sent, amused. *Have you recovered yet from her latest attempt to be helpful?*

If you're going to sit there, be useful, Saetan shot back.

Andulvar turned to Morton. "Did your cousin keep her promise?" When the boy gave him a blank look, he added, "Was she being polite?"

The tips of Morton's ears turned red. He shrugged helplessly. "For Karla . . . I guess so."

"Oh, Mother Night," Saetan muttered. Suddenly a thought swooped down on him, and he choked. He used the time needed to catch his breath to consider some rather nasty possibilities.

When he was finally in control again, he chose his words carefully. "Lord Morton, your uncle doesn't know you're here, does he?" Morton's nervous look was answer enough. "Where does he think you are?"

"Somewhere else."

Saetan studied Morton, fascinated by the subtle change in his posture. No longer a youth intimidated by his surroundings and the males he faced, but a Warlord protecting his young Queen. *You were wrong, boyo,* Saetan thought. *You've already chosen whom you serve.*

"Karla . . ." Morton gathered his thoughts. "It isn't easy for Karla. She wears Birthright Sapphire, and she's a Queen and a natural Black Widow as well as a Healer, and Uncle Hobart . . ."

Saetan tensed at the bitterness in Morton's blue eyes.

"She and Uncle Hobart don't get along," Morton finished lamely, looking away. When he looked back, he seemed so young and vulnerable. "I know Karla wants her to come visit like she used to, but couldn't Jaenelle just write a short note? Just to say hello?"

Saetan closed his golden eyes. *Everything has a price*, he thought. *Everything has a price.* He took a deep breath and opened his eyes. "I truly wish, with all of my being, that she could." He took another deep breath. "What I'm about to tell you must go no further than your cousin. I must have your pledge of silence."

Morton immediately nodded agreement.

"Jaenelle was seriously hurt two years ago. She can't write, she can't communicate in any way. She . . ." Saetan stopped, then resumed when he was sure he could keep his voice steady. "She doesn't know anyone."

Morton looked ill. "How?" he finally whispered.

Saetan groped for an answer. The change in Morton's expression told him he needn't have bothered. The boy had understood the silence.

"Then Karla was right," Morton said bitterly. "A male doesn't have to be that strong if he picks the right time."

Saetan snapped upright in his chair. "Is Karla being pressed to submit to a male? At *fifteen*?"

"No. I don't know. Maybe." Morton's hands clenched the arms of the chair. "She was safe enough when she lived with the Black Widows, but now that she's come back to the family estate . . ."

"Hell's fire, boy!" Saetan roared. "Even if they don't get along, why isn't your uncle protecting her?"

Morton bit his lip and said nothing.

Stunned, Saetan sank back in his chair. Not here, too. Not in Kaeleer. Didn't these fools realize what was lost when a Queen was destroyed that way?

"You have to go now," Saetan said gently.

Morton nodded and rose to leave.

"Tell Karla one other thing. If she needs it, I'll grant her sanctuary at the Hall and give her my protection. And you as well."

"Thank you," Morton said. Bowing to Saetan and Andulvar, he left.

Saetan grabbed his silver-headed cane and limped toward the door.

Andulvar got there first and pressed his hand against the door to keep it closed. "The Dark Council will be screaming for your blood if you give another girl your protection."

Saetan didn't speak for a long time. Then he gave Andulvar a purely malevolent smile. "If the Dark Council is so misguided they believe Hobart is a better guardian than I am, then they deserve to see some of Hell's more unusual landmarks, don't you think?"

3 / The Twisted Kingdom

There was no physical pain, but the agony was relentless.

Words lie. Blood doesn't.

You are my instrument.

Butchering whore.

He wandered through a mist-filled landscape full of shattered memories, shattered crystal chalices, shattered dreams.

Sometimes he heard a scream of despair.

Sometimes he even recognized his own voice.

Sometimes he caught a glimpse of a girl with long golden hair running away from him. He always followed, desperate to catch up with her, desperate to explain . . .

He couldn't remember what he needed to explain.

Don't be afraid, he called to her. Please, don't be afraid.

But she continued to run, and he continued to follow her through a landscape filled with twisting roads that ended nowhere and caverns that were strewn with bones and splashed with blood.

Down, always down.

He followed her, always begging her to wait, always pleading with her not to be afraid, always hoping to hear the sound of her voice, always yearning to hear her say his name.

If he could only remember what it was.

4 / Hell

Hekatah carefully arranged the folds of her full-length cloak while she waited for her demon guards to bring her the *cildru dyathe* boy. She sighed with satisfaction as her hands stroked the cloak's fur lining. Arcerian fur. A Warlord's fur. She could feel the rage and pain locked in his pelt.

The kindred. The four-footed Blood. Compared to humans, they had simple minds that couldn't conceive of greatness or ambition, but they were fiercely protective when they gave someone their loyalty—and equally fierce when they felt that loyalty was betrayed.

She had made a few little mistakes the last time she had tried to become the High Priestess of all the Realms, mistakes that had cost her the war between Terreille and Kaeleer 50,000 years ago. One mistake had been underestimating the strength of the Blood who lived in the Shadow Realm. The other mistake had been underestimating the kindred.

One of the first things she had done after she'd recovered from the shock of being demon-dead was to exterminate the kindred in Terreille. Some went into hiding and survived, but not enough of them. They would have had to breed with landen animals, and over time the interbreeding had probably produced a few creatures who were almost Blood, but never anything strong enough to wear a Jewel.

The wilder kindred in Kaeleer, however, had withdrawn to their own Territories after the war and had woven countless spells to protect their borders. By the time those fierce defenses had faded enough for anyone to survive passing through them, the kindred had become little more than myths.

Hekatah began to pace. Hell's fire! How long could it take for two grown males to catch a boy?

After a minute, she stopped pacing and once again arranged the folds of her cloak. She couldn't allow the boy to see any hint of her impatience. It might make him perversely stubborn. She stroked the cloak's fur lining, letting the feel of it soothe her.

During the centuries while she had waited for Terreille to ripen again into a worthy prize, she had helped the Territory of Little Terreille maintain a thread of contact with the Realm of Terreille. But it was only in the past few years that she'd established a foothold in Glacia via Lord Hobart's ambition.

She had chosen Glacia because it was a northern Territory whose people could be isolated more easily from the Blood in other Territories; it had Hobart, a male whose ambitions outstripped his abilities; and it had a Dark Altar. So for the first time in a very long time, she had a Gate at her disposal, and a way for carefully chosen males to slip into Kaeleer in order to hunt challenging prey.

That wasn't the only little game she was playing in Kaeleer, but the others required time and patience—and the assurance that nothing would interfere with her ambitions this time.

Which was why she was here on the *cildru dyathe*'s island.

She was just about to question the loyalty of her demon guards when they returned, dragging a struggling boy between them. With a savage curse, they pinned the boy against a tall, flat-sided boulder.

"Don't hurt him," Hekatah snapped.

"Yes, Priestess," one of the guards replied sullenly.

Hekatah studied the boy, who glared back at her. Char, the young Warlord leader of the *cildru dyathe*. Easy enough to see how he had come by that name. How had he been able to save so much of his body from the fire? He must have had a great deal of Craft skill for one so young. She should have realized that seven years ago when she had tangled with him the first time. Well, she could easily fix that misjudgment.

Hekatah approached slowly, enjoying the wariness in the boy's eyes. "I mean you no harm, Warlord," she crooned. "I just need your help. I know Jaenelle walks among the *cildru dyathe*. I want to see her."

What was left of Char's lips curled in a vicious smile. "Not all *cildru dyathe* are on this island."

Hekatah's gold eyes snapped with fury. "You lie. Summon her. *Now!*"

"The High Lord is coming," Char said. "He'll be here any moment."

"Why?" Hekatah demanded.

"Because I sent for him."

"*Why?*"

A strange light filled Char's eyes. "I saw a butterfly yesterday."

Hekatah wanted to scream in frustration. Instead, she raised her hand, her fingers curved into a claw. "If you want your eyes, little Warlord, you'll summon Jaenelle *now.*"

Char stared at her. "You truly wish to see her?"

"YES!"

Char tipped his head back and let out a strange, wild ululation.

Unnerved by the sound, Hekatah slapped him to make him stop.

"HEKATAH!"

Hekatah ran from the fury in Saetan's thundering voice. Then she glanced over her shoulder and stopped, shocked excitement making her nerves sizzle.

Saetan leaned heavily on a silver-headed cane, his golden eyes glittering with rage. There was more silver in the thick black hair, and his face was tight with exhaustion. He looked . . . worn-out.

And he was only wearing his Birthright Red Jewel.

She didn't even take the time for a fast descent to gather her full strength. She just raised her hand and unleashed the power in her Red-Jeweled ring at his weak leg.

His cry of pain as he fell was the most satisfying sound she'd heard in years.

"Seize him!" she screamed at her demons.

A cold, soft wind sighed across the island.

The guards hesitated for a moment, but when Saetan tried to get up and failed, they drew their knives and ran toward him.

The ground trembled slightly. Mist swirled around the rocks, around the barren earth.

Hekatah also ran toward Saetan, wanting to watch the knives cut deep, wanting to watch his blood run. A Guardian's blood! The richness, the strength in it! She would feast on him before dealing with that upstart little demon.

A howl rose from the abyss, a sound full of joy and pain, rage and celebration.

Then a tidal wave of dark power flooded the *cildru dyathe*'s island. Psychic lightning set Hell's twilight sky on fire. Thunder shook the land. The howling went on and on.

Hekatah fell to the ground and curled up as tight as she could.

Her demons screamed in nerve-shattering agony.

Go away, Hekatah pleaded silently. *Whatever you are, go away.*

Something icy and terrible brushed against her inner barriers, and Hekatah blanked her mind.

By the time it faded away, the witch storm had faded with it.

Hekatah pushed herself into a sitting position. Her throat worked convulsively when she saw what was left of her demons.

There was no sign of Saetan or Char.

Hekatah slowly got to her feet. Was that Jaenelle—or what was left of Jaenelle? Maybe she *wasn't cildru dyathe.* Maybe she had faded from demon to ghost and all that was left was that bodiless power.

It was just as well the girl was dead, Hekatah thought as she caught a White Wind and rode back to the stone building she claimed as her own. It was just as well that whatever was left of Jaenelle would be confined to the Dark Realm. Trying to control that savage power. . . . It was just as well the girl was dead.

Pain surrounded him, filled him. His head felt like it was stuffed with blankets. He clawed his way through, desperate to reach the muffled voices he heard around him: Andulvar's angry rumble, Char's distress.

Hell's fire! Why were they just sitting there? For the first time in two years, Jaenelle had responded to someone's call. Why weren't they trying to keep her within reach?

Because Jaenelle was gliding through the abyss too deep for anyone but him to feel her presence. But he couldn't just descend to the level of the Black and summon her. He had to be near her physically, he had to be with her to coax her into remaining with her body.

"Why did the witch storm hit him so bad?" Char asked fearfully.

"Because he's an ass," Andulvar growled in reply.

He redoubled his efforts to break through the muffling layers just so he could snarl at Andulvar. Maybe he *had* been channeling too much of the Black strength without giving his body a chance to recover. Maybe he *had* been foolish when he'd refused to drink fresh blood to maintain his strength. But that didn't give an Eyrien warrior the right to act like a stubborn, nagging Healer.

Jaenelle would have cornered him until he'd given in.

Jaenelle. So close. He might never have another chance.

He struggled harder. *Help me. I have to reach her. Help—* "me."

"High Lord!"

"Hell's fire, SaDiablo!"

Saetan grabbed Andulvar's arm and tried to pull himself into a sitting position. "Help me. Before it's too late."

"You need rest," Andulvar said.

"There isn't time!" Saetan tried to yell. It came out an infuriating croak. "Jaenelle's still close enough to reach."

"*What?*"

The next thing he knew he was sitting up with Andulvar supporting him and Char kneeling in front of him. He focused on the boy. "How did you summon her?"

"I don't know," Char wailed. "I don't know. I was just trying to keep Hekatah busy until you came. She kept demanding to see Jaenelle, so I thought . . . Jaenelle and I used to play 'chase me, find me' and that was the sound we used to make. I didn't know she would answer, High Lord. I've called like that lots of times since she went away, and she's never answered."

"Until now," Saetan said quietly. Why now? He finally noticed he was in a familiar bedroom. "We're at the Keep in Kaeleer?"

"Draca insisted on bringing you here," Andulvar said.

The Keep's Seneschal had given him a bedroom near the Queen's suite. Which meant he wasn't more than a few yards away from Jaenelle's body. Just chance? Or could Draca also feel Jaenelle's presence?

"Help me," Saetan whispered.

Andulvar half carried him the few yards down the corridor to the door where Draca waited.

"You will drink a cup of fressh blood when you return," Draca said.

If I return, Saetan thought grimly, as Andulvar helped him to the bed that held Jaenelle's frail body. There might not be another chance. He would bring her back or destroy himself trying.

As soon as he was alone with her, he took Jaenelle's head between his hands, drew every drop of power he had left in his Jewels, and made a quick descent into the abyss until he reached the level of the Black.

Jaenelle!

She continued her slow spiral glide deeper into the abyss. He didn't know if she was ignoring him or just couldn't hear him.

Jaenelle! Witch-child!

His strength was draining too quickly. The abyss pushed against his mind, the pressure quickly turning to pain.

You're safe, witch-child! Come back! You're safe!

She slipped farther and farther away from him. But little eddies of power washed back up to him, and he could taste the rage in them.

Chase me, find me. A child's game. He had been sending a message of love and safety into the abyss for two years. Char had been sending an invitation to play during that same time.

Silence.

In another moment, he would have to ascend or he would shatter.

Stillness.

Chase me, find me. Hadn't he really been playing the same game?

He waited, fighting for each second. *Witch-child.*

She slammed into him without warning. Caught in her spiraling fury, he didn't know if they were rising or descending.

He heard glass shatter in the physical world, heard someone scream. He felt something hit his chest, just below his heart, hard enough to take his breath away.

Not knowing what else to do, he opened his inner barriers fully, a gesture of complete surrender. He expected her to crash through him, rip him apart. Instead, he felt a startled curiosity and a feather-light touch that barely brushed against him.

Then she tossed him out of the abyss.

The abrupt return to the physical world left him dizzy, his senses scrambled. That had to be why he thought he saw a tiny spiral horn in the center of her forehead. That had to be why her ears looked delicately pointed, why she had a golden mane that looked like a cross between fur and human hair. That had to be why his heart felt as if it were beating frantically against someone's hand.

He closed his eyes, fighting the dizziness. When he opened them a moment later, all the changes in Jaenelle's appearance were gone, but there was still that odd feeling in his chest.

Gasping, he looked down as he felt fingers curl around his heart.

Jaenelle's hand was embedded in his chest. When she withdrew her hand, she would pull his heart out with it. No matter. It had been hers long before he'd ever met her. And it gave him an odd feeling of pride, remembering the frustration and delight he'd felt when he'd tried to teach her how to pass one solid object through another.

The fingers curled tighter.

Her eyes opened. They were fathomless sapphire pools that held no recognition, that held nothing but deep, inhuman rage.

Then she blinked. Her eyes clouded, hiding so many things. She blinked again and looked at him. "Saetan?" she said in a rusty voice.

His eyes filled with tears. "Witch-child," he whispered hoarsely.

He gasped when she moved her hand slightly.

She stared at his chest and frowned. "Oh." She slowly uncurled her fingers and withdrew her hand.

He expected her hand to be bloody, but it was clean. A quick internal check told him he would feel bruised for a few days, but she hadn't done any damage. He leaned forward until his forehead rested against hers.

"Witch-child," he whispered.

"Saetan? Are you crying?"

"Yes. No. I don't know."

"You should lie down. You feel kind of peaky."

Shifting his body until it was beside hers exhausted him. When she turned and snuggled against him, he wrapped his arms around her and held on. "I tried to reach you, witch-child," he murmured as he rested his cheek against her head.

"I know," she said sleepily. "I heard you sometimes, but I had to find all the pieces so I could put the crystal chalice back together."

"Did you put it back together?" he asked, hardly daring to breathe.

Jaenelle nodded. "Some of the pieces are cloudy and don't fit quite right yet." She paused. "Saetan? What happened?"

Dread filled him, and he didn't have the courage to answer that question honestly. What would she do if he told her what had happened? If she severed the link with her body and fled into the abyss again, he wasn't sure he would ever be able to convince her to return.

"You were hurt, sweetheart." His arms tightened around her. "But you're going to be fine. I'll help you. Nothing can hurt you, witch-child. You have to remember that. You're safe here."

Jaenelle frowned. "Where is here?"

"We're at the Keep. In Kaeleer."

"Oh." Her eyelids fluttered and closed.

Saetan squeezed her shoulder. Then he shook her. "Jaenelle? Jaenelle, no! Don't leave me. Please don't leave."

With effort, Jaenelle opened her eyes. "Leave? Oh, Saetan, I'm so tired. Do I really have to leave?"

He had to get control of himself. He had to stay calm so that she would feel safe. "You can stay here as long as you want."

"You'll stay, too?"

"I'll never leave you, witch-child. I swear it."

Jaenelle sighed. "You should get some sleep," she murmured.

Saetan listened to her deep, even breathing for a long time. He wanted to open his mind and reach for her, but he didn't need to. He could feel the difference in the body he still held.

So he reached out to Andulvar instead. *She's come back.*

A long silence. *Truly?*

Truly. And he would need his strength for the days ahead. *Tell the others. And tell Draca I'll take the cup of fresh blood now.*

5 / Kaeleer

Guided by instinct and a nagging uneasiness, Saetan entered Jaenelle's bedroom at the Keep without knocking.

She stood in front of a large, freestanding mirror, staring at the naked body reflected there.

Saetan closed the door and limped toward her. While she'd been away from her body, there had still been just enough of a link so that she could eat and could be led on gentle walks that had kept her muscles from atrophying. There had still been enough of a link for her body to slowly answer the rhythm of its own seasons.

Blood females tended to reach puberty later than landens, and witches' bodies required even more time to prepare for the physical changes that separated a girl from a woman. Inhibited by her absence, Jaenelle's body hadn't started changing until after her fourteenth birthday. But while her body was still in the early stages of transformation, it no longer looked like a twelve-year-old's.

Saetan stopped a few feet behind her. Her sapphire eyes met his in the mirror, and he had to work to keep his expression neutral.

Those eyes. Clear and feral and dangerous before she slipped on the mask of humanity. And it was a mask. It wasn't like the dissembling she used to do as a child to keep the fact that she was Witch a secret. This was a deliberate effort simply to be *human*. And that scared him.

"I should have told you," he said quietly. "I should have prepared you. But you've slept through most of the past four days, and I . . ." His voice trailed off.

"How long?" she asked in a voice full of caverns and midnight.

He had to clear his throat before he could answer. "Two years. Actually, a little more than that. You'll be fifteen in a few weeks."

She said nothing, and he didn't know how to fill the silence.

Then she turned around to face him. "Do you want to have sex with this body?"

Blood. So much blood.

His gorge rose. Her mask fell away. And no matter how hard he looked, he couldn't find Jaenelle in those sapphire eyes.

He had to give her an answer. He had to give her the *right* answer.

He took a deep breath and let it out slowly. "I'm your legal guardian now. Your adopted father, if you will. And fathers do not have sex with their daughters."

"Don't they?" she asked in a midnight whisper.

The floor disappeared under his feet. The room spun. He would have fallen if Jaenelle hadn't thrown her arms around his waist.

"Don't use Craft," he muttered through gritted teeth.

Too late. Jaenelle was already floating him to the couch. As he sank into it, she sat beside him and brushed her shoulder-length hair away from her neck. "You need fresh blood."

"No, I don't. I'm just a little dizzy." Besides, he'd been drinking a cup of fresh human blood twice a day for the past four days—almost as much as he usually consumed in a year.

"You need fresh blood." There was a definite edge in her voice.

What he needed was to find the bastard who had raped her and tear him apart inch by inch. "I don't need your blood, witch-child."

Her eyes flashed with anger. She bared her teeth. "There's nothing wrong with my blood, High Lord," she hissed. "It isn't tainted."

"Of course it isn't tainted," he snapped back.

"Then why won't you accept the gift? You never refused before."

There were clouds and shadows now in her sapphire eyes. It seemed that, for her, the price of humanity was vulnerability and insecurity.

Lifting her hand, he kissed her knuckles and wondered if he could delicately suggest that she put on a robe without her taking offense. *One thing at a time, SaDiablo.* "There are three reasons I don't want your blood right now. First, until you're stronger, you need every drop of it for yourself. Second, your body is changing from child to woman, and the potency of the blood changes, too. So let's test it before I find myself drinking liquid lightning."

That made her giggle.

"And third, Draca has also decided that I need fresh blood."

Jaenelle's eyes widened. "Oh, dear. Poor Papa." She bit her lip. "Is it all right if I call you that?" she asked in a small voice.

He put his arms around her and held her close. "I would be honored to be called 'Papa.'" He brushed his lips against her forehead. "The room is a little chilly, witch-child. Do you think you could put on a robe? And slippers?"

"You sound like a parent already," Jaenelle grumbled.

Saetan smiled. "I've waited a long time to fuss over a daughter. I intend to revel in it to the fullest."

"Oh, lucky me," Jaenelle growled.

He laughed. "No. Lucky *me.*"

6 / Kaeleer

Saetan stared at the tonic in the small ravenglass cup and sighed. He had the cup halfway to his lips when someone knocked on the door.

"Come," he said too eagerly.

Andulvar entered, followed by his grandson, Prothvar, and Mephis, Saetan's eldest son. Prothvar and Mephis, like Andulvar, had become demon-dead during that long-ago war between Terreille and Kaeleer. Geoffrey, the Keep's historian/librarian, entered last.

"Try this," Saetan said, holding out the cup to Andulvar.

"Why?" Andulvar asked, eyeing the cup. "What's in it?"

Damn Eyrien wariness. "It's a tonic Jaenelle made for me. She says I'm still looking peaky."

"You are," Andulvar growled. "So drink it."

Saetan ground his teeth.

"It doesn't smell bad," Prothvar said, pulling his wings tighter to his body when Saetan glared at him.

"It doesn't taste bad either," Saetan said, trying to be fair.

"Then what's the problem?" Geoffrey asked, crossing his arms. He frowned at the cup, his black eyebrows echoing his widow's peak. "Are you concerned that she doesn't have the training to make that kind of tonic? Do you think she's done it incorrectly?"

Saetan raised one eyebrow. "We're talking about Jaenelle."

"Ah," Geoffrey said, eyeing the cup with some trepidation. "Yes."

Saetan held the cup out to him. "Tell me what you think."

Andulvar braced his fists on his hips. "Why are you so eager to share it? If there's nothing wrong with it, why won't *you* drink it?"

"I do. I have. Every day for the past two weeks," Saetan grumbled. "But it's just so damn . . . potent." The last word was almost a plea.

Geoffrey accepted the cup, took a small sip, rolled the liquid on his tongue, and swallowed. As he handed the cup to Andulvar, he started gasping and pressed his hands to his stomach.

"Geoffrey?" Alarmed, Saetan grabbed Geoffrey's arm as the older Guardian swayed.

"Is it supposed to feel like that?" Geoffrey wheezed.

"Like what?" Saetan asked cautiously.

"Like an avalanche hitting your stomach."

Saetan sighed with relief. "It doesn't last long, and the tonic *does* have some astonishing curative powers, but . . ."

"The initial sensation is a bit unsettling."

"Exactly," Saetan said dryly.

Andulvar studied the two Guardians and shrugged. He took a sip, passed the cup to Prothvar, who took a sip and passed it to Mephis.

When the cup reached Saetan, it was still two-thirds full. He sighed, took a sip, and set the cup on an empty curio table.

Why couldn't Draca fill a table with useless bric-a-brac like everyone else? he thought sourly. At least then there would be a way to hide the damn thing since Jaenelle had put some kind of neat little spell on the cup that prevented it from being vanished.

"Hell's fire," Andulvar finally said.

"What does she put in it?" Mephis said, rubbing his stomach.

Prothvar eyed Geoffrey. "You know, you've almost got some color."

Geoffrey glared at the Eyrien Warlord.

"What did you all want to see me about?" Saetan asked.

That stopped them cold. Then they began talking all at once.

"You see, SaDiablo, the waif—"

"—it's a difficult time for a young girl, I do understand that—"

"—doesn't want to see us—"

"—suddenly so shy—"

Saetan raised his hand to silence their explanations.

Everything has a price. As he looked at them, he knew he had to tell them what the past two weeks had forced him to see. *Everything has a price, but, sweet Darkness, haven't we paid enough?*

"Jaenelle didn't heal." When no one responded, he wondered if he'd actually said it out loud.

"Explain, SaDiablo," Andulvar rumbled. "Her body is alive, and now that she's returned to it, it will get stronger."

"Yes," Saetan replied softly. "Her body is alive."

"Since she's obviously capable of doing more than basic Craft, her inner web must be intact," Geoffrey said.

"Her inner web is intact," Saetan agreed. Hell's fire. Why was he prolonging this? Because once he actually said it, it would be real.

He watched the knowledge—and the anger—fill Andulvar's eyes.

"The bastard who raped her managed to shatter the crystal chalice, didn't he?" Andulvar said slowly. "He shattered her mind, and that pushed her into the Twisted Kingdom." Pausing, he studied Saetan. "Or did it push her somewhere else?"

"Who knows what lies deep in the abyss?" Saetan said bitterly. "I don't. Was she lost in madness or simply walking roads the rest of us can't possibly comprehend? I don't know. I *do* know she is more and less and different than she was, and there are some days when it's hard to find anything left of the child we knew. She told me that she'd put the crystal chalice back together, and from what I can tell, she has. But she doesn't remember what happened at Cassandra's Altar. She doesn't remember anything that took place during the few months before that night. And she's hiding something. That's part of the reason she's withdrawing from us. Shadows and secrets. She's afraid to trust any of us because of those damn shadows and secrets."

Mephis finally broke the long silence. "Perhaps," he said slowly, "if she could be persuaded to see us in one of the public rooms, just for a few minutes at a time, it might help rebuild her trust in us. Especially if we don't push or ask any difficult questions." He added sadly, "And is being locked within herself while she lives in her body really any different than being lost in the abyss?"

"No," Saetan said softly. "It's not." It was a risk. Mother Night, was it a risk! "I'll talk to her."

Andulvar, Prothvar, Mephis, and Geoffrey left after agreeing to meet him in one of the smaller parlors. Saetan waited for several minutes before walking the few yards that separated his room from the Queen's suite. Once Jaenelle established her court, no males but her Consort, Steward, and Master of the Guard would be permitted in this wing unless they were summoned. Not even her legal guardian.

Saetan knocked quietly on her bedroom door. When he got no answer, he peeked into the room. Empty. He checked the adjoining sitting room. That was empty, too.

Running his fingers through his hair, he wondered where his wayward child had gone. He could sense that she was nearby. But he'd also learned that Jaenelle left such a strong psychic scent, it was sometimes difficult to locate her. Perhaps it had always been that way, but they'd never spent more than an hour or two together at any given time. Now her presence filled the huge Keep, and her dark, delicious psychic scent was a pleasure and a torment. To feel her, to yearn with all one's heart to embrace and serve her, and to be locked out of her life . . .

There could be no greater torture.

And it wasn't just for Andulvar, Mephis, Prothvar, and Geoffrey that he was willing to risk her emotional stability by asking for contact. There was one other, lately never far from his thoughts. If she didn't heal emotionally, if she could never endure a man's touch . . .

He wasn't the key that could unlock that final door. There was much he could do, but not that. He wasn't the key.

Daemon Sadi was.

Daemon . . . Daemon, where are you? Why haven't you come?

Saetan was about to retrace his steps, intending to find Draca—she always knew where *everyone* was in the Keep—when a sound made him turn toward a half-open door at the end of the corridor.

As he walked toward it, he noticed how much better his

leg felt since Jaenelle started dosing him with her tonic. If he could stomach it for a couple more weeks, he'd be able to put the cane away—and hopefully the tonic with it.

He had almost reached the door when someone inside the room let out a startled squawk. There was a loud *pop fizz boosh,* and then a lavender, gray, and rose cloud belched out of the room, followed by a feminine voice muttering, "Damn, damn, and double damn!"

The cloud began a slow descent to the floor.

Saetan held out his hand and stared at the chalky lavender, gray, and rose flecks that covered his skin and shirt cuff. Butterflies churned in his stomach, and they tickled, leaving him with an irrational desire to giggle and flee.

He swallowed the giggle, strapped a bit of mental steel to his backbone, and cautiously peered around the doorway.

Jaenelle stood by a large worktable, her arms crossed and her foot tapping as she frowned at the Craft book hovering above the table. The candle-lights on either side of the book gave off a pretty, stained-glass glow, softening the surrounding chaos. The entire room—and everything in it, including Jaenelle—was liberally dusted with lavender, gray, and rose. Only the book was clean. She must have put a shield around it before beginning . . . whatever it was.

"I really don't think I want to know about this," Saetan said dryly, wondering how Draca was going to react to the mess.

Jaenelle gave him an exasperated, amused look. "No, you really don't." Then she gave him her best unsure-but-game smile. "I don't suppose you'd like to help anyway?"

Hell's fire! During all the years when he'd been teaching her Craft and trying to unravel one of these quirky spells after the fact, he'd hoped for just this invitation.

"Unfortunately," he said, his voice full of wistful regret, "there's something else we have to discuss."

Jaenelle sat down, on air, hooking her heels on the nonexistent rung of a nonexistent stool, and gave him her full attention.

He remembered, too late, how unnerving it could be to have Jaenelle's undivided attention.

Saetan cleared his throat and glanced around the room,

hoping for inspiration. Maybe her workroom, with the tools of her Craft around her, was the best place to talk after all.

He stepped into the room and leaned against the door-frame. A good neutral place, not invading her territory but acknowledging a right to be there. "I'm concerned, witch-child," he said quietly.

Jaenelle cocked her head. "About what?"

"About you. About the way you avoid all of us. About the way you're shutting yourself away from everyone."

Ice filled her eyes. "Everyone has boundaries and inner barriers."

"I'm not talking about boundaries and inner barriers," he said, not quite able to keep his voice calm. "Of course everyone has them. They protect the inner web and the Self. But you've put up a *wall* between yourself and every-one else, excluding them from even simple contact."

"Perhaps you should be grateful for the wall, Saetan," Jaenelle said in a midnight voice that sent a shiver of fear up his spine.

Saetan. Not Papa. Saetan. And not the way she usually said his name. This sounded like a Queen formally ad-dressing a Warlord Prince.

He didn't know how to respond to her words or the warning.

She stepped off her invisible stool and turned away from him, resting her hands on the dusty table.

"Listen to me," he said, restraining the urgency he felt. "You can't lock yourself away like this. You can't spend the rest of your life in this room creating glorious spells that no one else will see. You're a Queen. You'll have to interact with your court."

"I'm not going to have a court."

Saetan stared at her, stunned. "Of course you'll have a court. You're a Queen."

Jaenelle flashed a look at him that made him cringe. "I'm not required to have a court. I checked. And I don't want to rule. I don't want to control anyone's life but my own."

"But you're Witch." The moment he said it, the room chilled.

"Yes," she said too softly. "I am." Then she turned around.

She dropped the mask of humanity—and the mask called flesh—and let him truly see her for the first time.

The tiny spiral horn in the center of her forehead. The golden mane that wasn't quite fur and wasn't quite hair. The delicately pointed ears. The hands that had sheathed claws. The legs that changed below the knee to accommodate the small hooves. The stripe of golden fur that ran down her spine and ended at the fawn tail that flicked over her buttocks. The exotic face and those sapphire eyes.

Having been Cassandra's Consort all those years ago, he thought he knew and understood Witch. Now he finally understood that Cassandra and the other Black-Jeweled Queens who had come before her had been *called* Witch. Jaenelle truly was the living myth, dreams made flesh.

How foolish he'd been to assume all the dreamers had been human.

"Exactly," Witch said softly, coldly.

"You're beautiful," he whispered. And so very, very dangerous.

She stared at him, puzzled, and he realized there would never be a better time to say what he had to say.

"We love you, Lady," he told her quietly. "We've always loved you, and it hurts more than words can express to be locked out of your life. You don't know how hard it was for us to wait for those few precious minutes that you could spend with us, to wonder and worry about you when you were gone, to feel jealous of people who didn't appreciate what you are. Now . . ." His voice broke. He pressed his lips together and took a deep breath. "We surrendered to you a long time ago. Not even you can change that. Do with us what you will." He hesitated, then added, "No, witch-child, we are *not* grateful for the wall."

He didn't wait for an answer. He left the room as swiftly as he could, tears shining in his eyes.

Behind him came a soft, anguished cry.

He couldn't stand their kindness. He couldn't stand their sympathy and understanding. Geoffrey had warmed a glass of yarbarah for him. Mephis had tucked a lap rug over his legs. Prothvar had stoked the fire to help take away the chill. Andulvar had stayed close to him, silent.

He'd started shaking the moment he had entered the safety of the parlor. He would have collapsed on the floor if Andulvar hadn't caught him and helped him to the chair. They had asked no questions, and except for a hoarsely whispered, "I don't know," he had told them nothing about what had happened—or about what he had seen.

And they had accepted it.

An hour later, feeling somewhat restored physically and emotionally, he still couldn't stand their kindness. What he couldn't stand even more was not knowing what was happening in that workroom.

The parlor door swung open.

Jaenelle stood on the threshold, holding a tray that contained two small carafes and five glasses. All her masks were back in place.

"Draca said you were all hiding in here," she said defensively.

"We're not exactly 'hiding,' witch-child," Saetan replied dryly. "And, if we are, there's room for one more. Want to join us?"

Her smile was shy and hesitant, but her coltish legs swiftly crossed the room until she stood beside Saetan's chair. Then she frowned and turned toward the door. "This room used to be larger."

"Your legs used to be shorter."

"That explains why the stairs feel so awkward," she muttered as she filled two glasses from one carafe and three from the other.

Saetan stared at the glass she gave him. His stomach cringed.

"Um," Prothvar said, as Jaenelle handed out the other glasses.

"Drink it," Jaenelle snapped. "You've all been looking peaky lately." When they hesitated, her voice became brittle. "It's just a tonic."

Andulvar took a sip.

Thank the Darkness for that Eyrien willingness to step

onto any kind of battlefield, Saetan thought as he, too, took a sip.

"How much of this do you make at one time, waif?" Andulvar rumbled.

"Why?" Jaenelle said warily.

"Well, you're quite right about us all feeling peaky. Probably wouldn't hurt to have another glass later on."

Saetan started coughing to hide his own dismay and give the others time to school their expressions. It was one thing for Andulvar to step onto the battlefield. It was quite another to drag them all with him.

Jaenelle fluffed her hair. "It starts to lose its potency an hour after it's made, but it's no trouble to make another batch later on."

Andulvar nodded, his expression serious. "Thank you."

Jaenelle smiled shyly and slipped out of the room.

Saetan waited until he was sure she was out of earshot before turning on Andulvar. "You unconscionable prick," he snarled.

"That's a big word coming from a man who's going to have to drink two glasses of this a day," Andulvar replied smugly.

"We could always pour it into the plants," Prothvar said, looking around for some greenery.

"I already tried that," Saetan growled. "Draca's only comment was that if another plant should suffer a sudden demise, she'd ask Jaenelle to look into it."

Andulvar chuckled, giving the other four men a reason to snarl at him. "Everyone expects Hayllians to be devious, but Eyriens are known for their forthright dealings. So when one of *us* acts deviously . . ."

"You did it so she'd have a reason to check up on us," Mephis said, eyeing his glass. "I thank you for that, Andulvar, but couldn't—"

Saetan sprang to his feet. "It loses its potency after an hour."

Andulvar raised his glass in a salute. "Just so."

Saetan smiled. "If we hold back half of each dose so that it's lost most of its potency and then mix it with the fresh dose . . ."

"We'll have a restorative tonic that has a tolerable potency," Geoffrey finished, looking pleased.

"If she finds out, she'll kill us," Prothvar grumbled.

Saetan raised an eyebrow. "All things considered, my fine demon, it's a little late to be concerned about *that*, don't you think?"

Prothvar almost blushed.

Saetan narrowed his golden eyes at Andulvar. "But we didn't know it would lose its potency until *after* you asked for a second dose."

Andulvar shrugged. "Most healing brews have to be taken shortly after they're made. It was worth the gamble." He smiled at Saetan with all the arrogance only an Eyrien male was capable of. "However, if you're admitting your balls aren't as big—"

Saetan said something pithy and to the point.

"Then there's no problem, is there?" Andulvar replied.

They looked at each other, centuries of friendship, rivalry, and understanding reflected in two pairs of golden eyes. They raised their glasses and waited for the others to follow suit.

"To Jaenelle," Saetan said.

"To Jaenelle," the others replied.

Then they sighed in unison and swallowed half their tonic.

7 / Kaeleer

Not quite content, Saetan watched the lights of Riada, the largest Blood village in Ebon Rih and the closest one to the Keep, shine up from the valley's fertile darkness like captured pieces of starlight.

He had watched the sun rise today. No, more than that. He had stood in one of the small formal gardens and had actually felt the sun's warmth on his face. For the first time in more centuries than he cared to count, there had been no lancing pain in his temples, no brutal stomach-twisting headache to tell him just how far he had stepped from the living, no weakening in his strength.

He was as physically strong now as when he first became a Guardian, first began walking that fine line between living and dead.

Jaenelle and her tonic had done that. Had done more than that.

He'd forgotten how sensual food could be, and over the past few days had savored the taste of rare beef and new potatoes, of roasted chicken and fresh vegetables. He'd forgotten how good sleep could feel, instead of that semiawake rest Guardians usually indulged in during the daylight hours.

He'd also forgotten how hunger pangs felt or how fuzzy-brained a man could be when he was beyond tired.

Everything has a price.

He smiled cautiously at Cassandra when she joined him at the window. "You look lovely tonight," he said, making a small gesture that took in her long black gown, the open-weave emerald shawl, and the way she'd styled her dusty-red hair.

"Too bad the Harpy didn't bother to dress for the occasion," Cassandra replied tartly. She wrinkled her nose. "She could have at least worn something around her throat."

"And you could have refrained from offering to lend her a high-necked gown," Saetan snapped. Then he clenched his teeth to trap the rest of the words. Titian didn't need a defender, especially after her slur about the delicate sensibilities of prissy aristo witches.

He watched the lights of Riada wink out, one by one.

Cassandra took a deep breath, let it out in a sigh. "It wasn't supposed to be like this," she said quietly. "The Black were never meant to be Birthright Jewels. I became a Guardian because I thought the next Witch would need a friend, someone to help her understand what she would become after making the Offering to the Darkness. But what has happened to Jaenelle has changed her so much she'll never be normal."

"*Normal?* Just what do you call 'normal,' Lady?"

She looked pointedly at the corner of the room where Andulvar, Prothvar, Mephis, and Geoffrey were trying to include Titian in the conversation and keep a respectful distance at the same time.

"Jaenelle just celebrated her fifteenth birthday. Instead of a party and a roomful of young friends, she spent the evening with demons, Guardians—and a Harpy. Can you honestly call that normal?"

"I've had this conversation before," Saetan growled. "And my answer is still the same: for her, that *is* normal."

Cassandra studied him for a moment before saying quietly, "Yes, you would see it that way, wouldn't you?"

He saw the room through a red haze before he got his temper tightly leashed. "Meaning what?"

"You became the High Lord of Hell while you were still living. You wouldn't see anything wrong with her having the *cildru dyathe* for playmates or having a Harpy teach her how to interact with males."

Saetan's breath whistled between his teeth. "When you foresaw her coming, you called her the daughter of my soul. But those were just words, weren't they? Just a way to ensure that I would become a Guardian so that my strength would be at your disposal for the protection of your apprentice, the young witch who would sit at your feet, awed by the attention of the Black-Jeweled Witch. Except it didn't work out that way. The one who came really *is* the daughter of my soul, and she is awed by no one and sits at no one's feet."

"She may be awed by no one," Cassandra said coldly, "but she also *has* no one." Then her voice softened. "And for that, I pity her."

She has me!

The quick, sharp look Cassandra gave him cut his heart.

Jaenelle had him. The Prince of the Darkness. The High Lord of Hell. More than any other reason, *that* was why Cassandra pitied her.

"We should join the others," Saetan said tightly, offering his arm. Despite the anger he felt, he couldn't turn his back on her.

Cassandra started to refuse his gesture of courtesy until she noticed Andulvar's and Titian's cold stares.

"Draca wants to talk with all of us," Andulvar growled

as soon as they approached. He immediately moved away from them, giving himself room to spread his wings. Giving himself room to fight.

Saetan watched him for a moment, then began reinforcing his own considerable defenses. They were different in many ways, but he'd always respected Andulvar's instincts.

Draca entered the room slowly, calmly. Her hands, as usual, were tucked into the long sleeves of her robe. She waited for them to be seated, waited until their attention was centered on her before pinning Saetan with her reptilian stare.

"The Lady iss fifteen today," Draca said.

"Yes," Saetan replied cautiously.

"Sshe wass pleassed with our ssmall offeringss."

It was sometimes difficult to perceive inflections in Draca's sibilant voice, but the words sounded more like a command than a question. "Yes," Saetan said, "I think she was."

A long silence. "It iss time for the Lady to leave the Keep. You are her legal guardian. You will make the arrangementss."

Saetan's throat tightened. The muscles in his chest constricted. "I had promised her that she could stay here."

"It iss time for the Lady to leave. Sshe will live with you at SsaDiablo Hall."

"I propose an alternative," Cassandra said quickly, pressing her fists into her lap. She didn't even glance at Saetan. "Jaenelle could live with me. Everyone knows who—and what—Saetan is, but I—"

Titian twisted around in her chair. "Do you really believe no one in the Shadow Realm knows you're a Guardian? Did you really think your masquerading as one of the living had fooled anyone?"

Anger flared in Cassandra's eyes. "I've always been careful—"

"You've always been a liar. At least the High Lord has been honest about what he is."

"But he *is* the High Lord—and that's the point."

"The *point* is you want to be the one who shapes Jaenelle just like Hekatah wants to shape Jaenelle, to mold her into an image of *your* choosing instead of letting her be what she is."

"How dare you speak to me like that? I'm a Black-Jeweled Queen!"

"You're not my Queen," Titian snarled.

"Ladies." Saetan's voice rolled through the room like soft thunder. He took a moment to steady his temper before turning his attention back to Draca.

"Sshe will live at the Hall," Draca said firmly. "It iss decided."

"Since you haven't discussed this with any of us until now, *who* decided this?" Cassandra said sharply.

"Lorn hass decided."

Saetan forgot how to breathe.

Hell's fire, Mother Night, and may the Darkness be merciful.

No one argued. No one made so much as a sound.

Saetan realized his hands were shaking. "Could I talk to him? There are some things he may not understand about—"

"He undersstandss, High Lord."

Saetan looked up at the Seneschal of Ebon Askavi.

"The time hass not yet come for you to meet him," Draca said. "But it *will* come." She tipped her head slightly. It was as much deference as she ever showed to anyone. Except, perhaps, to Jaenelle.

They watched her leave, listening to her slow, careful footsteps until the sound faded away completely.

Andulvar let his breath out in an explosive *ffooooh.* "When she wants to cut someone off at the knees, she's got an impressive knife."

Saetan leaned his head against the chair and closed his eyes. "Doesn't she though?"

Cassandra carefully rearranged her shawl and stood up, not looking at any of them. "If you'll excuse me, I'll retire now."

They rose and bid her good night.

Titian also excused herself. But before she left, she gave Saetan a sly smile. "Living at the Hall with Jaenelle will probably be difficult, High Lord, but not for the reasons you think."

"Mother Night," Saetan muttered before turning to the other men.

Mephis cleared his throat. "Telling the waif she has to leave isn't going to be easy. You don't have to do it alone."

"Yes, I do, Mephis," Saetan replied wearily. "I made her a promise. I'm the one who has to tell her I'm going to break it."

He said good night and slowly made his way through the stone corridors until he reached the stairs that would take him to Jaenelle's suite. Instead of climbing them, he leaned against the wall, shivering.

He had promised her that she could stay. He had *promised*.

But Lorn had decided.

It was long after midnight before he joined her in the private garden connected to her suite. She gave him a sleepy, relaxed smile and held out her hand. Gratefully, he linked his fingers through hers.

"It was a lovely party," Jaenelle said as they strolled through the garden. "I'm glad you invited Char and Titian." She hesitated. "And I'm sorry it was so difficult for Cassandra."

Saetan gave her a considering look through narrowed eyes.

She acknowledged the look with a shrug.

"How much did you hear?"

"Eavesdropping is rude," she said primly.

"An answer that neatly sidesteps the question," he replied dryly.

"I didn't *hear* anything. But I *felt* you all grumbling."

Saetan drifted closer to her. She smelled of wildflowers and sun-drenched meadows and fern-shaded pools of water. It was a scent that was gently wild and elusive, that captivated a male because it didn't try to capture him.

It relaxed him—and slightly aroused him.

Even knowing it was a Warlord Prince's natural response to a Queen he felt emotionally bound to, even knowing he would never cross the distinct line that separated a father's affection from a lover's passion, he still felt ashamed of his reaction.

He looked at her, wanting the sharp reminder of who she was and how young she was. But it was Witch who looked back at him, Witch whose hand tightened on his so that he couldn't break the physical link.

"I suppose even a wise man can sometimes be a fool," she said in her midnight voice.

"I would never—" His voice broke. "You know I would never—"

He saw a flicker of amusement in her ancient, haunted eyes.

"Yes, *I* know. Do you? You adore women, Saetan. You always have. You like to be near them. You like to touch them." She held up their hands.

"This is different. You're my daughter."

"And so you will keep your distance from Witch?" she asked sadly.

He pulled her into his arms and held her so tightly she let out a breathless squeak. "Never," he said fiercely.

"Papa?" Jaenelle said faintly. "Papa, I can't breathe."

He immediately loosened his hold but didn't let go.

Soft night sounds filled the garden. The spring wind sighed.

"This mood of yours has something to do with Cassandra, doesn't it?" Jaenelle asked.

"A little." He rested his cheek against her head. "We have to leave the Keep."

Her body tensed so much his ached in response.

"Why?" she finally asked, leaning back far enough to see his face.

"Because Lorn has decided we should live at the Hall."

"Oh." Then she added, "No wonder you're moody."

Saetan laughed. "Yes. Well. He does have a way of limiting one's options." He gently brushed her hair away from her face. "I do want to live at the Hall with you. I want that very much. But if you want to live somewhere else or have any reservations about leaving the Keep right now, I'll fight him over it."

Her eyes widened until they were huge. "Oh, dear. That wouldn't be a good idea, Saetan. He's *much* bigger than you."

Saetan tried to swallow. "I'll still fight him."

"Oh, dear." She took a deep breath. "Let's try living at the Hall."

"Thank you, witch-child," he said weakly.

She wrapped an arm around his waist. "You look a bit wobbly."

"Then I look better than I feel," he said, draping an arm around her shoulders. "Come along, little witch. The next few days are going to be hectic, and we'll both need our rest."

8 / Kaeleer

Saetan opened the front door of SaDiablo Hall and stepped into orchestrated chaos.

Maids flitted in every direction. Footmen lugged pieces of furniture from one room to another for no reason he could fathom. Gardeners trotted in with armloads of freshly cut flowers.

Standing in the center of the great hall, holding a *long* list in one hand while conducting the various people and parcels to their rightful places with the other, was Beale, his Red-Jeweled butler.

Somewhat bemused, Saetan walked toward Beale, hoping for an explanation. By the time he'd taken half a dozen steps, he realized that a walking obstacle had not been taken into account in this frenzied dance. Maids bumped into him, their annoyed expressions barely changing upon recognizing their employer, and their "Excuse me, High Lord," just short of being rude.

When he finally reached Beale, he gave his butler a sharp poke in the shoulder.

Beale glanced back, noticed Saetan's stony expression, and lowered his arms. A thud immediately followed, and a maid began wailing, "Now look what you've done."

Beale cleared his throat, tugged his vest down over his

girth, and waited, a slightly flushed but once more imperturbable butler.

"Tell me, Beale," Saetan crooned, "do you know who I am?"

Beale blinked. "You're the High Lord, High Lord."

"Ah, good. Since you recognize me, I must still be in human form."

"High Lord?"

"I don't look like a freestanding lamp, for example, so no one's going to try to tuck me into a corner and put a couple of candle-lights in my ears. And I won't be mistaken for an animated curio table that someone will leash to a chair so I don't wander off too far."

Beale's eyes bugged out a bit but he quickly recovered. "No, High Lord. You look exactly as you did yesterday."

Saetan crossed his arms and took his time considering this. "Do you suppose if I go into my study and stay there, I might escape being dusted, polished, or otherwise rearranged?"

"Oh, yes, High Lord. Your study was cleaned this morning."

"Will I recognize it?" Saetan murmured. He retreated to his study and sighed with relief. It was all the same furniture, and it was all arranged the same way.

Slipping out of the black tunic-styled jacket, he tossed it over the back of a chair, settled into the leather chair behind his desk, and rolled up the sleeves of his white silk shirt. Looking at the closed study door, he shook his head, but his eyes were a warm gold and his smile was an understanding one. After all, he had brought this on himself by telling them in advance.

Tomorrow, Jaenelle was coming home.

CHAPTER
FOUR

1 / Hell

"That gutter son of a whore is up to something. I can feel it."

Deciding it was better to say nothing, Greer sat back in the patched chair and watched Hekatah pace.

"For two glorious years he's barely been felt, let alone seen in Hell or Kaeleer. His strength was waning. I *know* it was. Now he's back, residing at the Hall in Kaeleer. *Residing.* Do you know how long it's been since he's made his presence felt in one of the living Realms?"

"Seventeen hundred years?" Greer replied.

Hekatah stopped pacing and nodded. "Seventeen hundred years. Ever since Daemon Sadi and Lucivar Yaslana were taken away from him." She closed her gold eyes and smiled maliciously. "How he must have howled when Dorothea denied him paternity at Sadi's Birthright Ceremony, but there was nothing he could do without sacrificing his precious honor. So he slunk away like a whipped dog, consoling himself that he still had the child Hayll's Black Widows couldn't claim." She opened her eyes and hugged herself. "But Prythian had already gotten to the boy's mother and told her all those wonderful half-truths one can tell the ignorant about Guardians. It was one of the few things that winged sow has ever done right." Her pleasure faded. "So why is he back?"

"Could—" Greer considered, shook his head.

Hekatah tapped her fingertips against her chin. "Has he

found another darling to replace his little pet? Or has he finally decided to turn Dhemlan into a feeding ground? Or is it something else?"

She walked toward him, her swaying hips and coquettish smile making him wish he'd known her when he could have done more than just appreciate what her movements implied.

"Greer," she crooned as she slipped her arms around his neck and pressed her breasts against him. "I want a little favor."

Greer waited, wary.

Hekatah's coquettish smile hardened. "Have your balls shriveled up so quickly, darling?"

Anger flashed in Greer's eyes. He hid it quickly. "You want me to go to the Hall in Kaeleer?"

"And risk losing you?" Hekatah pouted. "No, darling, there's no need for you to go to that nasty Hall. We have a loyal ally living in Halaway. He's wonderful at sifting out tidbits of information. Talk to him." Balancing on her toes, she lightly kissed Greer's lips. "I think you'll like him. You're two of a kind."

2 / Kaeleer

Beale opened the study door. "Lady Sylvia," he announced as he respectfully stepped aside for Halaway's Queen.

Meeting her in the middle of the room, Saetan offered both hands, palms down. "Lady."

"High Lord," she replied, placing her hands beneath his, palms up in formal greeting, leaving wrists vulnerable to nails.

Saetan kept his expression neutral, but he approved of the slight pressure pushing his hands upward, the subtle reminder of a Queen's strength. There were some Queens who deeply resented having to live with the bargain that the Dhemlan Queens in Terreille *and* Kaeleer had made with him thousands of years ago in order to protect the Dhemlan Territory in Terreille from Hayll's encroachment, who deeply resented being ruled by a male. There were some who had never understood that, in his own way, he had always served a Queen, that he had always served Witch.

Fortunately, Sylvia wasn't one of them.

She was the first Queen born in Halaway since her great-grandmother had ruled, and she was the pride of the village. The day after she had formed her court, she had come to the Hall and had informed him with forceful politeness that, while Halaway might exist to serve the Hall, it was her territory and they were her people, and if there was anything he wanted from her village she would do her utmost to honor his request—provided it was reasonable.

Saetan now offered her a warm but cautious smile as he led her to the half of his study that was furnished for less formal discussions.

After watching her perch on the edge of one of the overstuffed chairs, he took a seat on the black leather couch, putting the width of the low blackwood table between them. He picked up the decanter of yarbarah, filled one of the ravenglass goblets, and warmed it slowly over a tongue of witchfire before offering it to her.

As soon as she took the glass, he busily prepared one for himself so that he wouldn't insult her by laughing at her expression. She probably had the same look when one of her sons tried to hand her a large, ugly bug that only a small boy could find delightful.

"It's lamb's blood," he said mildly as he leaned back and crossed his legs at the knee.

"Oh." She smiled weakly. "Is that good?"

Her voice got husky when she was nervous, he noted with amusement.

"Yes, that's good. And probably far more to your liking than the human blood you feared was mixed with the wine."

She took a sip, trying hard not to gag.

"It's an acquired taste," Saetan said blandly. Had Jaenelle tasted the blood wine yet? If not, he'd have to correct that omission soon. "You've piqued my curiosity." He altered his deep voice so that it was coaxing, soothing. "Very few

Queens would willingly have an audience with me at midnight, let alone request one."

Sylvia carefully set her goblet on the table before pressing her hands against her legs. "I wanted a private meeting, High Lord."

"Why?"

Sylvia licked her lips, took a deep breath, and looked him in the eye. "Something's wrong in Halaway. Something subtle. I feel . . ." She frowned and shook her head, deeply troubled.

Saetan wanted to reach out and smooth away the sharp vertical line that appeared between her eyebrows. "What do you feel?"

Sylvia closed her eyes. "Ice on the river in the middle of summer. Earth leeched of its richness. Crops withering in the fields. The wind brings a smell of fear, but I can't trace the source." She opened her eyes and smiled self-consciously. "I apologize, High Lord. My former Consort used to say I made no sense when I explained things."

"Really?" Saetan replied too softly. "Perhaps you had the wrong Consort, Lady. Because I understand you all too well." He drained his goblet and set it on the table with exaggerated care. "Who among your people is being harmed the most?"

Sylvia took a deep breath. "The children."

A vicious snarl filled the room. It was only when Sylvia nervously glanced toward the door that Saetan realized the sound was coming from him. He stopped it abruptly, but the cold, sweet rage was still there. Taking a shuddering breath, he backed away from the killing edge.

"Excuse me." Giving her no time to make excuses to leave, Saetan walked out of his study, ordered refreshments, and then spent several minutes pacing the great hall until he had repaired the frayed leash that kept his temper in check. By the time he rejoined her, Beale had brought the tea and a plate of small, thin sandwiches.

She politely refused the sandwiches and didn't touch the tea he poured for her. Her uneasiness scraped at his temper. Hell's fire, he hated seeing that look in a woman's eyes.

Sylvia licked her lips. Her voice was very husky. "I'm

their Queen. It's my problem. I shouldn't have troubled you with it."

He slammed the cup and saucer down on the table so hard the saucer broke in half. Then he put some distance between them, giving himself room to pace but always staying close enough so that she couldn't reach the door before he did.

It shouldn't matter. He should be used to it. If she'd been afraid of him from the moment she stepped into the room, he could have handled it. But she hadn't been afraid. Damn her, she *hadn't* been afraid.

He spun around, keeping the couch and the table between them. "I have never harmed you or your people," he snarled. "I've used my strength, my Craft, my Jewels, and, yes, my temper to protect Dhemlan. Even when I wasn't visible, I still looked after you. There are many services—including highly personal services—that I could have required of you or any other Queen in this Territory, but I've never made those kinds of demands. I've accepted the responsibilities of ruling Dhemlan, and, damn you, I have *never* abused my position or my power."

Sylvia's brown skin was bleached of its warm, healthy color. Her hand shook when she lifted her cup to take a sip of tea. She set the cup down, lifted her chin, and squared her shoulders. "I met your daughter recently. I asked her if she found it difficult living with your temper. She looked genuinely baffled, and said, 'What temper?' "

Saetan stared at her for a moment, then the anger drained away. He rubbed the back of his neck, and said dryly, "Jaenelle has a unique way of looking at a great many things."

Before he could summon Beale, the teapot and used cups vanished. A moment later a fresh pot of tea appeared on the table, along with clean cups and saucers and a plate of pastries.

Saetan gave the door a speculative look before returning to the couch. He poured another cup of tea for Sylvia and one for himself.

"He didn't bring them in," Sylvia said quietly.

"I noticed," Saetan replied—and wondered just how

close his butler was standing to the study door. He put an
aural shield around the room.

"Maybe he felt intimidated."

Saetan snorted. "Any man who is happily married to
Mrs. Beale isn't intimidated by anyone—including me."

"I see your point." Sylvia picked up a sandwich and took
a bite.

Relieved that her color was back and she was no longer
afraid, he picked up his tea and leaned back. "I'll find out
what's happening in Halaway. And I'll stop it." He sipped
his tea to cover his hesitation, but the question had to be
asked. "When did it start?"

Sylvia looked at him sharply. "Your daughter isn't the
cause, High Lord. I met her only briefly one afternoon
when Mikal, my youngest son, and I were out walking; but
I know she isn't the cause." She fiddled with her cup, nervous again. "But she may be the catalyst. Maybe it's fairer
to say that it's her presence that has made me aware of it."

Saetan held his breath, waiting. Coaxing Jaenelle to try
the Halaway school for the last few weeks before summer
had been difficult. He'd hoped reconnecting with other children might stir her interest in contacting her old friends.
Instead, she'd become more withdrawn, more elusive. And
the politely phrased queries from Lord Menzar about her
formal education—or lack of it—had dismayed him because, except for the Craft he had taught her, he had no
idea how her education had been structured. But with each
day since they'd come to the Hall, he had seen the threads
he was trying to weave between himself and her unravel as
fast as he could weave them, and he had had no idea, no
clue as to why that was so. Until now.

"Why?"

Sylvia, lost in her own thoughts, stared at him, puzzled.

"Why is she the catalyst?" Saetan repeated.

"Oh." The vertical line between Sylvia's eyebrows reappeared as she concentrated. "She's . . . different."

Don't lash out at her, Saetan reminded himself. *Just listen.*

"Beron, my older son, has some classes with her, and
we've talked. Not that your household is fodder for gossip,
but she puzzles him so he asks me things."

"Why does she puzzle him?"

She nibbled on a sandwich, considering. "Beron says she's very shy, but if you can get her to talk, she says the most amazing things."

"I can believe that," Saetan said dryly.

"Sometimes when she's talking to someone or giving an answer in class, she'll stop in mid-sentence and cock her head, as if she's listening intensely to something no one else can hear. Sometimes when that happens, she'll pick up the sentence where she left off. Sometimes she'll withdraw into herself and won't speak for the rest of the day."

What voices did Jaenelle hear? Who—or what—called to her?

"Sometimes during a rest break, she'll walk away from the other children and not return until the next morning," Sylvia said.

She didn't return to the Hall, or he would have known about this before now. And she wasn't riding the Winds. He would have felt her absence if she had traveled beyond easy awareness. Mother Night, where did she go? Back into the abyss?

The possibility terrified him.

Sylvia took a deep breath. Took another. "Yesterday, the older students went on a trip to Marasten Gardens. Do you know it?"

"It's a large estate near the border of Dhemlan and Little Terreille. It has some of the finest gardens in Dhemlan."

"Yes." Sylvia had trouble swallowing the last bite of her sandwich. She carefully wiped her fingers on the linen napkin. "According to Beron, Jaenelle got separated from the others, although no one noticed until it was time to leave. He went back to look for her and . . . he found her kneeling beside a tree, weeping. She'd been digging, and her hands were scratched and bleeding." Sylvia stared at the teapot, breathing quickly. "Beron helped her up and reminded her that they weren't supposed to dig up the plants. And she said, 'I was planting it.' When he asked her why, she said, 'For remembrance.' "

The cold made Saetan's muscles ache, made his blood

sluggish. This wasn't the searing, cleansing cold of rage. This was fear. "Did Beron recognize the plant?"

"Yes. I had shown it to him only last year and explained what it was. None of it, thank the Darkness, grows in Halaway." Sylvia looked at him, deeply troubled. "High Lord, she was planting witchblood."

Why hadn't Jaenelle told him? "If the witchblood blooms . . ."

Sylvia looked horrified. "It won't unless. . . . It mustn't!"

Saetan spaced his words carefully, feeling too fragile to have even words collide. "I'll have that area investigated. Discreetly. And I'll take care of the problem in Halaway."

"Thank you." Sylvia fussed with the folds of her dress.

Saetan waited, forcing himself to be patient. He wanted to be alone, wanted time to think. But Sylvia obviously had something else on her mind. "What?"

"It's trivial in comparison."

"But?"

In one swift glance, Sylvia examined him from head to toe. "You have very good taste in clothes, High Lord."

Saetan rubbed his forehead, trying to find a connection. "Thank you." Hell's fire! How did women make these mental jumps so easily? *Why* did they make them?

"But you're probably not aware of what is considered fashionable for a young woman these days." It wasn't quite a question.

"If that's your way of telling me that Jaenelle looks like she got her wardrobe from an attic, then you're right. I think the Seneschal of the Keep opened every old trunk that was left there and let my wayward child pick and choose." It was a small subject, a safe subject. He became happily grumpy. "I wouldn't mind so much if any of them fit—that's not true, I *would* mind. She should have new clothes."

"Then why don't you take her shopping in Amdarh, or one of the nearby towns, or even Halaway?"

"Do you think I haven't tried?" he growled.

Sylvia made no comment for several moments. "I have two sons. They're very good boys—for boys—but they're not much fun to go shopping with." She gave him a twinkling little smile. "Perhaps if it was just two women having lunch and then looking around . . ."

Saetan called in a leather wallet and handed it to Sylvia. "Is that enough?"

Sylvia opened the wallet, riffled through the gold marks, and laughed. "I think we can get a decent wardrobe or three out of this."

He liked her laugh, liked the finely etched lines around her eyes. "You'll spend some of that on yourself, of course."

Sylvia gave him her best Queen stare. "I didn't suggest this with the expectation of being paid for helping a young Sister."

"I didn't offer it as payment, but if you feel uncomfortable about using some of it to please yourself, then do it to please me." He watched her expression change from anger to uneasiness, and he wondered who the fool had been who had made her unhappy. "Besides," he added gently, "you should set a proper example."

Sylvia vanished the wallet and stood up. "I will, naturally, provide you with receipts for all of the purchases."

"Naturally."

Saetan escorted her to the great hall. Taking her cape from Beale, he settled it carefully over her shoulders.

As they slowly walked to the door, Sylvia studied the carved wooden moldings that ran along the top of each wall. "I've only been here half a dozen times, if that. I never noticed the carvings before.

"Whoever carved these was very talented," she said. "Did he also make the sketches for all these creatures?"

"No." He heard the defensiveness in his voice and winced.

"You made the sketches." She studied the carvings with more interest, then muffled a laugh. "I think the woodcarver played a little with one of your sketches, High Lord. That little beasty has his eyes crossed and is sticking his tongue out—and he's placed just about where someone would stop after walking in. Apparently the beasty doesn't think much of your guests." She paused and studied him with as much interest as she'd just given the carving. "The woodcarver didn't play with your sketch, did he?"

Saetan felt his face heat. He bit back a growl. "No."

"I see," Sylvia said after a long moment. "It's been an interesting evening, High Lord."

Not sure how to interpret that remark, he escorted her into her carriage with a bit more haste than was proper.

When he could no longer hear the carriage wheels, he turned toward the open front door, wishing he could postpone the next conversation. But Jaenelle was more attuned to him during the dark hours, more revealing when hidden in shadows, more—

The sound snapped his thoughts. Holding his breath, Saetan looked toward the north woods that bordered the Hall's lawns and formal gardens. He waited, but the sound didn't come again.

"Did you hear it?" he asked Beale when he reached the door.

"Hear what, High Lord?"

Saetan shook his head. "Nothing. Probably a village dog strayed too far from home."

She was still awake, walking in the garden below her rooms.

Saetan drifted toward the waterfall and small pool in the center of the garden, letting her feel his presence without intruding on her silence. It was a good place to talk because the lights from her rooms on the second floor didn't quite reach the pool.

He settled comfortably on the edge of the pool and let the peace of a soft, early summer night and the murmur of water soothe him. While he waited for her, he idly stirred the water with his fingers and smiled.

He'd told her to landscape this inner garden for her own pleasure. The formal fountain had been the first thing to go. As he studied the water lilies, water celery, and dwarf cattails she'd planted in the pool and the ferns she'd planted around it, he wondered again if she had just wanted something that looked more natural or if she had been trying to re-create a place she had known.

"Do you think it's inappropriate?" Jaenelle asked, her voice drifting out of the shadows.

Saetan dipped his hand into the pool and raised the

cupped palm, watching the water trickle through his fingers.
"No, I was wishing I'd thought of it myself." He flicked
drops of water from his fingers and finally looked at her.

The dark-colored dress she was wearing faded into the
surrounding shadows, giving him the impression that her
face, one bare shoulder, and the golden hair were rising up
out of the night itself.

He looked away, focusing on a water lily but intensely
aware of her.

"I like the sound of water singing over stone," Jaenelle
said, coming a little closer. "It's restful."

*But not restful enough. How many things haunt you,
witch-child?*

Saetan listened to the water. He pitched his voice to
blend with it. "Have you planted witchblood before?"

She was silent so long he didn't think she would answer,
but when she did, her voice had that midnight, sepulchral
quality that always produced a shiver up his spine. "I've
planted it before."

Sensing her brittleness, he knew he was getting too close
to a soul-wound—and secrets. "Will it bloom in Marasten
Gardens?" he asked quietly, once more moving his fingers
slowly through the water.

Another long silence. "It will bloom."

Which meant a witch who had died violently was buried there.

Tread softly, he cautioned himself. This was dangerous
ground. He looked at her, needing to see what those ancient, haunted eyes would tell him. "Will we have to plant
it in Halaway?"

Jaenelle turned away. Her profile was all angles and shadows, an exotic face carved out of marble. "I don't know."
She stood very still. "Do you trust your instincts, Saetan?"

"Yes. But I trust yours more."

She had the strangest expression, but it was gone so swiftly
he didn't know what it meant. "Perhaps you shouldn't." She
laced her fingers together, pressing and pressing until dark
beads of blood dotted her hands where her nails pierced her
skin. "When I lived in Beldon Mor, I was often . . . ill. Hospi-

talized for weeks, sometimes months at a time." Then she added, "I wasn't physically ill, High Lord."

Breathe, damn you, breathe. Don't freeze up now. "Why didn't you ever mention this?"

Jaenelle laughed softly. The bitterness in it tore him apart. "I was afraid to tell you, afraid you wouldn't be my friend anymore, afraid you wouldn't teach me Craft if you knew." Her voice was low and pained. "And I was afraid you were just another manifestation of the illness, like the unicorns and the dragons and . . . the others."

Saetan swallowed his pain, his fear, his rage. There was no outlet for those feelings on a soft night like this. "I'm not part of a dreamscape, witch-child. If you take my hand, flesh will touch flesh. The Shadow Realm, and all who reside in it, are real." He saw her eyes fill with tears, but he couldn't tell if they were tears of pain or relief. While she had lived in Beldon Mor, her instincts had been brutalized until she no longer trusted them. She had recognized the danger in Halaway before Sylvia had, but she had doubted herself so much she hadn't been willing to admit it—just in case someone told her it wasn't real.

"Jaenelle," he said softly, "I won't act until I've verified what you tell me, but please, for the sake of those who are too young to protect themselves, tell me what you can."

Jaenelle walked away, her head down, her golden hair a veil around her face. Saetan turned around, giving her privacy without actually leaving. The stones he sat on felt cold and hard now. He gritted his teeth against the physical discomfort, knowing instinctively that if he moved she wouldn't be able to find the words he needed.

"Do you know a witch called the Dark Priestess?" Jaenelle whispered from the nearby shadows.

Saetan bared his teeth but kept his voice low and calm. "Yes."

"So does Lord Menzar."

Saetan stared at nothing, pressing his hands against the stones, relishing the pain of skin against rough edges. He didn't move, did nothing more than breathe until he heard Jaenelle climb the stairs that led to the balcony outside her rooms, heard the quiet click when she closed the glass door.

He still didn't move except to raise his golden eyes and watch the candle-lights dim one by one.

The last light in Jaenelle's room went out.

He sat beneath the night sky and listened to water sing over stone. "Games and lies," he whispered. "Well, I, too, know how to play games. You shouldn't have forgotten that, Hekatah. I don't like them, but you've just made the stakes high enough." He smiled, but it was too soft, too gentle. "And I know how to be patient. But someday I'm going to have a talk with Jaenelle's foolish Chaillot relatives, and then it will be blood and not water that will be singing over stone in a very . . . private . . . garden."

"Lock it."

Mephis SaDiablo reluctantly turned the key in the door of Saetan's private study deep beneath the Hall, the High Lord's chosen place for very private conversations. He took a moment to remind himself that he had done nothing wrong, that the man who had summoned him was his father as well as the Warlord Prince he served.

"Prince SaDiablo."

The deep voice pulled him toward the man sitting behind the desk.

It was a terrible face that watched him cross the room, so still, so expressionless, so contained. The silver in Saetan's thick black hair formed two graceful triangles at the temples, drawing one's gaze to the golden eyes. Those eyes now burned with an emotion so intense words like "hate" and "rage" were inadequate. There was only one way to describe the High Lord of Hell: cold.

Centuries of training helped Mephis take the last few necessary steps. Centuries and memories. As a boy, he had feared provoking his father's temper, but he'd never feared the man. The man had sung to him, laughed with him, listened seriously to childhood troubles, respected him. It wasn't until he was grown that he understood why the High Lord should be feared—and it wasn't until he was much older that he came to appreciate *when* the High Lord should be feared.

Like now.

"Sit." Saetan's voice had that singsong croon that was usually the last thing a man ever heard—except his own screams.

Mephis tried to find a comfortable position in the chair. The large blackwood desk that separated them offered little comfort. Saetan didn't need to touch a man to destroy him.

A little flicker of irritation leaped into Saetan's eyes. "Have some yarbarah." The decanter lifted from the desk, neatly pouring the blood wine into two glasses. Two tongues of witchfire popped into existence. The glasses tilted, traveled upward, and began turning slowly above the fires. When the yarbarah was warmed, one glass floated to Mephis while the other cradled itself in Saetan's waiting hand. "Rest easy, Mephis. I require your skills, nothing more."

Mephis sipped the yarbarah. "My skills, High Lord?"

Saetan smiled. It made him look vicious. "You are meticulous, you are thorough, and, most of all, I trust you." He paused. "I want you to find out everything you can about Lord Menzar, the administrator of Halaway's school."

"Am I looking for something in particular?"

The cold in the room intensified. "Let your instincts guide you." Saetan bared his teeth in a snarl. "But this is just between you and me, Mephis. I want no one asking questions about what you're seeking."

Mephis almost asked who would dare question the High Lord, but he already knew the answer. Hekatah. This had to do with Hekatah.

Mephis drained his glass and set it carefully on the blackwood desk. "Then with your permission, I'd like to begin now."

3 / Kaeleer

Luthvian hunched her shoulders against the intrusion and vigorously pounded the pestle into the mortar, ignoring the girl hovering in the doorway. If they didn't stop pestering her with their inane questions, she'd never get these tonics made.

"Finished your Craft lesson so soon?" Luthvian asked without turning around.

"No, Lady, but—"

"Then why are you bothering me?" Luthvian snapped, flinging the pestle into the mortar before advancing on the girl.

The girl cowered in the doorway but looked confused rather than frightened. "There's a man to see you."

Hell's fire, you'd think the girl had never seen a man before. "Is he bleeding all over the floor?"

"No, Lady, but—"

"Then put him in the healing room while I finish this."

"He's not here for a healing, Lady."

Luthvian ground her teeth. She was an Eyrien Black Widow and Healer. It grated her pride to have to teach Craft to these Rihlan girls. If she still lived in Terreille, they would have been her servants, not her pupils. Of course, if she still lived in Terreille, she would still be bartering her healing skills for a stringy rabbit or a loaf of stale bread. "If he's not here for—"

She shuddered. If she hadn't closed her inner barriers so tightly in order to shut out the frustrated bleating of her students, she would have felt him the moment he walked into her house. His dark scent was unmistakable.

Luthvian fought to keep her voice steady and unconcerned. "Tell the High Lord I'll be with him shortly."

The girl's eyes widened. She bolted down the hallway, caught a friend by the arm, and began whispering excitedly.

Luthvian quietly closed the door of her workroom. She let out a whimpering laugh and thrust her shaking hands into her work apron's pockets. That little two-legged sheep was trembling with excitement at the prospect of mouthing practiced courtesies to the High Lord of Hell. She was trembling too, but for a very different reason.

Oh, Tersa, in your madness perhaps you didn't know or care what spear was slipped into your sheath. I was young and frightened, but I wasn't mad. He made my body sing, and I thought . . . I thought . . .

Even after so many centuries, the truth still left a bitter taste in her mouth.

Luthvian removed her apron and smoothed out the wrinkles in her old dress as best she could. A hearth-witch would have known some little spell to make it look crisply ironed. A witch in personal service would have known some little spell to smooth and rebraid her long black hair in seconds. She was neither, and it was beneath a Healer's dignity to learn such mundane Craft. It was beneath a Black Widow's dignity to care whether a man—any man—expressed approval of how she dressed.

After locking her workroom and vanishing the key, Luthvian squared her shoulders and lifted her chin. There was only one way to find out why he was here.

As she walked down the main hallway that divided the lower floor of her house, Luthvian kept her pace slow and dignified as befitted a Sister of the Hourglass. Her workroom, healing room, dining room, kitchen, and storerooms took up the back part of the lower floor. Student workroom, study room, Craft library, and the parlor took up the front. Baths and bedrooms for her boarders were on the second floor. Her suite of rooms and a smaller suite for special guests filled the third floor.

She didn't keep live-in servants. Doun was just around the bend in the road, so her hired help went home each night to their own families.

Luthvian paused, not yet willing to open the parlor door. She was an Eyrien exiled among Rihlanders—an Eyrien who had been born without the wings that would have been an unspoken reminder that *she* came from the warrior race who ruled the mountains. So she snapped and snarled, never allowing the Rihlanders to become overly familiar. But that didn't mean she wanted to leave, that she didn't take some satisfaction in her work. She enjoyed the deference paid to her because she was a good Healer and a Black Widow. She had influence in Doun.

But her house didn't belong to her, and the land, like all the land in Ebon Rih, belonged to the Keep. Oh, the house had been built for her, to her specifications, but that didn't mean the owner couldn't show her the front door and lock it behind him.

Was that why he was here, to call in the debt and pay her back?

Taking a deep breath, Luthvian opened the parlor door, not fully prepared to meet her former lover.

He was surrounded by her students, the whole giggling, flirting, lash-batting lot of them. He didn't look bored or desperate to be rid of them, nor was he preening as a young buck might when faced with so much undiluted feminine attention. He was as he'd always been, a courteous listener who wouldn't interrupt inane chatter unless it was absolutely necessary, a man who could skillfully phrase a refusal.

She knew so well how skillfully he could phrase a refusal.

He saw her then. There was no anger in his gold eyes. There was also no warm smile of greeting. That told her enough. Whatever business he had with her was personal but not *personal*.

It made her furious, and a Black Widow in a temper wasn't a woman to tamper with. He saw the shift in her mood, acknowledged it with a slight lift of one eyebrow, and finally interrupted the girls' chatter.

"Ladies," he said in that deep, caressing voice, "I thank you for making my wait so delightful, but I mustn't keep you from your studies any longer." Without raising his voice, he managed to silence their vigorous protests. "Besides, Lady Luthvian's time is valuable."

Luthvian stepped away from the door just enough for them to scurry past her. Roxie, her oldest student, stopped in the doorway, looked over her shoulder, and fluttered her eyelashes at the High Lord.

Luthvian slammed the door in her face.

She waited for him to approach her with the cautious respect a male who serves the Hourglass always displays when approaching a Black Widow. When he didn't move, she blushed at the silent reminder that he didn't serve the Hourglass. He was still the High Priest, a Black Widow who outranked her.

She moved with studied casualness, as if getting close to him had no importance, but stopped with half the length of the room between them. Close enough. "How could you stand listening to that drivel?"

"I found it interesting—and highly educational," he added dryly.

"Ah," Luthvian said. "Did Roxie give you her tasteful or her colorfully detailed version of her Virgin Night? She's the only one old enough to have gone through the ceremony, and she primps and preens and explains to the other girls that she's really too tired for morning lessons these days because her lover's soooo demanding."

"She's very young," Saetan said quietly, "and—"

"She's vulgar," Luthvian snapped.

"—young girls can be foolish."

Tears pricked Luthvian's eyes. She wouldn't cry in front of him. Not again. "Is that what you thought of me?"

"No," Saetan said gently. "You were a natural Black Widow, driven by your intense need to express your Craft, and driven even harder by your need to survive. You were far from foolish."

"I was foolish enough to trust you!"

There was no expression in his golden eyes. "I told you who, and what, I was before I got into bed with you. I was there as an experienced consort to see a young witch through her Virgin Night so that when she woke in the morning the only thing broken was a membrane—not her mind, not her Jewels, not her spirit. It was a role I'd played many times before when I ruled the Dhemlan Territory in both Realms. I understood and honored the rules of that ceremony."

Luthvian grabbed a vase from a side table and flung it at his head. "Was impregnating her part of the understood rules?" she screamed.

Saetan caught the vase easily, then opened his hand and let it smash on the bare wood floor. His eyes blazed, and his voice roughened. "I truly didn't think I was still fertile. I didn't expect the spell's effects to last that long. And if you'll excuse an old man's memory, I distinctly remember asking if you'd been drinking the witch's brew to prevent pregnancy and I distinctly remember you saying that you had."

"What was I supposed to say?" Luthvian cried. "Every hour put me at risk of ending up destroyed under one of Dorothea's butchers. You were my only chance of survival. I knew I was close to my fertile time, but I had to take that risk!"

Saetan didn't move, didn't speak for a long time. "You knew there was a risk, you knew you'd done nothing to prevent it, you deliberately lied to me when I asked you, and *you still dare to blame me*?"

"Not for that," she screamed at him, "but for what came after." There was no understanding in his eyes. "You only cared about the baby. You didn't w-want to b-be with me anymore."

Saetan sighed and wandered over to the picture window, fixing his gaze on the low stone wall that surrounded the property. "Luthvian," he said wearily, "the man who guides a witch through her Virgin Night isn't meant to become her lover. That only happens when there's a strong bond between them beforehand, when they're already lovers in all but the physical sense. Most of the time—"

"You don't have to recite the rules, High Lord," Luthvian snapped.

"—after he rises from the bed, he may become a valued friend or no more than a soft memory. He cares about her—he has to care in order to keep her safe—but there can be a very big difference between caring and loving." He looked over his shoulder. "I cared about you, Luthvian. I gave you what I could. It just wasn't enough."

Luthvian hugged herself and wondered if she'd ever stop feeling the bitterness and disappointment. "No, it wasn't enough."

"You could have chosen another man. You should have. I told you that, even encouraged it."

Luthvian stared at him. *Hurt, damn you, hurt as much as I have.* "And how eager do you think those men were once they realized my son had been sired by the High Lord of Hell?"

The thrust went home, but the hurt and sorrow she saw in his eyes didn't make her feel better.

"I would have taken him, raised him. You knew that, too."

The old rage, the old uncertainties exploded out of her. "Raised him for what? For fodder? To have a steady supply of strong fresh blood? When you found out he was half Eyrien, you wanted to kill him!"

Saetan's eyes glittered. "You wanted to cut off his wings."

"So he'd have a chance at a decent life! Without them he would have passed for Dhemlan. He could have managed one of your estates. He could have been respected."

"Do you really think that would have been a fair trade? Living a lie of respectability against his never knowing about his Eyrien bloodline, never understanding the hunger in his soul when he felt the wind in his face, always wondering about longings that made no sense—until the day he looked at his firstborn and saw the wings. Or were you intending to clip each generation?"

"The wings would have been a throwback, an aberration."

Saetan was very, very still. "I will tell you again what I told you at his birth. He is Eyrien in his soul and that had to be honored above all else. If you had cut off his wings, then yes, I would have slit his throat in the cradle. Not because I wasn't prepared for it, which I wasn't since you took such pains not to tell me, but because he would have suffered too much."

Luthvian honed her temper to a cutting edge. "And you think he hasn't suffered? You don't know much about Lucivar, Saetan."

"And why didn't he grow up under my care, Luthvian?" he said too softly. "Who was responsible for *that*?"

The tears were back. The memories, the anguish, the guilt. "You didn't love me, and you didn't love him."

"Half right, my dear."

Luthvian gulped back a sob. She stared at the ceiling.

Saetan shook his head and sighed. "Even after all these years, trying to talk to each other is pointless. I'd better leave."

Luthvian wiped away the single tear that had escaped

her self-control. "You haven't said why you came here." For the first time, she looked at him without the past blurring the present. He looked older, weighed down by something.

"It would probably be too difficult for all of us."

She waited. His uneasiness, his unwillingness to broach the subject filled her with apprehension—and curiosity.

"I wanted to hire you as a Craft tutor for a young Queen who is also a natural Black Widow and Healer. She's very gifted, but her education has been quite . . . erratic. The lessons would have to be private and held at SaDiablo Hall."

"No," Luthvian said sharply. "Here. If I'm going to teach her, it will have to be here."

"If she came here, she would have to be escorted. Since you've always found Andulvar and Prothvar too Eyrien to tolerate, it would have to be me."

Luthvian tapped a finger against her lips. A Queen who was also a Healer *and* a Black Widow? What a potentially deadly combination of strengths. Truly a challenge worthy of her skills. "She would apprentice with me for the healing and Hourglass training?"

"No. She still has difficulty with much of the Craft we consider basic, and that's what I wanted her to work on with you. I'd be willing to extend her training with you to the healing Craft as well, if that's of interest to you, but I'll take care of the Hourglass's Craft."

Pride demanded a challenge. "Just who is this witch who requires a Black-Jeweled mentor?"

The Prince of the Darkness, the High Lord of Hell studied her, weighing, judging, and finally replied, "My daughter."

4 / Hell

Mephis dropped the file on the desk in Saetan's private study and began rubbing his hands as if to clean away some filth.

Saetan turned his hand in an opening gesture. The file

opened, revealing several sheets of Mephis's tightly packed writing.

"We're going to do something about him, aren't we?" Mephis snarled.

Saetan called in his half-moon glasses, settled them carefully on the bridge of his nose, and picked up the first sheet. "Let me read."

Mephis slammed his hands on the desk. "He's an obscenity!"

Saetan looked over his glasses at his eldest son, betraying none of the anger beginning to bloom. "Let me read, Mephis."

Mephis sprang away from the desk with a snarl and started pacing.

Saetan read the report and then read it again. Finally, he closed the file, vanished the glasses, and waited for Mephis to settle down.

Obscene was an inadequate word for Lord Menzar, the administrator of Halaway's school. Unfortunate accidents or illnesses had allowed Menzar to step into a position of authority at schools in several Districts in Dhemlan—accidents he couldn't be linked to, that had no scent of him. He always showed just enough deference to please, just enough self-assurance to convince others of his ability. And there he would be, carefully undercutting the ancient code of honor and snipping away at the fragile web of trust that bound men and women of the Blood.

What would happen to the Blood once that trust was destroyed? All one had to do was look at Terreille to see the answer.

Mephis stood before the desk, his hands clenched. "What are we going to do?"

"I'll take care of it, Mephis," Saetan said too softly. "If Menzar has been free to spread his poison this long, it's because I wasn't vigilant enough to detect him."

"What about all the Queens and their First Circles who also weren't vigilant enough to detect him when he was in their territories? You didn't ignore a warning that had been sent, you *never got* any warning until Sylvia came to you."

"The responsibility is still mine, Mephis." When Mephis

started to protest, Saetan cut him off. "What would you have me do? Give this information to the Queens now? Show them the evidence of how they'd been manipulated *by a man*? Do you want *them* to call in the debt?"

Mephis shuddered. "No, I don't want that. Their rage would burn for a long time over this."

"And would burn more than the man responsible for it." Saetan forced his voice to be gentle. "There are young witches—Queens, Black Widows, and Priestesses among them—coming of age in Dhemlan who bear the scars of what he's done. We'll have to tell some of the stronger males in those Districts what's happened so they'll be prepared and then do what we can to help them rebuild the trust Menzar destroyed." He shook his head sadly. "No, Mephis, if I'm not willing to accept the responsibilities then I should relinquish my claim to this land."

"His blood shouldn't be on your hands alone," Mephis said quietly.

Thank you, Mephis. I do thank you for that. "A formal execution never has more than one executioner." He paused, then asked, "Is there anyone dependent upon him?"

Mephis nodded. "He has a sister who looks after his house."

"A hearth-witch?"

Mephis's eyes were yellow stones. "Not by training or inclination from what I could determine. It seems he lets her live with him on sufferance—she, according to village gossip no doubt seeded by him, not having the wit or wisdom to be self-sufficient—and lets her pay for her room and board with all manner of domestic services." His voice left no doubt about what kind of services Menzar required.

"Do you think she has the wit and wisdom to be self-sufficient?"

Mephis shrugged. "I doubt she's ever had the chance to try. She doesn't wear Jewels. Whether she never had the potential or had it stripped from her . . . it's difficult to say at this point."

Hekatah, you train your servants well. "Use some of the family income to quietly provide her with an allowance equal to Menzar's wages. The house is leased? Pay the lease for a five-year period."

Mephis crossed his arms. "Without the rent to pay, it will be more money than she's ever had at her disposal."

"It'll give her the time and the means to rest. There's no reason she should pay for her brother's crimes. If her wits have been buried beneath Menzar's manipulation, they'll surface. If she's truly incapable of taking care of herself, we'll make other arrangements."

Mephis looked troubled. "About the execution . . ."

"I'll take care of it, Mephis." Saetan came around the desk and brushed his shoulder against his son's. "Besides, there's something else I want you to do." He waited until Mephis looked at him. "You still have the town house in Amdarh?"

"You know I do."

"And you still enjoy the theater?"

"Very much," Mephis said, puzzled. "I rent a box each season."

"Are there any plays that might intrigue a fifteen-year-old girl?"

Mephis smiled in understanding. "A couple of them next week."

Saetan's answering smile was chilling. "Well-timed, I think. An outing to Dhemlan's capital with her elder brother before her new tutors begin making demands on her time will suit our plans very well."

5 / Terreille

Lucivar's legs quivered from exhaustion and pain. Chained facing the back wall of his cell, he tried to rest his chest against it to lessen the strain on his legs, tried to ignore the tension in his shoulders and neck.

The tears came, slow and silent at first, then building into rib-squeezing, racking sobs of pent-up grief.

The surly guard had performed the beating. Not his back this time but his legs. Not a whip to cut, but a thick leather strap to pound against muscle stretched tight. Working to a slow drum rhythm, the guard had applied the strap with care, making each stroke overlap the one before so that no flesh was missed. Down and back, down and back. Except for the breath hissing between his teeth, Lucivar had made no sound. When it was finally done, he'd been hauled to his feet—feet too brutalized to take his weight—and fitted with Zuultah's latest toy: a metal chastity belt. It locked tight around his waist but the metal loop between his legs wasn't tight enough to cause discomfort. He'd puzzled over it for a moment before being forced to walk to his cell. There wasn't room for anything but the pain after that. And when he got to the cell, he understood only too well what was supposed to happen.

There was a new, thick-linked chain attached to the back wall. The bottom loop of the belt was pulled through a slot in the band around his waist, and the chain was locked to it. The chain wasn't long enough for him to do anything but stand, and if his legs buckled, it wouldn't be his waist absorbing his weight. No doubt Zuultah was being oiled and massaged while she waited for his scream of agony.

That wasn't reason enough to cry.

Slime mold had begun forming on his wings. Without a cleansing by a Healer, it would spread and spread until his wings were nothing more than greasy strings of membranous skin hanging from the frame. He couldn't spread his wings in the salt mine without being whipped, and now his hands were chained behind his back each night, locking his wings tight against a body coated with salt dust and dripping with sweat.

He'd told Daemon once he would rather lose his balls than his wings, and he had meant it.

But that wasn't reason enough to cry.

He hadn't seen the sun in over a year. Except for the few precious minutes each day when he was led from his cell to the salt mines and back again, he hadn't breathed clean air or felt a breeze against his skin. His world had become two dark, stinking holes—and a covered courtyard where he was stretched out on the stones and regularly beaten.

But that wasn't reason enough to cry.

He'd been punished before, beaten before, whipped before, locked in dark cells before. He'd been sold into service to cruel, twisted witches before. He'd always responded by fighting with all the savagery within him, becoming such a destructive force they'd send him back to Askavi in order to survive.

He hadn't once tried to escape from Pruul, hadn't once unleashed his volatile temper to rend and tear and destroy. Not that many years ago, Zuultah's and the guards' blood would have been splashed over the walls of this place and he would have stood in the rubble filling the night with an Eyrien battle cry of victory.

But that was when he'd still believed in the myth, the dream. That was when he'd still believed that one day he would meet the Queen who would accept him, understand him, value him. Meeting her had been his dream, a sweet, ever-blooming flower in his soul. The Lady of the Black Mountain. The Queen of Ebon Askavi. Witch.

Then the dream became flesh—and Daemon killed her.

That was reason to grieve. For the loss of the Lady he'd ached to serve, for the loss of the one man he thought he could trust.

Now there was only an emptiness, a despair so deep it covered his soul like the slime mold was covering his wings.

There was only one dream left.

The ache in his chest finally eased. Lucivar swallowed the last sob and opened his eyes.

He'd always known where he wanted to die and how he wanted to die. And it wasn't in the salt mines of Pruul.

Lucivar's legs vibrated from the strain. He sank his teeth into his lower lip until it bled. A couple more hours and the guards would release him to take him to the salt mines. More pain, more suffering.

He would whimper a little, cringe a little. Next week he would cringe a little more when a guard approached. Little by little they would forget what should never be forgotten about him. And then . . .

Lucivar smiled, his lips smeared with blood.

There was still a reason to live.

6 / Terreille

Dorothea SaDiablo stared at her Master of the Guard. "What do you mean you've called off the search?"

"He's not in Hayll, Priestess," Lord Valrik replied. "My men and I have searched every barn, every cottage, every Blood and landen village. We've been down every alley in every city. Daemon Sadi is not in Hayll, *has not been* in Hayll. I would stake my career on it."

Then you've lost. "You called off the search without my consent."

"Priestess, I'd give my life for you, but we've been chasing shadows. No one has seen him, Blood or landens. The men are weary. They need to be home with their families for a while."

"And ten months from now an army of mewling brats will be testimony to how weary your men are."

Valrik didn't answer.

Dorothea paced, tapping her fingertips against her chin. "So he isn't in Hayll. Start searching the neighboring Territories and—"

"We've no right to make such a search in another Territory."

"All those Territories stand in Hayll's shadow. The Queens wouldn't dare deny you access to their lands."

"The authority of the Queens ruling those Territories is weak as it is. We can't afford to undermine it."

Dorothea turned away from him. He was right, damn him. But she had to get him to do *something.* "Then you leave me at the mercy of the Sadist," she said with a tearful quiver in her voice.

"*No*, Priestess," Valrik said strenuously. "I've talked to the Masters of the Guard in all the neighboring Territories, made them aware of his bestial nature. They understand their own young are at risk. If they find him in their Territory, he won't get out alive."

Dorothea spun around. "I *never* gave you permission to kill him."

"He's a Warlord Prince. It's the only way we'll—"

"You must not kill him."

Dorothea swayed, pleased when Valrik put his arms around her and guided her to a chair. Wrapping her arms around his neck, she pulled his head down until their foreheads touched. "His death would have repercussions for all of us. He must be brought back to Hayll alive. You must at least supervise the search in the other Territories."

Valrik hesitated, then sighed. "I can't. For your sake and the sake of Hayll . . . I can't."

A good man. Older, experienced, respected, honorable.

Dorothea slid her right hand down his neck in a sensuous caress before driving her nails into his flesh and pumping all of her venom through the snake tooth.

Valrik pulled back, shocked, his hand clamped against his neck. "Priestess . . ." His eyes glazed. He stumbled back a step.

Dorothea daintily licked the blood from her fingers and smiled at him. "You said you would give your life for me. Now you have." She studied her nails, ignoring Valrik as he staggered out of the room, dying. Calling in a nail file, she smoothed a rough edge.

A pity to lose such an excellent Master of the Guard and a bother to have to replace him. She vanished the nail file and smiled. But at least Valrik, by example, would teach his successor a very necessary lesson: too much honor could get a man killed.

7 / Kaeleer

Saetan balled the freshly ironed shirt in his hands, massaging it into a mass of wrinkles. He shook it out, grimly satisfied with the results, and slipped it on.

He hated this. He had always hated this.

His black trousers and tunic jacket received the same treatment as the shirt. As he buttoned the jacket, he smiled wryly. Just as well he'd insisted that Helene and the rest of the staff take the evening off. If his prim housekeeper saw him dressed like this, she'd consider it a personal insult.

A strange thing, feelings. He was preparing for an execution and all he felt was relief that his appearance wouldn't bruise his housekeeper's pride.

No, not all. There was anger at the necessity and a simmering anxiety that, because of what he was about to do, he might look into sapphire eyes and see condemnation and disgust instead of warmth and love.

But she was with Mephis in Amdarh. She'd never know about tonight.

Saetan called in the cane he had put aside a few weeks ago.

Of course Jaenelle would know. She was too astute not to understand the meaning behind Menzar's sudden disappearance. But what would she think of him? What would it mean to her?

He had hoped—such a bittersweet thing!—that he could live here quietly and not give people reason to remember too sharply who and what he was. He had hoped to be just a father raising a Queen daughter.

It had never been that simple. Not for him.

No one had ever asked him why he'd been willing to fight on Dhemlan Terreille's behalf when Hayll had threatened that quiet land all of those long centuries ago. Both sides had assumed that ambition had been the driving force within him. But what had driven him had been far more seductive and far simpler: he had wanted a place to call home.

He had wanted land to care for, people to care for, children—his own and others—to fill his house with their laughter and exuberance. He had dreamed of a simple life where he would use his Craft to enrich, not destroy.

But a Black-Jeweled, Black Widow Warlord Prince who was already called the High Lord of Hell couldn't slip into the quiet life of a small village. So he'd named a price worthy of his strength, built SaDiablo Hall in all three Realms, ruled with an iron will and a compassionate heart, and yearned for the day when he would meet a woman whose love for him was stronger than her fear of him.

Instead, he had met and married Hekatah.

For a while, a very short while, he'd thought his dream had come true—until Mephis was born and she was sure he wouldn't walk away, wouldn't forsake his child. Even then, having pledged himself to her, he had tried to be a good husband, had tried even harder to be a good father. When she conceived a second time, he'd dared to hope again that she cared for him, wanted to build a life with him. But Hekatah had been in love only with her ambitions, and children were her payment for his support. It wasn't until she carried their third child that she finally understood he would never use his power to make her the undisputed High Priestess of all the Realms.

He never saw his third son. Only pieces.

Saetan closed his eyes, took a deep breath, and cast the small spell tied to a tangled web of illusions that he'd created earlier in the day. His leg muscles trembled. He opened his eyes and studied hands that now looked gnarled and had a slight but noticeable shake. "I hate this." He smiled slowly. He sounded like a querulous old man.

By the time he made his way to the public reception room, his back ached from being unnaturally hunched and his legs began to burn from the tension. But if Menzar was smart enough to suspect a trap, the physical discomfort would help hide the web's illusions.

Saetan stepped into the great hall and hissed softly at the man standing silently by the door. "I told you to take the evening off." There was no power in his voice, no soft thunder.

"It would not be appropriate for you to open the door when your guest arrives, High Lord," Beale replied.

"What guest? I'm not expecting anyone tonight."

"Mrs. Beale is visiting with her younger sister in Halaway. I will join them after your guest arrives, and we will dine out."

Saetan rested both hands on the cane and raised an eyebrow. "Mrs. Beale dines out?"

Beale's lips curved up a tiny bit. "On occasion. With reluctance."

Saetan's answering smile faded. "Join your lady, Lord Beale."

"After your guest has arrived."

"I'm not expect—"

"My nieces attend the Halaway school." The Red Jewel flared beneath Beale's white shirt.

Saetan sucked air through his teeth. This had to be done quietly. There was nothing the Dark Council could do to him directly, but if whispers of this reached them. . . . He stared at his Red-Jeweled Warlord butler. "How many know?"

"Know what, High Lord?" Beale replied gently.

Saetan continued to stare. Was he mistaken? No. For just a moment, there *had* been a wild, fierce satisfaction in Beale's eyes. The Beales would say nothing. Nothing at all. But they would celebrate.

"You'll be in your public study?" Beale asked.

Accepting his dismissal, Saetan retreated to his study. As he poured and warmed a glass of yarbarah, he noticed that his hands were shaking from more than the spell he'd cast.

Hayllian by birth, he had served in Terreillean courts, and had ruled, for the most part, in Terreille and then Hell. Despite his claim to the Dhemlan Territory in Kaeleer, he had been more like an absentee landlord, a visitor who only saw what visitors were allowed to see.

He knew what Terreille had thought of the High Lord. But this was Kaeleer, the Shadow Realm, a fiercer, wilder land that embraced a magic darker and stronger than Terreille could ever know.

Thank you, Beale, for the warning, the reminder. I won't forget again what ground I stand on. I won't forget what you've just shown me lies beneath the thin cloak of Protocol and civilized behavior. I won't forget . . . because this is the Blood that is drawn to Jaenelle.

Lord Menzar reached for the knocker but snatched his hand away at the last second. The bronze dragon head tucked tight against a thick, curving neck stared down at him, its green glass eyes glittering eerily in the torchlight. The knocker directly beneath it was a detailed, taloned foot curved around a smooth ball.

The Dark Priestess should have warned me.

Grabbing the foot with a sweaty hand, he pounded on the door once, twice, thrice before stepping back and glancing around. The torches created ever-changing shape-filled shadows, and he wished, again, that this meeting could have been held in the daylight hours.

He waved his hand to erase the useless thought and reached for the knocker again just as the door suddenly swung open. He almost stepped back from the large man blocking the doorway until he recognized the black suit and waistcoat that was a butler's uniform.

"You may tell the High Lord I'm here."

The butler didn't move, didn't speak.

Menzar surreptitiously chewed on his lower lip. The man was alive, wasn't he? Since he knew that many of Halaway's people worked for the Hall in one way or another, it hadn't occurred to him that the staff might be very different once the sun went down. Surely not with that girl here—although that might explain her eccentricities.

The butler finally stepped aside. "The High Lord is expecting you."

Menzar's relief at coming inside was short-lived. As shadow-filled as the outer steps, the great hall held a silence that was pregnant with interrupted rustling. He followed the butler to the end of the hall, disturbed by the lack of people. Where were the servants? In another wing, perhaps, or taking their supper? A place this size . . . half the village could be here and their presence would be swallowed up.

The butler opened the last right-hand door and announced him.

It was an interior room with no windows and no other visible door. Shaped like a reversed L, the long side had large chairs, a low blackwood table, a black leather couch, a Dharo carpet, candle-lights held in variously shaped wrought-iron holders, and powerful, somewhat disturbing paintings. The short leg . . .

Menzar gasped when he finally noticed the golden eyes shining out of the dark. A candle-light in the far corner began to glow softly. The short leg held a large blackwood desk. Behind it were floor-to-ceiling bookshelves. The walls on either side were covered with dark-red velvet. It felt different from the rest of the room. It felt dangerous.

The candle-lights brightened, chasing the shadows into the corners.

"Come where I can see you," said a querulous voice.

Menzar slowly approached the desk and almost laughed with relief. This was the High Lord? This shrunken, shaking, grizzled old man? This was the man whose name everyone feared to whisper?

Menzar bowed. "High Lord. It was kind of you to invite me to—"

"Kind? Bah! Didn't see any reason why I should torture my old bones when there's nothing wrong with your legs." Saetan waved a shaking hand toward the chair in front of the desk. "Sit down. Sit down. Tires me just to watch you stand there." While Menzar made himself comfortable, Saetan muttered and gestured to no one. Finally focusing on his guest, he snapped, "Well? What's she done now?"

Tamping down his jubilation, Menzar pretended to consider the question. "She hasn't been in school this week," he said politely. "I understand she'll be tutored from now on. I must point out that socializing with children her own age—"

"Tutors?" Saetan sputtered, thumping his cane on the floor. "Tutors?" Thump. Thump. "Why should I waste my coin on tutors? She's got all the teaching she needs to perform her duties."

"Duties?"

Saetan's mouth curved in a leering smile. "Her mind's a bit queered up and she's not much to look at, but in the dark she's sweet enough."

Menzar tried not to stare. The Dark Priestess's friend had hinted, but. . . . He'd seen no bite marks on the girl's neck. Well, there were other veins. What else might Saetan be doing—or what might she be required to do for him while he supped from a vein? Menzar could imagine several things. They all disgusted him. They all excited him.

Menzar clamped one hand over the other to keep them still. "What about the tutors?"

Saetan waved his hand, dismissing the words. "Had to say something when that bitch Sylvia came sniffing around asking about the girl." He narrowed his eyes. "You strike

me as a very discerning man, Lord Menzar. Would you like
to see my special room?"

Menzar's heart smashed against his chest. *If he invites
you to his private study, make an excuse, any excuse to leave.*
"Special room?"

"My special, special room. Where the girl and I . . .
play."

Menzar was about to refuse, but the doubts and the
warnings melted away. The High Lord was just a lecherous
old man. But no doubt a connoisseur of things Menzar had
only read about. "I'd like that."

The walk through the corridors was painfully slow. Saetan went down flights of stairs crabwise, muttering and cursing. Every time Menzar became uneasy about their descent,
a leering grin and a highly erotic tidbit vanished the
doubts again.

They finally arrived at a thick wooden door with a lock as
big as a man's fist. Menzar waited restlessly while Saetan's
shaking hand fit the key into the lock, and then he had to
help the High Lord push the heavy door open. Who helped
the High Lord at other times? That butler? Did the girl
follow him into the room like a well-trained pet or was she
restrained? Did Saetan require assistance? Did that butler
watch while he . . . Menzar licked his lips. The bed must
be like . . . he couldn't even begin to imagine what the bed
in this playroom would be like.

"Come in, come in," Saetan said querulously.

The torchlight from the corridor didn't penetrate the
room. Standing at the doorway, once more uncertain,
Menzar strained his eyes to see the furnishings, but the
room was filled with a thick, full darkness, a waiting darkness, something more than the absence of light.

Menzar couldn't decide whether to step back or step forward. Then he felt a phantom *something* whisper past him,
leaving a mist so fine it almost wasn't there. But that mist
was full of many things, and in his mind he saw a bouquet
of young faces, the faces of all the witches whose spirits he
had so carefully pruned. He'd always considered himself a
subtle gardener, but this room offered more. Much, much
more.

He stepped inside, drawn toward the center of the room by small phantom hands. Some playfully tugged, some caressed. The last one pressed firmly against his chest, stopping him from taking another step, before sliding down his belly and disappearing just before it reached his expectation.

His disappointment was as sharp as the sound of the lock snapping into place.

Cold. Dark. Silent.

"H-High Lord?"

"Yes, Lord Menzar," said a deep voice that rolled through the room like soft thunder. A seductive voice, caressing in the dark.

Menzar licked his lips. "I must be going now."

"That isn't possible."

"I have another appointment."

Slowly the darkness changed, lessened. A cold, silver light spread along the stone walls, floor, and ceiling, following the radial and tether lines of an immense web. On the back wall hung a huge, black metal spider, its hourglass made of faceted rubies. Attached to the silver web embedded in the stone were knives of every shape and size.

The only other thing in the room was a table.

Menzar's sphincter muscles tightened.

The table had a high lip and channels running to small holes in the corners. Glass tubing ran from the holes to glass jars.

Stop this. Stop it. He was letting his own fear beat him. He was letting this room intimidate him. That old man certainly wasn't intimidating. He could easily brush aside that doddering old fool.

Menzar turned around, ready to insist on leaving.

It took him a long moment to recognize the man leaning against the door, waiting.

"Everything has a price, Lord Menzar," Saetan crooned. "It's time to pay the debt."

The water swirling into the drain finally ran clear. Saetan twisted the dials to stop the hard spray that had been pounding him. He held on to the dials for balance, resting his head on his forearm.

It wasn't over. There were still the last details to attend to.

He toweled himself briskly, dropped the towel on the narrow bed as he passed through the small bedroom adjoining his private study deep beneath the Hall in the Dark Realm. A carafe of yarbarah waited for him on the large blackwood desk. He reached for it, hesitated, then called in a decanter of brandy. He filled a glass almost to the rim and drank it down. The brandy would give him a fierce headache, but it would also soften the edges, blur the memories and twisted fantasies that had burst from Menzar's mind like pus from a boil.

Brandy also didn't taste like blood, and the taste, the smell of blood wasn't something he could tolerate tonight.

He poured his second glass and stood naked in front of the unlit hearth, staring at Dujae's painting *Descent into Hell.* A gifted artist to have captured in ambiguous shapes that mixture of terror and joy the Blood felt when first entering the Dark Realm.

He poured his third glass. He had burned the clothes he'd worn. He had never been able to tolerate keeping the clothing worn for an execution. Some part of the fear and the pain always seemed to weave itself into the cloth. To be assaulted by it afterward . . .

The glass shattered in his hand. Snarling, he vanished the broken glass before returning to the small bedroom and hurriedly dressing in fresh clothes.

He had scrubbed Menzar off his body, but would he ever be able to cleanse Menzar's thoughts from his mind?

"You understand what to do?"

Two demons, once Halaway men, eyed the large, ornate wooden chest. "Yes, High Lord. It will been done precisely as you asked."

Saetan handed each of them a small bottle. "For your trouble."

"It's no trouble," one said. He pulled the cork from the bottle and sniffed. His eyes widened. "It's—"

"Payment."

The demon corked the bottle and smiled.

"The *cildru dyathe* don't want this."

Saetan set the small bottle on a flat rock that served as a table. He had distributed all the others. This was the last. "I'm not offering it to the rest of the *cildru dyathe*. Only you."

Char shifted his feet, uneasy. "We wait to fade into the Darkness," he said, but his blackened tongue licked what was left of his lips as he eyed the bottle.

"It's not the same for you," Saetan said. His stomach churned. Thin needles of pain speared his temples. "You care for the others, help them adjust and make the transitions. You fight to stay here, to give them a place. And I know when offerings are made in remembrance of a child who has gone, you don't refuse them." Saetan picked up the bottle and held it out to the boy. "It's appropriate for you to take this. More than you know."

Char slowly reached for the bottle, uncorked it, and sniffed. He took a tiny sip and gasped, delighted. "This is undiluted blood."

Saetan clamped his teeth tight against the nausea and pain. He stared at the bottle, hating it. "No. This is restitution."

8 / Hell

Hekatah stared at the large, ornate wooden chest and tapped the small piece of folded white paper against her chin.

Beautifully decorated with precious woods and gold inlay, the chest reeked of wealth, a sharp reminder of the way she'd once lived and the kind of luxury she believed was her due.

Using Craft, Hekatah probed the interior of the chest for the fifth time in an hour. Still nothing. Perhaps there *was* nothing more.

Opening the paper, she studied the elegant masculine script.

> Hekatah,
> Here is a token of my regard.
> Saetan

There *must* be something more. This was just the wrapping, no matter how expensive. Perhaps Saetan had finally realized how much he needed her. Perhaps he was tired of playing the beneficent patriarch and ready to claim what he—what they—should have claimed so long ago. Perhaps his damnable honor had been sufficiently tarnished by playing with the girl-pet he'd acquired in Kaeleer to take Jaenelle's place.

She'd savor those thoughts after she opened her present.

The brass key was still in the envelope. She shook it into her hand, knelt by the chest, and opened the brass lock.

Hekatah lifted the lid and frowned. Fragrant wood shavings filled the chest. She stared for a moment, then smiled indulgently. Packing, of course. With an excited little squeal, she plunged one hand into the shavings, rummaging for her gift.

The first thing she pulled out was a hand.

Dropping it, she scrambled away from the chest. Her throat worked convulsively as she stared at the hand now lying palm up, its fingers slightly curled. Finally curiosity overrode fear. On hands and knees, she inched forward.

Porcelain or marble would have shattered on the stone floor.

Flesh then.

For a moment, she was grateful it was a normal-looking hand, not maimed or misshaped.

Breathing harshly, Hekatah got to her feet and stared once more at the open chest. She waved her hand back and forth. Lifted by the Craft wind, the shavings spilled onto the floor.

Another hand. Forearms. Upper arms. Feet. Lower legs. Upper legs. Genitals. Torso. And in the corner, staring at her with empty eyes, was Lord Menzar's head.

Hekatah screamed, but even she couldn't say if it was from fear or rage. She stopped abruptly.

One warning. That was all he ever gave. But why?

Hekatah hugged herself and smiled. Through his work at the Halaway school, Menzar must have gotten a little too close to the High Lord's new choice little morsel.

Then she sighed. Saetan could be so possessive. Since Menzar had been careless enough to provoke him into an execution, it was doubtful the girl would be allowed outside SaDiablo Hall without a handpicked escort. And she knew from experience that anyone handpicked by Saetan for a particular duty wasn't amenable to bribes of any kind. So . . .

Hekatah sighed again. It would take a fair amount of persuasion to convince Greer to slip into the Hall to see the High Lord's new pet.

It was a good thing the girl whining in the next room was such a choice little tidbit.

9 / Terreille

Surreal strolled down the quiet, backwater street where no one asked questions. Men and women sat on front stoops, savoring the light breeze that made the sticky afternoon bearable. They didn't speak to her, and she, having spent two years of her childhood on a street like this, gave them the courtesy of walking by as if they weren't there.

As she reached the building where she had a top-floor flat, Surreal noticed the eyes that met hers for a brief moment. She casually shifted the heavy carry-basket from her right hand to her left while she watched one man cross the street and approach her cautiously.

Not the stiletto for this one, she decided. A slashing knife, if necessary. From the way he moved, he might still be healing from a deep wound on his left side. He'd try to protect it. But maybe not, if he was a Warlord experienced in fighting.

The man stopped a body length away. "Lady."

"Warlord."

She saw a tremor of fear in his eyes before he masked it. That she could identify his caste so easily, despite his efforts to hide it, told him that she was strong enough to win any dispute with him.

"That basket looks heavy," he said, still cautious.

"A couple of novels and tonight's dinner."

"I could carry it up for you . . . in a few minutes."

She understood the warning. Someone was waiting for her. If she survived the meeting, the Warlord would bring up the basket. If she didn't, he would divide the spoils among a select few in his building, thus buying a little help if he should need it in the future.

Surreal set the basket on the sidewalk and stepped back. "Ten minutes." When he nodded, she swiftly climbed the building's front steps. Then she paused long enough to put two Gray protective shields around herself and a Green shield over them. Hopefully whoever was waiting for her would respond to the lesser Green shield first. She also called in her largest hunting knife. If the attack was physical, the knife's blade would give her a little extra reach.

With her hand on the doorknob, she made a quick psychic probe of the entryway. No one. Nothing unusual.

A fast twist of the knob and she was inside, turning toward the back of the door. She kicked the door shut, keeping her back against a wall pocked with rusty letter boxes. Her large, gold-green eyes adjusted quickly to the gloomy entryway and equally dim stairwell. No sounds. And no obvious feel of danger.

Up the stairs quickly, keeping her mind open to eddies of mood or thought that might slip from an enemy's mind.

Up to the third floor, the fourth. Finally to the fifth.

Pressed in the opposite corner from her own door, Surreal probed once more—and finally felt it.

A dark psychic scent. Muted, altered somehow, but familiar.

Relieved—and a little annoyed—that there wouldn't be a fight, Surreal vanished the knife, unlocked her door, and went inside.

She hadn't seen him since he'd left Deje's Red Moon house more than two years ago. It didn't look like they'd been easy years. His black hair was long and raggedly cut. His clothes were dirty and torn. When he didn't respond to her briskly closing the door and just continued to stare at the sketch she'd recently purchased, she began to feel uneasy.

That lack of response was wrong. Very wrong. Reaching back, Surreal opened the door just enough not to have to fumble with locks.

"Sadi?"

He finally turned around. The golden eyes held no recognition, but they held something else that was familiar, if only she could remember where she'd seen that look before.

"Daemon?"

He continued to stare at her, as if he were struggling to remember. Then his expression cleared. "It's little Surreal." His voice—that beautiful, deep, seductive voice—was hoarse, rusty.

Little Surreal?

"You're not here alone, are you?" Daemon asked uneasily.

Starting across the room, she said sharply, "Of course I'm here alone. Who else would be here?"

"Where's your mother?"

Surreal froze. "My mother?"

"You're too young to be here alone."

Titian had been dead for centuries. He *knew* that. It was centuries ago that he and Tersa . . .

Tersa's eyes. Eyes that strained to make out the ghostly, gray shapes of reality through the mist of the Twisted Kingdom.

Mother Night, what had happened to him?

Keeping his distance, Daemon began edging toward the door. "I can't stay here. Not without your mother. I won't . . . I can't . . ."

"Daemon, wait." Surreal leaped between him and the door. Panic flashed in his eyes. "Mother had to go away for a few days with . . . with Tersa. I'd . . . I'd feel safer if you stayed."

Daemon tensed. "Has anyone tried to hurt you, Surreal?"

Hell's fire, not *that* tone of voice. Not with that Warlord coming up the stairs any minute with the basket.

"No," she said, hoping she sounded young but convincing. "But you and Tersa are as close as we have to family and I'm . . . lonely."

Daemon stared at the carpet.

"Besides," she added, wrinkling her nose, "you need a bath."

His head snapped up. He stared at her with such transparent hope and hunger it scared her. "Lady?" he whispered, reaching for her. "Lady?" He studied the hair entwined around his fingers and shook his head. "Black. It's not supposed to be black."

If she lied, would it help him? Would he know the difference? She closed her eyes, not sure she could stand the anguish she felt in him. "Daemon," she said gently, "I'm Surreal."

He stepped away from her, keening softly.

She led him to a chair, unable to think of anything else to do.

"So. You're a friend."

Surreal spun toward the door, feet braced in a fighting stance, the hunting knife back in her hand.

The Warlord stood in the doorway, the carry-basket at his feet.

"I'm a friend," Surreal said. "What are you?"

"Not an enemy." The Warlord eyed the knife. "Don't suppose you could put that away."

"Don't suppose I could."

He sighed. "He healed me and helped me get here."

"Are you going to complain about services rendered?"

"Hell's fire, no," the Warlord snapped. "He told me before he started that he wasn't sure he knew enough healing Craft to mend the damage. But I wasn't going to survive without help, and a Healer would have turned me in." He ran a hand through his short brown hair. "And even if he killed me, it would have been better than what my Lady would have done to me for leaving her service so abruptly." He gestured toward Daemon, who was curled in the chair, still keening softly. "I didn't realize he was . . ."

Surreal vanished the knife. The Warlord immediately picked up the basket, pressing his left hand to his side and grimacing.

"Asshole," Surreal snapped, hurrying to take the basket. "You shouldn't carry something this heavy while you're still healing."

She tugged. When he wouldn't let go of the basket, she snarled at him. "Idiot. Fool. At least use Craft to lighten the weight."

"Don't be a bitch." Clenching his teeth, the Warlord carried the basket to the table in the kitchen area. He turned to leave, then hesitated. "The story going around is that he killed a child."

Blood. So much blood. "He didn't."

"He thinks he did."

She couldn't see Daemon, but she could still hear him. "Damn."

"Do you think he'll ever come out of the Twisted Kingdom?"

Surreal stared at the basket. "No one ever has."

"Daemon." When she got no response, Surreal chewed her lower lip. Maybe she should let him sleep, if he was actually sleeping. No, the potatoes were baking, the steaks ready to broil, the salad made. He needed food as much as rest. Touch him? There was no telling what he might be seeing in the Twisted Kingdom, how he might interpret a gentle shake. She tried again, putting some snap in her voice. "Daemon."

Daemon opened his eyes. After a long minute, he reached for her. "Surreal," he said hoarsely.

She gripped his hand, wishing she knew some way to help him. When his grip loosened, she tightened hers and tugged. "Up. You need a shower before dinner."

He got to his feet with much of his fluid, feline grace, but when she led him into the bathroom, he stared at the fixtures as if he'd never seen them before. She lifted the toilet seat, hoping he remembered how to use that at least. When he still didn't move, she tugged him out of the jacket and shirt. It had never bothered her when Tersa displayed this childlike passivity. His lack of response frayed her temper. But when she reached for his belt, he snarled at her, his hand squeezing her wrist until she was sure the bones would break.

She snarled back. "Do it yourself then."

She saw the inward crumbling, the despair.

Loosening his hold on her wrist, he raised her hand and pressed his lips against it. "I'm sorry. I'm—" Releasing her, he looked beaten as he unbuckled the belt and began fumbling with his trousers.

Surreal fled.

A few minutes later the water pipes rattled and wheezed as he turned on the shower.

As she set the table, she wondered if he'd actually removed all his clothes. How long had he been like this? If this was what was left of a once-brilliant mind, how had he been able to heal that man?

Surreal paused, a plate half-resting on the table. Tersa had always had her islands of lucidity, usually around Craft. Once when the mad Black Widow had healed a deep gash in Surreal's leg, she'd responded to Titian's worry by saying, "One doesn't forget the basics." When the healing was done, however, Tersa couldn't even remember her own name.

A few minutes later, she was hovering in the hallway when she heard the muffled yelp that indicated the hot water had run out. The pipes rattled and wheezed as he shut off the water.

No other sound.

Swearing under her breath, Surreal pushed the bathroom door open. Daemon just stood in the tub, his head down.

"Dry yourself," Surreal said.

Flinching, he reached for a towel.

Struggling to keep her voice firm but quiet, she added, "I put out some clean clothes for you. When you've dried off, go put them on."

She retreated to the kitchen and busied herself with cooking the steaks while listening to the movements in the bedroom. She was putting the meat on their plates when Daemon appeared, properly dressed.

Surreal smiled her approval. "Now you look more like yourself."

"Jaenelle is dead," he said, his voice hard and flat.

She braced her hands on the table and absorbed the words that were worse than a physical blow. "How do you know?"

"Lucivar told me."

How could Lucivar, who was in Pruul, be sure of something she and Daemon couldn't be sure of? And who was there to ask? Cassandra had never returned to the Altar after that night, and Surreal didn't know who the Priest was, let alone where to start looking for him.

She cut the potatoes and fluffed them open. "I don't believe him." She looked up in time to see a lucid, arrested look in his eyes. Then it faded. He shook his head.

"She's dead."

"Maybe he was wrong." She took two servings of salad from the bowl and dressed them before sitting down and cutting into her steak. "Eat."

He took his place at the table. "He wouldn't lie to me."

Surreal plopped soured cream onto Daemon's baked potato and gritted her teeth. "I didn't say he lied. I said maybe he was wrong."

Daemon closed his eyes. After a couple of minutes, he opened them and stared at the meal before him. "You fixed dinner."

Gone. Turned down another path in that shattered inner landscape.

"Yes, Daemon," Surreal said quietly, willing herself not to cry. "I fixed dinner. So let's eat it while it's hot."

He helped her with the dishes.

As they worked, Surreal realized Daemon's madness was confined to emotions, to people, to that single tragedy he couldn't face. It was as if Titian had never died, as if Surreal hadn't spent three years whoring in back alleys before Daemon found her again and arranged for a proper education in a Red Moon house. He thought she was still a child, and he continued to fret about Titian's absence. But when she mentioned a book she was reading, he made a dry observation about her eclectic taste and proceeded to tell her about other books that might be of interest. It was the same with music, with art. They posed no threat to him, had no time frame, weren't part of the nightmare of Jaenelle bleeding on that Dark Altar.

Still, it was a strain to pretend to be a young girl, to pretend she didn't see the uncertainty and torment in his golden eyes. It was still early in the evening when she suggested they get some sleep.

She settled into bed with a sigh. Maybe Daemon was as relieved to be away from her as she was from him. On some level he knew she wasn't a child. Just as he knew she'd been with him at Cassandra's Altar.

Mist. Blood. So much blood. Shattered crystal chalices.
You are my instrument.
Words lie. Blood doesn't.
She walks among the cildru dyathe.
Maybe he was wrong.
He turned round and round.
Maybe he was wrong.
The mist opened, revealing a narrow path heading upward. He stared at it and shuddered. The path was lined with jagged rock that pointed sideways and down like great stone teeth. Anyone going down the path would brush against the smooth downward sides. Anyone going up . . .

He started to climb, leaving a little more of himself on each hungry point. A quarter of the way up, he finally noticed the sound, the roar of fast water. He looked up to see it burst over the high cliff above the path, come rushing toward him.

Not water. Blood. So much blood.

No room to turn. He scrambled backward, but the red flood caught him, smashed him against the stone words that had battered his mind for so long. Tumbling and lost, he caught a glimpse of calm land rising above the flood. He fought his way to that one small island of safety, grabbed at the long, sharp grass, and hauled himself up onto the crumbling ground. Shuddering, he held on to the island of *maybe.*

When the rush and roar finally stopped, he found himself

lying on a tiny, phallic-shaped island in the middle of a vast sea of blood.

Even before she was fully awake, Surreal called in her stiletto.

A soft, stealthy sound.

She slipped out of bed and opened her door a crack, listening.

Nothing.

Maybe it was only Daemon groping in the bathroom.

Gray, predawn light filled the short hallway. Keeping close to the wall, Surreal inspected the other rooms.

The bathroom was empty. So was Daemon's bedroom.

Swearing softly, Surreal examined his room. The bed looked like it had been through a storm, but the rest of the room was untouched. The only clothes missing were the ones she'd given him last night.

Nothing missing from the living area. Nothing missing— damn it!—from the kitchen.

Surreal vanished the stiletto before putting the kettle on for tea.

Tersa used to vanish for days, months, sometimes years before showing up at one of these hideaways. Surreal had intended to move on soon, but what if Daemon returned in a few days and found her gone? Would he remember her as a child and worry? Would he try to find her?

She made the tea and some toast. Taking them into the front room, she curled up on the couch with one of the thick novels she'd bought.

She would wait a few weeks before deciding. There was no hurry. There were plenty of men like the ones who had used Briarwood that she could hunt in this part of Terreille.

10 / Kaeleer

Stubbornly ignoring the steady stream of servants flowing past his study door toward the front rooms, Saetan reached for the next report.

They were only halfway up the drive. It would be another

quarter hour before the carriage pulled up to the steps. What had Mephis been thinking of when he'd decided to use the landing web at Halaway instead of the one a few yards from the Hall's front door?

Grinding his teeth, he flipped through the report, seeing nothing.

He was the Warlord Prince of Dhemlan, the High Lord of Hell. He should set an example, should act with dignity.

He dropped the report on his desk and left his study.

Screw dignity.

He crossed his arms and leaned against the wall at a point that was midway between his study and the front door. From there he could comfortably watch everything without being stepped on. Maybe.

Fighting to keep a straight face, Saetan listened to Beale accept one implausible excuse after another for why this footman or that maid just had to be in the great hall at that moment.

Intent on their busy chaos and excuses, no one noticed the front door open until a very rumpled Mephis said, "Beale, could you—Never mind, the footmen are already here. There are some packages—"

Mephis glared at the footmen scrambling out the door before he spotted Saetan. Weaving his way through the maids, Mephis walked over to Saetan, braced himself against the wall, and sighed wearily. "She'll be here in a minute. She pounced on Tarl as soon as the carriage stopped to consult him on the state of her garden."

"Lucky Tarl," Saetan murmured. When Mephis snorted, he studied his rumpled son. "A difficult trip?"

Mephis snorted again. "I never realized one young girl could turn an entire city upside down in just five days." He puffed his cheeks. "Fortunately, I'll only have to help with the paperwork. The negotiations will fall squarely into your lap . . . where they belong."

Saetan's eyebrow snapped up. "What negotiations? Mephis, what—"

A few footmen returned, carrying Jaenelle's luggage. The others . . .

Saetan watched with growing interest as smiling footmen

brought in armloads of brown-paper packages and headed for the labyrinth of corridors that would eventually take them to Jaenelle's suite.

"They aren't what you think," Mephis grumbled.

Since Mephis knew he'd been hoping Jaenelle would buy more clothes, Saetan growled in disappointment. Sylvia's idea of appropriate girl clothes hadn't included a single dress, and the only concession she and Jaenelle had made to his insistence that everyone at the Hall dress for dinner was *one* long black skirt and two blouses. When he had pointed out—and very reasonably, too—that trousers, shirts, and long sweaters weren't exactly feminine, Sylvia had given him a scalding lecture, the gist of it being that whatever a woman enjoyed wearing was feminine and anything she didn't enjoy wearing wasn't, and if he was too stubborn and old-fashioned to understand that, he could go soak his head in a bucket of cold water. He hadn't quite forgiven her yet for saying they would have to look hard to find a bucket big enough to fit his head into, but he admired the sass behind the remark.

Then Jaenelle bounded through the open door, dazzling Beale and the rest of the staff with a smile before politely asking Helene if she could have a sandwich and a glass of fruit juice sent to her suite.

She looks happy, Saetan thought, forgetting about everything else.

After Helene hurried off to the kitchen and Beale herded the remaining staff back to their duties, Saetan pushed away from the wall, opened his arms . . . and fought the sudden nausea as Menzar's fantasies and memories flooded his mind. He cringed at the thought of touching Jaenelle, of somehow dirtying the warmth and high spirits that flowed from her. He started to lower his arms, but she walked into them, gave him a rib-squeezing hug, and said, "Hello, Papa."

He held her tightly, breathing in her physical scent as well as the dark psychic scent he'd missed so keenly during the last few days.

For a moment, that dark scent became swift and penetrating.

But when she leaned back to look at him, her sapphire eyes told him nothing. He shivered with apprehension.

Jaenelle kissed his cheek. "I'm going to unpack. Mephis needs to talk." She turned to Mephis, who was still leaning wearily against the wall. "Thank you, Mephis. I had a grand time, and I'm sorry I caused you so much trouble."

Mephis gave her a warm hug. "It was a unique experience. Next time I'll be a little more prepared."

Jaenelle laughed. "You'd take me back to Amdarh?"

"Wouldn't dare let you go alone," Mephis grumped.

As soon as she was gone, Saetan slid an arm around Mephis's shoulders. "Come to my study. You could use a glass of yarbarah."

"I could use a year's sleep," Mephis grumbled.

Saetan led his eldest son to the leather couch and warmed a glass of yarbarah for him. Sitting on a footstool, Saetan rested Mephis's right foot on his thigh, removed the shoe and sock, and began a soothing foot massage. After a few silent minutes, Mephis roused enough to remember the yarbarah and take a sip.

Continuing his massage, Saetan said quietly, "So tell me."

"Where do you want me to start?"

Good question. "Do any of those packages contain clothes?" He couldn't keep the wistful note out of his voice.

Mephis's eyes gleamed wickedly. "One. She bought you a sweater." Then he yelped.

"Sorry," Saetan muttered, gently rubbing the just-squeezed toes while the mutter turned into a snarl. "I don't wear sweaters. I also don't wear nightshirts." He flinched as the words released more memories. Carefully setting Mephis's right foot down, he stripped off the left shoe and sock and began massaging that foot.

"It was difficult, wasn't it?" Mephis asked softly.

"It was difficult. But the debt's been paid." Saetan worked silently for another minute. "Why a sweater?"

Mephis sipped the yarbarah, letting the question hang. "She said you needed to slouch more, both physically and mentally."

Saetan's eyebrow snapped up.

"She said you'd never sprawl on the couch and take a nap if you were always dressed so formally."

Oh, Mother Night. "I'm not sure I know how to sprawl."

"Well, I heartily suggest you learn." Mephis sent the empty glass skimming through the air until it slid neatly onto a nearby table.

"You've got a mean streak in your nature, Mephis," Saetan growled. "What's in the damn packages?"

"Mostly books."

Saetan remembered not to squeeze the toes. "Books? Perhaps my old wits have gone begging, but I was under the impression we have a very large room full of books. Several, in fact. They're called libraries."

"Apparently not these kinds of books."

Saetan's stomach was full of butterflies. "What kind?"

"How should I know?" Mephis grumbled. "I didn't *see* most of them. I just paid for them. However . . ."

Saetan groaned.

". . . at every bookseller's shop—and we went to every one in Amdarh—the waif would ask for books about Tigrelan or Sceval or Pandar or Centauran, and when the booksellers showed her legends and myths about those places that were written by Dhemlan authors, she would politely—she was always polite, by the way—tell them she wasn't interested in books of legends unless they came directly from those people. Naturally the booksellers, and the crowd of customers that gathered during these discussions, would explain that those Territories were inaccessible places no one traded with. She would thank them for their help, and they, wanting to stay in her good graces and have continued access to my bank account, would say, 'Who is to say what is real and what is not? Who has seen these places?' And she would say, 'I have,' and pick up the books she'd already purchased and be out the door before the bookseller and customers could pick their jaws up from the floor."

Saetan groaned again.

"Want to hear about the music?"

Saetan released Mephis's foot and braced his head in his hands. "What about the music?"

"Dhemlan music stores don't have Scelt folk music or Pandar pipe music or . . ."

"Enough, Mephis." Saetan moaned. "They're all going to be on my doorstep wanting to know what kind of trade agreements might be possible with those Territories, aren't they?"

Mephis sighed, content. "I'm surprised we beat them here."

Saetan glared at his eldest son. "Did *anything* go as expected?"

"We had a delightful time at the theater. At least I'll be able to go back *there* without being snarled at." Mephis leaned forward. "One other thing. About music." He clasped his hands and hesitated. "Have you ever heard Jaenelle sing?"

Saetan probed his memory and finally shook his head. "She's got a lovely speaking voice so I just assumed. . . . Don't tell me she's tone-deaf or sings off-key."

"No." There was a strange expression in Mephis's eyes. "She doesn't sing off-key. She. . . . When you hear her, you'll understand."

"Please, Mephis, no more surprises tonight."

Mephis sighed. "She sings witchsongs . . . in the Old Tongue."

Saetan raised his head. "Authentic witchsongs?"

Mephis's eyes were teary bright. "Not like I've ever heard them sung before, but yes, authentic witchsongs."

"But how—" Pointless to ask how Jaenelle knew what she knew. "I think it's time I went up to see our way-ward child."

Mephis rose stiffly. He yawned and stretched. "If you find out what all that stuff is that I paid for, I'd like to know."

Saetan rubbed his temples and sighed.

"I bought you something. Did Mephis warn you?"

"He mentioned something," Saetan replied cautiously.

Her sapphire eyes twinkled as she solemnly handed him the box.

Saetan opened it and held up the sweater. Soft, thick,

black with deep pockets. He stripped off his jacket and shrugged into the sweater.

"Thank you, witch-child." He vanished the box and sank gracefully to the floor, finally stretching out his legs and propping himself up on one elbow. "Sufficiently slouched?"

Jaenelle laughed and plopped down beside him. "Quite sufficient."

"What else did you get?"

She didn't quite look him in the eye. "I bought some books."

Saetan eyed the piles of neatly stacked books that formed a large half-circle around her. "So I see." Reading the nearest spines, he recognized most of the Craft books. Copies were either in the family library or in his own private library. Same with the books on history, art, and music. They were the beginning of a young witch's library.

"I know the family has most of these, but I wanted copies of my own. It's hard to make notes in someone else's book."

Saetan experienced a hitch in his breathing. Notes. Handwritten guides that would help explain those breathtaking leaps she made when she was creating a spell. And he wouldn't have access to them. He gave himself a mental shake. *Fool. Just borrow the damn book.*

It hit him then, a bittersweet sadness. She would want a collection of her own to take with her when she was ready to establish her own household. So few years to savor before the Hall was empty again.

He pushed those thoughts aside and turned to the other stacks, the fiction. These were more interesting since a perusal of her choices would tell him a lot about Jaenelle's tastes and immediate interests. Trying to find a common thread was too bewildering, so he simply filed away the information. He considered himself an eclectic reader. He had no idea how to describe her. Some books struck him as being too young for her, some too gritty. Some he passed over with little interest, others reminded him of how long it had been since he'd browsed through a bookseller's shop for his own amusement. Lots of books about animals.

"Quite a collection," he finally said, placing the last book carefully on its stack. "What are those?" He pointed to the three books half-hidden under brown paper.

Blushing, Jaenelle mumbled, "Just books."

Saetan raised an eyebrow and waited.

With a resigned sigh, Jaenelle reached under the brown paper and thrust a book at him.

Odd. Sylvia had reacted much the same way when he'd called unexpectedly one evening and found her reading the same book. She hadn't heard him come in, and when she finally did glance up and notice him, she immediately stuffed the book behind a pillow and gave him the strong impression it would take an army to pull her away from her book-hiding pillow and nothing less would make her surrender it.

"It's a romantic novel," Jaenelle said in a small voice as he called in his half-moon glasses and started idly flipping the pages. "A couple of women in a bookseller's shop kept talking about it."

Romance. Passion. Sex.

He suppressed—barely—the urge to leap to his feet and twirl her around the room. A sign of emotional healing? Please, sweet Darkness, please let it be a sign of healing.

"You think it's silly." Her tone was defensive.

"Romance is never silly, witch-child. Well, sometimes it's silly, but not *silly*." He flipped more pages. "Besides, I used to read things like this. They were an important part of my education."

Jaenelle gaped at him. "Really?"

"Mmm. Of course, they were a bit more—" He scanned a page. He carefully closed the book. "Then again, maybe not." He removed his glasses and vanished them before they steamed up.

Jaenelle nervously fluffed her hair. "Papa, if I have any questions about things, would you be willing to answer them?"

"Of course, witch-child. I'll give you whatever help you want in Craft or your other subjects."

"Nooo. I meant . . ." She glanced at the book in front of him.

Hell's fire, Mother Night, and may the Darkness be merciful. The whole prospect filled him with delight and dread. Delight because he might be able to help her paint a different emotional canvas that would, he hoped balance the wounds the rape had caused. Dread because, no matter how knowledgeable he was about any subject, Jaenelle always viewed things from an angle totally outside his experience.

Menzar's thoughts, Menzar's imaginings flooded his mind again.

Saetan closed his eyes, fought to stop the images.

"He hurt you."

His body reacted to the midnight, sepulchral voice, to the instant chill in the room. "I was the one performing the execution, Lady. He's the one who is very, very dead."

The room got colder. The silence was more than silence.

"Did he suffer?" she asked too softly.

Mist. Darkness streaked with lightning. The edge of the abyss was very close and the ground was swiftly crumbling beneath his feet.

"Yes, he suffered."

She considered his answer. "Not enough," she finally said, getting to her feet.

Numbed, Saetan stared at the hand stretched toward him. Not enough? What had her Chaillot relatives done to her that she had no regrets about killing? Even he regretted taking a life.

"Come with me, Saetan." She watched him with her ancient, haunted eyes, waiting for him to turn away from her.

Never. He grasped her hand, letting her pull him to his feet. He would never turn away from her.

But he couldn't deny the shiver down his spine as he followed her to the music room that was on the same floor as their suites. He couldn't deny the instinctive wariness when he saw that the only light in the room came from two freestanding candelabras on either side of the piano. Candles, not candle-lights. Light that danced with every current of air, making the room look alien, sensual, and forbidding. The candles lit the piano keys and the music stand. The rest of the room belonged to the night.

Jaenelle called in a brown-paper package, opened it, and leafed through the music. "I found a lot of this tucked into back bins without any kind of preservation spell on them to protect them." She shook her head, annoyed, then handed him a sheet of music. "Can you play this?"

Saetan sat on the piano bench and opened the music. The paper was yellowed and fragile, the notation faded. Straining to see it in the flickering candlelight, he silently went through the piece, his fingers barely touching the keys. "I think I can get through it well enough."

Jaenelle stood behind one candelabra, becoming part of the shadows.

He played the introduction and stopped. Strange music. Unfamiliar and yet. . . . He began again.

Her voice rose, a molten sound. It soared, dove, spiraled around the notes he was playing and his soul soared, dove, spiraled with her voice. A Song of Sorrow, Death, and Healing. In the Old Tongue. A song of grieving . . . for both victims of an execution. Strange music. Soul-searing, heart-tearing, ancient, ancient music.

Witchsong. No, more than that. The songs of Witch.

He didn't know when he stopped playing, when his shaking hands could no longer find the keys, when the tears blinded him. He was caught in that voice as it lanced the memory of the execution and left a clean-bleeding wound—and then healed that.

Mephis, you were right.

"Saetan?"

Saetan blinked away the tears and took a shuddering breath. "I'm sorry, witch-child. I . . . I wasn't prepared."

Jaenelle opened her arms.

He stumbled around the piano, aching for her clean, loving embrace. Menzar was a fresh scar on his soul, one that would be with him forever, like so many others, but he no longer feared to hold her, no longer doubted the kind of love he felt for her.

He stroked her hair for a long time before gathering his courage to ask, "How did you know about this music?"

She pressed her face deeper into his shoulder. Finally she whispered, "It's part of what I am."

He felt the beginning of an inward retreat, a protective distancing between himself and her.

*No, my Queen. You say "It's part of what I am" with
conviction, but your retreat screams your doubt of acceptance. That I will not permit.*

He gently rapped her nose. "Do you know what else
you are?"

"What?"

"A very tired little witch."

She started to laugh and had to stifle a yawn. "Since
daylight is so draining for Mephis, we did most of our wandering after sunset, but I didn't want to waste the daytime
sleeping, so . . ." She yawned again.

"You *did* get some sleep, didn't you?"

"Mephis made me take naps," she grumbled. "He said
it was the only way he'd get any rest. I didn't think demons
needed to rest."

It was better not to answer that.

She was half-asleep by the time he guided her to her
room. As he removed her shoes and socks, she assured him
she was still awake enough to get ready for bed by herself
and he didn't need to fuss. She was sound asleep before he
reached her bedroom door.

He, on the other hand, was wide-awake and restless.

Letting himself out one of the Hall's back doors, Saetan
wandered across the carefully trimmed lawn, down a short
flight of wide stone steps, and followed the paths into the
wilder gardens. Leaves whispered in the light breeze. A
rabbit hopped across the path a body length in front of
him, watchful but not terribly concerned.

"You should be more wary, fluffball," Saetan said softly.
"You or some other member of your family has been
eating Mrs. Beale's young beans. If you cross her path,
you're going to end up the main dish one of these nights."

The rabbit swiveled its ears before disappearing under a
fire bush.

Saetan brushed his fingers against the orange-red leaves.
The fire bush was full of swollen buds almost ready to
bloom. Soon it would be covered with yellow flowers, like
flames rising above hot embers.

He took a deep breath and let it out in a sigh. There
was still a desk full of paperwork waiting for him.

Comfortably protected from the cool summer night, hi
hands warm in the sweater's deep pockets, Saetan strolled
back to the Hall. Just as he was climbing the stone step
below the lawn, he stopped, listened.

Beyond the wild gardens was the north woods.

He shook his head and resumed walking. "Damn dog."

CHAPTER
FIVE

1 / Kaeleer

Luthvian studied her reflection. The new dress hugged her trim figure but still didn't look deliberately provocative. Maybe letting her hair flow down her back looked too youthful. Maybe she should have done something about that white streak that made her look older.

Well, she *was* youthful, a little over 2,200 years old. And that white streak had been there since she was a small child, a reminder of her father's fists. Besides, Saetan would know if she tried to conceal it, and she certainly wasn't dressing up for *him*. She just wanted that daughter of his to recognize the caliber of witch who had agreed to train her.

With a last nervous glance at her dress, Luthvian went downstairs.

He was punctual, as usual.

Roxie pulled the door open at the first knock.

Luthvian wasn't sure if Roxie's alacrity was curiosity about the daughter or her desire to prove to the other girls that she had the skill to flirt with a dark-Jeweled Warlord Prince. Either way, it saved Luthvian from opening the door herself.

The daughter was a very satisfying surprise. She hadn't realized Saetan had adopted his little darling, but there wasn't a drop of Hayllian blood in the girl—and there was certainly none of his. Immature and lacking in social skills, Luthvian decided as she watched the brief greetings at the door. So what had possessed Saetan to give the girl his protection and care?

Then the girl turned toward Luthvian and smiled shyly, but the smile didn't reach those sapphire eyes. And there was no shyness in those eyes. They were filled with wariness and suppressed anger.

"Lady Luthvian," Saetan said as he approached her, "this is my daughter, Jaenelle Angelline."

"Sister," Jaenelle said, extending both hands in formal greeting.

Luthvian didn't like this assumption of equality, but she'd straighten that out privately, away from Saetan's protective presence. For now she returned the greeting and turned to Saetan. "Make yourself comfortable, High Lord." She tipped her chin toward the parlor.

"Perhaps you'd like a cup of tea, High Lord?" Roxie said, brushing against Saetan as she passed.

This wasn't the time or place to correct the ninny's ideas about Guardians, especially *this* Guardian, but it did surprise her when Saetan thanked Roxie for the offer and retreated into the parlor.

"You know," Roxie said, eyeing Jaenelle and smiling too brightly, "no one would ever believe you're the High Lord's daughter."

"Get the tea, Roxie," Luthvian snapped.

The girl flounced down the hall to the kitchen.

Jaenelle stared at the empty hallway. "Look beneath the skin," she whispered in a midnight voice.

Luthvian shivered. Even then she might have dismissed that sudden change in Jaenelle's voice as girlish theatrics if Saetan hadn't appeared at the parlor door, silently questioning and very tense.

Jaenelle smiled at him and shrugged.

Luthvian led her new pupil to her own workroom since Saetan had insisted the lessons be private. Maybe later, if the girl could catch up, she could do some of the lessons with the rest of the students.

"I understand we're to start with the very basics," Luthvian said, firmly closing the door.

"Yes," Jaenelle replied ruefully, fluffing her shoulder-length hair. She wrinkled her nose and smiled. "Papa has managed to teach me a few things, but I still have trouble with basic Craft."

Was the girl simpleminded or just totally lacking in ability?

Luthvian glanced at Jaenelle's neck, trying to detect a recent healing or a faint shadow of a bruise. If the girl was just fresh fodder, why bother training her at all? No, that made no sense, not if *he* was going to instruct Jaenelle in the Hourglass's Craft. Something was missing, something she didn't understand yet.

"Let's start with moving an object." Luthvian placed a red wooden ball on her empty worktable. "Point your finger at the ball."

Jaenelle groaned but obeyed.

Luthvian ignored the groan. Apparently Jaenelle was as much of a ninny as the rest of her students. "Imagine a stiff, thin thread coming out of your fingertip and attaching itself to the ball." Luthvian waited a moment. "Now imagine your strength running through the thread until it just touches the ball. Now imagine reeling in the thread so that the ball moves toward you."

The ball didn't move. The worktable, however, did. And the built-in cupboards that filled the workroom's back wall tried to.

"Stop!" Luthvian shouted.

Jaenelle stopped. She sighed.

Luthvian stared. If it had just been the worktable, she might have dismissed it as an attempt to show off. But the cupboards?

Luthvian called in four wooden blocks and four more wooden balls. Placing them on the worktable, she said, "Why don't you work by yourself for a minute. Concentrate on *lightly* making the connection between yourself and the object you're trying to move. I need to look in on the other students, then I'll be back."

Jaenelle obediently turned her attention to the blocks and balls.

Luthvian left the workroom in a hurry, her hands and

teeth clenched. There was only one person she wanted to look in on, and he'd damn well better have some answers.

She felt the chill in the front hallway before she heard the giggle.

"Roxie!" she snapped as she caught the doorway to stop her forward momentum. "You have spells to finish."

Roxie waved her hand airily. "Oh, I've just got one or two left."

"Then do them."

Roxie pouted and looked at Saetan for support.

There was no expression on his face. Worse, there was no expression in his eyes. Hell's fire! He was ready to rip out that lash-batting ninny's throat and she didn't even realize it!

Luthvian dragged Roxie out of the parlor and down the hall, finally shoving her toward the student workroom.

Roxie stamped her foot. "You can't treat me like this! My father's an important Warlord in Doun and my mother's—"

Luthvian squeezed Roxie's arm, and hissed, "Listen, you little fool. You're playing with someone you can't even begin to understand."

"He likes me."

"He wants to kill you."

Roxie looked stunned for a moment. Then a calculating look came into her eyes. "You're jealous."

It took all of her self-control not to slap the ninny hard enough to make her spin. "Go to the workroom and *stay* there." She waited until Roxie slammed the workroom door before returning to the parlor.

Pacing restlessly, Saetan was swearing under his breath as he raked his fingers through his hair. His anger didn't surprise her, but the effort he was making to keep it from being felt beyond this room did.

"I'm surprised you didn't give Roxie a real taste of your temper," Luthvian said, staying close to the door. "Why didn't you?"

"I have my reasons," he snarled.

"Reasons, High Lord? Or just one?"

Saetan snapped to a halt and looked past her. "Is the lesson over already?" he asked uneasily.

"She's practicing by herself." Luthvian hated talking to him when he was angry, so she decided to be blunt. "Why are you bothering to teach her the Hourglass's ways when she's still untrained?"

"I never said she was untrained," Saetan replied, starting to pace again. "I said she needed help with basic Craft."

"Until a witch has the basics, she can't do much else."

"Don't bet on it."

Saetan kept pacing, but it wasn't out of anger. Luthvian watched him and decided she didn't like seeing the High Lord nervous. She didn't like it at all. "What haven't you told me?"

"Everything. I wanted you to meet her first."

"She's got a lot of raw power for someone who doesn't wear Jewels."

"She wears Jewels. Believe me, Luthvian, Jaenelle wears Jewels."

"Then what—"

A loud whoop sent them hurrying to her workroom.

Saetan pushed the door open and froze. Luthvian started to push past him but ended up clinging to his arm for support.

The table was slowly revolving clockwise and also rotating as if it were on a spit. There were now a dozen wooden boxes, some flush to the table's top, others floating above it, and all of them were spinning slowly. Seven brightly colored wooden balls were performing an intricate dance around the boxes. And every single object was maintaining its position to that revolving, rotating table.

With a lot of effort, Luthvian thought she might be able to control something that intricate, but it should have taken years to acquire that kind of skill. You just didn't start with one ball you couldn't move and end up with this in a matter of minutes.

Saetan let out a groaning laugh.

"I think I'm getting the hang of this thread-to-object stuff," Jaenelle said as she glanced over her shoulder and grinned at them. Then she yelped as everything began to wobble and fall.

Luthvian extended her hand at the same moment Saetan extended his. She froze the smaller objects in place. He caught the table.

"Damn and blast!" Jaenelle plopped on air like a puppet with cut strings and glowered at the table, boxes, and balls.

Laughing, Saetan righted the table. "Never mind, witch-child. If you could do it perfectly on the first try, you wouldn't have much fun practicing, would you?"

"That's true," Jaenelle said with bouncing enthusiasm.

Luthvian vanished the boxes and balls, trying not to laugh at Saetan's immediate dismay. What did he think the girl would do? Try to manipulate an entire roomful of furniture?

Apparently so, because they were involved in a friendly argument about which room Jaenelle could use for practice.

"Definitely not the reception rooms," Saetan said. He sounded like a man who was desperately trying to believe the bog beneath his feet was firm ground. "There are empty rooms in the Hall and there's plenty of old furniture in the attics. Start with that. Please?"

Saetan saying please?

Jaenelle gave him a look of exasperated amusement. "All right. But only so you won't get into trouble with Beale and Helene."

Saetan let out a heartfelt sigh.

Jaenelle laughed and turned to Luthvian. "Thank you, Luthvian."

"You're welcome," Luthvian said weakly. Were all the lessons going to be like this? She wasn't sure how she felt about that. "We'll have your next lesson in two days," she added as they left the workroom.

Jaenelle wandered down the hall and studied the paintings. Was she really interested in the art or did she simply understand the adult need for private conversation after dealing with her?

"Can you survive it?" Saetan asked quietly.

Luthvian leaned toward him. "Is it always like this?"

"Oh, no," Saetan said dryly. "She was on her best behavior today. It's usually much worse."

Luthvian stifled a laugh. It was fun seeing him thrown off stride. He seemed so accessible, so . . .

The laughter died. He wasn't accessible. He was the High Lord, the Prince of the Darkness. And he had no heart.

Roxie came out of the student workroom. Luthvian wasn't sure what the girl had done to her dress, but there was a lot more cleavage showing than there'd been a short while ago.

Roxie looked at Saetan and licked her upper lip.

Although he was trying to hide it, Luthvian felt his revulsion and the beginning of hot anger. A moment later, those feelings were swept away by a bone-chilling cold that couldn't possibly come from a male.

Not even him.

"Leave him alone," Jaenelle said, her eyes fixed on Roxie.

There was something too feral, too predatory about the way Jaenelle approached Roxie. And that cold was rising from depths Luthvian didn't even want to imagine.

"We have to go," Saetan said quickly, grabbing Jaenelle's arm as she began to glide past him.

Jaenelle bared her teeth and snarled at him. It wasn't a sound that could possibly come from a human throat.

Saetan froze.

Luthvian watched them, too frightened to move or speak. She had no idea what was passing between them, but she kept hoping he was strong enough to contain Jaenelle's anger—and knew with dreadful certainty that he wasn't. He wore the Black Jewels, and he didn't outrank his daughter. May the Darkness be merciful!

The cold was gone as suddenly as it appeared.

Saetan released Jaenelle's arm and watched her until the front door closed behind her. Then he sagged against the wall.

As a Healer, Luthvian knew she should help him, but she couldn't make her legs move. That's when it finally struck her that the girls hadn't reacted to the cold or the danger, that the buzzing voices were speculating on the outward drama without any understanding at all.

"She's rather spoiled," Roxie said, giving Saetan her best pout.

He glared at her so malevolently she shrank back into the workroom, stepping on the other girls who were crowded around the doorway.

"Finish your spells," Luthvian said. "I'll check them in a minute." She closed the workroom door and rested her head against it.

"I'm sorry," Saetan said. He sounded exhausted.

"You shielded the girls, didn't you?"

Saetan gave her a tired smile. "I tried to shield you, too, but she rose past me too fast."

"Better that you didn't." Luthvian pushed away from the door and smoothed her gown. "But you were right. It was better having the first lesson and knowing what it will be like to teach her before coming to terms with what she is."

She saw his golden eyes change.

"And what do you think she is, Luthvian?" he asked too softly.

Look beneath the skin.

She looked him in the eye. "Your daughter."

Saetan strolled along the edge of the wide dirt road. Jaenelle was a little ways ahead of him and didn't seem to be in any hurry, so he didn't feel a pressing need to catch up with her. Besides, it was better to let her calm down before asking her what he needed to ask, and, since she was a Queen, the land would soothe her faster than he could.

In that, she was like every other Queen he'd ever known. No matter what other talents they had, the Queens were the ones most drawn to the land, the ones who most needed that contact with the earth. Even the ones who spent most of their time residing in larger cities had a garden where their feet could touch the living earth, quietly listening to all the land had to tell them.

So he strolled, relishing the ability once again to walk down a road on a summer morning and see the sun-kissed land. To his right was Doun's fenced-in common pastures, where all the villagers' cattle and horses grazed. To his left, just past the stone wall that surrounded Luthvian's lawn and gardens, was meadowland dotted with wildflowers. In the distance were stands of pine and spruce. Beyond them rose the mountains that ringed Ebon Rih.

Jaenelle stepped off the road and stopped, her back to all that was civilized, her sapphire eyes fixed on the wild. He approached her slowly, reluctant to disturb her meditation.

Nothing had happened at Luthvian's that could explain the intensity of Jaenelle's anger. Nothing had prepared him for that confrontation when she had turned on him, because part of her anger had been at him, and he still didn't know what he'd done to cause it.

She turned toward him, outwardly calm but still ready to fight.

Fight with a Queen when there's no other choice. Good, sound advice from the Steward of the first court he'd ever served in.

"What did you think of Luthvian?" Saetan asked as he offered Jaenelle his right arm.

Jaenelle studied him for a moment before linking arms with him. "She knows Craft." She wrinkled her nose and smiled. "I rather like her, even if she was a bit prickly today."

"Witch-child, Luthvian's always a bit prickly," Saetan said dryly.

"Ah. Especially with you?"

"We have a past." He waited for the inevitable questions, and became slightly uncomfortable when Jaenelle didn't ask any. Maybe past affairs weren't of interest to her. Or maybe she already had all the answers she required. "Why were you so angry with Roxie?"

"You're not a whore," Jaenelle snapped, pulling away from him.

Suddenly it seemed much darker, but when he looked up, the sky was just as blue as it had been a moment before and the clouds were still puffy and white. No, the storm gathering around him was standing a few feet away with her hands clenched and her feet spread in a fighting stance—and tears in her haunted eyes.

"No one said I was a whore," Saetan said quietly.

The tears spilled down Jaenelle's cheeks. "How could you let that bitch do that to you?" she screamed at him.

"Do what?" he snapped, failing to keep his frustration in check.

"How could you let her look at you like . . . force you . . ."

"FORCE ME? How in the name of Hell do you think that child could force me to do anything?"

"There are ways!"

"What ways? No one was ever stupid enough to try to force me even before I made the Offering, let alone since I began wearing the Black."

Jaenelle faltered.

"Listen to me, witch-child. Roxie is a young woman who's recently had her first sexual experience. Right now she thinks she owns the world and every male who looks at her will want to be her lover. In my younger years, I was a consort in a number of courts. I understand the game older, experienced men are expected to play. We're *supposed* to let girls practice on us because we have no interest in warming their beds. By our approval or disapproval, we help them understand how a man thinks and feels." He raked his fingers through his hair. "Although, I'll grant you, Roxie's a bit of a cunt."

Jaenelle scrubbed the tears from her face. "Then you didn't mind?"

Saetan sighed. "The truth? While listening to her giggling crudities, I was giving myself immense pleasure imagining what it would be like to hear her bones snapping."

"Oh."

"Come here, witch-child." He wrapped his arms around her, holding her tight while he rested his cheek on her head. "Who were you really angry for, Jaenelle? Who were you trying to protect?"

"I don't know. I sort of remember someone who had to submit to women like Roxie. It hurt him, and he hated it. It's not even a memory. More like a feeling because I can't

recall who or where or why I would have known someone
like that."

Which explained why she hadn't asked about Daemon.
He was too entwined with the trauma that had cost her
two years of her life, a trauma she'd locked away somewhere inside her. And all her memories of Daemon were
locked away with it.

Saetan asked himself, again, if he shouldn't tell her what
had happened. But he could only tell her a small part of
it. He couldn't tell her who had raped her because he still
didn't know. And he couldn't tell her what had happened
between her and Daemon while they were in the abyss.

And the truth was he was afraid to tell her anything
at all.

"Let's go home, witch-child," he whispered into her hair.
"Let's go home and explore the attics."

Jaenelle laughed shakily. "How will we explain this to
Helene?"

Saetan groaned. "I'm supposed to own the Hall, you
know. Besides, it's very large and has a lot of rooms. If
we're lucky, it'll take her a while to figure it out."

Jaenelle stepped back. "Race you home," she said, and
vanished.

Saetan hesitated. He took a long look at the meadow
with its wildflowers and the mountains in the distance.

He would give it a little while longer before he began
searching for Daemon Sadi.

2 / Kaeleer

Greer crept behind the row of junipers that bordered one
side of the lawn behind SaDiablo Hall. The sun was almost
up. If he didn't get to the south tower before the gardeners
began scurrying about, he'd have to hide in the woods
again. He might be demon-dead now, but he'd spent his
life in cities. The rustling quiet and blanket dark of a country night unnerved him, and despite not being able to sense
another presence, he couldn't shake the feeling he was

being watched. And then there was that damned howling that seemed to sing the night awake.

He couldn't believe someone like the High Lord didn't have guard spells around the Hall. How else could a place this size be protected? But the Dark Priestess had assured him that Saetan had always been too lax and arrogant to consider such things. Besides, the south tower had always been Hekatah's domain, and with each of her many renovations, she'd added secret stairways and false walls so that there were entire rooms tucked away that her own spells still kept carefully hidden. One of those rooms would keep him sheltered and shielded.

Provided he could reach it.

Slipping his hands into his coat pockets, Greer left the junipers' protection and walked purposefully toward the south tower. That was one of the rules of a good assassin: act as if you belong. If he was seen, he hoped he'd be dismissed as a tradesman or, better yet, a guest.

When he finally reached the door in the south tower, he began walking slowly to the left, his left hand feeling the stones for the catch that would open the secret entrance. Unfortunately, it had been so long, Hekatah couldn't remember exactly how far the entrance was from the door, especially since she'd made sure the alterations at the Kaeleer Hall didn't match the ones she'd made in Terreille.

Just when he thought he'd have to return to the door and start over, he found the chipped stone that held the hidden latch. A moment later, he was inside the tower, climbing a narrow stone stairway.

Shortly after that, he discovered just how far the Dark Priestess had misled him—or had misled herself.

There were no luxuriously furnished apartments in the south tower, no ornate beds, no elegant daybeds, no rugs, no drapes, no tables, no chairs. Room after room was empty and swept clean.

Greer put his left hand over the black silk scarf around his throat and pushed down the panic.

Swept clean and empty. Just like the secret staircase, which should have been thick with dust and cobwebs.

Which meant it wasn't as much of a secret as Hekatah thought.

He tried to tell himself it didn't matter since he was already dead, but he'd been in the Dark Realm long enough to have heard stories about what happened to demons who crossed the High Lord, and he didn't want to find out first-hand how much truth there was in those stories.

He returned to the chamber that had once belonged to Hekatah and began a systematic search for the hidden rooms.

They, too, were empty and clean. Either her spells had broken down over time or someone else had broken them.

There had to be somewhere he could hide! The sun was too high now, and even with the quantity of fresh blood he'd been consuming, the daylight weakened him, drained him. If all the rooms had been found . . .

At last he found a hidden room within a hidden room. More of a cubbyhole, really. Greer couldn't imagine what it had been used for, but it was disgustingly grimy and cobwebbed, and therefore safe.

With his back pressed into a corner, Greer wrapped his arms around his knees and began to wait.

3 / Kaeleer

Andulvar rapped sharply on the study door and walked in before getting a response. Swinging toward the back of the room, he stopped as Saetan quickly—and rather guiltily—hid the book he'd been reading.

Hell's fire, Andulvar thought as he settled into the chair facing the desk, when was the last time Saetan looked that relaxed? There he was, the High Lord of Hell, with his feet on the desk, wearing house slippers and a black sweater. Seeing him like that, Andulvar regretted that the days were long past when they could have gone to a tavern and wrangled over a couple of pitchers of ale.

Amused by Saetan's discomfort, Andulvar said, "Beale told me you were in here—taking care of correspondence, I believe he said."

"Ah, yes, the worthy Beale."

"Not many houses can claim a Red-Jeweled Warlord for a butler."

"Not many would want to," Saetan muttered, dropping his feet to the floor. "Yarbarah?"

"Please." Andulvar waited until Saetan poured and warmed the blood wine. "Since you're not doing correspondence, what are you doing? Besides hiding from your intimidating staff?"

"Reading," Saetan replied a bit stiffly.

Always the patient hunter, Andulvar waited. And waited. "Reading what?" he finally asked. His eyes narrowed. Was Saetan blushing?

"A novel." Saetan cleared his throat. "A rather . . . actually, a very erotic novel."

"Reminiscing?" Andulvar asked blandly.

Saetan growled. "Trying to anticipate. Adolescent girls ask the most terrifying questions."

"Better you than me."

"Coward."

"No argument there," Andulvar said, refusing to rise to the bait. Then he paused. "How are things going?"

"Why ask me?" Saetan propped his feet on the corner of the desk.

"You're the High Lord."

Saetan put a hand over his heart and sighed dramatically. "Ah, someone who remembers." He sipped the yarbarah. "Actually, if you want to know how things are going, you should ask Beale or Helene or Mrs. Beale. They're the triangle who run the Hall."

"A Blood triangle always has a fourth side."

"Yes, and whenever something comes up that requires 'Authority,' they prop me up, dust me off, and plunk me in the great hall to deal with it." Saetan's warm smile lit his golden eyes. "My chief functions are to be the Lady's loyal guardian and, since Beale would never deign to have his attire ruined by hysterics, to be a shoulder to cry on when Jaenelle throws her tutors off their stride—which seems to be averaging out to three or four times a week."

"The waif's doing all right then."

Saetan's smile vanished, replaced by a bleak, haunted expression. "No, she's not doing all right. Damn it, Andulvar, I'd hoped . . . She's trying so very, very hard. She's still Jaenelle. Still inquisitive and gentle and kind." He sighed. "But she's unable to respond to the overtures of friendship from the staff. Oh, I know." He waved a hand, dismissing an unspoken protest. "The relationship of servants to the Lady of the house is what it is. But it's not just them. Between that business with Menzar and the friction that exists between her and the rest of Luthvian's students, she's become timid. She avoids people whenever she can. Sylvia hasn't been able to coax her into another shopping trip, and that Lady has tried. She and her son, Beron, called a few days ago. Jaenelle managed to talk with them for about five minutes before bolting from the room.

"She has no friends, Andulvar. No one to laugh with, no one to do silly girl things with. She hasn't made the Offering yet, and she's already too aware of the gulf between herself and the rest of the Blood." Saetan slumped in his chair. "If only there was some way to get her to resume her life again."

"Why don't you invite that little ice harpy from Glacia to visit?" Andulvar said.

"Do you think she would be brave enough to come to the Hall?"

Andulvar snorted. "Considering the letter she wrote you, if you let that one through the door, she'll probably be stepping on your toes."

Saetan smiled wistfully. "I hope so, Andulvar. I do hope so."

Regretting that the easy mood would change, Andulvar drained his glass and set it carefully on the desk. "It's time you told me why you wanted me to come back to the Hall."

"Tarl was the one who suggested you might be able to help," Saetan said as he and Andulvar made their way to one of the walled gardens.

"I'm a hunter and a warrior, not a gardener, SaDiablo," Andulvar said gruffly. "How am I supposed to help him?"

"A large dog has staked out a territory in the north woods. I first heard it the night Sylvia told me there was something wrong in Halaway. It's killed a couple of young deer, but outside of that, the foresters haven't been able to find a trace of it. A few nights ago, it helped itself to a couple of chickens."

"Your foresters should be able to handle it."

Saetan opened the wooden gate that led into the low-walled garden. "Tarl found something else this morning." He nodded to the head gardener, who was standing near the back flower bed.

Tarl brushed his fingers against the brim of his cap and left.

Saetan pointed to the soft earth between two young plants. "That."

Andulvar stared at the clear, deep paw print for a long time before kneeling down and placing his hand beside it. "Damn, it's big."

Saetan knelt beside Andulvar. "That's what I thought, but this is your expertise. What really bothers me is it seems so deliberate, so carefully placed, as if it's a message or a signal of some kind."

"And who's supposed to be getting this message?" Andulvar rumbled. "Who would be expected to come in here and see it?"

"Since Lord Menzar's abrupt departure, Mephis has quietly checked everyone who serves the Hall, inside staff and out. He didn't find anything that would make me believe they can't be trusted."

Andulvar frowned thoughtfully at the print. "Could be a lover's signal for a secret tryst in the garden."

"Trust me, Andulvar," Saetan said dryly, "there are simpler and more effective ways of setting up a romantic adventure than this." He pointed to the paw print. "Besides, short of removing the dog's foot, how would anyone find the brute, bring it here, and convince it to leave one print in this exact spot?"

"I'm going to look around," Andulvar said abruptly.

While Andulvar studied the rest of the walled gardens in the waning daylight, Saetan studied the print. He'd managed to push aside the nagging worry until Andulvar had arrived, almost hoping the Eyrien would look at the print and shrug it off with an easy explanation. Now Andulvar was worried, and Saetan didn't like it. *Was* someone trying to set up a meeting? Or just lure someone away from the Hall?

Snarling softly, Saetan brushed dirt across the print until there was no trace of it. He got to his feet, brushed the dirt from his knees, glanced at the flower bed, and froze.

The paw print was as deep and as clear as it had been a minute ago.

"Andulvar!" Saetan dropped to his knees and smoothed dirt across the print again.

Andulvar rushed in, the air from his wings stirring the young plants, and knelt beside Saetan.

They watched in silence while the dirt rolled away from the print.

Andulvar swore viciously. "It's been spelled."

"Yes," Saetan said too softly. He used the equivalent strength of a White Jewel to obliterate the print again. When it came back just as quickly, he went to the Yellow, the next level of descent. Then he tried Tiger Eye, Rose, and Summer-sky. Finally, at the strength of the Purple Dusk Jewel, the print was barely discernible.

With a vicious swipe of his hand, Saetan used the strength of his Birthright Red to eliminate the print.

It didn't return.

"Someone wanted to be very sure this print wasn't carelessly erased," Saetan said, wiping his hand on the grass.

Andulvar rubbed his fist against his chin. "Keep the waif from wandering around by herself, even in these gardens. Prothvar and I aren't much help in the daylight, but we'll keep watch at night."

"You think someone's foolish enough to penetrate the Hall?"

"Looks like someone already has. That's not what's bothering me." Andulvar pointed to the now-smooth dirt. "That's not a dog, SaDiablo. It's a wolf. It's hard to believe a wolf would choose to get this close to humans, but even if it's being controlled by someone, what's the point of bringing it here?"

"Bait," Saetan said, immediately sending out a psychic call to Jaenelle. Her distracted acknowledgment reassured him that she was sufficiently engrossed in her studies to remain indoors.

"Bait for what?"

Instead of answering, Saetan made a sweeping probe of the Hall and the surrounding land. There was that muzziness in the south tower, the fading effects of the shielding spells Helene and Beale had broken as they cleared out the tower and uncovered Hekatah's secret rooms. There was also that odd ripple in the north woods.

Saetan probed a little longer and then stopped. Getting into the Hall had never been difficult. Getting out was another matter.

"Bait for what, SaDiablo?" Andulvar asked again.

"For a young girl who's lonely and loves animals."

4 / Kaeleer

Greer huddled in a corner of the secret cubbyhole, whimpering as that dark mind rolled through the very stones, probing, searching.

He struggled to keep his mind carefully blank as the surge of dark power washed over him. He couldn't safely bolt before sunset, but if he were caught here, how would he explain his presence? Having lost one little darling, Greer doubted any explanation would appease the High Lord right now.

When the psychic probe faded, Greer stretched out his legs and sighed. As much as he feared the High Lord, he didn't relish going back to Hekatah without any information. She would insist he try again.

It would have to be tonight. He would find the girl's room, look her over, and return to Hell. If Hekatah wanted to get any closer and risk coming face-to-face with Saetan, she could do it herself.

5 / Kaeleer

Saetan headed for his suite, hoping a little rest would bring inspiration. Earlier that evening, he'd tried to convince Jaenelle to contact some of her friends. He'd failed miserably and, in the process, had learned a lot about an adolescent witch's emotional volatility.

Wondering if he could enlist Sylvia as an ally in future emotional battles and still puzzling over the wolf print in the garden, he felt the warning signs a moment too late.

A psychic tidal wave of fear and rage crashed against his mind and sent him reeling into the wall. He clutched his head as knife-edged pain stabbed at his temples, and tasted blood as his teeth cut his lip.

Moaning at the merciless throbbing in his head, he sank to the floor and instinctively tried to strengthen his inner barriers against another mind-tearing assault.

When no other psychic wave crashed against his inner barriers, Saetan raised his head and probed cautiously. He stared at the door across the hall from where he huddled. "Witch-child?"

An agonized scream came from behind Jaenelle's door.

Saetan pushed himself to his feet, stumbled across the hall, and plunged into a room consumed by the most violent psychic storm he'd ever encountered. Except for a strong, swirling wind which bent the plants and twisted the curtains, the physical room appeared untouched, but it felt like it was filled with strands of spun glass that snapped as he passed through it, cutting the mind instead of the body.

Head down and shoulders hunched, Saetan gritted his teeth and forced himself, step by mind-slicing step, toward the bed, where Jaenelle thrashed and screamed.

When he touched her arm, she flung herself away from him.

Barely able to think, Saetan threw himself on top of her and wrapped his arms and legs around her. They rolled on the bed, tangled in the sheets she had shredded with her nails, while she fought and screamed. When she couldn't free her arms and legs, she half twisted in his arms, her teeth snapping a breath away from his throat.

"Jaenelle!" Saetan roared in her ear. "Jaenelle! It's Saetan!"

"Noooooo!"

Drawing on the reserved power in the Black Jewels, Saetan rolled once more, pinning Jaenelle between the bed and his body. He opened his inner barriers and sent out the message that she was safe, that he was with her, knowing if she struck him now, she'd destroy him.

Jaenelle brushed against his vulnerable mind and stopped moving.

Shaking, Saetan rested his cheek against her head. "I'm with you, witch-child," he whispered. "You're safe."

"Not safe," Jaenelle moaned. "Never safe."

Saetan clamped his teeth together, sickened by the images that suddenly flowed into his mind. He saw them all as she had once seen them. Marjane, hanging from the tree. Myrol and Rebecca, handless. Dannie and Dannie's leg. And Rose.

Tears rolled down his face as he held Jaenelle and made those agonizing memories his own. Now he finally understood what she'd endured as a child, what had been done to her, why she had never feared Hell or its citizens. As the memories flowed from her mind to his, he could see the building, the rooms, the garden, the tree.

And he remembered Char coming to him, troubled by a bridge and the maimed children who were traveling over it to the *cildru dyathe*'s island. A bridge Jaenelle had built once between Hell and . . . Briarwood.

The moment he thought the name, he felt Jaenelle's eyes open.

Suddenly there was impenetrable, swirling mist. It parted abruptly, and he looked down into the abyss. Every instinct urged him to flee, to get away from the cold rage and madness spiraling up from the depths.

But woven into the madness and rage were gentleness and magic, too. So he waited at the edge of the abyss for whatever would happen. He wouldn't run from his Queen.

The mist closed in again. He couldn't see her, but he felt her when Jaenelle rose from the abyss. And he shuddered as her sepulchral, midnight whisper rang through his mind.

Briarwood is the pretty poison. There is no cure for Briarwood.

Then she spiraled back down, and his mind was his own again.

Jaenelle stirred against him. "Saetan?" She sounded so young, so frail, so uncertain.

Saetan kissed her cheek. "I'm here, witch-child," he said hoarsely, cradling her to his chest. He gingerly probed the room, and quickly discovered using Craft wasn't going to be possible until the psychic storm completely faded.

"What . . ." Jaenelle said groggily.

"You were having a nightmare. Do you remember?"

A long silence. "No. What was it about?"

Saetan hesitated . . . and said nothing.

A boot scuffed on the balcony outside the open glass door. Someone hurried down the stairs.

Saetan's head snapped up. Since probing for the intruder's identity was useless, he frantically tore at the sheets tangled around his legs and sprang toward the balcony door. "PROTHVAR!" He tried to create a ball of witchlight to spotlight the garden, but Jaenelle's psychic storm absorbed his power, and the flash of light he managed left him night-blind.

On the far side of the garden, something snarled viciously. A man screamed. There was a brief, furious struggle, a blinding sizzle as the strength of two Jewels was unleashed and absorbed, the sound of odd-gaited footsteps, another snarl, and then a door slamming.

And then silence.

The bedroom door burst open. Saetan pivoted, his teeth bared, as Andulvar sprang into the room, an Eyrien war blade in his hand.

"Stay with her," Saetan snapped. He ran down the balcony stairs, reaching for the spells that would seal the Hall and prevent anyone from leaving. Then he swore. That tidal wave of power had shattered all of his spells—which meant the intruder could find a way out before they could hunt him down. And once he got away far enough from the effects of the storm, he could catch the Winds and just disappear.

"But where were you hiding that I didn't feel your presence before?" Saetan snarled, grinding his teeth in frustration as Prothvar landed beside him in the garden.

The Eyrien Warlord held out a torn black silk scarf. "I found this near the south tower."

Saetan stared at the scarf Greer had worn the first time he came to the Hall. His golden eyes glittered as he turned toward the south tower. "I've been too complacent about Hekatah's games and Hekatah's pets. But this pet has made one mistake too many."

"Hekatah!" Cursing, Prothvar dropped the scarf and wiped his hand on his trousers. Then he smiled. "I don't think her pet left as intact as he came. There are also wolf prints near the south tower."

Wolf. Saetan stared at the south tower. A wolf and Greer. Bait and an abductor? But that snarl, that clash of Jewels.

A movement on the balcony caught his eye.

Jaenelle looked down at them. Andulvar's arm was around her shoulders, tucking her close to his left side. His right hand still held the large, wicked-looking war blade.

"Papa, what's wrong?" Jaenelle called.

With a nod to Saetan, Prothvar vanished the scarf and slipped into the shadows to stand guard.

Saetan slowly crossed the garden and climbed the stairs, frustrated that the lingering effects of the witch storm made it impossible for him to use Craft to keep anyone else from reaching her rooms.

Andulvar stepped back as Jaenelle flung herself into Saetan's arms. He kissed her head, and the three of them went into her bedroom.

"What happened?" Jaenelle said, shivering as she watched Andulvar close the balcony doors and physically lock them.

That she had to ask indicated too much about her state of mind. Saetan hesitated. "It was nothing, witch-child," he finally said, holding her close. "An unexplained noise." But was it something she had seen or felt that had triggered those memories?

Andulvar and Saetan exchanged a look. The Eyrien Warlord Prince looked pointedly at the bed, then at the balcony doors.

Saetan nodded slightly. "Witch-child, your bed's a bit . . . rumpled. Since it's so late, rather than waking a maid to change it, why don't you stay in my room tonight?"

Jaenelle's head snapped up. There was shock, wariness, and fear in her eyes. "I could make up the bed."

"I'd rather you didn't."

Saetan felt her reach for his mind and waited. Unless she deliberately picked his thoughts, he could keep the reason for his concern from her but not the feeling of concern.

Jaenelle withdrew from him and nodded.

Relieved that she was still willing to trust him, Saetan led her to his suite across the hall and tucked her into his bed. After Andulvar left to check the south tower, he poured and warmed a glass of yarbarah, and settled into a chair nearby. A long time later, Jaenelle's breathing evened out, and he knew she was asleep.

A wolf, he thought as he watched over her. A friend or an enemy?

Saetan closed his eyes and rubbed his temples. The headache was subsiding, but the past hour had left him exhausted. Still, he kept seeing that print in the garden, a spelled message someone was supposed to understand.

But that snarl, *that clash of Jewels.*

Saetan snapped upright in the chair and stared at Jaenelle.

Not all the dreamers who had shaped this Witch had been human.

It fit. If it was true, it all fit.

Maybe, since Jaenelle hadn't gone to see her old friends, they were starting to come to her.

6 / Hell

Hekatah screamed at Greer, "What do you mean she's alive?"

"Just what I said," Greer replied as he inspected his torn arm. "The girl he's keeping at the Hall is that pale bitch granddaughter of Alexandra Angelline."

"But you destroyed her!"

"Apparently she survived."

Hekatah paced the small, dirty, sparsely furnished room. It couldn't be true. It just couldn't. She glanced at Greer, who was slumped in a chair. "You said it was dark, difficult to see. You never got into the room itself. It couldn't be the same girl. He told you she walked among the *cildru dyathe.*"

"He called her Jaenelle," Greer said, examining his foot.

Hekatah's eyes widened. "He lied about it." Her face turned ugly with rage and hate. "That gutter son of a whore *lied about it*!"

Then she remembered that terrifying presence on the *cildru dyathe*'s island. If the girl was really alive, she could still be shaped into the puppet Queen whom Hekatah needed to rule the Realms.

Hekatah ran her fingers over a scarred table. "Even if she survived physically, she's of little use to me if she has no power."

Cradling his torn arm, Greer took the bait. "She still has power. There was a fierce witch storm filling that room. It began before the High Lord entered. The Darkness only knows how he survived it."

Hekatah frowned. "What was he doing in her room at that hour?"

Greer shrugged. "It sounded like they were rolling around on the bed, and it wasn't a friendly tussle."

Hekatah stared at Greer but didn't see him. She saw Saetan, hot-blooded and hungry, easing his appetites—*all* his appetites—with that young, dark-blooded witch who should have belonged to her. A Guardian was still capable of that kind of pleasure. A Guardian . . . who valued honor. Oh, he could try to ignore the scandal and condemnation, but by the time she was done, she'd create such a firestorm around him even his most loyal servants would hate him.

But it had to be done delicately so that, unlike that fool Menzar, Saetan wouldn't be able to trace it back to her.

Hekatah studied Greer. The torn muscle in his forearm could be hidden by a coat, but that foot. . . . Whether it was snapped off and replaced with something artificial or left on and laced into a high boot, the dragging walk would be obvious—as were the maimed hands. A pity such a useful servant was so deformed and, therefore, so conspicuous. But he'd be able to perform this one last assignment. In fact, his deformities would work in her favor.

Hekatah allowed herself a brief smile before putting on her saddest expression. She sank to her knees beside Greer's chair. "Poor darling," she cooed, stroking his cheek with her fingertips, "I've let that bastard's schemes distract me from more important concerns."

"What concerns, Priestess?" Greer asked cautiously.

"Why, you, darling, and those ferocious wounds his beast inflicted on you." She wiped at her eyes as if they could still hold tears. "You know there's no way to heal these wounds now, don't you, darling?"

Greer looked away.

Hekatah leaned forward and kissed his cheek. "But don't worry. I have a plan that will pay Saetan back for everything."

"You wanted to see me, High Lord?"

Saetan's eyes glittered. He leaned against the blackwood desk in his private study in the Dark Realm and smiled at the Dea al Mon Harpy. "Titian, my dear," he crooned in a voice like soft thunder, "I have an assignment for you that I think will be very much to your liking."

CHAPTER
SIX

1 / Kaeleer

Saetan, along with the rest of the family, lingered at the dinner table, reluctant to have the meal and the camaraderie end.

At least some good had come from that unpleasant night last week. Jaenelle's nightmare had lanced the festering wound of those suppressed memories, easing a little of her emotional pain. He knew that soul wound wasn't healed, but for the first time since she'd returned from the abyss, she was more like the child they remembered than the haunted young woman she'd become.

"I think Beale would like to clear the table," Jaenelle said quietly, glancing at the butler standing at the dining room door.

"Then why don't we have coffee in the drawing room," Saetan suggested, pushing his chair back.

When Jaenelle walked toward the door, followed by Mephis, Andulvar, and Prothvar, he lingered a moment longer. It was so good to hear her laugh, so good to—

A movement at the window caught his attention. Immediately probing for the intruder, he took a step back when strangely scented, feral emotions pushed against his mind, challenging him, daring him to touch.

Anger. Frustration. Fear. And then . . .

The howl stopped conversations midword as Andulvar and Prothvar spun around, their hunting knives drawn. Saetan barely noticed them, too intent on Jaenelle's reaction.

She closed her eyes, took a deep breath, tipped her head back, and howled. It wasn't an exact imitation of the wolf's howl. It was eerier somehow because it turned into witch-song. A wild song.

And he realized, with a shivering sense of wonder, that she and the wolf had sung this song before, that they knew how to blend those two voices to create something alien and beautiful.

The wolf stopped howling. Jaenelle finished the song and smiled.

A large gray shape leaped through the window, passing through the glass. The wolf landed in the dining room, snarling at them.

With a welcoming cry, Jaenelle rushed past Andulvar and Prothvar, dropped to her knees, and threw her arms around the wolf's neck.

In that moment, Saetan caught the psychic scent he was searching for. The wolf was one of the legendary kindred. A Prince, but not, thank the Darkness, a Warlord Prince. He also caught a glimpse of the gold chain and the Purple Dusk Jewel hidden in the wolf's fur.

Still snarling, the wolf pressed against Jaenelle, urging her toward the window while it kept its body between her and the Eyriens.

Pushed off-balance, Jaenelle's arms tightened around the wolf's neck. "Smoke, you're being rude," she said in that quiet, firm Queen voice that no male in his right mind would defy.

Smoke gave her a quick lick and changed his snarl to a deep growl.

"What bad male?" Jaenelle scanned each concerned male face and shook her head. "Well, it wasn't one of them. This is my pack."

The growling stopped. There was intelligence and new interest in the wolf's eyes as he studied each man, then waved the tip of his tail once as a reluctant greeting.

Another brief pause. Jaenelle blushed. "No, none of them are my mate. I'm not old enough for a mate," she added hurriedly as Smoke gave them all a look of blatant disapproval. "This is Saetan, the High Lord. He's my sire.

My brother, Prince Mephis, is the High Lord's pup. And this is my uncle, Prince Andulvar, and my cousin, Lord Prothvar. And that's Lord Beale. Everyone, this is Prince Smoke."

As he greeted his kindred Brother, Saetan wondered which had startled the others more: kindred suddenly appearing, Jaenelle's conversing with a wolf, or the family labels she'd given them.

There was an awkward pause after the introductions. Andulvar and Prothvar glanced at him, then sheathed their knives, keeping their movements slow and deliberate. Mephis remained still but ready to respond, and Beale, hovering in the doorway, was silently awaiting instructions. Smoke looked uneasy, and there was a bruised, uncertain look in Jaenelle's eyes.

He had to do something quickly. But what did one say to a wolf? More important, what could he do to make Jaenelle's furry friend feel comfortable enough and welcome enough to want to stay? Well, what did one say to any guest?

"May I offer you some refreshments, Prince Smoke?" Said out loud, the name combined with a Blood title sounded silly to him even if it was an apt description of the wolf's coloring. Then again, maybe human names sounded just as silly to a wolf. Saetan raised an eyebrow at Beale and wondered how his stoic Warlord butler was going to react to a four-footed guest.

It was quickly apparent that any friend of Jaenelle's, whether he walked on two legs or four, would be treated as an honored guest.

Beale stepped forward, made his most formal bow, and addressed his inquiries to Jaenelle. "There is the beef roast from dinner, if Prince Smoke doesn't object to the meat being cooked."

Jaenelle looked amused, but her voice was steady and dignified. "Thank you, Beale. That would be quite acceptable."

"A bowl of cool water as well?"

Jaenelle just nodded.

"We'll be more comfortable in the drawing room," Sae-

tan said. He slowly approached Jaenelle, offering a hand
to help her to her feet.

Smoke tensed at his approach but didn't challenge him
or back away. The wolf didn't trust humans, didn't want
him close enough to touch Jaenelle, but was at a loss of
how to stop it without incurring his Lady's disapproval.

He's not so different from the rest of us, Saetan thought
as he escorted Jaenelle to the family drawing room.

Without conscious thought, the men waited for Jaenelle
to choose a seat before settling into chairs and couches far
enough away from her so the wolf wouldn't be upset and
close enough not to miss anything. Saetan sat opposite her
chair, aware that Smoke's attention was focused on him
and had been since the introductions were made.

He felt grateful for the distraction Beale provided moments later when the butler appeared with a silver serving
tray holding coffee for Jaenelle, yarbarah for the rest of
them, and bowls of meat and water for Smoke. Beale set
the bowls of meat and water in front of Smoke, placed the
tray on a table in front of Jaenelle, and, when no one indicated a further requirement, reluctantly left the room.

Smoke sniffed at the meat and water but remained seated
by Jaenelle's chair, pressed against her knees. Saetan added
the hefty dose of cream and sugar that Jaenelle liked in
her coffee, then poured and warmed yarbarah, passing the
glasses to the others before warming one for himself.

"Is Prince Smoke alone?" he asked Jaenelle. Until he
could find out how kindred communicated with humans, he
had no choice but to direct his questions to her.

Jaenelle watched Smoke studying the bowls and didn't
answer.

Saetan stiffened when he realized the wolf was doing
exactly what he would have done in unfamiliar and possibly
hostile territory—using Craft to probe the meat and drink,
looking for something that shouldn't be there. Looking for
poison. And he also realized who had taught the wolf to
look for poisons—which made him wonder why she'd
needed to teach that lesson in the first place.

"Well?" Jaenelle said quietly.

Smoke shifted his feet and made a sound that expressed uncertainty.

Jaenelle gave him an approving pat. "Those are herbs. Humans use them to alter the flavor of meat and vegetables." Then she laughed. "I don't know why we want to change the taste of meat. We just do."

Smoke selected a hunk of beef.

Jaenelle gave Saetan an amused smile, but there was sadness in her eyes and a touch of anxiety. "Smoke's pack is still in their home territory. He came alone because . . . because he wanted to see me, wanted to know if I'd come and visit his pack like I used to."

He missed you, witch-child. They all miss you. Saetan swirled the yarbarah in his glass. He understood her anxiety. Smoke was here instead of protecting his mate and young. That Jaenelle had taught them about poisons made it obvious that the kindred wolves faced dangers beyond natural ones. It would require some adjustments, but if Smoke was willing . . . "How much territory does a pack need?"

Jaenelle shrugged. "It depends. A fair amount. Why?"

"The family owns a considerable amount of land in Dhemlan, including the north woods. Even with the hunting rights I've granted the families in Halaway, there's plenty of game. Would that be sufficient territory for a pack?"

Jaenelle stared at him. "You want a wolf pack in the north woods?"

"If Smoke and his family would like to live there, why not?" Besides, the benefits certainly wouldn't be one-sided. He'd provide territory and protection for the wolf pack, and they'd provide companionship and protection for Jaenelle.

The silence that followed wasn't really silence but a conversation the rest of them couldn't hear. Jaenelle's expression was carefully neutral. Smoke's, as he studied each man in the room, was unreadable.

Finally Jaenelle looked at Saetan. "Humans don't like wolf-kind."

Saetan steepled his fingers and forced himself to breathe evenly. Jaenelle had rarely mentioned kindred. He knew she had visited the dream-weaving spiders in Arachna and once, when he'd first met her, she had mentioned unicorns. But Smoke's presence and the ease with which she and the wolf communicated spoke of a long-established relationship. What other kindred might know the sound of her voice, her dark psychic scent? What others might be willing to risk contact with humans in order to be with her again? Compared to what might be out there in those mist-enclosed Territories, what was a wolf?

The girl and the wolf waited for his answer.

"I rule this Territory," he said quietly. "And, as I said, the Hall and its land are personal property. If the humans don't want our kindred Brothers and Sisters as neighbors, then the humans can leave."

He wasn't sure if he was trying to reach out with his mind or if Smoke was trying to reach toward him, but he caught the edge of those alien, feral thoughts. Not thoughts, really, more like emotions filtered through a different lens but still readable. Surprise, followed by swift understanding and approval. Smoke, at least, knew exactly why the offer was being made.

Unfortunately, Jaenelle, reaching for her coffee, caught some of it, too. "What bad male?" she asked, frowning.

Smoke suddenly decided the meat was interesting.

From Jaenelle's annoyed expression, Saetan deduced the wolf had turned evasive. Since it wasn't a topic he wanted her to pursue, he decided to satisfy his own curiosity, aware of the effort Andulvar, Prothvar, and Mephis were making to sit quietly and not begin a barrage of questions. The kindred had always been elusive and timid about contact with humans, even before they had closed their borders. Now there was a wolf, kindred and wild, sitting in his drawing room.

"Prince Smoke is kindred?" Saetan asked, his tone more confirmation than question.

"Of course," Jaenelle said, surprised.

"And you can communicate with him?"

"Of course."

He felt the wave of frustration coming from the others

and clenched his teeth. *Remember who you're talking to.*
"How?"

Jaenelle looked puzzled. "Distaff to spear. The same way
I communicate with you." She fluffed her hair. "You can't
hear him?"

Saetan and the other men shook their heads.

Jaenelle looked at Smoke. "Can you hear them?"

Smoke looked at the human males and whuffed softly.

Jaenelle became indignant. "What do you mean I didn't
train them well? I didn't train them at all!"

Smoke's expression as he turned back to the meat was
smug.

Jaenelle muttered something uncomplimentary about
male thought processes, then said tartly, "Does the beef at
least meet with your approval?" She gave Saetan a brittle
smile. "Smoke says the beef is much better than the
squawky white birds." Her expression changed from annoyed to dismayed. "Squawky white birds? Chickens? You
ate Mrs. Beale's chickens?"

Smoke whined apologetically.

Saetan leaned back in his chair. Oh, it was so satisfying
to see her thrown off stride. "I'm sure Mrs. Beale was delighted to feed a guest—even if she wasn't aware of it," he
added dryly, remembering too well his cook's reaction
when she learned about the missing hens.

Jaenelle pressed her hands into her lap. "Yes. Well."
She nibbled her lower lip. "Communicating with kindred
isn't difficult."

"Really?" Saetan replied mildly, amused by the abrupt
return to the original topic of conversation.

"You just . . ." Jaenelle paused and finally shrugged.
"Shuck the human trappings and take one step to the side."

It wasn't the most enlightening set of instructions he'd
ever heard, but having seen beneath her mask of human
flesh, the phrase "shuck the human trappings" gave him
some uncomfortable things to wonder about. Was it more
comfortable, more natural for her to reach for kindred
minds? Or did she see kindred and human as equal
puzzles?

Alien and Other. Blood and more than Blood. Witch.

"What?" he asked, suddenly realizing they were all watching him.

"Do you want to try it?" Jaenelle asked gently.

Her haunted sapphire eyes, dark with their ancient wisdom, told him she knew exactly what troubled him. She didn't dismiss his concerns, which was sufficient acknowledgment that he had a reason to be concerned. And no reason at all.

Saetan smiled. "Yes, I'd like to try it."

Jaenelle touched the minds of the four men just outside the first inner barrier and showed them how to reach a mind that wasn't human.

It was simple, really. Rather like walking down a narrow, hedged-in lane, sidestepping through a gap in the hedge, and discovering that there was another well-worn path on the other side. Human trappings were nothing more than a narrow view of communication. He—and Andulvar, Prothvar, and Mephis, and maybe Smoke as well—would always be aware of the hedge and would have to travel through a gap. For Jaenelle, it was just one wide avenue.

Human. Smoke sounded pleased.

Filled with wonder, Saetan smiled. *Wolf.*

Smoke's thoughts were fascinating. Happiness because Jaenelle was glad to see him. Relief that the humans accepted him. Anticipation of bringing his pack to a safe place—clouded by darker images of kindred being hunted, and the need to understand these humans in order to protect themselves. Curiosity about how humans marked their territory since he hadn't smelled any scent markers in this stone place. And a yearning to water a few trees himself.

"I think we should go for a walk," Jaenelle said, standing quickly.

The human males stepped through the gaps in the mental hedge, their thoughts once more their own.

"After your walk, there's no reason Smoke has to return to the woods tonight," Saetan said casually, ignoring the sharp look Jaenelle gave him. "If your room's too warm, he could always bed down on the balcony or in your garden."

I will keep the bad male away from the Lady.

Apparently Smoke was accustomed to sliding through

the mental hedge. Saetan also noticed the wolf sent the thought on a spear thread, male to male, so that Jaenelle couldn't pick it up.

Thank you, Saetan replied. "Finished tomorrow's studies?"

Jaenelle wrinkled her nose at him and bid them all good night, Smoke eagerly trotting beside her as they headed for an outside door.

Saetan turned to the others.

Andulvar whistled softly. "Sweet Darkness, SaDiablo. Kindred."

"Kindred," Saetan agreed, smiling.

Andulvar and Mephis returned the smile.

Prothvar drew his hunting knife from its sheath and studied the blade. "I'll go with him to bring the pack home."

Images of hunters and traps pushed away the smiles.

"Yes," Saetan said too quietly, "do that."

2 / Terreille

Seething that her afternoon's intended amusement was now spoiled, Dorothea SaDiablo gave the young Warlord who was her current toy-boy a final, throat-swabbing kiss before dismissing him. Her eyes narrowed at the hasty way he fixed his clothes and left her sitting room. Well, she would take care of that little discipline problem tonight.

Rising gracefully from the ornate gold-and-cream daybed, she swished her hips provocatively as she walked to a table and poured a glass of wine. She drained half the glass before turning to face her son—and caught him pressing a fist into his lower back, trying to ease the chronic ache. She turned away, knowing her face reflected the revulsion she felt now every time she looked at him.

"What do you want, Kartane?"

"Did you find out anything?" he asked hesitantly.

"There's nothing to find out," Dorothea replied sharply, setting the glass down before it broke in her hand. "There's nothing wrong with you." Which was a lie. Anyone who looked at him knew it was a lie.

"There must be some reason why—"

"There is nothing wrong with you." Or, more truthfully, nothing she could do about it. But there was no need to tell him that.

"There has to be something," Kartane persisted. "Some spell—"

"Where?" Dorothea said angrily, turning to face him. "Show me where. There is nothing, I tell you, *nothing.*"

"Mother—"

Dorothea slapped him hard across the face. "Don't call me that."

Kartane stiffened and said nothing else.

Dorothea took a deep breath and ran her hands along her hips, smoothing the gown. Then she looked at him, not bothering to hide her disgust. "I'll continue to look into the matter. However, I have other appointments right now."

Kartane bowed, accepting the dismissal.

As soon as she was alone, Dorothea reached for the wine and swore when she saw how badly her hand was shaking.

Kartane's "illness" was getting worse, and there wasn't a damn thing she could do. The best Healers in Hayll couldn't find a physical reason for his body's deterioration because there wasn't one. But she'd pushed the Healers until a few months ago, when Kartane's screams had woken her and she'd learned about the dreams.

It always came back to that girl. Greer's death, Kartane's illness, Daemon's breaking the Ring of Obedience, Hekatah's obsession.

It always came back to that girl.

So she had gone to Chaillot secretly and had discovered that all the males who had been associated with a place called Briarwood were suffering in similar ways. One man screamed at least once a day that his hands were being cut off, despite being able to see them, move them. Two others babbled about a leg.

Furious, she had gone to Briarwood, which had been abandoned by then, to search for the tangled web of dreams and visions that she was sure had ensnared them all.

Her efforts had failed. The only thing she had been able to draw from Briarwood's wood and stone was ghostly, taunting laughter. No, not quite the only thing. After she had been there an hour, fear had thickened the air—fear and a sense of expectant waiting. She could have pried a little more, pushed a little harder. If she had, she was sure she would have found a strand that would have led her into the web. She was also sure she wouldn't have found a way out again.

It always came back to that girl.

She had returned home, dismissed the Healers, and begun insisting there was nothing wrong with him whenever Kartane pushed for her help.

She would keep on insisting, not only because there was nothing she could do, but because it would serve another purpose. Once Kartane felt certain he would get no help from her, he would look elsewhere. He would look for the one person he had always run to as a child whenever he needed help.

And sooner or later, he would find Daemon Sadi for her.

3 / Kaeleer

Saetan stormed through the corridors, heading for the garden room that opened onto a terrace at the back of the Hall.

Three days since Jaenelle, Prothvar, and Smoke had left to bring Smoke's pack to the Hall! Three gut-twisting, worried days full of thoughts of hunters and poison and how young she must have been when she'd first met the kindred, had first started teaching them to avoid man-made traps without a thought of what might happen to her if she'd been caught in one of those traps—or the other kinds of traps a Blood male might set for a young witch.

But she had been caught in "that kind of trap," hadn't she? He hadn't kept her safe from that one.

Now, finally, she was home. Had been home since just before dawn and *still* remained in the gardens bordering the north woods, *still* hadn't come up to the Hall to let him know she was all right.

Saetan flung open the glass doors, strode out onto the

terrace, and sucked the late afternoon air through his clenched teeth. Teetering at the edge of the flagstones, he tasted that held breath and shuddered.

The air was saturated with Jaenelle's feelings. Anguish, grief, rage. And a hint of the abyss.

Saetan stepped back from the terrace edge, his anger bleached by the primal storm building at the border of the north woods. It had gone wrong. Somehow, it had gone very wrong.

As anxiety replaced anger, as he wavered between waiting for her to come to him and going out to find her, he finally caught the quality of the silence, the dangerous silence.

Step by careful step, he retreated to the glass doors.

She was home. That's what mattered. Andulvar and Mephis would be rising with the dusk. Prothvar would rise, too, meet them in the study and tell them what happened.

There was no reason to intrude on her precarious self-control.

Because he didn't want to find out what would happen if the silence shattered.

Prothvar moved as if he'd endured a three-day beating.

Perhaps he had, Saetan thought as he watched the demon-dead Warlord warm a glass of yarbarah.

Prothvar lifted the glass to drink, but didn't. "They're dead."

Mephis made a sound of protest and dismay. Andulvar angrily demanded an explanation.

Saetan, remembering the dangerous silence that had filled the air, barely heard them. If he'd asked her about the wolf print earlier, if Smoke hadn't had to wait so long to reach her . . .

"All of them?" His voice broke, hushing Andulvar and Mephis.

Prothvar shook his head wearily. "Lady Ash and two pups survived. That's all that was left of a strong pack when the hunters were through harvesting pelts."

"They can't be the only kindred wolves left."

"No, Jaenelle said there are others. And we did find two

young wolves from another pack. Two young, terrified Warlords."

"Mother Night," Saetan whispered, sinking into a chair.

Andulvar snapped his wings open and shut. "Why didn't you gather them up and get out of there?"

Prothvar spun to face his grandfather. "Don't you think I tried? Don't you—" He closed his eyes and shuddered. "Two of the dead ones had made the change to demons. They had been skinned and their feet had been cut off, but they still—"

"Enough!" Saetan shouted.

Silence. Brittle, brittle silence. Time enough to hear the details. Time enough to add another nightmare to the list.

Moving as if he would shatter, Saetan led Prothvar to a chair.

They let him talk, let him exorcise the past three days. Saetan rubbed Prothvar's neck and shoulders, giving voiceless comfort. Andulvar knelt beside the chair and held his grandson's hand. Mephis kept the glass of yarbarah filled. And Prothvar talked, grieving because the kindred were innocent in a way the human Blood were not.

Someone else needed that kind of comfort. Someone else needed their strength. But she was still in the garden with the kindred and, like the kindred, was not yet able to accept what they offered.

"Is that all?" Saetan asked when Prothvar finally stopped talking.

"No, High Lord." Prothvar swallowed, choked. "Jaenelle disappeared for several hours before we left. She wouldn't tell me where she'd been or why she'd gone. When I pushed, she said, 'If they want pelts, they'll have pelts.' "

Saetan squeezed Prothvar's shoulders, not sure if he was giving comfort or taking it. "I understand."

Andulvar pulled Prothvar to his feet. "Come on, boyo. You need clean air beneath your wings."

When the Eyriens were gone, Mephis said, "You understand what the waif meant?"

Saetan stared at nothing. "Do you have commitments this evening?"

"No."

"Find some."

Mephis hesitated, then bowed. "As you wish, High Lord."

Silence. Brittle, brittle silence.

Oh, he understood exactly what she'd meant. Beware the golden spider who spins a tangled web. The Black Widow's web. Arachna's web. Beware the fair-haired Lady when she glides through the abyss clothed in spilled blood.

If the hunters never returned, nothing would happen. But they would return. Whoever they were, wherever they'd come from, they would return, and one kindred wolf would die and awaken the tangled web.

The hunters would still get their harvest, would still do the killing and the cutting and the skinning. Only one, confused and frightened, would leave with the bounty, and once he'd returned to wherever he'd come from, then, and only then, would the web release him and show him that the pelts he'd harvested didn't belong to wolf-kind.

4 / Kaeleer

Lord Jorval rubbed his hands gleefully. It was almost too good to be true. A scandal of this magnitude could topple anyone, even someone so firmly entrenched as the High Lord.

Remembering his new responsibilities, Jorval altered his expression to one more suitable to a member of the Dark Council.

This was a very serious charge, and the stranger with the maimed hands had admitted that he had no evidence except what he'd seen. After what the High Lord had done to the man's hands before dismissing him from service, it was understandable why he refused to stand before the Dark Council and testify against the High Lord in person. Still, something should be done about the girl.

A strong young Queen, the stranger had said. A Queen who could, with proper guidance, be a great asset to the Realm. All that glorious potential was being twisted by the High Lord's perversions, being forced to submit to . . .

Jorval jerked his thoughts away from those kinds of images.

The girl needed someone who could advise her and channel that power in the right direction. She needed someone she could depend on. And since she wasn't *that* young, maybe she needed more than that from her legal guardian. She might even expect, *want,* that kind of behavior . . .

But getting the girl away from Saetan would require a delicate touch. And the stranger had warned him about moving too quickly. A Dhemlan Queen could officially protest the High Lord's treatment of the girl, but Jorval didn't know any of them except by name or reputation. No, somehow the Dark Council itself had to be pressured into calling the High Lord to account.

And they could, couldn't they? After all, the Dark Council had granted the High Lord guardianship, and no one had forgotten what he'd done to gain that guardianship. It wouldn't be unusual for the Council to express concern about the girl's welfare.

A few words here. A hesitant question there. Strenuous protests that it was only a foul, unsubstantiated rumor. By the time it finally reached Dhemlan and the High Lord, no one would have any idea where the rumor started. Then they would see if even Saetan could withstand the rage of all the Queens in Kaeleer.

And he, Lord Jorval of Goth, the capital of Little Terreille, would be ready to assume his new and greater responsibilities.

5 / Kaeleer

The pushing turned into a shove. "Wake up, SaDiablo."

Saetan tried to pull the covers over his bare shoulder and pushed his head deeper into the pillows. "Go away."

A fist punched his shoulder.

Snarling, he braced himself on one elbow as Andulvar tossed a pair of trousers and a dressing robe onto the bed.

"Hurry," Andulvar said. "Before it's gone."

Before what was gone?

Rubbing his eyes, Saetan wondered if he might be allowed to splash some water on his face to wake up, but he had the distinct impression that if he didn't dress quickly, Andulvar would drag him through the corridors wearing nothing but his skin.

"The sun's up," Saetan muttered as he pulled on his clothes. "You should have retired by now."

"You were the one who pointed out that Jaenelle's presence has altered the Hall so that demons aren't affected by daylight as long as we stay inside," Andulvar said as he led Saetan through the corridors.

"That's the last time I tell you anything," Saetan growled.

When they reached a second floor room at the front of the Hall, Andulvar cautiously parted the drapes. "Stop grumbling and look."

Giving his eyes a final rub, Saetan braced one hand against the window frame and peered through the opening in the drapes.

Early morning. Clear, sunny. The gravel drive was partially raked. The landing web was swept. But the work looked interrupted, as if something had caused the outdoor staff to withdraw. They were still outside, and he picked up their excitement despite their shields. It was as if they were trying, almost hopefully, to go undetected.

Frowning, Saetan looked toward the left and saw a white stallion grazing on the front lawn, its hindquarters facing the windows. Not plain white, Saetan decided. Cream, with a milk-white mane and tail.

"Where did he come from?" Saetan looked inquiringly at Andulvar.

Andulvar snorted softly. "Probably from Sceval."

"What?" Saetan looked outside again at the same moment the stallion raised his head and turned toward the Hall. "Mother Night," he whispered, clutching the drapes. "Mother Night."

The ivory horn rose from the majestic head. Around the horn's base, glinting in the morning sun, was a gold ring. Attached to the ring was an Opal Jewel.

"That's a Warlord Prince having breakfast on your front lawn," Andulvar said in a neutral voice.

Saetan stared at his friend in disbelief. True, Andulvar had seen the stallion first and had time to take in the wonder of it, but was he really so jaded that the wonder could pass so quickly? There was a *unicorn* on the front lawn! A . . . kindred Warlord Prince.

Saetan braced himself against the wall. "Hell's fire, Mother Night, and may the Darkness be merciful."

"Think the waif knows about him?" Andulvar asked.

The question was answered by a wild, joyous whoop as Jaenelle sprinted across the gravel drive and slid to a stop a foot away from that magnificent, deadly horn.

The stallion arched his neck, raised his tail like a white silk banner, and danced around Jaenelle for a minute. Then he lowered his head and nuzzled her palms.

Saetan watched them, hoping nothing would disturb the lovely picture of a girl and unicorn meeting on a clear summer morning.

The picture shattered when Smoke streaked across the lawn.

The stallion knocked Jaenelle aside, laid his ears back, lowered that deadly horn, and began pawing the ground. Smoke skidded to a stop and bared his teeth in challenge.

Jaenelle grabbed a handful of the unicorn's mane and thrust out her other hand to stop Smoke. Whatever she said made the animals hesitate.

Finally, Smoke took a cautious step forward. The unicorn did the same. Muzzle touched muzzle.

Looking amused but exasperated, Jaenelle mounted the unicorn—and then scrambled to keep her seat when he took off at a gallop.

He stopped abruptly and looked back at her.

Jaenelle fluffed her hair and said something.

The stallion shook his head.

She became more emphatic.

The stallion shook his head and stamped one foot.

Finally, looking annoyed and embarrassed, she wrapped her hands in the long white mane and settled herself on his back.

The stallion walked away from the Hall, staying on the grass next to the drive. When they turned back toward the Hall, he changed to an easy canter. When they started the second loop, Smoke joined them.

"Come on," Saetan said.

He and Andulvar hurried to the great hall. Most of the house staff were pressed against the windows of the drawing rooms on either side of the hall, and Beale was peering through a crack in the front door.

"Open the door, Beale."

Startled by Saetan's voice, Beale jerked away from the door.

Pretending he didn't see Beale struggling to assume a proper stoic expression, Saetan swung the door open and stepped out while Andulvar stayed in the shadowy doorway.

She looked beautiful with her wind-tossed golden hair and her face lit from within by happiness. She belonged on a unicorn's back with a wolf beside her. He felt a pang of regret that she was cantering over a clipped lawn instead of in a wild glade. It was as if, by bringing her here, he had somehow clipped her wings—and he wondered if it were true. Then she saw him, and the stallion turned toward the door.

Reminding himself that he wore the darker Jewel, Saetan tried to relax—and couldn't. A Blood Prince, even a wolf, would accept his relationship with Jaenelle simply because he, a Warlord Prince, claimed her. Another Warlord Prince would challenge that claim, especially if it might interfere with his own, until the Lady acknowledged it.

As he went down the steps to meet them, Saetan felt the challenge being issued from the other side of the mental hedge, a demand that he acknowledge the stallion's prior claim. He silently met the challenge, opening himself just enough for the other Warlord Prince to feel his strength. But he didn't deny the unicorn's claim to Jaenelle.

Interested, the stallion pricked his ears.

"Papa, this is Prince Kaetien," Jaenelle said as she stroked the stallion's neck. "He was the first friend I made in Kaeleer."

Oh, yes. A *very* prior claim. And not one to be taken lightly. In the Old Tongue, "kaetien" meant "white fire," and he didn't doubt for a moment that the name fit this four-footed Brother.

"Kaetien," Jaenelle said, "this is the High Lord, my sire."

Kaetien backed away from the Saetan, his ears tight to his head.

"No, no," Jaenelle said hurriedly. "He's not *that* one. He's my *adopted* sire. He was the friend who was teaching me Craft, and now I'm living with him here."

The stallion snorted, relaxed.

Watching them, Saetan kept his feelings carefully hidden. He wouldn't push—yet—but sometime soon he and Kaetien were going to have a little talk about Jaenelle's sire.

Kaetien pawed the gravel as two young grooms slowly approached. The older of the two brushed his fingers against his cap brim. "Do you think the Prince would like some feed and a little grooming?"

Jaenelle hesitated, then smiled as she continued to stroke Kaetien's neck. "I should have my breakfast now," she said quietly. She tried to finger-comb her hair and made a face. "And I could use some grooming myself."

Kaetien tossed his head in what could be interpreted as agreement.

Jaenelle dismounted and ran up the steps. Then she spun around, her hands on her hips and fire in her eyes. "I did not fall off! I just wasn't balanced."

Kaetien looked at her and snorted.

"My legs are not weak, there's nothing wrong with my seat, and I'll thank you to keep your nose in your own feed bag! *I do so eat!*" She looked at Saetan. "Don't I?" She narrowed her eyes. "Don't I?"

Since silence was his safest choice, Saetan didn't reply.

Jaenelle narrowed her eyes a little more and snarled, "Males."

Satisfied, Kaetien followed the grooms to the stables.

Muttering under her breath, Jaenelle stomped past Andulvar and Beale and headed for the breakfast room.

With a cheerful whuff, Smoke continued his morning rounds.

"He deliberately baited her," Andulvar said from the doorway.

"It would seem so," Saetan agreed, chuckling. They headed for the breakfast room—slowly. "But isn't it comforting to know that some of our Brothers have developed a wonderful knack for badgering her."

"That particular Brother probably knows how much ground he can cover in a flat-out gallop."

Saetan smiled. "I imagine they both know."

She was sitting at the breakfast table, shredding a piece of toast.

Saetan cautiously took a seat on the opposite side of the table, poured a cup of tea, and felt grateful toast was the only thing she seemed interested in shredding.

"Thanks for backing me up," she said tartly.

"You wouldn't want me to lie to another Warlord Prince, would you?"

Jaenelle glared at him. "I'd forgotten how bossy Kaetien can be."

"He can't help it," he said soothingly. "It's part of what he is."

"Not all unicorns are bossy."

"I was thinking of Warlord Princes."

She looked startled. Then she smiled. "You should know." She reached for another piece of toast and began shredding it, her mood suddenly pensive. "Papa? Do you really think they'd come?"

His hand stuttered but he got the cup to his lips. "Your human friends?" he asked calmly.

She nodded.

He reached across the table and covered her restless hands with his. "There's only one way to find out, witch-child. Write the invitations, and I'll see that they're delivered."

Jaenelle wiped her hands on her napkin. "I'm going to see how Kaetien's doing."

Saetan picked at his breakfast steak for a while, drank

another cup of tea, and finally gave up. He needed to talk to someone, needed to share the apprehension and excitement fizzing in his stomach. He'd tell Cassandra, of course, but their communication was always formal now and he didn't want to be formal. He wanted to yip and chase his tail. Sylvia? She liked Jaenelle and would welcome the news—all the news—but it was too early to drop in on her.

That left him with one choice.

Saetan grinned.

Andulvar would be comfortably settled in by now. A punch in the shoulder would do him good.

6 / Hell

Titian cleaned her knife with a scrap from the black coat while the other Harpies hacked up the meat and tossed the pieces to the pack of Hounds waiting in a half circle around the body.

The body twitched and still feebly struggled, but the bastard could no longer scream for help and the muted sounds he made filled her with satisfaction. A demon couldn't feel pain the way the living did, but pain was a cumulative thing, and he hadn't been dead long enough for his nerves to forget the sensation.

A Harpy tossed a large chunk of thigh toward the pack. The pack leader snatched it in midair and backed away with his prize, snarling. The rest of the pack re-formed the half circle and waited their turn. The Hound bitches watched their pups gnaw at fingers and toes.

Demons weren't usually the Hell Hounds' meat. There was better prey for these large, black-furred, red-eyed hunters, prey as native to this cold, forever-twilight Realm as the Hounds themselves. But this demon's flesh was saturated with too much fresh blood—blood Titian knew hadn't come from voluntary offerings.

It had taken a while to hunt him down. He hadn't strayed far from Hekatah since the High Lord had made his request. Until tonight.

There were no Gates in Hekatah's territory, and the closest two were now fiercely guarded. One was beside the Hall, a place Hekatah no longer dared approach, and the other was in the Harpies' territory, Titian's territory. Not a place for the unwary, no matter how arrogant. That meant Hekatah and her minions had to travel a long distance on the Winds to reach another Gate, or they had to take risks.

Tonight, Greer took a risk and paid for it.

If he'd had time to use his Jewels, it might have turned out differently, but he'd been allowed to reach the Dark Altar and go through the Gate unchallenged, so he had no reason to expect they'd be waiting for his return. Once he'd left the Sanctuary, the Harpy attacks had come so fast and so fierce all he could do was shield himself and try to escape. Even so, a number of Harpies burned themselves out and vanished to become a whisper in the Darkness. Titian didn't grieve for them. Their twilight existence had dissolved in fierce joy.

In the end it was one frightened mind against so many enraged ones probing for weakness, while Titian's trained Hounds constantly lunged at the body, forcing Greer to use more and more of the reserved strength in his Jewels to keep them away. The Harpies broke through his inner barriers at the same moment Titian's arrow drove through his body and pinned it to a tree.

As the Harpies pulled the body away from the tree and began carving up the meat, Titian picked through Greer's mind as delicately as if she were picking the meat from a cracked nut. She saw the children he'd feasted on. She saw the narrow bed, the blood on the sheets, the familiar young face that had been bruised by his maimed hands. She saw Surreal's horn-handled dagger driving into his heart, slicing his throat. She saw him smiling at her when his own knife had slit *her* throat centuries ago. And she saw where he'd been tonight.

Titian sheathed the knife and checked the blade of the small ax propped beside her.

She regretted not bringing him down before he reached Little Terreille. If Greer's assessment of Lord Jorval was correct, the whispers would begin soon.

A Guardian wasn't a natural being in a living Realm.

There would always be whispering and wondering—especially when that Guardian was also the High Lord of Hell. And she could guess well enough how the Kaeleer Queens were going to react to the rumors.

She would visit her kinswomen, tell them what she wanted from them if the opportunity presented itself. That would help.

Titian picked up her ax. The Harpies moved aside for their Queen.

The limbs were gone. The torso was empty. The eyes still held a glimmer of intelligence, a glimmer of Self. Not much, but enough.

With three precise strokes, Titian split Greer's skull. Using the blade, she opened one of the splits until it was wide enough for her fingers. Then she tore the bone away.

She looked into Greer's eyes. Still enough there.

Whistling for the pack leader, she walked away, smiling, while the Hound began feasting on the brain.

7 / Kaeleer

Saetan brushed his hair for the third time because it gave him something to do. Like buffing his long, black-tinted nails twice. Like changing his jacket and then changing back to the first one.

He stopped himself from reaching for the hairbrush again, straightened his already straight jacket, and sighed.

Would the children come?

He hadn't requested a reply to the invitation because he had wanted to give the children as much time as possible to gather their courage or wear down their elders' arguments—and because he was afraid of what rejection dribbling in day after day might do to Jaenelle.

As he had promised, he or other members of the family had delivered all the invitations. Some had been left at the child's residence. Most had been left at message stones, the piles of rocks just inside a Territory's border where travelers or traders could leave a message requesting a meeting. He had no idea how messages left in those places reached the intended person, and he doubted those children would be here this afternoon. He didn't know what to expect from the children in the accessible Territories. He only hoped Andulvar was right and that little witch from Glacia would be here, stepping on his toes.

Taking a deep breath that still came out as a sigh, Saetan left his suite to join the rest of the family and Cassandra in the great hall.

Everyone was there except Jaenelle and Sylvia. Halaway's Queen had been delighted when he'd told her about the party and had used her considerable enthusiasm to browbeat Jaenelle into a shopping trip for a new outfit. They didn't come back with a dress, but he'd had to admit, grudgingly, that the soft, full, sapphire pants and long, flowing jacket were very feminine-looking, even if the skimpy gold-and-silver top worn beneath the jacket. . . . As a man, he approved of the top; as a father, it made him grind his teeth.

As soon as she saw him, Cassandra took his arm and led him away from the other men. "Do you think it's wise for everyone to be out here?" she asked quietly. "Won't it be too intimidating?"

"And whom would you ask to leave?" Saetan replied, knowing full well he was one of the people she thought should be absent.

After receiving his note, Cassandra had arrived to help with the preparations, but she'd acted too forcedly cheerful, as if she were really preparing for the moment when Jaenelle would face an empty drawing room. Sylvia, on the other hand, had thrown herself into the preparations and had bristled at anyone who dared to express a doubt.

A wise man would have locked himself in his study and stayed there. Only a fool would have left two witches alone when they were constantly circling and spitting at each other like angry cats.

When Cassandra didn't answer his question, Saetan took his place in the great hall. Andulvar was one step behind him on his left. Mephis and Prothvar were on Andulvar's left and a little to the side so that they weren't part of the official greetings. Cassandra stood on Saetan's right, one step behind. By rights she should have stood beside him, Black with Black, and he was only too aware of why she was using an option of Protocol to distance herself from him.

Saetan turned toward the sound of feet racing down the staircase in the informal drawing room.

Sylvia burst into the great hall, looking a little too lovely with her golden eyes shining and her cheeks flushed. "The wolf pups hid Jaenelle's shoes and it took a while to find them," she said breathlessly. "She's on her way down, but I didn't want to be late."

Saetan smiled at her. "You're not—"

A clock struck three times.

Cassandra made a quiet, unhappy sound and stepped away from him.

For the first time since he'd told her about the party, Sylvia's eyes filled with concern.

They all stood in the great hall, silently waiting, while Beale stood woodenly by the front door and the footmen who would take the outer garments stared straight ahead.

The minutes ticked past.

Sylvia rubbed her forehead and sighed. "I'd better go up—"

"We don't need any more of *your* kind of help," Cassandra said coldly as she brushed past Sylvia. "You set her up for this."

Sylvia grabbed Cassandra's arm and spun her around. "Maybe I was too enthusiastic, but you did everything but say outright that she would never have a friend for the rest of her life!"

"Ladies," Saetan warned, stepping toward them.

"What could you possibly know about wearing the Black?" Cassandra snapped. "I *lived* with that isolation—"

"La—"

BOOM!

"Hell's fire," Andulvar muttered.

BOOM!

Beale leaped to open the front door while it was still intact.

She swept into the great hall, stopping where the sunlight

coming from the lead glass window above the double doors produced a natural spotlight. Tall and slim, she wore severely tailored, dark blue trousers, a loose jacket, and heeled boots. Her white-blond hair rose in spiky peaks above her head like sculptured ice. Darkened eyebrows and lashes framed ice-blue eyes.

"Sisters," she said, giving Sylvia and Cassandra a perfunctory nod that couldn't quite be called insolent. Then her eyes raked over Saetan from head to toe.

Saetan held his breath. Even if Lord Morton hadn't slunk in behind her, he would have bet this was Karla, the young Glacian Queen.

"Well," Karla said, "you're not bad-looking for a corpse."

Before he could reply, Jaenelle's serene but amused voice said, "You're only half-right, darling. He's not a corpse."

Karla whirled toward the informal drawing room, where Jaenelle leaned against the doorway, her fingers hooked in the jacket thrown over one shoulder.

Karla let out a screech that raised the hairs on Saetan's neck.

"You've got tits!" Karla pulled open the blue jacket, revealing a silver, just as skimpy top. "So do I, if you call these lovely little bee stings tits." Smiling the wickedest smile Saetan had ever seen, she turned back to him. "What do you think?"

He didn't stop to think. "Are you asking if I think they're lovely or if I think they're bee strings?"

Karla closed the jacket, crossed her arms, and narrowed those ice-blue eyes. "Sassy, isn't he?"

"Well, he *is* a Warlord Prince," Jaenelle replied.

Ice-blue eyes met sapphire eyes. Both girls smiled.

Karla shrugged. "Oh, all right. I'll be a polite guest." She stepped up to Saetan, and that wicked smile bloomed. "Kiss kiss."

He refused to give her the satisfaction of seeing him wince.

Karla turned away from him and headed for Jaenelle. "*You've* got some explaining to do. I had to figure out all those damn spells by myself." She swept Jaenelle into the drawing room and closed the door.

Saetan stared at his shoe. "Damn it, she *did* step on my toes," he muttered before realizing Morton had come close enough to hear him.

"H-High Lord."

"Lord Morton, I have only one thing to say to you."

"Sir?" Morton tried to suppress a shiver.

Saetan tried to suppress a rueful smile and couldn't. "You have my heartfelt sympathy."

Morton melted with relief. "Thank you, sir. I could use it."

"Help yourself to the refreshments in there," Saetan said, making a slight gesture toward the closed door. "And if they start making plans to knock down any walls, let me know."

BANG!

For one panicked moment, Saetan thought the caution had been made too late. Then he realized someone was, more or less, knocking on the front door.

If Karla was ice, this one was fire, with her dark red hair flowing down her back, her green eyes flashing, and a swirling gown that looked like an autumn woods in motion. She headed for Saetan but veered when Jaenelle and Karla poked their heads out of the drawing room. Grinning, she held up a cloth bundle. "I wasn't sure if we would end up in the stables or digging in the garden, so I brought some real clothes."

Saetan stifled a growl. Didn't *any* of them like to dress up?

The girls disappeared into the drawing room—and closed the door.

The youth who'd come in with the fire witch was tall, good-looking, and a couple of years older. He had curly brown hair and blue eyes. Smiling, he extended one hand in informal greeting.

With his stomach sinking toward his heels, Saetan clasped the offered hand. There were a lot of ways he could describe those blue eyes. They all meant trouble.

"You must be the High Lord," the young Warlord said

with a smile. "I'm Khardeen, from the isle of Scelt." He
jerked his thumb toward the drawing room. "That's
Morghann."

The drawing room door opened. Jaenelle approached
them hesitantly. Then she held out both hands in formal
greeting. "Hello, Khary."

Khary looked at the offered hands and turned back to
Saetan. "Did Jaenelle ever tell you about her adventure
with my uncle's stone—"

"Khary," Jaenelle gasped, glancing nervously at Saetan.

"Hmm?" Khary smiled at her. "Did you know that a
proper hug can toss a thought right out of a man's head?
It's a well-known fact. I'm surprised you hadn't heard of
it."

Jaenelle had been balanced on the balls of her feet, ready
to bolt. Now her heels came down and her eyes narrowed. "Really."

Watching the two of them, Saetan decided the prudent
thing was to stand still and keep his mouth shut.

Seconds passed. When Jaenelle didn't move, Khardeen
turned back to him. "You see, my—"

Jaenelle moved.

"You don't have to hug *all* the air out of me," Khary
said as he carefully wrapped his arms around her.

"Now what were you going to say?" Jaenelle asked
ominously.

"About what?" Khary replied sweetly.

Laughing, Jaenelle threw her arms around his neck. "I'm
glad you came, Khardeen. I've missed you."

Khary gently untangled himself. "We'll have plenty of
time to catch up on things. Right now you'd better get back
to your sisters or I'll get the sharp side of Morghann's
tongue for the rest of the day."

"Compared to Karla, Morghann's tongue doesn't have a
sharp side."

"All the more reason then."

With another nervous glance at Saetan, Jaenelle bolted
for the drawing room. She had just reached it when someone knocked on the door. It almost sounded polite.

They must have appeared on the landing web within seconds of each other and approached the door en masse because he knew this group didn't come from the same Territories. And since they spared him no more than an uneasy glance before focusing on Jaenelle, he was forced to deduce who they were by the names on the invitations.

The satyrs from Pandar were Zylona and Jonah. The small, pixie-faced darling with the dusky hair and iridescent wings who was perched on Jonah's shoulder was Katrine from Philan, one of the Paw Islands. The black-haired, gray-eyed youth who strongly reminded Saetan of the young wolves now living in the north woods was Aaron from Dharo. Sabrina, a hazel-eyed brunette, was also from Dharo. The two tawny-skinned, dark-striped youngsters were Grezande and Elan from Tigrelan.

The last of the group—a petite witch with a lusciously rounded figure, soft brown eyes, and dark brown hair— hugged Jaenelle, shyly approached him, and introduced herself as Kalush from Nharkhava.

There was a sweetness about her that made Saetan want to cuddle her. Instead, he slid his hands beneath her offered ones in formal greeting, and said, "I'm honored to meet you, Lady Kalush."

"High Lord." She had a husky voice that would do wonderfully bad things to young men's libidos. He pitied her father.

Beale, looking slightly dazed, started to close the door when it was yanked out of his grasp.

Saetan pushed Kalush toward Andulvar and tensed.

The centaurs walked in.

The young witch, Astar, headed for the girls. The Warlord Prince continued down the great hall until he was standing in front of Saetan.

"High Lord." The greeting sounded more like a challenge.

"Prince Sceron."

Sceron was a few years older than the others, old enough to have begun filling out the massive shoulders and the powerfully built upper body. The rest of him would have done any stallion proud.

There was an unasked question in Sceron's eyes, and an anger in him that seemed ready to blaze into rage.

Jaenelle stepped into that frozen silence, balled her hand into a fist, and drove it into Sceron's upper arm.

Sceron grabbed her and lifted her until they were eye to eye.

"That's for not saying hello," Jaenelle said.

Sceron studied her face and finally smiled. "You are well?"

"I was better before you rumpled me."

Laughing, Sceron put her down.

Someone gasped.

Saetan felt a shiver run up his spine and looked toward the door.

Because he hadn't expected them to come, he hadn't thought about how the others would react to their presence. But they had come. The Children of the Wood. The Dea al Mon.

They both had the slender, sinewy build that was as inherent to their race as the delicately pointed ears. Both wore their silver hair long and unbound. Both had the large, forest-blue eyes, although the girl's had a touch more gray.

The girl, Gabrielle, stopped just inside the door. The boy—oh, no, it would be extremely foolish to think of Chaosti as a boy—came forward slowly, silently.

Saetan fought the instincts that always came to the fore at the appearance of an unknown Warlord Prince. Because they hadn't approached him, Elan and Aaron hadn't pricked those instincts. Sceron had just managed to scratch the surface. But this one, calmly staring at him with those large eyes, made all the aggressiveness and territoriality that was part of a Warlord Prine boil to the surface.

Saetan felt himself rising to the killing edge, and knew Chaosti was also rising, but instinct was driving him too hard to hold it back.

"Chaosti," Jaenelle said in her midnight voice.

Chaosti slowly turned to face her.

"He's my father, Chaosti," Jaenelle said. "By my choice."

After a long moment, Chaosti placed a hand over his heart. "By your choice, cousin," he replied in a deceptively quiet tenor voice.

Jaenelle led the girls into the informal drawing room and closed the door.

The males let out a collective sigh of relief.

Chaosti turned to face Saetan. "She's been away so long and has been deeply missed. Titian said you weren't to blame, but—"

"But I'm the High Lord," Saetan said with a trace of bitterness.

"No," Chaosti replied, smiling coolly, "you are not Dea al Mon."

Saetan felt his body relax. "Why do you call her 'cousin'?"

"Gabrielle and I belong to the same clan. Grandmammy Teele is the matriarch. She also adopted Jaenelle." Chaosti's smile turned feral. "So you are kin of my kin—which makes you Titian's kin as well."

Saetan wheezed.

Khardeen approached them. "If we want anything to eat, I think we're going to have to fight for it," he said to Chaosti.

"I'll accept any challenge a male wants to make," Chaosti snapped.

"The girls are between us and the food."

Chaosti sighed. "Challenging another male would be easier."

"Safer, too."

"Gentlemen," Beale said. "Refreshments are also being served in the formal drawing room."

"Have you ever heard that red-haired witches have hot tempers?" Khardeen asked as he and Chaosti followed the other males into the formal drawing room.

"There are no red-haired witches among the Dea al Mon," Chaosti replied, "and they *all* have hot tempers."

"Ah. Well, then."

The door closed behind them.

Saetan jumped when a hand squeezed his shoulder.

"You all right?" Andulvar asked quietly.

"Am I still standing up?"

"You're vertical."

"Thank the Darkness." Saetan looked around. He and Andulvar were the only ones left in the great hall. "Let's hide in my study."

"Agreed."

They drank two glasses of yarbarah and finally relaxed when an hour had passed without any shrieks, bangs, or booms.

"Mother Night." Saetan wearily striped off his jacket and slumped in one of the comfortable, oversized chairs.

"By my count," Andulvar said as he refilled the glasses, "including the waif, you've got ten adolescent witches in one room—Queens every one of them, and two besides Jaenelle who are natural Black Widows."

"Karla and Gabrielle. I noticed." Saetan closed his eyes.

"In the other room, you have seven young males, four of whom are Warlord Princes."

"I noticed that, too. It makes a very interesting First Circle, don't you think?"

Andulvar muttered in Eyrien. Saetan chose not to translate it.

"Where do you think the others went?" Andulvar asked.

"If Mephis and Prothvar have any sense at all, they're hiding somewhere. Sylvia is no doubt passing out nutcakes and sandwiches. Cassandra?" Saetan shrugged. "I don't thinks she was prepared for this."

"Were you?"

"Shit." When someone tapped on the study door, Saetan thought about sitting up straighter, then decided not to bother. "Come."

A smiling Khardeen entered and placed sixteen sealed envelopes on the blackwood table. "I told Jaenelle I'd drop these off to you. We're going out to meet the wolves and the unicorn."

"Finished devouring the kitchen already?" Saetan asked as he picked up one of the envelopes.

"At least until dinner."

"Plant your feet, Warlord," Saetan said, stopping Khardeen's hasty retreat. He broke the formal seal, called in his half-moon glasses, and read the message. Then he stared at Khary. "This is from Lady Duana."

"Mmm," Khary said, rocking on his heels. "Morghann's grandmother."

"The Queen of Scelt is Morghann's grandmother?"

Khary stuffed his hands into his pockets. "Mmm."

Saetan placed his glasses carefully on the table. "Let's skip the hunt and just tree the prey. Do all these letters say the same thing?"

"What's that, High Lord?" Khary asked innocently.

"All of these letters give permission for an extended visit?"

"So I gathered."

"Define 'extended visit.' "

"Not long. Just the rest of the summer."

Saetan couldn't speak. Wasn't sure what he'd say if he could.

"Everything is being taken care of," Khary said soothingly. "Lord Beale and Lady Helene are taking care of the room assignments right now, so there's nothing for you to worry about."

"Noth—" Saetan's voice cracked.

"And it *is* a reasonable compromise, High Lord. You get to spend time with her and we get to spend time with her. Besides, the Hall is the only place big enough for all of us. And, as my uncle pointed out, having all of us in one place would surely drive a man to drink, and that being the case, he'd rather it be you than him."

Saetan made a weak gesture of dismissal and waited until the door was safely closed before bracing his head in his hands. "Mother Night."

CHAPTER
SEVEN

1 / Kaeleer

Saetan steepled his fingers and stared at Sylvia. "I beg your pardon?"

"You have to talk to Tersa," Sylvia said again.

Damn her. Why was she being so insistent?

With difficulty, he leashed his temper. It wasn't Sylvia's fault. She had no way of knowing how he and Tersa were connected.

"Would you like some wine?" he finally asked, his deep voice betraying too much of his heart.

Sylvia eyed the decanter on the corner of his desk. "If that's brandy, why don't you pour yourself a glass and hand me the decanter."

Saetan filled two brandy snifters and floated one to her.

Sylvia took a generous swallow and choked a little.

"That's not exactly the way to drink good brandy," he said dryly, but he slugged back a good portion of his own glass, despite the headache he knew it would give him. "All right. Tell me about Tersa."

Sylvia leaned forward, her arms braced on the chair, both hands cupped around the snifter. "I'm not a child, Saetan. I understand that some people slip into the Twisted Kingdom and some people are shoved—and a very brave few make a deliberate choice. And I know most Black Widows who become lost in the Twisted Kingdom aren't harmful to others. In their own way, they're extraordinarily wise."

"But?"

Sylvia pressed her lips together. "Mikal, my youngest son, spends quite a bit of time with her. He thinks she's wonderful." She finished the brandy and held out her glass for a refill. "Lately she's been calling him Daemon."

Her voice was so low, so husky he had to strain to hear her. He wished, bitterly, that he hadn't heard.

"Mikal shrugs it off," Sylvia continued after taking another large swallow of brandy. "He says anyone stuffed that full of interesting things to say could easily get confused about everyday things, and she'd probably known a boy named Daemon and used to tell him the same kind of interesting stuff."

She never got the chance. He was already lost, to both of us, by the time he was Mikal's age. "But?"

"The last couple of times Mikal's gone to see her, she keeps telling him to be careful." Sylvia closed her eyes and frowned in concentration. "She says the bridge is very fragile, and she'll keep sending the sticks." She opened her eyes and poured herself another brandy. "Sometimes she just holds Mikal and cries. She keeps sticks she's collected from every yard in the village in a big basket in her kitchen and panics if anyone goes near them. But she can't, or won't, tell Mikal or me why the sticks are important. I've had every bridge around Halaway checked and they're all sound, even the smallest footbridge. I thought maybe she'd tell you."

Would she tell him? Would she let him broach the one subject she refused to discuss with him? When he went to see her, one hour each week, Tersa talked about her garden; she told him what she'd had for dinner; she showed him a piece of needlepoint she was working on; she talked about Jaenelle. But she wouldn't talk about their son.

"I'll try," he said quietly.

Sylvia put her empty glass on the desk and stood up, swaying.

Saetan went around the desk, cupped his hand under her elbow, and led her to the door. "You should go home and take a nap."

"I never take naps."

"After that much brandy, I doubt you'll have a choice."

"My metabolism will burn it up fast enough." Sylvia hiccuped.

"Uh-huh. Did you realize you called me Saetan?"

She turned so fast she fell against him. He liked the feel of her. It disturbed him that he liked the feel of her.

"I'm sorry, High Lord. I'm sorry."

"Are you?" he asked softly. "I'm not sure I am."

Sylvia stared at him. She hesitated. She said nothing.

He let her go.

"You're going out?"

Jaenelle leaned against the wall opposite his bedroom door, her finger tucked between the pages of a Craft book to hold her place.

Amused, Saetan raised an eyebrow. It was usually the parent who insisted on knowing his offspring's whereabouts, not the other way around. "I'm going to see Tersa."

"Why? This isn't your usual evening to see her."

He caught the slight edge in her voice, the subtle warning. "Am I that predictable?" he asked, smiling.

Jaenelle didn't smile back.

Before her own catastrophic plunge into the abyss or wherever she'd spent those two years, Jaenelle had gone into the Twisted Kingdom and had led Tersa back to the blurred boundary that separated madness and sanity. That was as far as Tersa could go—or was willing to go.

Jaenelle had helped her regain a little of the real world. Now that they were living near each other, Jaenelle continued to help Tersa fill in the pieces that made up the physical world. Small things. Simple things. Trees and flowers. The feel of loam between strong fingers. The pleasure of a bowl of soup and a thick slice of fresh-baked bread.

"Sylvia came to see me this afternoon," he said slowly, trying to understand the chill emanating from Jaenelle. "She thinks Tersa's upset about something, so I wanted to look in on her."

Jaenelle's sapphire eyes were as deep and still as a bottomless lake. "Don't push where you're not welcome, High Lord," Witch said.

He wondered if she knew how much her eyes revealed. "You'd prefer I not see her?" he asked respectfully.

Her eyes changed. "See her if you like," his daughter replied. "But don't invade her privacy."

"There's no wine." Tersa opened and closed cupboards, looking more and more confused. "The woman didn't buy the wine. She always buys a bottle of wine on fourth-day so it will be here for you. She didn't buy the wine, and tomorrow I was going to draw a picture of my garden and show it to you, but third-day's gone and I don't know where I put it."

Saetan sat at the pine kitchen table, his body saturated with sorrow until it felt too heavy to move. He'd joked about being predictable. He hadn't realized that his predictability was one of Tersa's touchstones, a means by which she separated the days. Jaenelle had known and had let him come to learn the lesson for himself.

With his hands braced on the table, he pushed himself up from the chair. Every movement was an effort, but he reached Tersa, who was still opening cupboards and muttering, seated her at the table, put a kettle on the stove, and, after a little exploring in the cupboards, made them both a cup of chamomile tea.

As he put the cup in front of her, he brushed the tangled black hair away from her face. He couldn't remember a time when Tersa's hair didn't look as if she'd washed it and let it dry in the wind, as if her fingers were the only comb it had ever known. He suspected it wasn't madness but intensity that made her indifferent. And he wondered if that wasn't one of the reasons, when he'd finally agreed to that contract with the Hayllian Hourglass to sire a child, that he'd chosen Tersa, who was already broken, already teetering on the edge of madness. He'd spent over an hour brushing her hair that first night. He'd brushed her hair every night of the week he'd bedded her, enjoying the feel of it between his fingers, the gentle pull of the brush.

Now, sitting across from her, his hands around the mug, he said, "I came early, Tersa. You didn't lose third-day. This is second-day."

Tersa frowned. "Second-day? You don't come on second-day."

"I wanted to talk to you. I didn't want to wait until fourth-day. I'll come back on fourth-day to see your drawing."

Some of the confusion left her gold eyes. She sipped her tea.

The pine table was empty except for a small azure vase holding three red roses.

Tersa gently touched the petals. "The boy picked these for me."

"Which boy is that?" Saetan said quietly.

"Mikal. Sylvia's boy. He comes to visit. Did she tell you?"

"I thought you might mean Daemon."

Tersa snorted. "Daemon's not a boy now. Besides, he's far away." Her eyes became clouded, farseeing. "And the island has no flowers."

"But you call Mikal Daemon."

Tersa shrugged. "Sometimes it's nice to pretend that I'm telling him stories. Jaenelle says it's all right to pretend."

A cold finger whispered down his spine. "You've told Jaenelle about Daemon?"

"Of course not," Tersa said irritably. "She's not ready to know about him. All the threads are not yet in place."

"What threads—"

"The lover is the father's mirror. The brother stands between. The mirror spins, spins, spins. Blood. So much blood. He clings to the island of maybe. The bridge will have to rise from the sea. The threads are not yet in place."

"Tersa, where is Daemon?"

Tersa blinked, drew a shuddering breath. She stared at him, frowning. "The boy's name is Mikal."

He wanted to shout at her, *Where's my son? Why hasn't he gone to the Keep or come through one of the Gates? What's he waiting for?* Useless to shout at her. She couldn't translate what she'd seen any better than she had. One thing he did understand. All the threads were not yet in place. Until they were, all he could do was wait.

"What are the sticks for, Tersa?"

"Sticks?" Tersa looked at the basket of sticks in the corner of the kitchen. "They have no purpose." She shrugged. "Kindling?"

She withdrew from him, exhausted by the effort of keeping the stones of reality and madness from grinding her soul.

"Is there anything I can do for you?" he asked, preparing to leave.

Tersa hesitated. "It would anger you."

Right now, he didn't feel capable of that strong an emotion. "It won't anger me. I promise."

"Would you . . . Would you hold me for a minute?"

It rocked him. He, who had always craved physical affection, had never thought to offer her an embrace.

He closed his arms around her. She wrapped her arms around his back and rested her head on his shoulder.

"I don't miss the rutting, but it feels good to be held by a man."

Saetan gently kissed her tangled hair. "Why didn't you mention it before? I didn't know you wanted to be held."

"Now you do."

2 / Kaeleer

The Dark Council whispered.

At first it was only a thoughtful look, a troubled frown. The High Lord had done many things in his long life—look what he'd done to the Council itself in order to become the girl's guardian—but it was hard to believe he was capable of *that*. He had always insisted that the strength of a Territory, the strength of the Realm, depended on the strength of its witches, especially its Queens. To think he would do such things with a vulnerable girl, a dark young Queen . . .

Oh, yes, they had inquired about the girl before now, but the High Lord had always responded tersely. The girl was ill. She could have no visitors. She was being privately tutored.

Where had the girl been during the past two years? What had she been subjected to? Was Jorval sure?

No, Lord Jorval insisted, he was not sure. It was only a spurious rumor made by a dismissed servant. There was no reason to suspect it wasn't just as the High Lord had said. The girl probably *was* ill, an invalid of some kind, perhaps too emotionally or physically fragile for the stimulation of visitors.

The High Lord had made no mention of the girl being ill until the Council requested to see her the first time.

Jorval stroked his dark beard with a thin hand and shook his head. There was no evidence. Only the word of a man who couldn't be found.

Murmurs, speculations, whisssspers.

3 / The Twisted Kingdom

He clung to the sharp grass on the crumbling island of *maybe* and watched the sticks float toward him. They were evenly spaced like the boards of a rope bridge strung across the endless sea. But the footing would be precarious at best, and there were no ropes to hang on to. If he tried to use them, he would sink beneath the vast sea of blood.

He was going to sink anyway. The island continued to crumble. Eventually there wouldn't be enough left to hold him.

He was tired. He was willing to let it suck him down.

The sticks broke formation, swirled and re-formed, swirled and re-formed over and over again into rough letters.

You are my instrument.

Words lie. Blood doesn't.

Butchering whore.

He tried to scramble away from that side of the island, but the other side kept crumbling, crumbling. There was only enough room now for him to lie there, helpless.

Something moved beneath the sea of blood, disturbing the sticks and their endless words. The sticks swirled around his small island, bumped against the crumbling edges of *maybe*, and piled up against each other to form a fragile, protective wall.

He leaned over the edge and watched the face float upward, sapphire eyes staring at nothing, golden hair spread out like a fan.

The lips moved: *Daemon.*

He reached down and gently lifted the face out of the sea of blood. Not a head, just a face, as smooth and lifeless as a mask.

The lips moved again. The word sounded like the sigh of the night wind, like a caress. *Daemon.*

The face dissolved, oozed through his fingers.

Sobbing, he tried to hold it, tried to re-form it into that beloved face. The harder he tried, the quicker it slipped through his fingers until there was nothing left.

Shadows in the bloody sea. A woman's face, full of compassion and understanding, surrounded by a mass of tangled black hair.

Wait, she said. *Wait. The threads are not yet in place.*

She vanished in the ripples.

Finally, there was an easy thing to do, a thing without pain, without fear.

Making himself as comfortable as possible, he settled down to wait.

4 / Kaeleer

Saetan wondered if there was something wrong with the bookcases behind his desk or if there was something wrong with his butler, because Beale had been staring at the same spot for almost a minute.

"High Lord," Beale said stiffly, still staring at the bookcases.

"Beale," Saetan replied cautiously.

"There's a Warlord to see you."

Saetan carefully set his glasses on top of the papers covering his desk, and folded his hands to keep them from shaking. "Is he cringing?"

Beale's lips twitched. "No, High Lord."

Saetan sagged in his chair. "Thank the Darkness. At least he's not here because of something the girls have done."

"I don't believe the Ladies are involved, High Lord."

"Then send him in."

The Warlord who entered the study was a head taller than Saetan, twice as wide, and solid muscle. His hands were big enough to engulf a man's skull and strong enough to crush one. He looked like a rough man who would wrench what he wanted from the land or from other people. But beneath that massive body and roaring voice was a heart filled with simple joy and a soul too sensitive to bear harsh treatment.

He was Dujae. Five hundred years ago, he had been the finest artist in Kaeleer. Now he was a demon.

Saetan knew it was hypocritical to be angry with Dujae for coming here since Mephis, Andulvar, and Prothvar were all frequently in residence at the Hall since Jaenelle had returned with him, and they all had contact with the children. Even so, keeping the Dark Realm separated from the living Realms had always been a knife-edged dance, and he was uncomfortably aware that, even when living, he'd straddled that line. Now with all the children spending the summer at the Hall and the Dark Council pressuring him for an interview with Jaenelle, having demons coming into Kaeleer for an audience with him was beyond tolerance.

"Twice a month I hold an audience in Hell for any who wish to come before me," he said coldly. "You've no business here, Lord Dujae."

Dujae stared at the floor, his long, thick fingers pulling at the brim of the shabby blue cap he held in his hands. "I know, High Lord. Forgive me. I should not have come here, but I could not wait."

Saetan could, and did.

Dujae crushed the cap in his hands. When he finally looked up, there was only despair in his eyes. "I am so tired, High Lord. There is nothing left to paint, no one to teach, to share with. No purpose, no joy. There is nothing. Please, High Lord."

Saetan closed his eyes, his anger forgotten. It happened sometimes. Hell was a cold, cruel, blasted Realm, but it

had its measure of kindness. It was a place where the Blood
could make peace with their lives, a suspended time to take
care of unfinished business. Some did nothing with that last
gift, enduring weeks or years or centuries of tedium before
finally fading into the Darkness. Others embraced that time
to nurture talents they'd ignored while living or chosen to
forsake in order to follow another road. Others, cut off
before they were finished, continued as they had lived.
Dujae had died in his prime, suddenly, unexpectedly. When
he realized he could still paint, he had accepted being
demon-dead with a joyous heart.

Now he was asking Saetan to release him from the dead
flesh, to consume the last of his psychic strength and let
him become a whisper in the Darkness.

It happened sometimes. Not often, thankfully, but sometimes the desire to continue faded before the psychic
strength. When that happened, a demon came to him and
asked for a swift release. And because he was the High
Lord, he honored those requests.

Saetan opened his eyes and blinked hard to clear his
vision. "Dujae, are you sure?"

"I'm—"

Karla exploded into the room. "That overbearing, over-
dressed, overscented sewer rat says my drawing is defi-
cient!" Her eyes filled with tears as she flung a sketch pad
onto Saetan's desk.

He vanished his glasses before the sketch pad landed
on them.

"He's a grubby-minded prick," Karla wailed. "This isn't
my life's work, this isn't my road. This is supposed to be
fun!"

Saetan surged out of his chair. There had been so many
tutors coming and going in the past three weeks he couldn't
remember this particular ass's name, but if the man could
reduce Karla to tears, he was probably shredding Kalush
and Morghann, to say nothing of Jaenelle.

Dujae reached for the sketch pad.

"No!" Karla dove for the pad, too upset to remember
she could vanish it before Dujae's hand closed around it.

Her forehead hit Dujae's arm. She stumbled backward

into Saetan. He wrapped his arms around her and ground his teeth, hating the anguish pouring out of her.

Dujae studied the sketch. He shook his head slowly. "This is terrible," he rumbled, flipping the pages back to earlier sketches. "Obscene," he roared. He shook the sketch pad at Karla. "You call him sewer rat? You are too kind, Lady. He's a—"

"Dujae," Saetan warned, first to prevent Dujae from possibly teaching Karla a pithy phrase she didn't already know and second because he'd felt Karla perk up.

Dujae looked at Saetan and took a deep breath. "He is not a good instructor," he finished lamely.

Karla sniffed. "You don't think my drawings are good either."

Dujae flipped to the last sketch. "What is this?" he demanded, stabbing the paper with his finger.

Karla pulled her shoulders back and narrowed her eyes.

Saetan stifled a groan and held on tighter.

"It's a vase," she said coolly.

"Vase. Bah!" Dujae ripped the page from the pad, crumpled it, and threw it over his shoulder. He pointed at Karla.

Did Dujae realize just how close his finger was to Karla's teeth?

"You are a Queen, yes?" Dujae continued to roar. "You do this for fun when you are finished with the hard lessons of your Craft, yes? You do this because Ladies must learn many things to be good Queens, yes? You do not make polite, itsy-bitsy drawings." He scrunched up his shoulders, scrunched up his face, tucked his wrist under his chin, and made tiny scratching motions. "Bah!" He pulled Karla out of Saetan's arms, spun her around, engulfed her hand in his own, and began making large, circular motions. "There is fire in your heart, yes? That fire needs charcoal and a large pad to express itself. Then when you want to draw a vase, you draw a vase."

"B-but—" Karla stammered, watching her hand sweep round and round.

"That vase you try to draw, that is someone else's vase. Use it as a model. Models are good. Then you draw YOUR

VASE, the one that reveals the fire, the one that says I am a witch, I am a Queen, I am—" Dujae finally hesitated.

"Karla," she said meekly.

"KARLA!" Dujae roared.

"What's going on?" Jaenelle asked from the doorway. Gabrielle stood beside her.

Saetan settled on the corner of his desk and crossed his arms, resigned to whatever the little darlings were about to do.

Seeing the other girls, Dujae released Karla and stepped back.

"Do we have any charcoal?" Karla asked, wiping her eyes.

"We have some, but Lord Stuffy says charcoal is messy and not the proper medium for Ladies," Gabrielle said tartly.

Saetan stared at Gabrielle and wondered what sort of idiot he'd hired as an art instructor.

Then he felt the blood rush out of his head. He gripped the desk, willing himself not to faint. He'd never fainted. This would be a very bad time to start.

With the other girls around them, he hadn't recognized the triangle of power. Karla, Gabrielle, Jaenelle. Three strong Queens who were also natural Black Widows.

May the Darkness be merciful, he thought. *That trio could tear apart anything or anyone or build anything they wanted.*

"High Lord?"

Saetan blinked. He took a deep breath. His lungs still worked, sort of. Finally sure he wasn't going to keel over, he looked around. Dujae was the only one left in the room.

Dujae twisted his cap. "I did not mean to interfere."

"Too late now," Saetan muttered.

Three blond heads appeared at the study door.

"Hey," Karla said. "We've got the charcoal and large sketch pads. Aren't you coming?"

Dujae continued to twist his cap. "I cannot, Ladies."

"Why not?" Jaenelle asked as the three of them entered the study.

Dujae looked beseechingly at Saetan, who refused to look at anything but the point of his shoe.

"I—I am Dujae, Lady."

Jaenelle looked pleased. "You painted *Descent into Hell.*"

Dujae's eyes widened.

"Why can't you give us drawing lessons?" Gabrielle said.

"I am a demon."

Silence.

Karla cocked a hip and crossed her arms. "What, there's some rule that says drawing has to be taught in the daytime? Besides, the sun's up now and you're here."

"That's because the Hall retains enough dark power so that sunlight doesn't bother the demon-dead when they're inside," Jaenelle said.

"So that's not a problem," Karla said.

"And if you don't want to be here during the daylight hours, candle-lights or balls of witchlight would make a room bright enough to work in," Gabrielle said.

Dujae looked helplessly at Saetan. Saetan studied his other shoe.

"Is your ego so puffed up that it's beneath you to teach a few little witches how to draw?" Karla asked with sweet malevolence.

"Puffed up? No, no, Ladies, I would be honored but—"

"But?" Jaenelle asked softly in her midnight voice.

Dujae shuddered. Saetan shivered.

"I am a demon."

Silence.

Finally Karla snorted. "If you don't want to teach us, just say so, but stop using a paltry excuse to weasel out of it."

They left, closing the study door behind them.

Dujae twisted his cap.

Saetan stared at his shoe. "Dujae," he said quietly, "it takes a strong but sensitive personality to deal with these young Ladies, not to mention talent. If you decide to become their art instructor, I can either provide you with wages which, I admit, aren't much use in the Dark Realm, or you can add whatever you want for your own projects to the list of supplies you'll provide me for them. However, if you decide to decline"—he looked Dujae in the eye—"*you* can go out there and try to explain it to them."

There was panic in Dujae's eyes. There was also only one door out of the study.

"But, High Lord, I am a demon."

"Didn't impress them, did it?"

Dujae sagged. "No." Then he shrugged and smiled. "It has been a long time since I have done portraits, and they have interesting faces, yes? And too much fire to be wasted on polite, itsy-bitsy drawings."

Saetan waited half an hour before strolling into the great hall. Staying well in the background, he watched the coven.

The girls were sitting on the floor in a circle, busily sketching a still life of vase, apple, and trinket box. Dujae squatted next to Kalush, explaining something in a rumbling murmur before turning to Morghann, who had a stick of charcoal poised above her sketch pad.

Jaenelle put down her pad, wiped her fingers on the towel she was sharing with Karla, and approached him, smiling, nothing more than a delightful, delighted woman-child enjoying a creative endeavor.

Saetan slipped an arm around her waist. "The truth, witch-child," he said quietly. "Was the other one really a bad instructor?"

Jaenelle ran her finger down the gold chain that held his Birthright Red Jewel. "He wasn't right for us, any of us, and—"

He wouldn't let her duck her head, wouldn't let her hide the eyes he was learning to read so well, that told him so much. "And?"

"He was afraid of me," she whispered. "Not just me," she quickly amended. "He didn't like being around Queens. Even Kalush made him uneasy. So he was always saying things like 'ladies' do this and 'ladies' don't do that. Hell's fire, Saetan, we aren't 'ladies,' we don't want to be 'ladies.' We're witches."

He wrapped his arms around her. "Why didn't you tell me?" He seemed to be asking that a lot lately.

Jaenelle shrugged. "We hadn't gotten around to telling you that the music instructor and the dancing instructor already bolted this week."

Saetan let out a chuckling sigh. "Well, lessons and summertime are probably a bad combination anyway." He kissed her hair. "Dujae came here because he wanted to be released."

"Not really. He just needed something to spark his interest again."

Saetan watched Dujae move around the circle, gesturing, rumbling encouragement, frowning as he studied Karla's sketch before saying something that made her laugh. There was no despair in Dujae's eyes now, no hint of the pain that had driven him to seek out the High Lord.

"We aren't puppet masters, witch-child," Saetan murmured. "We're very powerful, but we must be careful about pulling strings to make other people dance."

"Depends on why the strings are being pulled, don't you think?" She looked at him with those ancient sapphire eyes and smiled. "Besides, we just overrode a silly excuse. If it was his time, he would have gone."

She returned to her spot on the floor, Karla on her right, Gabrielle on her left.

He returned to his study and warmed a glass of yarbarah.

Puppet masters. Manipulators. Hekatah and her schemes. Jaenelle and her sensitivity to other hearts. Such a fine, fragile line, with intent the only difference.

He picked up the latest letter from the Dark Council. There was something beneath the terse words that disturbed him, but it was too vague for him to define. He couldn't put them off much longer. A few more weeks at most. What then?

Such a fine, fragile line.

What then?

5 / Kaeleer

Jaenelle picked up a small vial and tapped three amethyst-colored granules into the large glass bowl on the worktable. "Why are members of the Dark Council coming here?"

Saetan eyed the thick, bubbling liquid that covered the bottom third of the bowl and sincerely hoped the stuff wasn't a new tonic. "Since my legal guardianship was granted by the Council, they want to look in on us to see how we live."

"If they're members of the Council, they're also Jeweled Blood. They should know how we live." Jaenelle picked up a vial of red powder and held it up to the light.

Saetan crossed his arms and leaned against the wall. He wouldn't, couldn't tell her about the latest "request" from the Council. Their strident insistence had made it easy to read between the lines. They weren't just coming to look in on a guardian and his ward. They were coming to pass judgment on him.

"I'm not going to have to wear a dress, am I?" Jaenelle growled as she dipped her little finger into the vial of red powder. Using her nail as a scoop, she tapped the powder into the bowl.

Saetan bit his tongue before the lie could slip out. "No. They said they wanted to see a normal afternoon."

Jaenelle looked at him over her shoulder. "Have we ever had a normal afternoon?"

"No," Saetan said mournfully. "We have typical afternoons, but I don't think anyone would consider them normal."

Her silvery, velvet-coated laugh filled the room. "Poor Papa. Well, since I don't have to dress up and simper, I'll try not to offend their delicate sensibilities." She handed him a vial of black powder. "Put a pinch of that in the bowl and stand back."

The butterflies in his stomach were having a grand time. "What happens then?"

Jaenelle laced her fingers. "Well, if I mixed the powders in the right proportions to the spell, it'll create an impressive illusion."

Saetan looked from his nervously smiling daughter to the bowl on the table to the vial in his hand. "And if you didn't mix them in the right proportions?"

"It'll blow up the table."

An hour later, as he lay in a deep, hot bath, soaking the soreness out of his muscles, he had to give her full marks for her fast reflexes and the strength of her protective shields. Except for knocking them both to the floor, the explosion hadn't damaged anything in the room—except the glass bowl and the table. And he had to admit that the shape that had started rising out of the bowl had been impressive.

Two days from now, the Dark Council would come to the Hall. He would show them courtesy and endure their presence because, in the end, it didn't matter what they thought. No one was going to take her away from him. If the Council had to learn that lesson twice, so be it.

He doubted it would come to that. Remembering the awe-filled moment between the shape starting to rise from the mist and the table exploding, he let out a moan that turned into a chuckle. The Dark Council wanted to spend a typical afternoon with Jaenelle?

The poor fools would never survive it.

CHAPTER
EIGHT

1 / Kaeleer

It started going wrong the moment the two members of the Dark Council walked through the front door, looked around, and shivered.

SaDiablo Hall was a dark-gray structure that rose above the land and cast a long shadow. He'd built it to be imposing, but hadn't planned on having a stony-faced, Red-Jeweled butler frightening his guests before they even crossed the threshold. As for the chill in the air . . . Helene had let him know, with stiff courtesy, what she thought of the Council coming to poke and pry into her domain, and all of the servants had spent the day scurrying away from the kitchen and Mrs. Beale.

Dark-Jeweled houses always had Blood servants, but when *all* the witches in a household decided to express their displeasure, the phrase "cold comfort" took on a whole new meaning.

"Good afternoon," Saetan said, coming forward to greet the two men.

The elder of the two bowed. "We appreciate your taking the time to see us, High Lord. I'm Lord Magstrom. This is Lord Friall."

Saetan liked Lord Magstrom. A man in his twilight years, he had a kind face framed by a cloud of white hair and blue eyes that probably twinkled most of the time. Those eyes were serious now but not condemning. Lord Magstrom, at least, would make his decision based on his own integrity and honor.

Lord Friall, on the other hand, had already decided. Weedy-looking for all the hair cream and finery, he kept glancing around with distaste and dabbing his lips with a scented, lace-edged handkerchief.

Saetan led them to the formal drawing room to the right of the great hall. It was a large room, but the furniture was arranged so that tall, painted screens could be placed across its width to divide it. The screens were in place, making this section appear cozy. The plastered walls were painted ivory. All the pictures were serene watercolors. The furniture was dark but not heavy and comfortably arranged over subtly patterned Dharo carpets. There was a bouquet of fresh flowers on a table near the windows. Saetan watched Lord Magstrom tactfully look over the room and knew the man was as pleased with the tasteful decorations as he was.

"It's a delightful room, High Lord," Lord Magstrom said as he accepted a seat. "Do you use it often?"

Saetan shoved his hands into his sweater pockets. "No," he said after a slight but noticeable hesitation. "We don't have many formal guests." He turned toward a movement in the doorway. "Ah, Beale."

The butler stood in the doorway, empty-handed.

Saetan raised an eyebrow. "Refreshments for our guests?"

"They'll be ready momentarily, High Lord." Beale bowed and retreated, leaving the door open.

Saetan was tempted to close the door but decided against it. No point forcing Beale to demean himself by listening at the keyhole.

"Have we come at an awkward time?" Lord Friall asked, looking pointedly at Saetan's casual attire while he continued to pat his lips with the scented handkerchief.

Perfume won't help what's troubling you, Lord Friall, Saetan thought coldly. *My psychic scent permeates the very stones of the Hall.* Saetan glanced down at the white cotton shirt unbuttoned low enough so that the Black Jewel around his neck wasn't completely hidden, the black cotton trousers that were already rumpled, and the sweater. "I gather you were expecting a more formal meeting. However, since I had understood that the Council wanted some indication of our usual living arrangements, those two expectations are incompatible."

"Surely—" Friall began, but he was cut off by Beale bringing in the refreshment tray.

Saetan studied the tray. It was sparse by Mrs. Beale's usual standards. There were plenty of sandwiches but none of the nutcakes or spiced tarts. "I don't suppose Mrs. Beale would—"

Beale set the tray on a table with an almost-inaudible thump.

"No," Saetan said dryly, "I don't suppose she would." He poured the coffee and offered the sandwiches while he tried to ignore the twinkle in Lord Magstrom's eyes. Settling into a corner of the couch where he could keep an eye on the door, he smiled at Lord Friall and wondered if his clenched teeth would survive the afternoon. "You were saying?"

"Surely—"

The front door slammed.

Catching the psychic scent and the emotional undercurrents, Saetan whistled a sharp command and resigned himself to disaster.

A moment later, Karla stuck her head around the corner. "Kiss kiss," she said, doing her best to look innocent.

Having already dealt with several of the coven's spells that had gone awry, Karla trying to look innocent scared him silly. But, if he was lucky, he might never have to know what she'd been up to.

Karla pointed toward the ceiling. "I'm late for my art lesson."

Saetan groaned softly and massaged his temple. Had he remembered to tell Dujae not to come today? "Please ask Jaenelle to come down. These gentlemen would like to see her."

Karla's ice-blue eyes swept over Magstrom and Friall. "Why?" She jerked her chin toward Lord Magstrom. "The grandfather looks harmless enough, but why would she want to talk to a fribble?"

Friall sputtered.

Lord Magstrom raised his cup to hide his smile.

Saetan was sure half his teeth were going to shatter. "Now."

"Oh, all right. Kiss kiss," Karla said, and was gone.

"Lady Karla is a friend of your ward?" Lord Magstrom asked mildly.

"Yes." Saetan's lips twitched. "She and Jaenelle's other friends are staying with us for the summer—if I survive it."

Lord Magstrom blinked.

"She's a little bitch," Friall sputtered, dabbing his lips with his handkerchief. "Hardly a suitable companion for your ward."

"Karla's a Queen and a natural Black Widow," Saetan said coldly, "as well as a Healer. She's an exuberant—but formidable—young lady. Like my daughter."

He caught Lord Magstrom's arrested look. Hadn't the Council checked the register at the Keep? As soon as Jaenelle had returned to them, he and Geoffrey had prepared the listing for her. They had agreed not to include the Territory—or Realm—where she had been born, or anything else that could lead someone back to her Chaillot relatives, but they *had* included that the Black was her Birthright Jewel. Didn't the Council know who, and what, they were dealing with? Or had the Tribunal chosen not to tell these men?

Lord Magstrom accepted another cup of coffee. "Your . . . daughter . . . is a Black Widow Queen? And a Healer as well?"

"Yes," Saetan replied. "Didn't the Council mention it?"

Lord Magstrom looked troubled. "No, they didn't. Perhaps—"

A woman let out a screech that made all three men jump. As Lord Magstrom dabbed at the spilled coffee and murmured apologies, a young wolf leaped into the drawing room. Friall let out a screech of his own and leaped behind his chair. Veering away from the screeching human, the wolf bounded behind the couch, came around the other side, and finally pressed himself against Saetan's legs, his head and one paw in Saetan's lap and a pleading expression in his eyes.

Saetan reminded himself that, compared to most days, they were having a quiet afternoon. He rubbed the young wolf's head and sighed. "Now what have you done?"

"I'll tell you what he's done." A red-faced woman filled the drawing room doorway.

Friall whimpered.

The wolf whined.

Lord Magstrom stared.

Mother Night, Mother Night, Mother Night. "Ah, Mrs. Beale," Saetan said calmly while he pressed a damp palm into the wolf's fur.

Mrs. Beale wasn't fat. She was just . . . *large*. And she didn't need to use Craft to lift a fifty-pound sack of flour with one hand.

Mrs. Beale pointed a finger at the wolf. "That walking muff just ate the chickens I was preparing for tonight's dinner."

Saetan looked down at the wolf. "Bad muff," he said mildly.

The wolf whined, but the tip of his tail dusted the floor.

Saetan sighed and turned his attention back to the huffing woman. "If there's no time to prepare more of our own, perhaps you could send someone to the butcher's in Halaway?"

Mrs. Beale huffed even more and said in a voice that rattled the windows, "Those chickens had been marinating in my special plum wine sauce since last night."

"Must have been tasty," Saetan murmured.

The wolf licked his chops and whuffed softly.

Mrs. Beale growled.

"What about a different meat?" Saetan said quickly. "I'm sure our young friend could find a couple of rabbits."

"Rabbits?" Mrs. Beale waved her hand, slicing the air in several directions. "I'm to fill *rabbits* with my nut and rice stuffing?"

"No, of course not. How foolish of me. A stew perhaps? I noticed last week that Jaenelle and Karla had second helpings of your stew."

"Noticed myself that that serving dish had come back empty," Mrs. Beale muttered. She pointed at the wolf. "Two rabbits. And not scrawny ones either." She turned on her heel and stomped away.

Lord Magstrom sighed gustily.

Lord Friall stumbled into his chair.

Saetan wondered if he had any bone left in his legs. This was turning into a typical afternoon after all. He scratched the wolf behind the ears. "You understand?" He held up two fingers. "Two plump bunnies for Mrs. Beale. Tarl says there are plenty of them fattening themselves up in the vegetable garden." He gave the wolf a last scratch. "Off with you."

After nuzzling Saetan's hand, the wolf trotted out the door.

"You let a woman like that work here when there are children in the house?" Friall sputtered. "And you keep a wolf for a pet?"

"Mrs. Beale is an excellent cook," Saetan replied mildly. *Besides,* he added silently, *who would have the balls to dismiss her?* "And the wolf isn't a pet. He's kindred. Several of them live with us. Another sandwich, Lord Magstrom?"

Looking a bit dazed, Lord Magstrom took another sandwich, stared at it for a moment, then set it on his plate.

"What's going on?" Jaenelle asked. Smiling politely at Magstrom and Friall, she settled next to Saetan on the couch.

"We're having bunny stew for dinner instead of chicken."

"Ah. That explains Mrs. Beale." Her lips twitched. "I suppose I should explain human territoriality to the wolves to avoid further misunderstandings."

"At least Mrs. Beale's territory," Saetan said, smiling at his fair-haired daughter, aware that the way Jaenelle sat so close to him was open to misinterpretation.

"Is that your usual way of dressing, Lady Angelline?" Lord Friall asked, once more dabbing his lips with his handkerchief.

Jaenelle looked at the baggy overalls she had acquired from one the gardeners and the white silk shirt Saetan had unknowingly donated to her wardrobe. She lifted one loose braid and studied the feathers, small bells, and seashells attached to the strips of leather woven into her hair. Then her eyes swept over Friall. "Sometimes," she said coolly. "Do you always dress like that?"

"Of course," Friall said proudly.

"Why?"

Friall stared at her.

Remember their delicate sensibilities, witch-child.

Screw their delicate sensibilities.

Saetan flinched. Her mood had shifted.

He dropped one arm around her shoulders. "Lord Magstrom would like to ask you a few questions." Hopefully the older Warlord felt the emotional currents in the room and would tread carefully.

"Before the interrogation begins, may I ask you something?"

Lord Magstrom fiddled with his cup. "This isn't an interrogation, Lady," he said gently.

"Really?" she said in her midnight voice.

Magstrom shivered. His hand shook as he set his cup on the table.

Hoping to divert her, Saetan groaned theatrically. "What do you want to ask?"

Her sapphire eyes studied him. Concern faded to exasperated amusement. "It isn't that bad."

"That's what you said the last time."

Jaenelle gave him her best unsure-but-game smile. "Dujae wants to know if we can have a wall."

He tried not to panic. "A wall? Dujae wants one of my walls?"

"Yes."

Saetan pressed his fingertips against his temple. Something was clogging his throat. He wasn't sure if it was a shriek or a laugh. "Why does Dujae want a wall?"

"We're going to paint it." She pondered this for a moment. "Well, I guess saying we're going to paint it isn't quite accurate. We're going to draw on it. Dujae says we need to think more expansively and the only way to do that is to have an expansive canvas to work on and the only thing big enough is a wall."

Uh-huh. "I see." Saetan looked around the tastefully decorated room and sighed. "There are lots of empty rooms here. Why don't you pick one in the same wing as the rumpus room."

Jaenelle frowned. "We don't have a rumpus room."

Saetan tweaked one of her braids. "You wouldn't say that if you'd ever been in the room under it while you were all doing . . . whatever."

Jaenelle gave him a look of amused tolerance. "Thank you, Papa." She bussed his cheek and bounded off the couch.

Saetan grabbed the back of her overalls and pulled her down beside him. "Dujae can wait a bit. Lord Magstrom has a few questions."

The cold fire was back in her eyes, but she settled against him on the couch, her hands demurely in her lap, and gave the two men a look of polite impatience.

Saetan nodded at Lord Magstrom.

His hands loosely clasped on the arms of the chair, Lord Magstrom smiled at Jaenelle. "Is art a favorite study of yours, Lady Angelline?" he asked politely. "I have a grand-daughter about your age who enjoys 'mucking about with colors,' as she puts it."

At the mention of a granddaughter, Jaenelle looked at Lord Magstrom with interest. "I enjoy drawing, but not as much as music," she said after a moment's thought. "Much more than mathematics." She wrinkled her nose. "But then, anything's better than mathematics."

"Arnora holds mathematics in the same high regard," Lord Magstrom said seriously, but his blue eyes twinkled.

Jaenelle's lips twitched. "Does she? A sensible witch."

"What other subjects do you enjoy?"

"Learning about plants and gardening and healing and weaponry and equitation is fun . . . and languages. And dancing. Dancing's wonderful, don't you think? And of course there's Craft, but that's not really a lesson, is it?"

"Not really a lesson?" Lord Magstrom looked startled.

He accepted another cup of coffee. "With so much studying, you don't have much time to socialize," he said slowly.

Jaenelle frowned and looked at Saetan.

"I believe Lord Magstrom is referring to dances and other public gatherings," he said carefully.

Her frown deepened. "Why do we need to go out for dancing? We've got enough people here who play instruments and we dance whenever we want to. Besides, I promised Morghann I'd spend a few days in Scelt with her when they have the harvest dances, and Kalush's family invited me to go to the theater with them, and Gabrielle—"

"Dujae," Friall said tightly. "Dujae is teaching you to draw?"

Saetan squeezed Jaenelle's shoulder but she shrugged away from him.

"Yes, Dujae is teaching me to draw," Jaenelle said, the chill back in her voice.

"Dujae is dead."

"For centuries now."

Friall dabbed at his lips. "You study drawing with a demon?"

"Just because he's a demon doesn't make him less of an artist."

"But he's a *demon*."

Jaenelle shrugged dismissively. "So are Char and Titian and a number of my other friends. Who I call a friend is no business of yours, Lord Friall."

"No business," Friall sputtered. "It most certainly *is* the Council's business. It was a show of faith that the Council allowed something like the High Lord to keep a young girl in the first place—"

"*Something* like the High Lord?"

"—and to soil a young girl's sensibilities by forcing her to consort with demons—"

"He never forces me. *No one* forces me."

"—and submit to his own lustful attentions—"

The room exploded.

There was no time to think, no time to protect himself from the spiraling fury rising out the abyss.

Drawing everything he could from his Black Jewels, Saetan threw himself on Jaenelle as she lunged for Friall. Wild, vicious sounds erupted from her as she fought to break free and reach the Warlord, who stared at her in shock while windows shattered, paintings crashed to the floor, plaster cracked as psychic lightning scored the walls, and the furniture was ripped to pieces.

Hanging on grimly, Saetan let the room go, using his strength to shield the other men, using himself as a buffer between Jaenelle's rage and flesh. She wasn't trying to hurt him. That was the terrifying irony. She was simply trying to get past the barriers he was placing between her and Friall. He opened his mind, intending to press against her inner barriers and force her to feel a little of the pain he was enduring. But there were no barriers. There was only the abyss and a long, mind-shattering fall.

*Please, witch-child. *Please!**

She came at him with frightening speed, cocooned him in black mist, and then brought him up to the depth of the Red Jewel before she turned and glided back down into the comfortable sanctuary of the abyss.

Silence.

Stillness.

His head throbbed mercilessly. His tongue hurt. His mouth was full of blood. He felt too brittle to move. But his mind was intact.

She loved him. She wouldn't deliberately hurt him. She loved him.

Pulling that thought around his bruised mind and battered body like a warm cloak, Saetan surrendered to oblivion.

Lord Magstrom woke to a none-too-gentle slap. Blinking to clear his vision, he focused on the dark wings and stern face.

"Drink this," the Eyrien snapped, shoving a glass into Magstrom's hands. He stepped back, fists braced on his hips. "Your companion is finally coming around. He's lucky to be here at all."

Magstrom gratefully sipped his drink and looked around. Except for the chairs he and Friall were sitting in, the room was empty. The painted screens that divided the room were gone. The furniture on the other side was tumbled but intact. If not for the black streaks on the ivory walls that looked like lightning gone to ground, he might have thought they'd been moved to a different room, that it had been a hallucination of some kind.

He'd heard of Andulvar Yaslana, the Demon Prince. He knew it was a measure of his own terror that he found shivering comfort in having an Ebon-gray-Jeweled demon standing over him. "The High Lord?" he asked.

Andulvar stared at him. "He almost shattered the Black trying to keep you safe. He's exhausted, but he'll recover with a few days of rest." Then he snorted. "Besides, it'll give the waif an excuse to dose him with one of her restorative tonics, and that, thank the Darkness, should keep her from thinking too much about what happened."

"What did happen?"

Andulvar nodded at Friall. Beale was still waving smelling salts under Friall's nose, but the butler's expression strongly suggested he'd rather toss the intruder onto the drive and be done with it. "He pissed her off. Not a smart thing to do."

"Then she's unstable? Dangerous?"

Andulvar slowly spread his dark wings. He looked huge. And there was no concern in his gold eyes, only an unspoken threat.

"Simply by being Blood, we're all dangerous, Lord Magstrom," Andulvar growled softly. "She belongs to the family, and we belong to her. Never forget that." He folded his wings and crouched beside Magstrom's chair. "But in truth, Saetan's the only thing that stands between you and her. Don't forget that either."

An hour later, Magstrom and Friall's coach rolled down the well-kept drive, then onto the road that ran through Halaway.

It was dusk on a late summer afternoon. Wildflowers painted meadows with bright colors. Trees stretched their branches high above the road, creating cool tunnels. It was beautiful land, lovingly tended, shadowed for thousands of years by SaDiablo Hall and the man who ruled there.

Shadowed and protected.

Magstrom shivered. He was a Warlord who wore Summer-sky Jewels. He acted as the caretaker of the village where he'd been born and where he'd contentedly spent his life. Until he'd been asked to serve on the Dark Council, his dealings with those who wore darker Jewels had been diplomatic and, fortunately, seldom. The Blood in Goth, Little Terreille's capital, were interested in court intrigue, not in a village that looked across a river into the wooded land of Dea al Mon.

But now a curtain had been drawn back, just a little, and he had seen dark power, truly dark power.

Saetan's the only thing that stands between you and her.

The girl had to stay with the High Lord, Magstrom thought as the coach rolled through Halaway to the landing web where they would catch the Winds and go home. For all their sakes, she had to stay.

Saetan woke slowly as someone settled on the end of his bed. Grunting, he propped himself up on one elbow and stroked the candle-light on the bedside table just enough to dimly light the room.

Jaenelle sat cross-legged on his bed, her eyes haunted, her face pinched and pale. She handed him a glass. "Drink this. It'll help soothe your nerves."

He took a sip and then another. It tasted of moonlight, summer heat, and cool water. "This is wonderful, witch-child. You should have a glass yourself."

"I've had two." She tried to smile but couldn't quite manage it. She fluffed her hair and bit her lower lip. "Saetan, I don't like what happened today. I don't like what . . . almost happened today."

He drained the glass, set it on the bedside table, and reached for her hand. "I'm glad. Killing should never be easy, witch-child. It should leave a scar on your soul. Sometimes it's necessary. Sometimes there's no choice if we're trying to defend what we cherish. But if there's an alternative, take it."

"They'd come here to condemn you, to hurt you. They had no right."

"I've been insulted by fools before. I survived."

Even in the dim light he saw her eyes change.

"Just because he was using words instead of a knife, you can't dismiss it, Saetan. He hurt you."

"Of course he hurt me," Saetan snapped. "Being accused of—" He closed his eyes and squeezed her hand. "I don't tolerate fools, Jaenelle, but I also don't kill them for being fools. I simply keep them out of my life." He sat up and took her other hand. "I am your sword and your shield, Lady. You don't have to kill."

Witch studied him with her ancient, haunted sapphire eyes. "You'll take the scars on your soul so that mine remains unmarked?"

"Everything has a price," he said gently. "Those kinds of scars are part of being a Warlord Prince. You're at a crossroads, witch-child. You can use your power to heal or to harm. It's your choice."

"One or the other?"

He kissed her hand. "Not always. As I said, sometimes destruction is necessary. But I think you're more suited to healing. It's the road I'd choose for you."

Jaenelle fluffed her hair. "Well, I do like making healing brews."

"I noticed," he said dryly.

She laughed, but the amusement quickly faded. "What will the Dark Council do?"

He leaned back on his pillows. "There's nothing they can do. I won't let them take you away from your family and friends."

She kissed his cheek. The last thing she said before she left his bedroom was, "And I won't let them put more scars on your soul."

2 / Kaeleer

He had expected it, even prepared for it. It still hurt.

Jaenelle stood silently in the petitioner's circle, her fingers demurely laced in front of her, her eyes fixed on the seal carved into the front of the blackwood bench where the Tribunal sat. She wore a dress she had borrowed from one of her friends, and her hair was pulled back in a tight, neat braid.

Knowing the Council watched his every move, Saetan stared at nothing, waiting for the Tribunal to begin their vicious little game.

Because he had anticipated the Council's decision, he'd allowed no one but Andulvar to come with them. Andulvar could take care of himself. He would take care of Jaenelle. The moment the Tribunal announced the Council's verdict, the moment Jaenelle protested and turned to him for help . . .

Everything has a price.

Over 50,000 years ago, he'd been instrumental in creating the Dark Council. Now he'd destroy it. One word from her, and it would be done.

The First Tribune began to speak.

Saetan didn't listen. He scanned the faces of the Council. Some of the witches looked more troubled than angry. But most of their eyes glittered like feral, slithery things gathered for the kill. He knew some of them. Others were new, replacements for the fools who had challenged him once before in this room. As he watched them watching him, his regret at his decision to destroy them trickled away. They had no right to take his daughter away from him.

"—and so it's the careful opinion of this Council that appointing a new guardian would be in your best interest."

Tensed, Saetan waited for Jaenelle to turn to him. He'd gone deep into the Black before they'd reached the Council chambers. There were dark Jewels here that might hold out long enough to try to attack, but the Black unleashed would shatter every mind caught in the explosion of psychic energy. Andulvar was strong enough to ride out the psychic storm. Jaenelle would be held safe, protected in the eye of the storm.

Saetan took a deep breath.

Jaenelle looked at the First Tribune. "Very well," she said quietly, clearly. "When the sun next rises, you may appoint a new guardian—unless you reconsider your decision before then."

Saetan stared at her. No. No! She was the daughter of his soul, his Queen. She couldn't, wouldn't walk away from him.

She did.

She didn't look at him when she turned and walked down the center of the chamber to the doors at the far end. When she reached the doors, she sidestepped away from Andulvar's outstretched hand.

The doors closed.

Voices murmured. Colors swirled. Bodies moved past him.

He couldn't move. He'd thought he was too old for illusions, too heart-bruised to hope, too hardened to dream. He'd been wrong. Now he swallowed the bitterness of hope, choked on the ashes of dreams.

She didn't want him.

He wanted to die, wanted, desperately, that final death before pain and grief overwhelmed him.

"Let's get out of here, SaDiablo."

Andulvar led him away from the smug faces and the glittering eyes.

Tonight, before the sun rose again, he would find a way to die.

He'd forgotten the children would be waiting for him.

"Where's Jaenelle?" Karla asked, trying to look past him and Andulvar as they entered the family drawing room.

He wanted to slink away to his suite, where he could lick his wounds in private and decide how to accomplish the end.

He would lose them, too. They'd have no reason to visit, no reason to talk with him once Jaenelle was gone.

Tears pricked his eyes. Grief squeezed his throat.

"Uncle Saetan?" Gabrielle asked, searching his face.

Saetan cringed.

"What happened?" Morghann demanded. "Where's Jaenelle?"

Andulvar finally answered. "The Dark Council is going to choose another guardian. Jaenelle's not coming back."

"WHAT?" they yelled in unison.

Their voices pummeled him, questioning, demanding. He was going to lose all of these children who had crept into his heart over the past few weeks, whom he'd foolishly allowed himself to love.

Karla raised her hand. The room was instantly silent. Gabrielle moved forward until the two girls stood shoulder to shoulder.

"The Council appointed another guardian," Karla said, spacing out the words as she narrowed her eyes.

"Yes," Saetan whispered. His legs were going to buckle. He had to get away from them before his legs buckled.

"They must be mad," Gabrielle said. "What did Jaenelle say?"

Saetan forced himself to focus on Karla and Gabrielle. It would be the last time he would ever see them. But he couldn't answer them, couldn't get the damning words out.

Andulvar guided Saetan to a couch and pushed him down. "She said they could appoint a new guardian in the morning."

"Were those her exact words?" Gabrielle asked sharply.

"What difference does it make?" Andulvar snarled. "She made the decision to walk away from—"

"Damn your wings, you son of a whoring bitch," Karla screamed at him. *"What did she say?"*

"Stop it!" Saetan shouted. He couldn't stand having them argue, having the last hour with them tainted by anger. "She said—" His voice cracked. He clamped his hands between his knees, but it didn't stop them from shaking. "She said when the sun next rose they could appoint another guardian unless they reconsidered their decision by then."

The mood in the room changed to a little uneasiness blended with strong approval and calm acceptance. Puzzled, Saetan watched them.

Karla plopped down on the couch beside him and wrapped her arms around one of his. "In that case, we'll all stay right here and wait with you."

"Thank you, but I'd rather be alone." Saetan tried to rise, but Chaosti's stare unnerved him so badly he couldn't find his legs.

"No, you wouldn't," Gabrielle said, squeezing past Andulvar so that she could settle on the other side of him.

"I want to be alone right now," Saetan said, trying, but failing, to get that soft thunder into his voice.

Chaosti, Khary, and Aaron formed a wall in front of him, flanked by the other young males. Morghann and the rest of the coven circled the couch, trapping him.

"We're not going to let you do something stupid, Uncle Saetan," Karla said gently. Her wicked smile bloomed. "At least wait until the sun next rises. You're not going to want to miss it."

Saetan stared at her. She knew what he intended to do. Defeated, he closed his eyes. Today, tomorrow, what difference did it make? But not while they were still here. He wouldn't do that to them.

Satisfied, Karla and Gabrielle snuggled close to him while the other girls drifted toward the other couches.

Khary rubbed his hands together. "Why don't I see if Mrs. Beale is willing to brew up some tea?"

"Sandwiches would be good, too," Aaron said enthusiastically. "And some spiced tarts, if we didn't finish them. I'll go with you."

SaDiablo? Andulvar said on an Ebon-gray spear thread.

Saetan kept his eyes closed. *I won't do anything stupid.*

Andulvar hesitated. *I'll tell Mephis and Prothvar.*

No reason to answer. No answer to give. Because of him, Jaenelle would be lost to all of them. Would her new guardian welcome the wolves and the unicorns? Would he welcome the Dea al Mon and Tigre, the centaurs and satyrs? Or would she be forced to sneak an hour with them now and then, as she had done as a child?

As the hours passed and the children dozed in chairs or on the floor around him, he let it all go. He'd savor this time with them, savor the weight and warmth of Karla's and Gabrielle's heads nestled on his shoulders. Time enough to deal with the pain . . . after the sun rose.

"Wake up, SaDiablo."

Saetan sensed Andulvar's urgency but didn't want to respond, didn't want to tear the veil of sleep where he'd found a little comfort.

"Damn it, Saetan," Andulvar hissed, *"wake up."*

Reluctantly, Saetan opened his eyes. At first he felt grateful that Andulvar stood in front of him, blocking his view of the windows and the traitorous morning. Then he realized the candle-lights were lit, and necessary, and there was a flicker of fear in the Eyrien's eyes.

Andulvar stepped aside.

Saetan rubbed his eyes. Sometime during the night Karla and Gabrielle had slumped from his shoulders and were now using his thighs for pillows. He couldn't feel his legs.

He finally looked at the windows.

It was dark.

Why was Andulvar shoving him awake in the middle of the night?

Saetan glanced at the clock on the mantle and froze. Eight o'clock.

"Mrs. Beale wants to know if she should serve breakfast," Andulvar said, his voice strained.

The boys began to stir.

"Breakfast?" Khary said, stifling a yawn as he ran his fingers through his curly brown hair. "Breakfast sounds grand."

"But," Saetan stammered. The clock was wrong. It had to be wrong. "But it's still dark."

Chaosti, the Child of the Wood, the Dea al Mon Warlord Prince, gave him a fierce, satisfied smile. "Yes, it is."

A duet of giggles followed Chaosti's words as Karla and Gabrielle pushed themselves upright.

Saetan's heart pounded. The room spun slowly. He'd thought the Council's eyes had held a feral glitter, but that had been tame compared to these children who smiled at him, waiting.

"Black as midnight," Gabrielle said with sweet venom.

"Caught on the edge of midnight," Karla added. She rested her forearm on his shoulder and leaned toward him. "How long do you think it's going to take the Council to reconsider their decision, High Lord? A day? Maybe two?" She shrugged and rose. "Let's find breakfast."

With Andulvar in the lead, the children drifted out of the family drawing room, chatting and unconcerned.

Watching them, Saetan remembered something Titian had told him years before. *They know what she is.* He saw Khardeen, Aaron, and Chaosti exchange a look before Khary and Aaron followed the others. Chaosti stayed by the window, waiting.

Another triangle of power, Saetan thought as he approached the window. Almost as strong and just as deadly. May the Darkness help whoever stood in their way. "You knew," he said quietly as he stared out the window at the moonless, starless, unbroken night. "You knew."

"Of course," Chaosti said, smiling. "Didn't you?"

"No."

Chaosti's smile faded. "Then we owe you an apology, High Lord. We thought you were worried about what was going to happen. We didn't realize you didn't understand."

"How did you know?"

"She warned them when she set the terms. 'When the sun next rises.'" Chaosti shrugged. "Obviously the sun wasn't going to rise."

Saetan closed his eyes. He was the Black-Jeweled High Lord of Hell, the Prince of the Darkness. He wasn't sure that was a sufficient match for these children. "You're not afraid of her, are you?"

Chaosti looked startled. "Afraid of Jaenelle? Why should I be? She's my friend, my Sister, and my cousin. And she's the Queen." He tipped his head. "Are you?"

"Sometimes. Sometimes I'm very afraid of what she might do."

"Being afraid of what she might do isn't the same as being afraid of Jaenelle." Chaosti hesitated, then added, "She loves you, High Lord. You are her father, by her choice. Did you really think she'd let you go unless that's what you wanted?"

Saetan waited until Chaosti joined the others before answering.

Yes. May the Darkness help him, yes. He'd let his feelings tangle up his intellect. He'd been prepared to destroy the Council in order to keep her. He should have remembered what she'd said about not letting the Council put more scars on his soul.

She had stopped the Council, and she had stopped him.

It shamed him that he hadn't understood what Karla, Gabrielle, Chaosti, and the others had known as soon as they heard the phrasing she'd used. Loving her as he did, living with her while she stretched daily toward the Queen she'd become, he should have known.

Feeling better, he headed for the breakfast room.

There was just one thing that still troubled him, still produced a nagging twinge between his shoulder blades.

How in the name of Hell had Jaenelle done it?

3 / Hell

Hekatah stared out the window at the sere landscape. Like the other Realms, Hell followed the seasons, but even in summer, it was still a cold, forever-twilight land.

It had gone wrong again. Somehow, it had gone wrong.

She'd counted on the Council's being able to separate Saetan and Jaenelle. She hadn't foreseen the girl resisting in such a spectacular, frightening way.

The girl. So much power waiting to be tapped. There had to be a way to reach her, had to be some kind of bait with which to entice her.

As the thought took shape, Hekatah began to smile.

Love. A young man's ardor pitted against a father's affection. For all her power, the girl was a soft-hearted idiot. Torn between her own desires and another's needs—needs she could safely accommodate since she'd already been opened—she'd comply. Wouldn't she? If the male was skilled and attractive? After a while, with the help of an addictive aphrodisiac, she'd need the mounting far more than she'd need a father. Rejection would be all the discipline required if she balked at something her beloved wanted. All that dark, lovely power offered to a cock and balls who would, of course, be controlled by Hekatah.

Hekatah nibbled on her thumbnail.

This game required patience. If she was frightened of

sexual overtures and repelled all advances. . . . No need to worry about that. Saetan would never tolerate it, would never permit her to become frigid. He strongly believed in sexual pleasure—as strongly as he believed in fidelity. The latter had been a nuisance. The former guaranteed his little darling would be ripe for the picking in a year or two.

Smiling, Hekatah turned away from the window.

At least that gutter son of a whore was good for something.

4 / Kaeleer

Saetan handed Lord Magstrom a glass of brandy before settling into the chair behind his blackwood desk. It was barely afternoon, but after three "days" of unyielding night, he doubted many men were going to quibble about when they tossed back the first glass.

Saetan steepled his fingers. At least the fools in the Council had the sense to send Lord Magstrom. He wouldn't have granted an audience to anyone else. But he didn't like the Warlord's haggard appearance, and he hoped the elderly man would fully recover from the strain of the past three days. He'd spent most of his long life living between sunset and sunrise, and even he found this unnatural darkness a strain on his nerves. "You wanted to see me, Lord Magstrom?"

Lord Magstrom's hand shook as he sipped the brandy. "The Council is very upset. They don't like being held hostage this way, but they've asked me to put a proposal before you."

"I'm not the one you have to negotiate with, Warlord. Jaenelle set the terms, not me."

Lord Magstrom looked shocked. "We assumed—"

"You assumed wrong. Even I don't have the power to do this."

Lord Magstrom closed his eyes. His breathing was too rapid, too shallow. "Do you know where she is?"

"I think she's at Ebon Askavi."

"Why would she go there?"

"It's her home."

"Mother Night," Magstrom whispered. "Mother Night." He drained the glass of brandy. "Do you think we'll be able to see her?"

"I don't know." No point telling Magstrom that he'd already tried to see Jaenelle and, for the first time in his life, had been politely but firmly refused entrance to the Keep.

"Would she talk to us?"

"I don't know."

"Would—Would you talk to her?"

Saetan stared at Magstrom, momentarily shocked before fiery cold rage washed through him. "Why should I?" he said too softly.

"For the sake of the Realm."

"You *bastard*!" Saetan's nails scored the blackwood desk. "You try to take my daughter away from me and you expect *me* to smooth it over? Did you learn nothing from your last visit? No. You just chose to tear apart the life she's starting to build again with no thought to what it might do to her. You try to tear out my heart, and then when you discover there are penalties for playing your vicious little games, you want me fix it. You dismissed me as her guardian. If you want to end this, *you* go up to Ebon Askavi and *you* face what's waiting for you there. And in case you don't yet realize who you're dealing with, I'll tell you. Witch is waiting for you, Magstrom. Witch in all her dark glory. And the Lady isn't pleased."

Magstrom moaned and collapsed in the chair.

"Damn." Saetan took a deep breath and leashed his temper as he filled another glass with two fingers of brandy, called in a small vial from his stock of healing powders, and tapped in the proper dosage. Cradling Magstrom's head, he said, "Drink this. It'll help."

When Magstrom was once more aware and breathing easier, Saetan returned to his own chair. Bracing his head in his hands, he stared at the nail marks on the desk. "I'll take her the Council's proposal exactly as it's given to me, and I'll bring back her answer exactly as it's given to me. I'll do nothing more."

"After what you said, why would you do that?"

"You wouldn't understand," Saetan snapped.

Magstrom was silent for a moment. "I think I need to understand."

Saetan ran his fingers through his thick black hair and closed his golden eyes. He took a deep breath. If their positions were reversed, wouldn't he want an answer? "I stand at the window and worry about the sparrows and the finches and all the other creatures of the day, all the innocents who can't comprehend why the daylight doesn't come. I cradle a flower in my hand, hoping it will survive, and feel the land grow colder with each passing hour. I'm not going for the Council or even the Blood. I'm going to plead for the sparrows and the trees." He opened his eyes. "Now do you understand?"

"Yes, High Lord, I do." Lord Magstrom smiled. "How fortunate that the Council agreed to let me negotiate the terms of the proposal. If you and I can reach an agreement, perhaps it will be acceptable to the Lady as well."

Saetan tried, but he couldn't return the smile. They'd never seen Jaenelle's sapphire eyes change, never seen her turn from child to Queen, never seen Witch. "Perhaps."

He'd felt grateful when Draca granted him entrance to the Keep. He didn't feel quite so grateful about it when Jaenelle pounced on him the moment he entered her workroom.

"Do you understand this?" she demanded, thrusting a Craft book into his hands and pointing to a paragraph.

His insides churning, he called in his half-moon glasses, positioned them carefully on his nose, and obediently read the paragraph. "It seems simple enough," he said after a moment.

Jaenelle plopped on air, spraddle-legged. "I knew it," she muttered, crossing her arms. "I knew it was written in male."

Saetan vanished his glasses. "I beg your pardon?"

"It's gibberish. Geoffrey understands it but can't explain it so that it makes sense, and you understand it. Therefore, it's written in male—only comprehensible to a mind attached to a cock and balls."

"Considering his age, I don't think Geoffrey's balls are the problem, witch-child," Saetan said dryly.

Jaenelle snarled.

Stay here, a part of him whispered. *Stay with her in this place, in this way. They don't love you, never cared about you unless they wanted something from you. Don't ask her. Let it go. Stay.*

Saetan closed the book and held it tight to his chest. "Jaenelle, we have to talk."

Jaenelle fluffed her hair and eyed the closed book.

"We have to talk," he insisted.

"About what?"

That she'd pretend not to know pricked his temper. "Kaeleer, for a start. You have to break the spell or the web or whatever you did."

"When it ends is the Council's choice."

He ignored the warning in her voice. "The Council asked me—"

"You're here on behalf of the *Council*?"

Between one breath and the next, he watched a disgruntled young witch change into a sleek, predatory Queen. Even her clothes changed as she furiously paced the length of her workroom. By the time she finally stopped in front of him, her face was a cold, beautiful mask, her eyes held the depth of the abyss, her nails were painted a red so dark it was almost black, and her hair was a golden cloud caught up at the sides by silver combs. Her gown seemed to be made of smoke and cobwebs, and a Black Jewel hung above her breasts.

She'd gotten one of her Black Jewels set, he thought as his heart pounded. When had she done *that*?

He looked into her ancient eyes, silently challenging.

"Damn you, Saetan," she said with no emotion, no heat.

"I live for your pleasure, Lady. Do with me what you will. But release Kaeleer from midnight. The innocent don't deserve to suffer."

"And whom do you call innocent?" she asked in her midnight voice.

"The sparrows, the trees, the land," he answered quietly.

"What have they done to deserve having the sun taken away?"

He saw the hurt in her eyes before she yanked the book out of his hands and turned away.

"Don't be daft, Saetan. I would never hurt the land."

Never hurt the land. Never hurt the land. Never never never.

Saetan watched the air currents in the room. They were pretty. Reds, violets, indigos. It didn't matter that air currents didn't have color. Didn't even matter if he was hallucinating. They were pretty.

"Is there a chair in this room?" He wondered if she heard him. He wondered if he said the words out loud.

Jaenelle's voice made the colors dance. "Didn't you get *any* rest?"

A chair hugged him, warm against his back. A thick shawl wrapped around his shoulders, a throw covered his legs. A healing brew spiked with brandy thawed his tight muscles. Warm, gentle hands smoothed back his hair, caressed his face. And a voice, full of summer winds and midnight, said his name over and over.

He needn't fear her. There was nothing to fear. He needed to take these things in stride and not become distraught over the magnitude of her spells. After all, she was still wearing her Birthright Jewels, still cutting her Craft baby teeth. When she made the Offering . . .

He whimpered. She shushed him.

Cocooned in the warmth, he found his footing again. "The sun's been rising for the sparrows and the trees hasn't it, witch-child?"

"Of course," she said, settling on the arm of the chair.

"In fact, it's been rising for everything but the Blood."

"Yeesss."

"All the Blood?"

Jaenelle fluffed her hair and snarled. "I couldn't get the species separated so I had to lump them all together. But I did send messages to the kindred so they'd know it was temporary," she added hurriedly. "At least, I hope it's temporary."

Saetan snapped upright in the chair. "You did this without knowing for sure you could undo it?"

Jaenelle frowned at him. "Of course I can undo it. *Whether* I undo it depends on the Council."

"Ah." He needed to sleep for a week—as soon as he saw the sun rise. "The Council asked me to tell you that they've reconsidered."

"Oh." Jaenelle shifted on the chair arm. The layers of her gown split, revealing her entire leg.

She had nice legs, his fair-haired daughter. Strong and lean. He'd strangle the first boy who tried to slip his hand beneath her skirt and stroke that silky inner thigh.

"Would you help me translate that paragraph?" Jaenelle asked.

"Don't you have something to do first?"

"No. It has to be done at the proper hour, Saetan," she added as his eyebrow started to rise.

"Then we might as well fill the time."

They were still struggling with that paragraph two hours later. He was almost willing to agree that there were some things that couldn't be translated between genders, but he kept trying to explain it anyway because it filled him with perverse delight.

Despite her strength and intuition, there were still, thank the Darkness, a few things his fair-haired Lady couldn't do.

PART III

CHAPTER
NINE

1 / Terreille

He had been in the salt mines of Pruul for five years.
Now it was time to die.

In order to reach the fierce, clean death he'd promised
himself, he had to get beyond Zuultah's ability to pull him
down with the Ring of Obedience. It wouldn't be difficult.
Thinking him cowed, the guards didn't pay much attention
to him anymore, and Zuultah had gotten lax in her use of
the Ring. By the time they remembered what they never
should have forgotten about him, it would be far too late.

Lucivar yanked the pick out of the guard's belly and
drove it into the man's brain, sending just enough Ebon-
gray power through the metal to finish the kill by shattering
the guard's mind and Jewels.

Baring his teeth in a feral smile, he snapped the chains
that had held him for the past five years. Then he called
in his Ebon-gray Jewels and the wide leather belt that held
his hunting knife and his Eyrien war blade. A lot of foolish
Queens over the centuries had tried to force him to surrender those weapons. He'd endured the punishment and the
pain and had never admitted they were always within
reach—at least until he used them.

Unsheathing the war blade, he ran toward the mine's
entrance.

The first two guards died before they realized he was
there.

The next two blew apart when he struck with the Ebon-gray.

The rest were entangled by frantic slaves trying to get out of the way of an enraged Warlord Prince.

Fighting his way clear of the tangled bodies, he reached the mine entrance and ran across the slave compound, mentally preparing himself for a blind leap into the Darkness, hoping that, like an arrow released from a bow, he'd fly straight and true to the closest Wind and freedom.

Nerve-searing agony from the Ring of Obedience shredded his concentration at the same moment a crossbow bolt went through his thigh, breaking his stride. Howling with rage, he unleashed a wide band of power through his Ebon-gray ring, ripping the pursuing guards apart, body and mind. Another blast of pain from the Ring tore through him. He pivoted on his good leg, braced himself, and aimed a surge of power at Zuultah's house.

The house exploded. Stones smashed into surrounding buildings.

The pain from the Ring stopped abruptly. Lucivar probed swiftly and swore. The bitch was alive. Stunned and hurt, but still alive. He hesitated, wanting that kill. A weak strike at his inner barriers pulled his attention back to the surviving guards. They ran toward him, trying to braid their Jewels' strength in order to overwhelm him.

Fools. He could tear them apart piece by piece, and would have for the joy of paying pain back with pain, but by now someone would have sent out a call for help and if Zuultah came to enough to use the Ring of Obedience . . .

Battle lust sang in his veins, numbing physical pain. Maybe it would be better to die fighting, to turn the Arava Desert into a sea of blood. The closest Wind was a long, blind leap away. But, Hell's fire, if Jaenelle could do it when she was seven, then he could do it now.

Blood. So much blood.

Bitterness centered him, decided him.

Unleashing one more blast of power from the Ebon-gray, he gathered himself and leaped into the Darkness.

*   *   *

Bracing himself against the well, Lucivar filled the dipper again with sweet, cool water and drank slowly, savoring every swallow. Filling the dipper a last time, he limped to the nearby remains of a stone wall and settled himself as comfortably as possible.

That blind leap into the Darkness had cost him. Zuultah had roused enough to send another bolt through the Ring of Obedience just as he'd launched himself into the Darkness, and he'd drained half the strength in his Ebon-gray Jewels making the desperate reach for the Winds.

He sipped the water and stubbornly ignored what his body screamed at him. Hunger. Pain. A desperate need to sleep.

A hunting party from Pruul was three, maybe four hours behind him. He could have lost them, but it would have taken time he didn't have. A message relayed from mind to mind would reach Prythian, Askavi's High Priestess, faster than he could travel right now, and he didn't want to be caught by Eyrien warriors before he reached the Khaldharon Run.

And, if at all possible, there was a debt he wanted to call in.

Lucivar secured the dipper to the well and emptied the bucket. Satisfied that everything was as he'd found it, he faced south and sent out a summons on an Ebon-gray thread, pushing for his maximum range.

Sadi!

He waited a minute, then turned to face southeast.

Sadi!

After another restless minute, he turned east.

Sadi!

A flicker. Faint, different somehow, but still familiar.

Lucivar sighed like a satisfied lover. It was a fitting place for the Sadist to go to ground—in more ways than one. Plenty of broken, tumbled rock among those ruins. Some of them should be large enough to use as a makeshift altar. Oh, yes, a very fitting place.

Smiling, he caught the Red Wind and headed east.

Except for stories about Andulvar Yaslana, Lucivar had never had much interest in history. But Daemon had once

insisted that SaDiablo Hall in Terreille had been intact until
about 1,600 years ago, that something had happened—not
an attack, but something—that had broken the preservation
spells that had held for more than 50,000 years and had
begun the building's decay.

Treading carefully through the broken ruins, Lucivar
thought Daemon might have been right. There was a deep
emptiness about the place, as if its energy had been deliberately bled out. The stones felt dead. No, not dead. Starved.
Every time he touched one as he made his way toward an
inner courtyard, it felt as if the stone was trying to suck his
strength into itself.

He followed the smell of woodsmoke, shaking off his
uneasiness. He hadn't come here to ponder phantoms. He'd
be one soon enough.

Baring his teeth in a feral smile, he unsheathed the war
blade and stepped into the courtyard, staying back from
the circle of firelight.

"Hello, Bastard."

Daemon slowly looked up from the fire and just as slowly
pinpointed the sound. When he finally did, his smile was
gentle and weary.

"Hello, Prick. Have you come to kill me?" Daemon's
voice sounded rusty, as if he hadn't spoken for a long time.

Concern warred with anger until it became another flavor
of anger. And the difference in Daemon's psychic scent
bothered him. "Yes."

Nodding, Daemon stood up and removed his torn jacket.

Lucivar's eyes narrowed as Daemon unbuttoned the remaining buttons on his shirt, pulled the shirt aside to ex-
pose his chest, and stepped around the fire to stand where
the light best favored the attacker. It felt wrong. Everything
felt wrong. Daemon knew enough about basic survival and
living off the land—Hell's fire, *he* had seen to that—to have
kept himself in better condition than this. Lucivar studied
the dirty, ragged clothes, Daemon's half-starved body shivering in the firelight, the calm, almost hopeful look in those
bruised, exhausted eyes, and ground his teeth. The only
other person he'd ever met who was that indifferent to her
physical well-being was Tersa.

Maybe Daemon's voice wasn't rusty from disuse but hoarse from screaming himself awake at night.

"You're caught in it, aren't you?" Lucivar asked quietly. "You're tangled up in the Twisted Kingdom."

Daemon trembled. "Lucivar, please. You promised you'd kill me."

Lucivar's eyes glittered. "Do you feel her under you, Daemon? Do you feel that young flesh bruising under your hands? Do you feel her blood on your thighs while you drive into her, tearing her apart?" He stepped forward. "Do you?"

Daemon cringed. "I didn't . . ." He raised a shaking hand, twisting his fingers in the thick tangle of hair. "There's so much blood. It never goes away. The words never go away. Lucivar, please."

Making sure he had Daemon's attention, Lucivar stepped back and sheathed the war blade. "Killing you would be a kindness you don't deserve. You owe her every drop of pain that can be wrung out of you for the rest of your life and, Daemon, I wish you a very long life."

Daemon wiped his face with his sleeve, leaving a dirt smear across his cheek. "Maybe the next time we meet you can—"

"I'm dying," Lucivar snapped. "There won't be a next time."

There was a flicker of understanding in Daemon's eyes.

Something clogged Lucivar's throat. Tears pricked his eyes. There would be no reconciliation, no understanding, no forgiveness. Just a bitterness that would last beyond the flesh.

Lucivar limped out of the courtyard as fast as he could, using Craft to support his wounded leg. As he picked his way through the broken stones toward the remains of the landing web, he heard a cry so full of anguish the stones seemed to shudder. He stumbled to the web, gasping and tear-blind, unwilling to turn back, unwilling to leave.

But just before he caught the Gray Wind that would take him to Askavi and the final run, he looked at the ruins of the Hall and whispered, "Good-bye, Daemon."

*   *   *

Lucivar stood on the canyon rim at the halfway point in the Khaldharon Run, waiting for the sun to rise enough to light the canyon far below him.

Craft was the only thing keeping him on his feet now, the only thing that would let him use the greasy, tattered mess his wings had become after the slime mold had devoured them.

Intent on watching the sun rise, he also watched the small, dark shapes flying toward him—Eyrien warriors coming for the kill.

He looked down the Khaldharon Run, judging shadows and visibility. Not good. Foolish to throw himself into that dangerous intermingling of wind and the darker Winds when he couldn't distinguish the jagged canyon walls from the shadows, couldn't judge the curves that would create sudden wind shifts, when his wings barely functioned. At best it would be a suicide run.

Which was exactly why he was there.

The small, dark shapes flying toward him got larger, closer.

To the south of him, the sunlight touched the rock formation called the Sleeping Dragons. One faced north, the other south. The Khaldharon Run ended there and the mystery began, because no one who had entered one of those yawning, cavernous mouths had ever returned.

Several miles south of the Sleeping Dragons, the sun kissed the Black Mountain, Ebon Askavi, where Witch, his young, dreamed-of Queen would have lived if she'd never met Daemon Sadi.

The Eyrien warriors were close enough now for him to hear their threats and curses.

Smiling, he unfurled his wings, raised his fist, and let out an Eyrien war cry that silenced everything.

Then he dove into the Khaldharon Run.

It was as exhilarating, and as bad, as he'd thought it would be.

Even with Craft, his tattered wings didn't provide the balance he needed. Before he could compensate, the wind that howled through the canyon smashed him into the side wall, breaking his ribs and his right shoulder. Screaming defiance, he twisted away from the rock, pouring the strength of the Ebon-gray into his body as he plunged back into the center of the wild mingling of forces.

Just as the other Eyriens dove into the Run, he caught the Red thread and began the headlong race toward the Sleeping Dragons.

Instead of cutting in and out of the looping, twisting Winds within his range of strength to make a run as close to the canyon center as possible, he held to the Red, following it through narrow cuts of rock, pulling his wings tight to arrow through weatherworn holes that scraped his skin off as he passed through them.

His right foot hung awkwardly from the ripped ankle. The outer half of his left wing hung useless; the frame snapped when a gust of wind shoved him against a rock. The muscles in his back were torn from forcing his wings to do what they could no longer do. A deep, slicing belly wound pushed his guts out below the wide leather belt.

He shook his head, trying to clear blood out of his eyes, and let out a triumphant roar as he gauged his entry between the sharp stones that looked like petrified teeth.

A final gust of wind pushed him down as he shot through the Dragon's mouth. A "tooth" opened his left leg from hip to knee.

He drove into swirling mist, determined to reach the other side before he emptied the Jewels and his strength gave out.

Movement caught his eye. A startled face. Wings.

"Lucivar!"

He pushed to his limit, aware of the pursuers gaining on him.

"LUCIVAR!"

The other mouth had to be. . . . There! But . . .

Two tunnels. The left one held lightened twilight. The right one was filled with a soft dawn.

Darkness would hide him better. He swung toward the twilight.

A rush of wings on his left. A hand grabbing at him.

He kicked, twisted away, and drove for the right-hand tunnel.

"*LUU-CI-VAARRR!*"

Past the teeth and out, driving upward past the canyon rim toward the morning sky, pumping useless wings out of stubborn pride.

And there was Askavi, looking as he imagined it might have looked a long time ago. The muddy trickle he'd flown over was now a deep, clear river. Barren rock was softened by spring wildflowers. Beyond the Run, sunlight glinted off small lakes and twisting streams.

Pain flooded his senses. Blood mixed with tears.

Askavi. Home. Finally home.

He pumped his wings a last time, arched his body in a slow, painfully graceful backward curve, folded his wings, and plummeted toward the deep, clear water below.

2 / The Twisted Kingdom

The wind tried to rip him off the tiny island that was his only resting place in this endless, unforgiving sea. Waves smashed down on him, soaking him in blood. So much blood.

You are my instrument.

Words lie. Blood doesn't.

The words circled him, mental sharks closing in to tear out another piece of his soul.

Gasping, he choked on a mouthful of bloody foam as he dug his fingers into rock that suddenly softened. He screamed as the rock beneath his hands turned into pulpy, violet-black bruises.

Butchering whore.

Nooooo!

I loved her! he screamed. *I *love* her! I never meant her harm.*

You are my instrument.

Words lie. Blood doesn't.

Butchering whore.

The words leaped playfully over the island, slicing him deeper and deeper with each pass.

Pain deepening anguish deepening agony deepening pain until there was no pain at all.

Or, perhaps, no one left to feel it.

3 / Terreille

Surreal stared at the dirty, trembling wreck that had once been the most dangerous, beautiful man in the Realm. Before he could shy away, she pulled him into the flat, threw every physical bolt on the door, and then Gray-locked it for good measure. After a moment's thought, she put a Gray shield on all the windows to lessen the chance of a severed artery or a five-story uncontrolled dive.

Then she took a good look at him and wondered if a severed artery would be such a bad thing. He'd been mad the last time she'd seen him. Now he looked as if he'd been sliced open and scooped out as well.

"Daemon?" She walked toward him, slowly.

He shook, unable to control it. His bruised-looking eyes, empty of everything but pain, filled with tears. "He's dead."

Surreal sat on the couch and tugged on his arm until he sat beside her. "Who's dead?" Who would matter enough to produce this reaction?

"Lucivar. Lucivar's *dead*!" He buried his head in her lap and wept like a heartsick child.

Surreal patted Daemon's greasy, tangled hair, unable to think of one consoling thing to say. Lucivar had been important to Daemon. His death mattered to Daemon. But even thinking of expressing sympathy made her want to gag. As far as she was concerned, Lucivar was also responsible for some of the soul wounds that had pushed Daemon over the edge, and now the bastard's death might be the fatal slice.

When the sobs diminished to quiet sniffles, she called in a handkerchief and stuffed it into his hand. She'd do a lot of things for Sadi, but she'd be damned if she'd blow his nose for him.

Finally cried out, he sat next to her, saying nothing. She sat quietly and stared at the windows.

This backwater street was safe enough. She'd returned several times since Daemon's last visit, staying longer and longer each time. It felt comfortable here. She and Wyman, the Warlord Daemon had healed, had developed a casual friendship that kept loneliness at bay. Here, with someone looking after him, maybe Daemon could heal a little.

"Daemon? Would you stay here with me for a while?" Watching him, she couldn't tell what he was thinking, even *if* he was thinking.

Eventually, he said, "If you want."

She thought she saw a faint flicker of understanding. "You promise to stay?" she pressed. "You promise not to leave without telling me?"

The flicker died. "There's nowhere else to go."

4 / Kaeleer

A light breeze. Sunlight warming his hand. Birdsong. Firm comfort under him. Soft cotton over him.

Lucivar slowly opened his eyes and stared at the white ceiling and the smooth, exposed beams. Where . . . ?

Out of habit, he immediately looked for ways out of the room. Two windows covered by white curtains embroidered with morning glories. A door on the wall opposite the bed he was lying on.

Then he noticed the rest of the room. The pine bedside table and dresser. The piece of driftwood turned into a lamp. A cabinet, its top bare except for a simple brass stand for holding music crystals. An open workbasket stuffed with skeins of yarn and floss. A large, worn, forest-green chair and matching hassock. A needlework frame covered with white material. An overstuffed bookcase. Braided, earth-tone rugs. Two framed charcoal sketches—head views of a unicorn and a wolf.

Lucivar's lip curled automatically when he caught the feminine psychic scent that saturated the walls and wood.

Then he frowned. For some reason, that psychic scent didn't repulse him.

He looked around the room again, confused. This was Hell?

A door opened in the room beyond. He heard a woman's voice say, "All right, go look, but don't wake him."

He closed his eyes. The door opened. Nails clicked on the wood floor. Something snuffled his shoulder. He kept his muscles relaxed, feigning sleep while his senses strained to identify the thing.

Fur against his bare skin. A cold, wet nose sniffing his ear.

Then a snort that made him twitch, followed by satisfied silence.

Giving in to curiosity and the warrior's need to identify an enemy, Lucivar opened his eyes and returned the wolf's intent gaze for a moment before it let out a pleased whuff and trotted out the door.

He barely had time to gather his wits when the woman pushed the door fully open and leaned against the doorway. "So you've finally decided to rejoin the living."

She sounded amused, but if the rest of her was anything to go by, the hoarseness in her voice was caused by strain, fatigue, and overuse. Painfully thin. The way the trousers and shirt hung on her, she'd probably dropped the weight far too fast to be healthy. The long, loose braid of gold hair looked as dull as her skin, and there were dark smudges under those beautiful, ancient sapphire eyes.

Lucivar blinked. Swallowed hard. Finally remembered to breathe. "Cat?" he whispered. He raised his hand in a mute plea.

She raised one eyebrow and walked toward him. "I know you said you would find me when I was seventeen, but I had no idea you would do it in such a dramatic fashion."

The moment she touched his hand, he pulled her down on top of him and wrapped his arms around her squirming body, laughing and crying, ignoring her muffled protests as he said, "Cat, Cat, Cat, oowww!"

Jaenelle scrambled off the bed and out of reach, breathing hard.

Lucivar rubbed his shoulder. "You bit me." He didn't mind the bite—well, yes, he did—but he didn't like her pulling away from him.

"I *told* you I couldn't breathe."

"Do we need to?" he asked, still rubbing his shoulder. Judging by the look in her eyes, if she were actually feline, she'd be puffed to twice her size.

"I don't know, Lucivar," she said in a voice that could scorch a desert. "I could always remove your lungs and we'd find out firsthand if breathing is optional."

The tiny doubt that she might not be kidding was sufficient to make him swallow the flippant remark he was about to make. Besides, he had enough confusing things to think about, not to mention doing something about the urgent, basic message his body was now sending. Hell's fire, he'd never imagined being dead would feel so much like being alive.

He rolled onto his side, wondering if his muscles were always going to feel so limp—weren't there *any* advantages to being a demon?—and thrust his legs out from under the covers.

"Lucivar," Jaenelle said in a midnight voice.

He gave her a measuring look and decided to ignore the dangerous glitter in her eyes. He levered himself upright, pulled the sheet across his lap, and grinned weakly. "I've always been proud of my accuracy and aim, Cat, but even I can't water the flowers from here."

Thankfully, he didn't understand anything she said after the first Eyrien curse she flung at him.

She slung his arm over her shoulders, wrapped her arm around his waist, and pulled him to his feet. "Just take it slow. I've got most of your weight."

"The males who serve here should be doing this, not you," Lucivar snarled as they shuffled to the door, not sure if he was more embarrassed about being naked or needing her support.

"There aren't any. Hey!"

He almost overbalanced both of them reaching for the door, but he needed to tighten his hand around something. His darling Cat was here alone, unprotected, with no one but a wolf for company? Taking care of his . . . "You're a young woman," he said through clenched teeth.

"I'm a fully qualified Healer." She tugged at his waist. It didn't do any good. "You were easier to take care of before you woke up."

He snarled at her.

"Lucivar," Jaenelle said in that voice Healers used on irascible patients and idiots, "you've been in a healing sleep for the past three weeks. Taking that into consideration as well as what it took to put you back together, I think I've seen every inch of you more than once. Now, are you going to dribble on the floor like an untrained puppy or are we going to get to where you wanted to go?"

A fierce desire to get well enough to stand on his own two feet so that he could strangle her got him to the bathroom. Pride made him snarl her out the door. Stubbornness kept him upright long enough to do what was necessary, tie a bath towel around his waist, and reach the bathroom door.

By then his energy and useful emotions were tapped out, so he didn't protest when Jaenelle helped him walk to a stool near a large pine table in the cabin's main room. She moved behind him, her hands firm and gentle as they explored his back. He kept his eyes fixed on the outside door, not ready yet to ask about the healing. Then he felt one of his wings slowly unfurl, guided by those same gentle hands.

The wing closed. The other stretched out. As she came around to the front, he turned his head and stared at a wing that was healthy and whole. Stunned, he bit his lip and blinked back tears.

Jaenelle glanced at his face, then returned her attention to the wing. "You were lucky," she said quietly. "In another week there wouldn't have been enough healthy tissue left to rebuild them."

Rebuild them? Considering the damage the slime mold and the salt mines had done, even the best Eyrien Healers would have cut off the wings. How could she rebuild them?

Mother Night, he was tired, but there were too many things here that didn't fit his expectations. He desperately needed to understand and didn't know where to begin.

Then Jaenelle bent over to look at the lower part of the wing and the jewelry around her neck swung out of her shirt. Later he'd ask why Witch was wearing a Sapphire Jewel. Right now, all his attention was caught by the hourglass pendant that hung above the Jewel.

The hourglass was the Black Widows' symbol, both a declaration and a warning about the witch who wore it. An apprentice wore a pendant with the gold dust sealed in the top half of the glass. A journeymaid's pendant had the gold dust evenly divided between top and bottom. A fully trained Black Widow wore an hourglass with all the gold dust in the bottom chamber.

"When did you become a fully trained Black Widow?"

The air around him cooled. "Does it bother you that I am?"

Obviously it bothered some people. "No, just curious."

She gave him a quick smile of apology and continued her inspection. The air returned to normal. "Last year."

"And you became a qualified Healer?"

She carefully folded the wing and started checking his right shoulder. "Last year."

Lucivar whistled. "Busy year."

Jaenelle laughed. "Papa says he's thrilled he survived it."

He could almost hear the blade against the whetstone as his temper rose to the killing edge. She had a father, a family, and yet lived without human companionship, not even a servant. Exiled here because of the Hourglass? Or because she was Witch? Once he was fit again, this father of hers would have a few things to adjust to—like the Warlord Prince who now served her.

"Lucivar." Jaenelle's voice seemed as far away as the hand squeezing his taut shoulder. "Lucivar, what's wrong?"

Time moved slowly at the killing edge, measured by the beat of a war drum heart. The world became filled with individual, razor-sharp details. A blade would flow through muscle, humble bone. And the mouth would fill with the living wine as teeth sank into a throat.

"*Lucivar.*"

Lucivar blinked. Felt the tension in Jaenelle's fingers as she gripped his shoulders. He backed from the edge, step by mental step, while the wildness in him howled to run free. Senses dulled by the salt mines of Pruul were reborn. The land called him, seducing him with scents and sounds. She seduced him, too. Not for sex, but for another kind of bond, in its own way just as powerful. He wanted to rub against her so that her physical scent was on his skin. He wanted to rub against her so that *his* physical scent on *her* warned others that a powerful male had some claim to her, was claimed by her. He wanted . . .

He turned his head, catching her finger between his teeth, exerting enough force to display dominance without actually hurting her. Her hand relaxed in submission, embracing the wild darkness within him. And because she *could* embrace it, he surrendered everything.

A minute later, completely returned to the mundane world, he noticed the open outer door and the three wolves standing on the covered porch, studying him with sharp interest.

Jaenelle, now inspecting his collarbone and chest muscles, glanced at the wolves and shook her head. "No, he can't come out and play."

Making disappointed-sounding whuffs, the wolves went back outside.

He studied the land framed by the open door. "I never thought Hell would look like this," he said softly.

"Hell doesn't." She slapped his hand when he tried to stop her from probing his hip and thigh.

Forcefully reminding himself that he shouldn't smack a Healer, he gritted his teeth and tried again to find some answers. "I didn't know that demon-dead children grew up or that demons could be healed."

She gave him a penetrating look before examining his other leg. Heat and power flowed from her hands. "*Cildru dyathe* don't and demons can't. But I'm not *cildru dyathe* and you're not a demon—although you did your damnedest to become one," she added tartly. She pulled up a straight-backed chair, sat down facing him, and took his hands in hers. "Lucivar, you're not dead. This isn't the Dark Realm."

He'd been so sure. "Then . . . where are we?"

"We're in Askavi. In Kaeleer." She watched him anxiously.

"The Shadow Realm?" Lucivar whistled softly. Two tunnels. One a lightening twilight, the other a soft dawn. The Dark Realm and the Shadow. He grinned at her. "Since we're not dead, can we go exploring?"

He watched, intrigued, as she tried to force her answering grin into a sober, professional expression.

"When you're fully healed," she said sternly, then spoiled it with a silvery, velvet-coated laugh. "Oh, Lucivar, the dragons who live on the Fyreborn Islands are going to love you. You not only have wings, you're big enough to wave whomp."

"Wave what?"

Her eyes widened and her teeth caught her lower lip. "Umm. Never mind," she said too brightly, bouncing off her chair.

He caught the back of her shirt. After a brief tussle that left him breathing hard and left her looking more than a little rumpled, she was once again slumped in the chair.

"Why are you living here, Cat?"

"What's wrong with it?" she said defensively. "It's a good place."

Lucivar narrowed his eyes. "I didn't say it wasn't."

She leaned forward, studying his face. "You're not one of those males who gets hysterical about every little thing, are you?"

He leaned forward, forearms braced on thighs, and smiled his lazy, arrogant smile. "I never get hysterical."

"Uh-huh."

The smile showed a hint of teeth. "Why, Cat?"

"Wolves can be real tattletales, did you know that?" She looked at him hopefully. When he didn't say anything, she fluffed her hair and sighed. "You see, there are times when I need to get away from everyone and just be with the land, and I used to come and camp out here for a few days, but during one of those trips it rained and I was sleeping on the wet ground and got chilled and the wolves went running off to tell Papa and he said he appreciated my need to spend some time with the land but he saw no reason why

I couldn't have the option of some shelter and I said that a lean-to would probably be a reasonable idea so he had this cabin built." She paused and gave him an apprehensive smile. "Papa and I have rather different definitions of 'lean-to.'"

Looking at the large stone hearth and the solid walls and ceiling, and then at the woman-child sitting in front of him with her hands pressed between her knees, Lucivar reluctantly let go of the knot of anger he'd felt for this unknown father of hers. "Frankly, Cat, I like your papa's definition better."

She scowled at him.

Black Widow and Healer she might be, but she was also almost grown, with enough of the endearing awkwardness of the young to still remind him of a kitten trying to pounce on a large, hoppy bug.

"So you don't live here all the time?" he asked carefully.

Jaenelle shook her head. "The family has several residences in Dhemlan. Most of the time I live at the family seat." She gave him a look he couldn't read. "My father is the Warlord Prince of Dhemlan—among other things."

A man of wealth and position then. Probably not the sort who'd want a half-breed bastard as a companion for his daughter. Well, he'd deal with that when the time came.

"Lucivar." She fixed her eyes on the open door and chewed her lip.

He sympathized with her. This was sometimes the hardest part of the healing, telling the patient honestly what could—and could not—be mended. "The wings are just decorative, aren't they?"

"No!" She took a deep breath. "The injuries were severe. All of them, not just the wings. I've done the healing, but what happens now depends, in large part, on you. I estimate it will take another three months for your back and wings to heal completely." She chewed her lip. "But, Lucivar, there's no margin for error in this. I had to pull everything you had to give for this healing. If you reinjure *anything*, the damage may be permanent."

He reached for her hand, caressed her fingers with his

thumb. "And if I do it your way?" He watched her carefully. There were no false promises in those sapphire eyes.

"If you do it my way, three months from now we'll make the Run."

He lowered his head. Not because he didn't want her to see the tears, but because he needed a private moment to savor the hope.

When he had himself under control again, he smiled at her.

She smiled back, understanding. "Would you like a cup of tea?" When he nodded, she bounced out of the chair and went through the door to the right of the stone hearth.

"Any chance of persuading my Healer to add a bit of food to that?"

Jaenelle's head popped out of the kitchen doorway. "How does a large slice of fresh bread soaked in beef broth sound?"

About as edible as the table leg. "Do I have any choices?"

"No."

"Sounds wonderful."

She returned a few minutes later, helped him shift from the stool to a straight-backed chair that supported his back, then placed a large mug on the pine table. "It's a healing brew."

His lip curled in a silent snarl. Every healing brew he'd ever had forced down his throat had always tasted like brambles and piss, and he'd reached the opinion that Healers made them that way as a penalty for being hurt or ill.

"You don't get anything else until you drink it," Jaenelle added with a distasteful lack of sympathy.

Lucivar lifted the cup and sniffed cautiously. It smelled . . . different. He took a sip, held it in his mouth for a moment, then closed his eyes and swallowed. And wondered how she'd distilled into a healing brew the solid strength of the Askavi mountains, the trees and grasses and flowers that fleshed out the earth beneath, the rivers that flowed through the land.

"This is wonderful," he murmured.

"I'm pleased you approve."

"Really, it is," he insisted, responding to the laughter in her voice. "These things usually taste awful, and this tastes good."

Her laughter turned to puzzlement. "They're supposed to taste good, Lucivar. Otherwise, no one would want to drink them."

Not being able to argue with that, he said nothing, content to sip the brew. He was even content enough to feel a mild tolerance for the bowl of broth-soaked bread that Jaenelle placed in front of him, a tolerance that sharpened considerably when he noticed the slivers of beef sprinkled over the bread.

Then he noticed she was going to eat the same thing.

"I'm not the only one you drained to the limit in order to do this healing, am I, Cat?" he said quietly, unable to completely mask the anger underneath. How dare she risk herself this way, when there was no one to look after her?

Her cheeks colored faintly. She fiddled with her spoon, poked at the bread, and finally shrugged. "It was worth it."

He stabbed at the bread as another thought occurred to him. He'd let that wait for a moment. He tasted the bread and broth. "Not only do you make a good healing brew, you're also a decent cook."

She smacked the bread with her spoon, sending up a small geyser of broth. Wiping up the mess, she let out a hurt sniff and glared at him. "Mrs. Beale made this. I can't cook."

Lucivar took another mouthful and shrugged. "Cooking isn't that difficult." Then he looked up and wondered if a grown man had ever been beaten to death with a soup spoon.

"You can cook?" she asked ominously. Then she huffed. "Why do so many males know how to cook?"

He bit his tongue to keep from saying, "self-preservation." He ate a couple more spoonfuls of bread and broth. "I'll teach you to cook—on one condition."

"What condition?"

In the moment before he answered, he sensed a brittle fragility within her, but he could only respond as the Warlord Prince he was. "The bed's big enough for both of us," he said quietly, aware of how quickly she paled. "If you're not comfortable with that, fine. But if someone's going to sleep in front of the hearth, it's going to be me."

He saw the flash of temper, quickly reined in.

"You need the bed," she said through gritted teeth. "The healing isn't done yet."

"Since there's no one else here to look after you, I, as a Warlord Prince, have the duty and the privilege of overseeing your care." He was invoking ancient customs long ignored in Terreille, but he knew by her frustrated snarl that they still applied in Kaeleer.

"All right," she said, hiding her shaking hands in her lap. "We'll share the bed."

"And the blankets," he added.

The hostile look combined with the suppressed smile told him she wasn't sure what to think about him. That was all right. He wasn't sure, either.

"I suppose you want a pillow, too."

He smiled that lazy, arrogant smile. "Of course. And I promise not to kick you if you snore."

With her command of the Eyrien language, the girl could have made a Master of a hunting camp blush.

It hit him later, when he was comfortably settled on his belly in the bed, his wings open and gently supported, and Jaenelle and the wolves were out doing walkies—a silly word that struck him as an accurate description of the intricate, furry dance three wolves would perform around her while taking a late afternoon stroll.

He had made the Khaldharon Run intending to die and, instead, not only had survived but had found the living myth, his dreamed-of Queen.

Even as he smiled, the tears began, hot and bitter.

He was alive. And Jaenelle was alive. But Daemon . . .

He didn't know what had happened at Cassandra's Altar, or how that sheet had gotten drenched with Jaenelle's blood, or what Daemon had done, but he was beginning to understand what it had cost.

Pressing his face into the pillow to muffle the sobs, squeezing his eyes shut to deny the images his mind con-

jured, he saw Daemon. In Pruul that night, exhausted but
determined. In the ruins of SaDiablo Hall in Terreille,
burned out by the nightmare of madness and ready to die.
He heard again Daemon's frightened, enraged denial.
Heard again that anguished cry rising from the broken
stones.

If he hadn't been so chained by bitterness that night, if
he'd left with Daemon, they would have found a way
through the Gates. Together, they would have. And they
would have found her and had these years with her, watching her grow up, participating in the experiences that would
transform a child into a woman, a Queen.

He would still do that. He would be with her during the
final years of that transformation and would know the joy
of serving her.

But Daemon . . .

Lucivar bit the pillow, muffling his own scream of
anguish.

But Daemon . . .

CHAPTER
TEN

1 / Kaeleer

Lucivar stood at the edge of the woods, not quite ready to step across the line that divided forest shadow from sun-drenched meadow. The day was warm enough to appreciate shade. Besides, Jaenelle was away on some kind of obligatory trip so there was no reason to hurry back.

Smoke trotted up, chose a tree, lifted a leg, and looked expectantly at Lucivar.

"I marked territory a ways back," Lucivar said.

Smoke's snort was a clear indication of what wolves thought about a human's ability to mark territory properly.

Amused, Lucivar waited until Smoke trotted off before stepping into the sunlight and spreading his wings to let them dry fully. The spring-fed pool Jaenelle had shown him wasn't quite warm enough yet, but he'd enjoyed the brisk dip.

He fanned his wings slowly, savoring the movement. He was halfway through the healing. If everything continued to go well, next week he would test his wings in flight. It was hard to be patient, but, at the end of the day, when he felt the good, quiet ache in his muscles, he knew Jaenelle was setting the right pace for the healing.

Folding his wings, Lucivar set off for the cabin at an easy pace.

Lulled by earlier physical activity and the day's warmth, it took him a moment to realize something wasn't right about the way the two young wolves raced toward him.

Jaenelle had taught him how to communicate with the kindred, and he'd been flattered when she'd told him they were highly selective about which humans they would speak to. But now, bracing himself as the wolves ran toward him, he wondered how much their opinion of him depended upon her presence.

A minute later he was engulfed in fur, fighting for balance while the wolf behind him wrapped its forelegs around his waist and pushed him forward and the one in front of him placed its paws on his shoulders and leaned hard against him, earnestly licking his face and whimpering for reassurance.

Their thoughts banged against his mind, too upset to be coherent.

The Lady had returned. The bad thing was going to happen. They were afraid. Smoke guarding, waiting for Lucivar. Lucivar come now. He was human. He would help the Lady.

Lucivar got untangled enough to start walking quickly toward the cabin. They didn't say she was hurt, so she wasn't wounded. But something bad was going to happen. Something that made them afraid to enter the cabin and be with her.

He remembered how uneasy Smoke had been when Jaenelle told them she was leaving for a few days.

Something bad. Something a human would make better.

He sincerely hoped they were right.

He opened the cabin door and understood why the wolves were afraid.

She sat in the rocking chair in front of the hearth, just staring.

The psychic pain in the room staggered him. The psychic shield around her felt deceptively passive, as easy to brush aside as a cobweb. Beneath the passivity, however, lay something that, if unleashed, would extract a brutal price.

Pulling his wings in tight, Lucivar carefully circled around the shield until he stood in front of her.

The Black Jewel around her neck glowed with deadly fire.

He shook, not sure if he was afraid for himself or for her. He closed his eyes and made rash promises to the Darkness to keep from being sick on the spot.

Having lived in Terreille most of his life, he recognized someone who had been tortured. He didn't think she'd been physically harmed, but there were subtle kinds of abuse that were just as destructive. Certainly, her body had paid a terrible price over the past four days. The weight she'd put on had been consumed along with the muscle she'd built up by working with him. Her skin was stretched too tight over her face and looked fragile enough to tear. Her eyes . . .

He couldn't stand what he saw in those eyes.

She sat there, quietly bleeding to death from a soul wound, and he didn't know how to help her, didn't know if there was anything he *could* do that would help her.

"Cat?" he called softly. "Cat?"

He felt her revulsion when she finally looked at him, saw the emotions writhing and twisting in those haunted, bottomless eyes.

She blinked. Sank her teeth into her lower lip hard enough to draw blood. Blinked again. "Lucivar." Neither a question nor a statement, but an identification painfully drawn up from some deep well inside her. "Lucivar." Tears filled her eyes. "Lucivar?" A plea for comfort.

"Drop the shield, Cat." He watched her struggle to understand him. Sweet Darkness, she was so young. "Drop the shield. Let me in."

The shield dissolved. So did she. But she was in his arms before the first heart-tearing sob began. He settled them in the rocking chair and held her tight, murmuring soothing nothings, trying to rub warmth into icy limbs.

When the sobs eased to sniffles, he rubbed his cheek against her hair. "Cat, I think I should take you to your father's house."

"No!" She pushed at him, struggling to get free.

Her nails could have opened him to the bone. The venom in her snake tooth could have killed him twice over. One surge of the Black Jewels could have blown apart his inner barriers and left him a drooling husk.

Instead, she struggled futilely against a stronger body. That told him more about her temperament than anything else she might have done—and also explained why this had happened in the first place. Her temper had probably slipped once and the result had scared the shit out of her. Now she didn't trust herself to display *any* anger—even in self-defense. Well, he *could* do something about *that.*

"Cat—"

"No." She gave one more push. Then, too weak to fight anymore, she collapsed against him.

"Why?" He could think of one reason she was afraid to go home.

The words spilled out of her. "I know I look bad. I know. That's why I can't go home now. If Papa saw me, he'd be upset. He'd want to know what happened, and I can't tell him that, Lucivar. I can't. He'd be so angry, and he'd have another fight with the Dark Council and they'd just cause more trouble for him."

To Lucivar's way of thinking, having her father explode in a murderous rage over what had been done to her would be all to the good. Unfortunately, Jaenelle didn't share his way of thinking. She'd rather endure something that devastated her than cause trouble between her beloved papa and the Dark Council. That might suit her and the Dark Council and her papa, but it didn't suit him.

"That's not good enough, Cat," he said, keeping his voice low. "Either you tell me what happened, or I bundle you up and take you to your father right now."

Jaenelle sniffed. "You don't know where he is."

"Oh, I'm sure if I create enough of a fuss, someone will be happy to tell me where to find the Warlord Prince of Dhemlan."

Jaenelle studied his face. "You're a prick, Lucivar."

He smiled that lazy, arrogant smile. "I told you that the first time we met." He waited a minute, hoping he wouldn't have to prod her and knowing he would. "Which is it going to be, Cat?"

She squirmed. He could understand that. If someone had cornered him the way he'd cornered her, he'd squirm, too. He sensed she wanted physical distance between them before explaining, but he figured he'd hear something closer to the truth if she remained captured on his lap.

Finally giving up, she fluffed her hair and sighed. "When I was twelve, I was hurt very badly—"

Was that how they had explained the rape to her? Being hurt?

"—and Papa became my legal guardian." She seemed to have a hard time breathing, and her voice thinned until, even sitting that close, he had to strain to hear her. "I woke up—came back to my body—two years later. I . . . was different when I came back, but Papa helped me rebuild my life piece by piece. He found teachers for me and encouraged my old friends to visit and he u-understood me." Her voice turned bitter. "But the Dark Council didn't think Papa was a suitable guardian and they tried to take me away from him and the rest of the family, so I stopped them and they had to let me stay with Papa."

Stopped them. Lucivar turned over the possibilities of how she could have stopped them. Apparently, she hadn't done quite enough.

"To placate the Council, I agreed to spend one week each season socializing with the aristo families in Little Terreille."

"Which doesn't explain why you came back in this condition," Lucivar said quietly. He rubbed her arm, trying to warm her up. He was sweating. She still shivered.

"It's like living in Terreille again," she whispered. The haunted look filled her eyes. "No, worse than that. It's like living in—" She paused, puzzled.

"Even aristos in Little Terreille have to eat," he said gently.

Her eyes glazed over. Her voice sounded hollow. "Can't trust the food. Never trust the food. Even if you test it, you can't always sense the badness until it's too late. Can't sleep. Mustn't sleep. But they get to you anyway. Lies are true, and truth is punished. Bad girl. Sick-mind girl to make up such lies."

An icy fist pressed into Lucivar's lower back as he wondered what nightmare in the inner landscape she was wandering through right now.

Capturing her chin between his thumb and finger, Lucivar turned her head, forcing her to look at him. "You're not a bad girl, you're not sick, and you don't lie," he said firmly.

She blinked. Confusion filled her eyes. "What?"

Would she understand if he told her what she'd said? He doubted it. "So the food is lousy and you don't sleep well. That still doesn't explain why you came back in this shape. What did they do to you, Cat?"

"Nothing," she whispered, closing her eyes. Her throat worked convulsively. "It's just that boys expect to be kissed and—"

"They expect *what*?" Lucivar snarled.

"—I'm f-f-frigid and—"

"Frigid!" Lucivar roared, ignoring her frightened squeak. "You're seventeen years old. Those strutting little sons of whoring bitches shouldn't be trying *anything* with you that would even bring up the question of whether or not you're 'frigid.' And where in the name of Hell were the chaperons?"

He rocked furiously, petting her hair with one hand while his other arm tightened protectively around her. Her yip of pain when he accidentally pinched her arm snapped him out of a red haze. He muttered an apology, resettled her in his lap, and began rocking at a more soothing tempo. After a couple of minutes, he shook his head.

"Frigid," he said with a snort of disgust. "Well, Cat, if objecting to having someone slobber on you or grope and squeeze you is their definition of frigid, then I'm frigid, too. They have no right to use you, no matter what they say. Any man who tells you otherwise deserves a knife between the ribs." He gave her a considering look, then shook his head. "You'd probably find it hard to gut a man. That's all right. I don't."

Jaenelle stared at him, wide-eyed.

He wrapped his hand around the back of her neck and massaged gently. "Listen to me, Cat, because I'll only say this once. You're the finest Lady I've ever met and the dearest friend I've ever had. Besides that, I love you like a brother, and any bastard who hurts my little sister is going to answer to me."

"Y-you can't," she whispered. "The agreement—"

"I'm not part of that damn agreement." He gave her a little shake, wondering how he could get that frail, bruised look out of her eyes. Then he squelched a grin. He'd do what he'd do with any feline he wanted to spark—rub her the wrong way. "Besides, Lady," he said in a courteous snarl, "you broke a solemn promise to me, and breaking a promise to a Warlord Prince is a serious offense."

Her eyes flashed fire. He could almost feel her back arch and the nonexistent fur stand on end. Maybe he wouldn't have to dig that hard to bring a little of her temper to the surface.

"I never did!"

"Yes, you did. I distinctly remember teaching you what to do—"

"They weren't standing behind me!"

Lucivar narrowed his eyes. "You don't have any human male friends?"

"Of course I do!"

"And not one of them has ever taken you behind the barn and taught you what to do with your knee?"

Her fingernails suddenly required her attention.

"That's what I thought," Lucivar said dryly. "So I'll give you a choice. If one of those fine, rutting aristo males does something you don't like, you can give him a hard knee in the balls or I can start with his feet and end with his neck and break every bone in between."

"You couldn't."

"It's not that difficult. I've done it before."

He waited a minute, then tapped her chin. She closed her mouth.

Then she seemed to shrink into herself. "But, Lucivar," she said weakly, "what if it's my fault that he's aroused and needs relief?"

He snorted, amused. "You didn't actually fall for that, did you?"

Her eyes narrowed to slits.

"I don't know how things are in Kaeleer, but it used to

be, in Terreille, that a young man could register at a Red Moon house and not only get his 'relief' but also learn how to do more than a thirty-second poke and hump."

She made a choking sound that might have been a suppressed laugh.

"And if they can't afford a Red Moon house, they can get their own 'relief' easily enough."

"How?"

Lucivar suppressed a grin. Sometimes catching her interest was as easy as rolling a ball of yarn in front of a kitten. "I'm not sure an older brother is the right person to explain that," he said primly.

She studied him. "You don't like sex, do you?"

"Not my experience of it, no." He traced her fingers, needing to be honest. "But I've always thought that if I cared about a woman, it would be wonderful to give her that kind of pleasure." He shook himself and set her on her feet. "Enough of this. You need to eat and get your strength back. There's beef soup and a loaf of fresh bread."

Jaenelle paled. "It won't stay down. It never does after . . ."

"Try."

When they sat down to eat, she managed three spoonfuls of soup and one mouthful of bread before she bolted into the bathroom.

His own appetite gone, Lucivar cleared the table. He was pouring the soup back into the pan when Smoke slunk into the kitchen.

Lucivar?

Lucivar lifted his bowl of soup. "You want some of this?"

Smoke ignored the offer. *Bad dreams come now. Hurt the Lady. She not talk to us, not see us, not want males near. Not eat, not sleep, walk walk walk, snarl at us. Bad dreams now, Lucivar.*

Do the bad dreams always come after one of these visits? Lucivar asked, narrowing his thoughts to a spear thread.

Smoke bared his teeth in a silent snarl. *Always.*

Lucivar's stomach clenched. So it didn't end once she got

away from Little Terreille. *How long?* The kindred had a fluid sense of time, but Smoke, at least, understood basic divisions of day and night.

Smoke cocked his head. *Night, day, night, day . . . maybe night.*

So she'd spend tonight and the next two days trying to outrun the nightmares hovering at the edge of her vision by depleting an already exhausted body that she would mercilessly flog until it collapsed under the strain of no food, no water, no rest. What kind of dreams could drive a young woman to such masochistic cruelty?

He found out that night.

The change in her breathing snapped him out of a light sleep. Propping himself up on one arm, he reached for her shoulder.

Can't wake when bad dreams come. Standing at the foot of the bed, Smoke's eyes caught the moonlight.

Why?

Not see us. Not know us. All dreams.

Lucivar swore under his breath. If every sound, every touch got sucked into the dreamscape . . .

Jaenelle's body arched like a tightly strung bow.

He studied the clenched, straining muscles and swore again. She'd be hurting sore in the morning.

The tension went out of her body. She collapsed against the mattress, twitching, moaning, sweat-soaked.

He had to wake her up. If it took throwing her into a cold shower or walking her around the meadow for the rest of the night, he was going to wake her up.

He reached out again . . . and she began to talk.

Every word was a physical blow as the memories poured out.

His head bowed, his body flinching, he listened as she talked about and to Marjane, Myrol and Rebecca, Dannie, and, especially, Rose. He listened to the horrors a child had witnessed and endured in a place called Briarwood. He listened to the names of the men who had hurt her, hurt them all. And he suffered with her as she relived the rape that had torn her apart physically and had shattered her mind, the rape that had made her desperately try to sever the link between body and spirit.

As she plunged once again into an abyss beyond reach, she took a deep, ragged breath, murmured a name, and was still.

He watched her for several minutes until he felt reasonably sure she was just sleeping deeply. Then he went into the bathroom and was quietly, but thoroughly, sick.

He rinsed out his mouth, padded into the kitchen, and poured a generous dose of whiskey. Naked, he stepped onto the porch and let the night air dry the sweat from his skin while he sipped his drink.

Smoke came out of the cabin, standing so close his fur tickled Lucivar's bare leg. The two young wolves remained huddled at the far end of the porch.

She never remembers, does she? Lucivar asked Smoke.

No. The Darkness is kind.

Maybe she just wasn't ready to face those memories. He certainly wasn't going to push her. But he had the uneasy feeling that the day would come when someone or something would force that door open and she would have to face her past. Until then, there were some things he would hold in silence—and he hoped she would forgive him.

He'd heard pain when she'd talked about the men who had hurt her. He'd heard pain when she'd talked about the man who had raped her.

But the only time she'd mentioned Daemon, his name had sounded like a promise, like a caress.

Blinking back tears and leashing his guilt, Lucivar finished the whiskey and turned to go back inside.

2 / Kaeleer

Lucivar settled on the tree stump that marked the usual halfway point for walkies. Summer was over. The healing was complete. Two days ago, he had successfully made the Khaldharon Run. Yesterday, he and Jaenelle had gone to the Fyreborn Islands to play with the small dragons who lived there. He would have happily spent today being lazy, but something had pushed Jaenelle out of the cabin the moment they'd returned this morning, and the way she shied away from his questions told him it had to do with him.

Well, if you couldn't entice the kitten with a ball of yarn, you certainly could provoke her with a fast dunk in a tub of cold water.

"You could have warned me, Cat."

Jaenelle bristled. "I *told* you to watch your angle when you whomped that wave." Her eyes flicked to his right side. She chewed her lower lip. "Lucivar, that bruise looks awfully nasty. Are you sure—"

"I wasn't talking about the wave," Lucivar said through his teeth. "I was talking about the pickleberries."

"Oh." Jaenelle sat down near the tree stump. She gave him a slanty-eyed look. "Well, I did think the name was sufficient warning so that a person wouldn't just sink his teeth into one."

"I was thirsty. You said they were juicy."

"They are," Jaenelle pointed out so reasonably that he wanted to belt her. She wrapped her arms around her knees. "The dragons were extremely impressed by the sounds you made. They wondered if you were demonstrating territorial claims or a mating challenge."

Lucivar shuddered at the memory of biting into that aptly named fruit. Juicy, yes. When he'd bitten into it, the juice had flooded his mouth with golden sweetness for a moment before the tartness made his teeth curl and his throat close. He'd stomped and howled so much he could understand why the dragons thought he'd been showing them examples of Eyrien display. To add to the insult, the dragons had chomped on pickleberries throughout that whole damn performance while Jaenelle had nibbled daintily and watched with wide-eyed apprehension.

The little traitor. She was sitting close enough to reach, the trusting little fool. No weapons. He wanted his bare hands on her. Strangling would be too quick, too permanent. Pulling her across his lap and whacking her ass until his hand got hot . . .

She shifted her hips, putting her just out of reach.

Lucivar bared his teeth in a smile, acknowledging the movement.

Shifting a little farther, she began to pluck grass. "I gave Mrs. Beale a pickleberry once," she said in a small voice.

Lucivar stared at the meadow. Over the past three months, he'd heard plenty of stories about the cook who worked for Jaenelle's family. "Did you tell her what it's called?"

"No." A small, pleased smile curved Jaenelle's lips.

He clenched his teeth. "What happened?"

"Well, Papa asked me if I had any idea why those sounds were coming from the kitchen and I said I did have some idea and he said 'I see,' stuffed me into one of our private Coaches, and told Khary to take me to Morghann's house since Scelt was on the other side of the Realm."

Struggling to keep a straight face, Lucivar clamped his right hand over his left wrist hard enough to hurt. It helped.

"The next morning, Mrs. Beale cornered Papa in his study and told him that I'd given her a sample of a new kind of fruit and, having thought about it, she'd decided that it would enhance the flavor of a number of common dishes and she'd appreciate having some. Then she set a wicker basket on Papa's desk and Papa had to tell her that he didn't know where the fruit came from and Mrs. Beale pointed out that, obviously, I did, and Papa just as politely pointed out that I was not at home at the moment and Mrs. Beale suggested that he and her wicker basket go find me and bring back the desired fruit. So he did and we did and because the Fyreborn Islands are a closed Territory, Mrs. Beale is envied by other cooks for her ability to produce this unique taste in the food she prepares."

Lucivar rubbed his head vigorously, then smoothed back his shoulder-length black hair. "Does Mrs. Beale outrank your father?"

"Not by a long shot," Jaenelle said tartly, and then added plaintively, "It's just that she's rather . . . *large*."

"I'd like to meet Mrs. Beale. I think I'm in love." He looked at Jaenelle's horrified expression, fell off the stump, and laughed himself silly. He laughed even harder when she poked him, and said worriedly, "You were joking, weren't you, Lucivar? Lucivar?"

With a whoop, he yanked her down on top of him and wrapped his arms around her tight enough to hold her and loose enough not to panic her. "You should have been Eyrien," he said once his laughter had settled to a quiet simmer. "You've got the brass for it."

Then he smoothed her hair away from her face. "What is it, Cat?" he asked quietly. "What am I going to find so bitter to swallow that you wanted to give me this burst of sweetness first?"

Jaenelle traced his collarbone. "You're healed now."

He could almost taste her reluctance. "So?"

She rolled away from him and leaped to her feet, a movement so graceful nothing tame could have made it.

He rose more slowly, snapped his wings open to clear away the dust and bits of grass, settled on the tree stump again, and waited.

"Even after the war between Terreille and Kaeleer, people came through the Gates," Jaenelle said quietly, her eyes fixed on the horizon. "Mostly those who'd been born in the wrong place and were seeking 'home.' And there's always been some trading between Terreille and Little Terreille.

"A couple of years ago, the Dark Council decided to allow more open contact with Terreille, and aristo Blood began pouring in to see the Shadow Realm. The number of lower-ranking Blood wanting to immigrate to Kaeleer should have warned the Council about what courts are like in Terreille, but Little Terreille opened its arms to embrace the kinship ties. However, Kaeleer is not Terreille. Blood Law and Protocol can be . . . understood differently.

"Too many Terreilleans refused to understand that what they could get away with in Terreille isn't tolerated in Kaeleer, and they died.

"A year ago, in Dharo, three Terreillean males raped a young witch for sport. Raped her until her mind was so broken there was no one left to sing back to the body. She was my age."

Lucivar concentrated on his clenched hands, forcing them to open. "Did they catch the bastards who did it?"

Jaenelle smiled grimly. "The Dharo males executed those men. Then they banished the rest of the Terreilleans in Dharo, sending them back to Little Terreille. Within six months, the fatality rate for Terreilleans in most Territories was over ninety percent. Even in Little Terreille it was over half. Since the slaughter strained good feelings between the Realms, the Dark Council passed some rules of immigration. Now, a Terreillean who wants to immigrate has to serve a Kaeleer witch to her satisfaction for a specified time. Non-Jeweled Blood have to serve for eighteen months. The lighter Jewels have to serve three years, the darker Jewels five. Queens and Warlord Princes of any rank have to serve five years."

Lucivar felt sick. His body shook. He felt detached sympathy for it. *To her satisfaction.* That meant the bitch could do anything to him and he would have to allow it if he wanted to stay in Kaeleer.

He tried to laugh. It sounded panicked.

She knelt beside him and petted him anxiously. "Lucivar, it won't be so bad. Truly. The Queens. . . . Serving in Kaeleer isn't like serving in Terreille. I know all of the Territory Queens. I'll help you find someone who suits you, someone you'll enjoy serving."

"Why can't I serve you?" He spread his hands over her shoulders, needing her to be his anchor as he fought against hurt and panic. "You like me—at least some of the time. And we work well together."

"Oh, Lucivar," Jaenelle said gently, cupping his face in her hands. "I always like you. Even when you're being a pain in the ass. But you should have the experience of serving in a Kaeleer court."

"You'll be setting up your court in a year or two."

"I'm not going to have a court. I don't want to have that kind of power over someone else's life. Besides, you don't want to serve me. You don't know about me, don't understand—"

He lost patience. "What? That you're Witch?"

She looked shocked.

He rubbed her shoulders, and said dryly, "Wearing the Black at your age makes it rather obvious, Cat. Anyway, I've known who, and what, you were since I met you." He tried to smile. "The night we met, I'd asked the Darkness for a strong Queen I'd be proud to serve, and there you were. Of course, you were a bit younger than I'd imagined, but I wasn't going to be picky about it. Cat, please. I've waited a lifetime to serve you. I'll do anything you want. Please don't send me away."

Jaenelle closed her eyes and rested her head against his chest. "It's not that easy, Lucivar. Even if you can accept what I am—"

"I *do* accept what you are."

"There are other reasons why you might not be willing to serve me."

Something inside him settled. He understood the custom of passing tests or challenges in order to earn a privilege. Whether she realized it or not, she was offering him a chance. "How many?"

She looked at him blankly.

"How many reasons? Set a number, now. If I can accept them, then I can choose to serve you. That's fair."

She gave him a strange look. "And will you be honest with yourself as well as with me about whether you can really accept them?"

"Yes."

She pulled away from him, sitting just out of reach. After several minutes of tense silence, she said, "Three."

Three. Not a dozen or so to natter about. Just three. Which meant he had to take them seriously. "All right. When?"

Jaenelle flowed to her feet. "Now. Pack a bag and plan to stay overnight." She headed for the cabin at a swift pace.

Lucivar followed her but didn't try to catch up. Three tests would determine the next five years of his life.

She'd be fair. Whether she liked the end result or not, she'd be fair. And so would he.

As he approached the cabin, the wolves ran out to greet him, offering furry comfort to the adopted member of their pack.

Lucivar buried his hands in their fur. If he had to serve someone else, would he ever see them again?

He would be honest. He wouldn't abuse her trust in him.

But he was going to win.

3 / Kaeleer

Lucivar's heart pounded against his chest. He had never been inside the Keep, not even an outside courtyard. A half-breed bastard wasn't worthy of entering this place. If he'd learned nothing else in the Eyrien hunting camps, he'd learned that, no matter what Jewels he wore or how skilled he was with weapons, his birth made him unworthy to lick the boots of the ones who lived in Ebon Askavi, the Black Mountain.

Now he was here, walking beside Jaenelle through massive rooms with vaulted ceilings, through open courtyards and gardens, through a labyrinth of wide corridors—and the prickle between his shoulder blades told him that something had been watching him since he entered the Keep. Something that flitted inside the stone, hid inside shadows, created shadows where shadows shouldn't exist. Not malevolent—at least, not yet. But the stories about what guarded the Keep were the fireside tales that frightened young boys sleepless.

Lucivar twitched his shoulders and followed his Lady.

By the time they reached the upper levels that appeared to be more inhabited, Lucivar began wistfully eyeing the benches and chairs that lined the corridors and promising himself a drink of water from the next indoor fountain or decorative waterfall they came to.

Jaenelle had said nothing since they'd stepped off the landing web in the outer courtyard. Her silence was supportive but not comforting. He understood that. Ebon Askavi was Witch's home. If he served her, he had to come to terms with the place without leaning on her.

She reached an intersection of corridors, glanced left, and smiled. "Hello, Draca. This is Lucivar Yaslana. Lucivar, this is Draca, the Keep's Seneschal."

Draca's psychic scent, filled with great age and old, dark power, unnerved him as much as the reptilian cast of her features. He bowed respectfully, but was too nervous to speak a proper greeting.

Her unblinking eyes stared at him. He caught a whiff of emotion that unraveled his nerves even more. For some reason, he amused her.

"Sso, you have finally come," Draca said. When Lucivar didn't answer, she turned to Jaenelle. "He iss sshy?"

"Hardly that," Jaenelle said dryly, looking amused. "But a bit overwhelmed, I think. I gave him the long tour of the Keep."

"And he iss sstill sstanding?" Draca sounded approving.

Lucivar would have appreciated her approval more if his legs weren't shaking so badly.

"We have guestss. Sscholarss. You will wissh to dine privately?"

"Yes, thank you," Jaenelle said.

Draca stepped aside, moving with careful, ancient grace. "I will let you continue your journey." She stared at Lucivar again. "Welcome, Prince Yasslana."

Jaenelle led him down another maze of corridors. "There's someone else I want you to meet. By then, Draca will have a guest room ready for you, one with a whirlbath. It'll be good for those tight leg muscles." She studied his face. "Did she intimidate you?"

He'd promised honesty. "Yes."

Jaenelle shook her head, baffled. "Everyone says that. I don't understand. She's a marvelous person when you get to know her."

He glanced at the Black Jewel hanging above the V neckline of her slim, black tunic-sweater and decided against trying to explain it.

After another flight of stairs and several twists and turns, Jaenelle finally stopped in front of a door. He sincerely hoped their destination was behind it. A door stood open at the end of the corridor. Voices drifted out of the room, enthusiastic and hot, but not angry. Must be the scholars.

Ignoring the voices, Jaenelle opened the door, and they stepped into part of the Keep's library. A large blackwood table filled one side of the room. At the other end were comfortable chairs and small tables. The back wall was a series of large arches. Beyond them, stacks of reference books stretched out of sight. The arch on the far right was fitted with a wooden door.

"The rest of the library is general reference, Craft, folklore, and history," Jaenelle said. "Things anyone can come and use. These rooms contain the older reference material, the more esoteric Craft texts, and the Blood registers, and can only be used with Geoffrey's permission."

"Geoffrey?"

"Yes?" said a quiet baritone voice.

He was the palest man Lucivar had ever seen. Skin like polished marble combined with black hair, black eyes, black clothes, and deep red lips that looked inviting in an unnerving sort of way. But there was something strange about his psychic scent, something inexplicably different. Almost as if the man weren't . . .

Guardian.

The word slammed into Lucivar, freezing his lungs.

Guardian. One of the living dead.

Jaenelle made the introductions. Then she smiled at Geoffrey. "Why don't you get acquainted? There's something I want to look up."

Geoffrey looked pained. "At least tell me the name of the volume before you leave. The last time I couldn't tell your father where you 'looked something up,' he treated me to some eloquent phrases that would have made me blush if I was still capable of doing it."

Jaenelle patted Geoffrey's shoulder and kissed his cheek. "I'll bring the book out and even mark the page for you."

"So kind of you."

Laughing, Jaenelle disappeared into the stacks.

Geoffrey turned to Lucivar. "So. You've finally come."

Why did they make him feel like he'd kept them waiting?

Geoffrey lifted a decanter. "Would you like some yarbarah? Or some other refreshment?"

With some effort, Lucivar found his voice. "Yarbarah's fine."

"Have you ever drunk yarbarah?" Geoffrey asked drolly.

"It's drunk during some Eyrien ceremonies." Of course, the cup used for those ceremonies held a mouthful of the blood wine. Geoffrey, he noted apprehensively, was filling and warming two wineglasses.

"It's lamb," Geoffrey said, handing a glass to Lucivar and settling into a chair beside the table.

Lucivar gratefully sank into a chair opposite Geoffrey and sipped the yarbarah. There was more blood in the mixture than was used in the ceremonies, the wine more full-bodied.

"How do you like it?" Geoffrey's black eyes sparkled.

"It's . . ." Lucivar struggled to find something mild to say.

"Different," Geoffrey suggested. "It's an acquired taste, and here we drink it for other reasons than ceremonial."

Guardian. Was the blood mixed with the wine ever human? Lucivar took another swallow and decided he wasn't curious enough to ask.

"Why have you never come to the Keep, Lucivar?"

Lucivar set the glass down carefully. "I was under the impression a half-breed bastard wouldn't be welcome here."

"I see," Geoffrey said mildly. "Except for those who care for the Keep, who has the right to decide who is welcome and who is not?"

Lucivar forced himself to meet Geoffrey's eyes. "I'm a half-breed bastard," he said again, as if that should explain everything.

"Half-breed." Geoffrey sounded as if he were turning the word over and over. "The way you say it, it sounds insulting. Perhaps dual bloodline would be a more accurate way to think of it." He leaned back, cradling the wineglass in both hands. "Has it ever occurred to you that, without that other bloodline, you wouldn't be the man you are? That you wouldn't have the intelligence and strength you have?" He waved his glass at Lucivar's Ebon-gray Jewel. "That you never would have worn those? For all that you are Eyrien, Lucivar, you are also your father's son."

Lucivar froze. "You know my father?" he asked in a choked voice.

"We've been friends for many years."

It was there, in front of him. All he had to do was ask. It took him two tries to get the word out. "Who?"

"The Prince of the Darkness," Geoffrey said gently. "The High Lord of Hell. It's Saetan's bloodline that runs through your veins."

Lucivar closed his eyes. No wonder his paternity had never been registered. Who would have believed a woman who claimed to be seeded by the High Lord? And if anyone *had* believed her, imagine the panic that would have caused. Saetan still walked the Realms. Mother Night!

Had Daemon ever learned who had sired them? He would have been pleased with *this* paternal bloodline.

The thought lanced through him. He locked it away.

At least there was one thing he was still sure of. Maybe. He looked at Geoffrey, afraid of either answer. "I'm still a bastard."

Geoffrey sighed. "I'm reluctant to pull the rest of the ground out from under you but, no, you're not. He formally registered you the day after you were born. Here, at the Keep."

He wasn't a bastard. They . . . "Daemon?" Had he said it out loud?

"Registered as well."

Mother Night. They weren't bastards. He scrambled, clawing for solid ground that kept turning into quicksand under him. "Doesn't make any difference since no one else knew."

"Have you ever been encouraged to play stud, Lucivar?"

Encouraged, pressured, imprisoned, punished, drugged, beaten, forced. They'd been able to use him, but they'd never been able to breed him. He'd never known if the reason was physical or if, somehow, his own rage had kept him sterile. He'd wondered sometimes why they'd wanted his seed so badly. Knowing who had sired him and the potential strength of any offspring he might produce. . . . Yes, they'd overlook a great deal to have him sire offspring for specific covens, specific aristo houses with failing bloodlines.

He gulped the yarbarah. Cold, it tasted thick. Shaking

and choking, he wondered if his stomach was going to stay down.

A small water glass and another decanter appeared. "Here," Geoffrey said as he quickly filled the glass and shoved it into Lucivar's hand. "I believe whiskey is the proper drink for this kind of shock."

The whiskey cleansed his mouth and burned all the way down. He held out the glass for a refill.

By the time he drained his fourth glass, he was still shaking, but he also felt fuzzy and numb. He liked fuzzy and numb.

"What did you do to Lucivar?" Jaenelle asked, dropping the book on the table. "I thought I was the only one who made him look like that."

"Fuzzy and numb," Lucivar murmured, resting his head against her.

"So I see," Jaenelle replied, petting him.

A soft warmth surrounded him. That felt nice, too.

"Come on, Lucivar," Jaenelle said. "Let's tuck you into a bed."

He didn't want her to think four paltry glasses of whiskey could put him under the table, so he stood up.

The last things he clearly remembered seeing before the room began moving in unpredictable ways were Geoffrey's gentle smile and the understanding in Jaenelle's eyes.

4 / Kaeleer

Jaenelle was gone before he woke the next morning, leaving him to deal with a throbbing head and the emotional upheaval on his own. When he'd found out she'd left him at the Keep, he'd come close to hating her, silently accusing her of being cold, cruel, and unfeeling.

He spent the two days she was gone exploring the Keep and the mountain called Ebon Askavi. He returned for meals because he was expected to, spoke only when required, and retreated to his room each evening. The wolves offered silent company. He petted and brushed them and, finally, asked the question that had bothered him.

Yes, Smoke told him reluctantly, Lucivar had cried. Heart pain. Caught-in-a-trap pain. The Lady had petted and petted, sung and sung.

It had been more than a dream, then.

In one of the dreamscapes Black Widows spun so well, Jaenelle had met the boy he had been and had drawn the poison from the soul wound. He had wept for the boy, for the things he hadn't been allowed to do, for the things he hadn't been allowed to be. But he didn't weep for the man he'd become. "Ah, Lucivar," she'd said regretfully as they'd walked through the dreamscape. "I can heal the scars on your body, but I can't heal the scars of the soul. Not yours, not mine. You have to learn to live with them. You have to choose to live beyond them."

He couldn't remember anything else in the dream. Perhaps he wasn't meant to. But because of it, he didn't weep for the man he'd become.

Lucivar and Jaenelle stood on the wall of one of the Keep's outer courtyards, looking out over the valley.

Jaenelle pointed to the village below them. "Riada is the largest village in Ebon Rih. Agio is at the northern end of the valley. Doun is at the southern end. There are also several landen villages and a number of independent farmsteads, Blood and landen." She brushed stray hairs from her face. "Outside of Doun, there's a large stone house. The property's surrounded by a stone wall. You can't miss it."

He waited. "Is that where we're going?" he finally asked.

"I'm going back to the cabin. You're going to that house."

"Why?"

She kept her eyes fixed on the valley. "Your mother lives there."

A large, three-story, stone house. A low stone wall separating two acres of tended land from the wildflowers and grasses. Vegetable garden, herb garden, flower gardens, rock garden. In one corner, a stand of trees that whispered, "forest."

A solid place that should have welcomed. A place that gave no comfort. Conflicting emotions too familiar, even after all this time.

Sweet Darkness, don't let it be her.

Of course, it was her. And he wondered why she had abandoned him when he was so young he couldn't remember her and then tolerated his visits as a youth without ever once hinting that she was his mother.

He pushed the kitchen door wide open but remained outside. Until he crossed the threshold, she wouldn't realize he was there. How many times had he suggested that she extend her territorial shield a few feet beyond the stone walls she lived in so she'd have some warning of an intruder? One time less than she'd rejected the suggestion.

Her back was to the door as she fussed with something on the counter. He recognized her anyway by that distinctive white streak in her black hair and the stiff, angry way she always moved.

He stepped into the kitchen. "Hello, Luthvian."

She whirled around, a long-bladed kitchen knife in her hand. He knew it wasn't personal. She'd caught the psychic scent of a grown male and had reached automatically for a knife.

She stared at him, her gold eyes growing wider and wider, filming with tears. "Lucivar," she whispered. She took a step toward him. Then another. She made a funny little sound between a laugh and a sob. "She did it. She actually did it." She reached for him.

Lucivar flicked a glance at the knife and didn't move toward her.

Confusion swiftly changed to anger and changed back again. He saw the moment she realized she was pointing a knife at him.

Shaking her head, Luthvian dropped the knife on the kitchen table.

Lucivar stepped farther into the kitchen.

Her tear-bright eyes roamed over him, not like a Healer studying her Sister's Craft but like a woman who truly cared. She pressed one trembling hand against her mouth and reached for him with the other.

Hopeful, heart full, he linked his hand with hers.

And she changed. As she always did, had done since the first time the youth she'd tolerated like a stray-turned-sometimes-pet showed up on her doorstep wearing the traditional dress of an Eyrien warrior, and he'd learned, painfully, that the Black Widow Healer he'd thought of as a friend didn't feel the same way about him after she could no longer call him "boy" and believe it.

Now, as she backed away from him, her eyes filled with wary distrust, he realized for the first time how young she was. Age and maturity became slippery things for the long-lived races. There was rapid growth followed by long plateaus. The white streak in her hair, her Craft skills, her temper and attitude had all helped him believe she was a mature woman granting him her company, a woman centuries older than he. And she was centuries older—and had been just old enough to breed and successfully carry a child to term.

"Why do you despise Eyrien males so much?" he asked quietly.

"My father was one."

Sadly, she didn't have to explain it any better than that.

Then he saw her do what she'd done a hundred times before—subtly shift the way her eyes focused. It was as if she created a sight shield that vanished his wings and left him without the one physical attribute that separated Eyriens from Dhemlans and Hayllians.

Swallowing his anger and a small lump of fear, he pulled out a kitchen chair and straddled it. "Even if I'd lost my wings, I'd still be an Eyrien warrior."

Moving restlessly around the kitchen, Luthvian picked up the knife and shoved it back in the knife rack. "If you'd grown up someplace where males learned how to be decent men instead of brutes—" She wiped her hands on her hips. "But you grew up in the hunting camps like the rest of them. Yes, even without your wings, you'd still be an Eyrien warrior. It's too late for you to be anything else."

He heard the bitterness, the sorrow. He heard the things that were unsaid. "If you felt that strongly, why didn't you

do something?" He kept his voice neutral. His heart was
being bruised to pulp.

She looked at him, emotions flashing through her eyes.
Resignation. Anxiety. Fear. She pulled a chair close to his
and sat down. "I had to, Lucivar," she said, pleading. "Giving you to Prythian was a mistake, but at the time I thought
it was the only way to hide you from—"

him.

She touched his hand and then pulled away as if burned.
"I wanted to keep you safe. She promised you would be
safe," she added bitterly. Then her voice turned eager.
"But you're here now, and we can be together." She waved
her hand, silencing him before he could speak. "Oh, I know
about the immigration rule, but I've been here long enough
to count as a Kaeleer witch. The work wouldn't be hard,
and you'd have plenty of time to be out on the land. I know
you like that." She smiled too brightly. "You wouldn't even
have to live in the house. We could build a small cabin
nearby so that you would have privacy."

Privacy for what? he wondered coldly as the inside
kitchen door opened. He felt walls and chains closing in
on him.

"What do you want, Roxie?" Luthvian snapped.

Roxie stared at him, her lips turning up in a pouty smile.
"Who are you?" she asked, eyeing him hungrily.

"None of your business," Luthvian said tightly. "Get
back to your lessons. *Now.*"

Roxie smiled at him, her finger tracing the V neckline of
her dress. It made his blood burn, but not the way she
imagined.

Lucivar's hands curled into fists. He'd smashed that look
off a lot of faces over the centuries. There was battle-fire
in the voice he kept low and controlled. "Get the slut out
of here before I break her neck."

Roxie's eyes widened in shock.

Luthvian surged out of her chair, tossed Roxie out of the
kitchen, and slammed the door.

Fine tremors ran through him. "Well, now I know why
I need privacy. It would be an extra selling point for your
school, wouldn't it? Your students would have the use of

a strong Warlord Prince. You could assure fretful parents that their daughters would have a safe Virgin Night. I wouldn't dare provide anything else since the witch I serve has to be served *to her satisfaction*."

"It wouldn't be like that," Luthvian insisted, gripping the back of a chair. "You'd get something out of it, too. Hell's fire, Lucivar, you're a Warlord Prince. You need sexual relief on a regular basis just to keep your temper in check."

"I've never needed it before," he snarled, "and I don't need it now. I can keep my temper in check just fine—when I choose to."

"Then you don't choose to very often!"

"No, I don't. Especially when I'm being forced into a bed."

Luthvian smashed the chair against the table. She bared her teeth. "Forced to. Oh, yes, it's such an onerous task to give a little pleasure, isn't it? Forced to! You sound like—" *your father*.

He'd tolerated her temper before, withstood her tantrums before. He'd tried to be understanding. He was trying hard now. What he couldn't understand was why a man like the High Lord had ever wanted to mount and breed such a troubled young woman.

"Tell me about my father, Luthvian."

Desperation and a keening rage flooded the kitchen. "It's past. It's done. He's not part of our lives."

"Tell me."

"He didn't want us! *He didn't love us!* He threatened to slit your throat in the cradle if I didn't do what he wanted." The length of the table stood between them. She stood there, shaking, hugging herself.

So young. So troubled. And he couldn't help her. They would destroy each other inside of a week if he tried to stay here with her.

She gave him a wavering smile. "We can be together. You can stay—"

"I'm already in service." He hadn't meant for it to come out so harshly, but it was kinder than saying he would never serve her.

Vulnerability crystallized into rejection, rejection froze

into rage. "Jaenelle," Luthvian said, her voice dangerously empty. "She has a gift for wrapping males around her little finger." She braced her hands on the table. "You want to know about your father? Go ask precious Jaenelle. She knows him better than I ever did."

Lucivar snapped to his feet, knocking the chair over. "No."

Luthvian smiled with pleased malice. "Be careful how you play with your sire's toys, little Prince. He just might snip your balls off. Not that it would matter."

Never taking his eyes off her, Lucivar righted the chair and backed away to the outer kitchen door. Years of training kept him surefooted as he crossed the threshold. One more step. Two.

The door slammed in his face.

A moment later, he heard dishes smashing on the floor.

She knows him better than I ever did.

It was late afternoon by the time he reached the cabin. He was dirty, hungry, and shaking from physical and emotional fatigue.

He approached slowly but couldn't bring himself to step onto the porch where Jaenelle sat reading.

She closed the book and looked at him.

Wise eyes. Ancient eyes. Haunting and haunted eyes.

He forced the words out. "I want to meet my father. Now."

She studied him. When she finally answered, her gentle compassion inflicted pain he had no defense against. "Are you sure, Lucivar?"

No, he wasn't sure! "Yes, I'm sure."

Jaenelle remained seated. "Then there's something you need to understand before we go."

He heard the warning underneath the gentleness and compassion.

"Lucivar, your father is also my adopted father."

Frozen, he stared at her, finally understanding. He could accept them both or walk away from both, but he wouldn't be allowed to serve her and battle with a man who already had a claim on her love.

She'd been right when she'd said there were reasons he might not be able or willing to serve her. The Keep he could handle. He could deal with Luthvian as well. But the High Lord?

There was only one way to find out.

"Let's go," he said.

5 / Kaeleer

Jaenelle stepped off the landing web. "This is the family seat."

Lucivar reluctantly stepped off the web. A few months ago, he'd walked through the ruins of SaDiablo Hall in Terreille. Ruins didn't prepare a man for this dark-gray mountain of a building. Hell's fire, an entire court could live in the place and not get in each other's way.

Then the significance of her living at the Hall finally hit him, and he turned and stared at her as if he'd never seen her before.

All of those amusing stories she had told him about her loving, beleaguered papa—she had been talking about Saetan. The Prince of the Darkness. The High Lord of Hell. The man who had built the cabin for her, who had helped her rebuild her life. He couldn't reconcile the conflicting images of the man any better than he could reconcile the Hall with the manor house he'd imagined.

And he would never reconcile anything by just standing there.

"Come on, Cat. Let's knock on the door."

The door opened before they reached the top step. The large man standing in the doorway had the stoic, unflappable expression of an upper servant, but he also wore a Red Jewel.

"Hello, Beale," Jaenelle said as she breezed through the door.

Beale's lips turned up in the tiniest hint of a smile. "Lady."

The smile disappeared when Lucivar walked in. "Prince," Beale said, bowing the exact, polite distance.

The lazy, arrogant smile came automatically. "Lord Beale." He put enough bite in his voice to warn the other man not to tangle with him, but not enough to issue a challenge. He'd never challenged a servant in his life. On the other hand, he'd never met a Red-Jeweled Warlord who was a butler by profession.

Ignoring the subtle, stiff-legged displays of dominance, Jaenelle called in the luggage and dumped it on the floor. "Beale? Would you ask Helene to prepare a suite in the family wing for Prince Yaslana?"

"It would be my pleasure, Lady."

Jaenelle pointed toward the back of the great hall. "Papa?"

"In his study."

Lucivar followed Jaenelle to the last right-hand door, trying, unsuccessfully, to think of another reason besides amusement for the sudden gleam in Beale's eyes.

Jaenelle tapped on the door and went in before anyone answered. Lucivar followed close on her heels and then stumbled as the man standing in front of the blackwood desk turned around.

Daemon.

While they stared at each other, both too startled to respond, Lucivar took in the details that denied the gut reaction.

The dark psychic scent was similar, yet subtly different. The man before him was an inch or two shorter than Daemon and more slender in build, but moved with the same feline grace. The thick black hair was silvered at the temples. His face—lined by laughter as well as by the weight of burdens—belonged to a man at the end of his prime or a little beyond. But that face. Masculine. Handsome. The warmer, rougher model for Daemon's cold, polished beauty. And the final touch—the long, black-tinted nails and the Black-Jeweled ring.

Saetan crossed his arms, leaned back against the desk, and said mildly, "Witch-child, I'm going to throttle you."

Instinctively, Lucivar bared his teeth and stepped forward to protect his Queen.

Jaenelle's aggrieved, adolescent wail stopped him cold.

"That's the sixth time in two weeks and I've barely been home!"

Anger flooded Lucivar. How dare the High Lord threaten her!

Except his darling Cat didn't seem the least bit intimidated and Saetan seemed to be fighting hard to keep a straight face.

"Sixth time?" Saetan said, his deep voice still mild but laced with an undercurrent of amusement.

"Twice from Prothvar, twice from Uncle Andulvar—"

All the blood drained out of Lucivar's head. *Uncle Andulvar?*

"—once from Mephis, and now you."

Saetan's lips twitched. "Prothvar always wants to throttle you so that's no surprise, and you do have a knack for provoking Andulvar, but what did you do to annoy Mephis?"

Jaenelle stuffed her hands in her trouser pockets. "I don't know," she grumped. "He said he couldn't discuss it while I was in the room."

Saetan's rich, warm laugh filled the room. When his laughter and Jaenelle's temper were both at a simmer, he looked knowingly at Lucivar. "And I suppose Lucivar has never threatened to throttle you, so he wouldn't understand the impulse to express the desire even when there was no intention of ever carrying it out."

"Oh, no," Jaenelle replied. "He just threatens to wallop me."

Saetan stiffened. "I beg your pardon?" he asked softly, coldly.

Lucivar shifted back into a fighting stance.

Startled, Jaenelle looked at both of them. "You're going to argue about the *word* when you mean the same thing?"

"Stay out of this, Cat," Lucivar snarled, watching his adversary.

Snarling back, she threw a punch at him with enough temper behind it that it could have broken his jaw if he hadn't dodged it.

The tussle that followed was just turning into fun when Saetan roared, "Enough!" He glared at them until they separated, then he rubbed his temples and growled, "How in the name of Hell did the two of you manage to live together and survive?"

Eyeing Jaenelle warily, Lucivar grinned. "She's harder to pin now."

"Don't rub it in," Jaenelle muttered.

Saetan sighed. "You might have warned me, witch-child."

Jaenelle laced her fingers together. "Well, there really wasn't any way for Lucivar to be prepared, so I figured if you both were unprepared, you'd start out on even ground."

They stared at her.

She gave them her best unsure-but-game smile.

"Witch-child, go terrify someone else for a while."

After Jaenelle slipped out of the room, they studied one another.

"You look a lot better than the last time I saw you," Saetan said, breaking the silence, "but you still look ready to keel over." He pushed away from the desk. "Care for some brandy?"

Turning toward the less formal side of the room, Lucivar settled into a chair designed to accommodate Eyrien wings and accepted the glass of brandy. "And when was the last time you saw me?"

Saetan sat on the couch and crossed his legs. He toyed with the brandy glass. "Shortly after Prothvar brought you to the cabin. If he hadn't been standing guard duty at the Sleeping Dragons, if he hadn't managed to reach you before—" He stroked the rim of the glass with a fingertip. "I don't think you realize how severe the injuries were. The internal damage, the broken bones . . . your wings."

Lucivar sipped his brandy. No, he hadn't realized. He'd known it was bad, but once he was in the Khaldharon Run, he'd stopped caring what happened physically. If what Saetan said was true . . .

"So you let a seventeen-year-old Healer take it on alone," he said, struggling to keep a tight rein on his rising anger. "You let her do that much healing, knowing what it would do to her, and left her without so much as a helper or servant to look after *her*."

Saetan's eyes filled with anger that was just as tightly leashed. "*I* was there to take care of her. I was there all the time she put you back together. I was there to coax her to eat when she could. I was there to watch the web during the resting times so she could get a little sleep. And when you finally started rising from the healing sleep, I held her and fed her spoonfuls of honeyed tea while she wept from exhaustion and pain because her throat was so raw from singing the healing web. I left the day before you woke because you had enough to deal with without having to come to terms with me. How dare you assume—" Saetan clamped his teeth together.

Dangerous, shaky ground. There might be a great many things he could no longer afford to assume.

Lucivar refilled his glass. "Since there was so much damage, wouldn't it have been better to split the healing between two Healers?" He kept his voice carefully neutral. "Luthvian's a temperamental bitch most of the time, but she's a good Healer."

Saetan hesitated. "She offered. I wouldn't let her because your wings were involved."

"She would have removed them." A small lump of fear settled in Lucivar's stomach.

"Jaenelle was sure she could rebuild them, but it would require a systemic healing—one Healer singing the web because everything had to be pulled into it. There could be no diversions, no hesitations, no lack of commitment to the whole. Doing it Luthvian's way, the two of them could have healed everything but your wings. Jaenelle's way was all or nothing—either you came out of it whole or you didn't survive."

Lucivar could see them—two strong-willed women standing on either side of a bed that held his mangled body. "You decided."

Saetan drained his glass and refilled it. "I decided."

"Why? You threatened to slit my throat in the cradle. Why fight for me now?"

"Because you're my son. But I would have slit your

throat." Saetan's voice was strained. "May the Darkness help me, if she'd cut off your wings, I would have."

Cut off your wings. Lucivar felt sick. "Why did you breed her?"

Saetan set the glass down and raked his fingers through his hair. "I didn't mean to. When I agreed to see her through her Virgin Night, I honestly didn't think I was still fertile, and she swore that she'd been drinking the brew to prevent pregnancy, swore it wasn't her fertile time. And she never told me she was Eyrien." He looked up, his eyes filled with pain. "I didn't know. Lucivar, I swear by all I am, until I saw the wings, I didn't know. But you're Eyrien in your soul. Altering your physical appearance would have changed nothing."

Lucivar drained his glass and wondered if he dared ask. This meeting was bruising Saetan as badly as it was bruising him—if not worse. But he had come here to ask so that he could make an honest decision. "Couldn't you have been there sometimes? Even in secret?"

"If you have some objection to my not being part of your life, take it up with your mother. That was her choice, not mine." Saetan closed his eyes. His fingers tightened around his glass. "For reasons I've never been able to explain rationally to myself, I agreed to try to breed with a Black Widow in order to bring a strong, dark bloodline back into the long-lived races. Dorothea was the Hayllian Hourglass's choice but not mine." He hesitated. "Have you ever met Tersa?"

"Yes."

"An extraordinarily gifted witch. Dorothea would never have become the force she is in Terreille if Tersa had survived her Virgin Night. Tersa was my choice. And Tersa became pregnant."

With Daemon. Had Daemon ever known, ever guessed?

"A couple of weeks later, she asked me to see a friend through her Virgin Night, a young Black Widow with strong potential who, if I refused, would end up broken and shattered. I was still capable of performing the service, and I wouldn't have refused Tersa anything within reason. *Everyone* was willing to accommodate Tersa at that point.

No one wanted her to become distressed enough to miscarry since there would be no second chances.

"A few weeks after I saw Luthvian through her Virgin Night, she told me she was pregnant with my child. There was an empty house on the estate, about a mile from the Hall. I insisted she and Tersa live there instead of with Dorothea's court. Tersa wasn't much older than Luthvian, but she understood a great deal more, especially about Guardians. She was content with the companionship I offered. Luthvian was more high-strung and had discovered the pleasure of the bed. She craved sex. For a while, I could still provide the kind of intimacy she wanted. By the time I couldn't, she had lost interest. But after she healed from the birthing, the hunger returned. By then, I could satisfy her in other ways but not the way she craved.

"Between the fights about raising you in Dhemlan, as she wanted, or raising you in Askavi, where I believed you needed to be, and my sexual inability, our relationship became strained to the point that, when she was spoon-fed half-truths about Guardians, she chose to believe them.

"Dorothea timed her schemes well. With Prythian's help, I lost both of you. Within a day, I lost both of you."

Not Luthvian. Daemon.

A sigh shuddered out of Saetan. "Lucivar, for what it's worth, I've never regretted your existence. I've regretted the pain you've endured, but not you. And I'm very glad you survived."

Unable to think of anything to say, Lucivar nodded.

Saetan hesitated. "Would you tell me something, if you can?"

Lucivar knew what Saetan was going to ask. He wasn't sure what he thought about the man who had sired him, but for this moment at least, he could look beyond the titles and the power and see a man asking about one of his children.

He closed his eyes, and said, "He's in the Twisted Kingdom."

Saetan lay on the couch in his study, desperately glad to be alone.

Everything has a price.

He just hadn't expected the price to be so high.

Regrets were useless. And guilt was useless. A Warlord Prince's first duty was to his Queen. But Daemon . . .

Shards of memories floated through him, pricking his heart.

Tersa ripely pregnant, holding his hand against her belly.

Luthvian's constant circle of anger and sexual hunger.

Daemon sitting in his lap while he read a bedtime story.

Lucivar fluttering around the room, laughing gleefully while just staying out of his reach.

Jaenelle turning his study upside down the first time he tried to show her how to use Craft to retrieve her shoes.

Tersa's madness. Luthvian's fury.

Lucivar lying on the bed in the cabin, his body torn apart.

Daemon, lying on Cassandra's Altar, his mind so terribly fragile.

Jaenelle rising out of the abyss after two heartbreaking years.

Fragments. Like Daemon's mind.

Which explained why, during the careful searches he had made over the past two years, he hadn't been able to find this son who was like a mirror. He'd been looking in the wrong place.

A regret slipped in, as useless as any other.

He might be able to find Daemon, but the one person who could have brought Daemon out of the Twisted Kingdom without question was Jaenelle. And Jaenelle was the one person who couldn't know what he intended to do.

CHAPTER
ELEVEN

1 / Kaeleer

Waiting for dinner, Saetan's stomach tightened another notch.

Jaenelle had been home for a week, helping Lucivar adjust to the family—and helping the family adjust to Lucivar—when a pointed letter from the Dark Council arrived, reminding her that she had not finished her visit to Little Terreille.

He still didn't understand Lucivar's cryptic remark, "Knees or bones, Cat," but Jaenelle had stomped out of the Hall spitting Eyrien curses, and Lucivar had seemed grimly pleased.

That had been three days ago.

She had returned abruptly that afternoon, snarled at Beale, "Tell Lucivar I used my knee," and had locked herself in her room.

Disturbed, Beale had informed him of her return and the comment meant for Lucivar, and had added that the Lady seemed unwell.

Jaenelle always seemed unwell after a visit to Little Terreille. He'd never been able to pry the reason for that out of her. Nothing she said about the activities she'd participated in explained the strained, haunted look in her eyes, the weight loss, the restless nights afterward, or the inability to eat.

The only person besides Beale who saw Jaenelle after she returned was Karla. And Karla, teary-eyed and distressed, had picked a fight with the one person she could count on to give her a battle—Lucivar.

After enduring a vicious harangue about males, Lucivar had hauled her out to the lawn, handed her one of the Eyrien sticks, and let her try to whack him. He'd pushed and taunted her until her muscles and emotions finally gave out. He'd offered no explanation, and the fury in his eyes had warned all of them not to ask.

The dining room door opened. Andulvar, Prothvar, and Mephis joined him, the concern in their eyes needing no words.

Karla arrived a minute later, moving stiffly. Lucivar came in behind her, threw an arm around her shoulders—which, amazingly, produced no temperamental explosion—and helped her into a chair.

Beale appeared, looking as strained as Saetan felt, and said, "The Lady says she will be unable to join you for dinner."

Lucivar pulled out the chair on Saetan's right. "Tell the Lady she's joining us for dinner. She can come down on her own two feet or over my shoulder. Her choice."

Beale's eyes widened.

A low growl of displeasure came, unexpectedly, from Mephis.

The room smelled dangerous.

Wanting to avoid the confrontation building up between the men in the family, Saetan nodded to Beale, silently backing Lucivar.

Beale hastily retreated.

Lucivar just leaned against the chair and waited.

Jaenelle appeared a few minutes later, her face drained of color except for the dark smudges underneath her eyes.

Smiling that lazy, arrogant smile, Lucivar pulled out the chair beside his and waited.

Jaenelle swallowed hard. "I—I'm sorry. I can't."

She moved fast. Lucivar moved faster.

In stunned silence, they watched him drag her to her place at the table and dump her in the chair. She immediately shot upward, smacking into the fist he calmly held above her head. Dazed, she didn't protest when he pushed her chair up to the table and sat down beside her.

Saetan sat down, torn between his concern for Jaenelle and his desire to treat Lucivar to the same kind of affection.

Andulvar, Prothvar, and Mephis took their seats, bristling. If Lucivar noticed the anger being directed at him, he ignored it.

The arrogance of not acknowledging the displeasure of males of equal or darker rank galled Saetan, but he held his tongue and his temper. There would be time to unleash both later.

"You're going to eat," Lucivar said calmly.

Jaenelle stared at the place setting in front of her. "I can't."

"Cat, if we have to dump the soup on the floor so that you can puke into the tureen, then that's what we'll do. But you're going to eat."

Jaenelle snarled at him.

A pale, shaky footman brought the soup.

Lucivar put a ladle full into her bowl and filled his own halfway. He picked up his spoon and waited.

Her snarl grew louder as she reluctantly picked up her spoon.

After a narrow-eyed, considering look at Lucivar, Karla asked a question about a Craft lesson she was working on.

Mephis responded, and the discussion covered the first course.

Jaenelle ate one spoonful of soup.

Andulvar shifted in his seat, rustling his wings.

Saetan flicked a glance at Andulvar, warning him to keep still. He'd caught the scent of feminine anger. He'd caught Lucivar's tightly focused awareness of Jaenelle and her rising temper—a temper Lucivar was able to provoke with frightening ease.

With each dish offered in the second course, Lucivar selected food for her, pricked at her, scraped away her self-control.

"Liver?" Lucivar asked.

"Only if it's yours," she snapped, her eyes glittering queerly.

Lucivar smiled slightly.

By the end of the second course, Jaenelle was an explosion waiting for a spark, and Saetan couldn't understand the point of taunting her.

Until the meat course.

Lucivar slipped a small piece of prime rib onto her plate and then stacked two large pieces on his own.

Jaenelle stared at the tender, pink-centered meat for a long moment. Then she picked up her knife and fork and began to eat with single-minded intensity. When the meat was gone, she turned to her right and looked at Karla's plate.

Karla's face paled to a ghastly white.

When Jaenelle turned to her left and Saetan got a good look at her eyes, he realized that Lucivar had turned the meal into a violent, brilliantly choreographed dance designed to bring the predatory side of Witch to the surface.

Finally her attention fixed on Lucivar's plate. Snarling softly, she licked her lips and raised her fork.

Keeping his movements slow and deliberate, Lucivar transferred the second piece of prime rib from his plate to hers.

She stabbed the meat with her fork and bared her teeth at him.

Lucivar withdrew his utensils and hands and calmly resumed his meal while Jaenelle devoured the meat.

By the time they reached the fruit and cheese course, Jaenelle's attention was entirely focused on Lucivar and his offerings of food. When he held up the last grape, she stared at it for a moment, then wrinkled her nose and sat back with a contented sigh.

And the woman-child Saetan knew and loved returned.

For the first time since the meal began, Lucivar looked at the other men sitting at the table, and Saetan felt keen sympathy for this son with the battle-weary look in his golden eyes.

After the coffee was served, Lucivar took a deep breath and turned to Jaenelle. "By the way, you owe me a piece of jewelry."

"What jewelry?" Jaenelle asked, baffled.

"Kaeleer's equivalent to the Ring of Obedience."

She choked on her coffee.

Lucivar thumped her back until she gave him a teary-eyed glare. He smiled at her. "Will you tell them, or shall I?"

Jaenelle looked at the men who made up her family. She hunched her shoulders, and said in a small voice, "In order to fill the immigration requirement, Lucivar's going to serve me for the next five years."

This time Saetan choked.

"And?" Lucivar prodded.

"I'll come up with something," Jaenelle said testily. "Although why you want to wear one of those Rings is beyond me."

"I did a little checking while you were gone. Males have to wear a Restraining Ring as part of the immigration requirements."

Jaenelle let out an exasperated snort. "Lucivar, who's going to be foolish enough to ask you to prove you're wearing one?"

"That Ring is physical proof that I serve you, and I want it."

Jaenelle gave Saetan one fleeting, pleading look—which he ignored. "All right. I'll come up with something," she growled, pushing her chair back. "Karla and I are going to take a walk."

Karla, gathering her wits faster than the men could, moaned to her feet and shuffled after Jaenelle.

Andulvar, Prothvar, and Mephis swiftly found excuses to leave.

After the brandy and yarbarah were brought to the table, Saetan dismissed the footmen, grimly amused by their strained eagerness to return to the servants' hall. His staff didn't gossip to outsiders—Beale and Helene saw to that—but only a fool would think they didn't talk among themselves. Lucivar's arrival had caused quite a stir. Lucivar in service to their Lady . . .

If tonight was a sample of what to expect, it was going to be an interesting—and long—five years.

"You play an intriguing game," Saetan said quietly as he warmed a glass of yarbarah. "And a dangerous one."

Lucivar shrugged. "Not so dangerous, as long as I don't push her past surface temper."

Saetan studied Lucivar's carefully neutral expression. "But do you understand who, and what, lies beneath that surface temper?"

Lucivar smiled tiredly. "I know who she is." He sipped his brandy. "You don't approve of my serving her, do you?"

Saetan rolled his glass between his hands. "You've been able to do more in three months to improve her physical and emotional health than I've been able to do in two years. That galls a little."

"You laid a stronger foundation than you realize." Lucivar grinned. "Besides, a father's supposed to be strong, supportive, and protective. Older brothers, on the other hand, are naturally a pain in the ass and are inclined to be overprotective bullies."

Saetan smiled. "You're an overprotective bully?"

"So I'm told frequently and with great vigor."

Saetan's smiled faded. "Be careful, Lucivar. She has some deep emotional scars you're not aware of."

"I know about the rape—and about Briarwood. When she's pushed too hard, she talks in her sleep." Lucivar refilled his glass and met Saetan's cool stare. "I slept with her. I didn't mount her."

Slept with her. Saetan kept a tight rein on his temper while he sifted through the implications of that statement and weighed it against the amount of physical contact Jaenelle allowed Lucivar without retreating into that chilling emotional blankness that always scared the rest of them. "She didn't object?" he asked carefully.

Lucivar snorted. "Of course she objected. What woman wouldn't after being hurt that badly? But she objected more to having her patient sleeping in front of the hearth, and I objected just as strongly to having the Healer who saved my life sleeping in front of the hearth. So we reached an agreement. I didn't complain about the way she hogged the pillows, tangled the covers, sprawled over more than her share of the bed, made those cute little noises that we don't call snoring no matter what it sounds like, and growled at everything and everyone until she had her first cup of coffee. And she didn't complain about the way I hogged the pillows, tangled the covers, sprawled over more than my share of the bed, made funny noises that woke her up and stopped the minute she was awake, and tended to be overly cheerful in the morning. And we both agreed that neither of us wanted the other for sex."

Which, for Jaenelle, would have made the difference.

"Do you pay much attention to who immigrates to Kaeleer?" Lucivar asked suddenly.

"Not much," Saetan replied cautiously.

Lucivar studied his brandy. "You wouldn't know if a Hayllian named Greer came in, would you?"

The question chilled him. "Greer is dead."

Lucivar fixed his eyes on the dining room wall. "Being the High Lord of Hell, you could arrange a meeting, couldn't you?"

Why was Lucivar straining to breathe evenly?

"Greer is *dead,* not just a citizen of the Dark Realm."

Lucivar's jaw tightened. "Damn."

Saetan clenched his teeth. Sweet Darkness, how was Lucivar involved with Greer? "Why are you so interested in him?"

Lucivar's hands curled into tight fists. "He was the bastard who raped Jaenelle."

Saetan's temper exploded. The dining room windows shattered. Zigzag cracks raced across the ceiling. Swearing viciously, he rechanneled the power to strike the drive out front, turning the gravel into powder.

Greer. Another link between Hekatah and Dorothea.

Saetan sank his nails into the table, tearing through the wood again and again, an unsatisfying exercise since he wanted *flesh* beneath his nails.

The training was too deeply ingrained in him. Damn the Darkness, it was too deeply ingrained. He couldn't kill a witch in cold blood. And if he was going to break the code of honor he'd lived by all his life, he should have done it more than five years ago when it might have made a difference, might have saved Jaenelle. Not now, when she already bore the scars. Not now, when it wouldn't change anything.

Hands clamped on his wrists. Tightened. Tightened some more.

"High Lord."

He should have torn that bastard apart the first time Greer asked about Jaenelle. Should have shredded his mind. What was *wrong* with him? Had he become too tame, too docile? What was he doing, trying to appease those puny fools in the Dark Council when they were doing something that hurt his daughter, his Queen?

"High Lord."

And who was this fool who dared lay hands on the Prince of the Darkness, the High Lord of Hell? No more. *No more.*

"*Father.*"

Saetan gulped air, fought to clear his head. Lucivar. Lucivar was pinning his arms to the table.

Someone pounded on the door. "Saetan! Lucivar!"

Jaenelle. Sweet Darkness, not Jaenelle. He couldn't see her now.

"SAETAN!"

"Please," he whispered. "Don't let her—"

The door shattered.

"Get out, Cat," Lucivar snapped.

"What—"

"OUT!"

Andulvar's voice. "Go upstairs, waif. We'll take care of this."

Voices arguing, fading.

"Yarbarah?" Lucivar asked after a long, tense silence.

Saetan shuddered, shook his head. Until he was settled, if he tasted blood, he would want it hot from the vein. "Brandy."

Lucivar pressed a glass into his hand.

Saetan gulped the brandy. "You should have gotten out of here."

Lucivar raised his glass with an unsteady hand and offered a wobbly grin. "I've had some experience tangling with the Black. All in all, you're not too bad. Daemon always scared the shit out of me when he turned savage." He drained his glass and refilled both of them. "I hope you didn't redecorate in here recently. You're going to have to do it again, but it doesn't look like the room's going to fall in on us."

"The girls didn't like the wallpaper anyway." Ten good reasons to hold his temper. Ten good reasons to unleash it. And always, always, for Blood males like him, the fine line he had to walk to hold on to the balance between two conflicting instincts. "The Harpies executed Greer," he said abruptly. "They have a distinct sensibility when it comes to that sort of thing."

Lucivar nodded.

Steady. He would need to be steady for the days ahead. "Lucivar, see if you can persuade Jaenelle to show you Sceval. You should meet Kaetien and the other unicorns."

Lucivar regarded him steadily. "Why?"

"I have some business I want to take care of. I'll need to stay at the Keep in Terreille for a few days, and I'd prefer it if Jaenelle wasn't around to ask questions or wonder where I was."

Lucivar considered this for a minute. "Do you think you can do it?"

Saetan sighed wearily. "I won't know until I try."

2 / Terreille

Saetan carefully secured his Black-Jeweled ring to the center of the large tangled web. It had taken two days of searching through Geoffrey's Hourglass archives to find the answer. It had taken two more to construct the web. He'd given himself two nerve-fraying days more to rest and slowly gather his strength.

Draca had said nothing when he'd asked for a guest room and workroom at the Terreille Keep, but the workroom had been supplied with a frame large enough to hold the tangled web. Geoffrey had said nothing about the requested books, but he had added a couple of books Saetan wouldn't have thought of.

Saetan took a deep breath. It was time.

Normally a Black Widow needed physical contact to guide someone out of the Twisted Kingdom. But sometimes blood-ties could cross boundaries otherwise impossible to cross, and no one had a stronger tie to Daemon than he did. The tie of father to son; more, the bond of that night at Cassandra's Altar.

And the Blood shall sing to the Blood.

Pricking his finger, Saetan placed a drop of blood on the four anchor threads that held the web to its wooden frame. The blood flowed down the top threads, and up the bottom threads. Just as the drops reached his ring, Saetan lightly touched the Black Jewel, smearing it with blood.

The web glowed. Saetan sang the spell that opened the dreamscape that would lead him to the one he sought.

A tortured landscape, full of blood and shattered crystal chalices.

Taking another deep breath, Saetan focused his eyes on the Black-Jeweled ring and began the inward journey into madness.

Daemon.

He raised his head.

The words circled, waiting for him. The edges of the tiny island crumbled a little more.

Daemon.

He knew that voice. *You are my instrument.*

Daemon!

He looked up. Flattened himself against the pulpy ground.

A hand hovered over him, reached for him. A light-brown hand with long, black-tinted nails. A wrist appeared. Part of a forearm. Straining to reach him.

He knew that voice. He knew that hand. He hated them.

Daemon, reach for me. I can show you the road back.

Words lie. Blood doesn't.

The hand shook with the effort to reach him.

Daemon, let me help you. Please.

Inches separated them. All he had to do was raise his hand and he could leave this island.

His fingers twitched.

Daemon, trust me. I can help you.

Blood. So much blood. A sea of it. He would drown in it. Because he'd trusted that voice once and he'd done something . . . he'd done . . .

LIAR! he screamed. *I'll never trust you!*

Daemon. An anguished plea.

NEVER!

The hand began to fade.

Fear swamped him. He didn't want to be alone in this sea of blood with the words circling, waiting to slice into him again and again. He wanted to grab the hand and hold tight, wanted whatever lies might ease this pain for a little while.

But he owed someone this pain because he'd done something . . .

Butchering whore.

That voice, that hand had tricked him into hurting someone. But, sweet Darkness, how he wanted to trust, wanted to hold on.

Daemon. A whisper of sound.

The hand faded, withdrew.

He waited.

The words circled and circled. The island crumbled a little more.

He waited. The hand didn't return.

He pressed himself against the pulpy ground and wept in relief.

Saetan sank to his knees. The threads of the tangled web were blackened, crumbling. He caught his ring as it fell from the center of the web and slipped it on his finger.

So close. A hand span at most. A moment of trust. That's all it would have taken to begin the journey out of that pain and madness.

That's all it would have taken.

Stretching out on the cold stone floor, Saetan pillowed his head on his arms and wept bitterly.

3 / Kaeleer

Saetan looked at Lucivar and shook his head.

"Well," Lucivar said, his voice tight, "you tried." After a minute he added, "You're wanted in the kitchen."

"In the kitchen? Why?" Saetan asked as Lucivar herded him toward Mrs. Beale's undisputed territory.

Lucivar smiled and dropped a friendly hand on Saetan's shoulder.

The gesture filled him with foreboding. "How was your trip?"

"Traveling with Cat is an experience."

"Do I really want to know about this?"

"No," Lucivar said cheerfully, "but you're going to anyway."

Jaenelle sat cross-legged on the kitchen floor. A brown-and-white Sceltie puppy tumbled about in front of her. Her lap was full of a large, white . . . kitten?

"Hello, Papa," Jaenelle said meekly.

Papa High Lord, said the puppy. When Saetan didn't answer, the puppy looked at Jaenelle. *Papa High Lord?*

"Kindred." Saetan cleared his throat. His voice went back to a deep baritone. "The Scelties are kindred?"

"Not all of them," Jaenelle said defensively.

"About the same ratio of Blood to landen as other species," Lucivar said, grinning. "You're taking this a lot better than Khardeen did. He sat down in the middle of the road and became hysterical. We had to drag him over to the side before he got run over by a cart."

A muffled chuckle-snort came from the direction of the worktable where Mrs. Beale was busily chopping up some meat.

"And with that one little explanation, the humans suddenly realized why some of the Scelties matured so late and had a longer life span," Lucivar added with annoying cheerfulness. "After Ladvarian made it clear that Cat belonged to him—"

Mine! said the puppy.

The kitten lifted a large, white, furry paw and squashed the puppy.

Ours! said the puppy, wriggling out from beneath the paw.

"—we fixed a strong sedative for the Warlord who had just discovered that his bitch was also a Priestess."

"Mother Night." Saetan switched to a Red spear thread. *Why does a male Sceltie have a name with an Eyrien feminine ending?*

That's what he said his name is. Who am I to argue?

"After that," Lucivar continued, "Khary dragged us to Tuathal to see Lady Duana, who had a few pointed things to say about not being told there were kindred in her Territory."

Yes, he was sure the Queen of Scelt would have had quite a few things to say—and would have a few more to say to *him.*

Jaenelle hid her face in the kitten's fur.

Lucivar, damn his soul, seemed to be enjoying this now that he could dump it into someone else's lap.

Since Jaenelle wasn't jumping into the conversation, Lucivar continued the tale. "In the invigorating discussion that followed, it came out that there are also two breeds of horses who are kindred."

Saetan swayed. Lucivar propped him up.

The Scelts were noted horsemen. Khary's and Morghann's families especially were passionate about horses.

"Imagine how surprised people were when they discovered their horses could talk back to them," Lucivar said.

Saetan knelt beside Jaenelle. At least if he fainted now he wouldn't fall so far. "And our feline Brother?"

Jaenelle's fingers tightened in the kitten's fur. Her eyes held a dark, dangerous look. "Kaelas is Arcerian. He's an orphan. His mother was killed by hunters."

Kaelas. In the Old Tongue, the word meant "white death." It usually referred to a kind of snowstorm that came with little warning—swift, violent, and deadly.

Saetan switched to a spear thread again. *I suppose no one named him, either.*

Nope, Lucivar replied.

Saetan didn't like the sober caution in Lucivar's tone. He reached out to pet the kitten.

Kaelas took a swipe at him.

"Hey!" Jaenelle said sharply. "Don't swat the High Lord."

Kaelas snarled, displaying an impressive set of baby teeth. The claws weren't anything to shrug off either.

"Here you are, sweeties," Mrs. Beale cooed, setting two bowls on the kitchen floor. "Some meat and warm milk."

Saetan eyed his cook. This was the same woman who always cornered him whenever the wolf pups chased the bunnies through her garden? Then he looked at the bowl of chopped meat and frowned. "Isn't that the cold roast you were going to serve for lunch?"

Mrs. Beale glared at him. Lucivar prudently stepped behind him.

Abandoning the kitchen to Mrs. Beale and her charges, Saetan headed for his suite. Lucivar went with him.

"The puppy's cute," Saetan said. If that was the best he could do, he definitely needed to rest.

"Don't let puppy cute fool you," Lucivar said quietly. "He's a Warlord, and there's a shrewd intelligence inside that furry little head. Combine that with a large Warlord Prince predator and you've got a partnership that needs to be handled with care."

Saetan stopped at the door of his suite. "Lucivar, just how big do Arcerian cats get?"

Lucivar grinned. "Let's just say you ought to start putting strengthening spells on the furniture now."

"Mother Night," Saetan muttered, stumbling to his bed. The paperwork on his desk could wait. He didn't need to look for trouble.

He'd just started to doze off when he felt eyes staring at him. Rolling over, Saetan blinked at Ladvarian and Kaelas. Someone—he snorted—had already taught Ladvarian to air walk. True, the puppy wobbled, but he was, after all, a puppy.

Groaning, Saetan rolled back over, hoping they would go away.

Two bodies landed on the bed.

Well, he didn't have to worry about rolling over on the

Sceltie. He wasn't going to roll anywhere with Kaelas pressed against his back—except, perhaps, onto the floor.

And where was Jaenelle?

The Lady, he was told, was taking a bath. They wanted a nap. Since Papa High Lord was taking a nap, they would stay with him.

With grim determination, Saetan closed his eyes.

He didn't need to look for trouble. It had just pounced on him.

CHAPTER
TWELVE

1 / Kaeleer

Carrying a glass globe and a small glass bowl, both cobalt blue, Tersa walked a few feet into her backyard, her bare feet sinking into ankle-deep snow. The full moon played hide-and-seek among the clouds, much as the vision had eluded her throughout the day. She had lived within visions for so many centuries, she understood that this one needed to be given a physical shape before revealing itself.

Letting her body be the dreamscape's instrument, she used Craft to sail the globe and bowl through the air. When they reached the center of the lawn, they settled quietly into the snow.

She took a step toward them, then looked down. Her nightgown brushed the snow, disturbing it. That wouldn't do. Pulling it off, she tossed it near the cottage's back door and walked toward the globe and bowl. She stopped. Yes. This was the right place to begin.

One long stride to keep the snow pristine between her shuffled footsteps from the cottage and the footsteps that would guide the vision. Placing one foot carefully in front of the other, heel to toe, she waited. There was something else, something more.

Using Craft to sharpen a fingernail, she cut the instep of each foot deep enough for the blood to run freely. Then she walked the vision's pattern. When it brought her back to her first footstep, she leaped to reach the snow disturbed by shuffled footsteps.

As she turned to see the pattern, the journeymaid Black Widow who was staying with her for a few weeks called out, "Tersa? What are you doing outside at this time of night?"

Snarling, Tersa whirled back to face the young witch.

The journeymaid studied her face for a moment. Fetching the discarded nightgown, she tore it into strips, wrapped Tersa's feet to absorb the blood, then moved aside.

Urgency pushed Tersa up the stairs to her bedroom. Opening the curtains, she looked down at the yard and the lines she had drawn in the snow with her blood.

Two sides of a triangle, strong and connected. The father and the brother. The third side, the father's mirror, was separated from the other two and the middle was worn away. If it broke fully, that side would never be strong enough again to complete the triangle.

Moonlight and shadows filled the yard. The cobalt globe and bowl that rested in the center of the triangle became sapphire eyes.

"Yes," Tersa whispered. "The threads are now in place. It's time."

Receiving Jaenelle's silent permission, Saetan entered her sitting room. He glanced at the dark bedroom where Kaelas and Ladvarian were awake and anxious. Which meant Lucivar would be appearing soon. In the five months since he'd begun serving her, Lucivar had become extraordinarily sensitive to Jaenelle's moods.

Saetan sat down on the hassock in front of the overstuffed chair where Jaenelle was curled up. "Bad dream?" he asked. She'd had quite a few restless nights and bad dreams in the past few weeks.

"A dream," she agreed. She hesitated for a moment. "I was standing in front of a cloudy crystal door. I couldn't see what was behind it, wasn't sure I *wanted* to see. But someone kept trying to hand me a gold key, and I knew that if I took it, the door would open and then I would *have* to know what was hidden behind it."

"Did you take the key?" He kept his voice soft and soothing while his heart began to pound in his chest.

"I woke up before I touched it." She smiled wearily.

This was the first time she remembered one of those dreams upon waking. He had a good idea what memories were hidden behind that crystal door. Which meant they needed to talk about her past soon. But not tonight. "Would you like a brew to help you sleep?"

"No, thank you. I'll be all right."

He kissed her forehead and left the room.

Lucivar waited for him in the corridor. "Problem?" Lucivar asked.

"Perhaps." Saetan took a deep breath, let it out slowly. "Let's go down to the study. There's something we need to discuss."

2 / Kaeleer

"Cat!" Lucivar rushed into the great hall. He didn't know what had set her off, but after talking with Saetan last night, he wasn't about to let her go anywhere by herself.

Fortunately, Beale was equally reluctant to let the Lady rush out the door without telling someone her destination.

Caught between them, Jaenelle unleashed her frustration with enough force to make all the windows rattle. "Damn you both! I have to *go.*"

"Fine." Lucivar approached her slowly, holding his hands up in a placating gesture. "I'm going with you. Where are we going?"

Jaenelle raked her fingers through her hair. "Halaway. Sylvia just sent a message. Something's wrong with Tersa."

Lucivar exchanged a look with Beale. The butler nodded. Saetan and Mephis would be back at any moment from their meeting with Lady Zhara, the Queen of Amdarh, Dhemlan's capital—and Beale would remain in the great hall until they arrived.

"Let me go!" Jaenelle wailed.

Thank the Darkness, it didn't occur to her to use force against them. She could easily eliminate what amounted to token resistance.

"In a minute," Lucivar said, swallowing hard when her

eyes turned stormy. "You can't go out in your socks. There's snow on the ground."

Jaenelle swore. Lucivar called in her winter boots and handed them to her while a breathless footman brought her winter coat and the belted, wool cape with wing slits that served as a coat for him.

A minute later, they were flying toward Tersa's cottage.

The journeymaid Black Widow who was staying with Tersa flung the door open as soon as they landed. "In the bedroom," she said in a worried voice. "Lady Sylvia is with her."

Jaenelle raced up to the bedroom with Lucivar right behind her.

Seeing them, Sylvia sagged against the dresser, the relief in her face overshadowed by stark concern. Lucivar put his arm around her, uneasy about the way she clung to him.

Jaenelle circled the bed to face Tersa, who was frantically packing a small trunk. Scattered among the clothing strewn on the bed were books, candles, and a few things Lucivar recognized as tools only a Black Widow would own.

"Tersa," Jaenelle said in a quiet, commanding voice.

Tersa shook her head. "I have to find him. It's time now."

"Who do you have to find?"

"The boy. My son. Daemon."

Lucivar's heart clogged his throat as he watched Jaenelle pale.

"Daemon." Jaenelle shuddered. "The gold key."

"I have to find him." Tersa's voice rang with frustration and fear. "If the pain doesn't end soon, it will destroy him."

Jaenelle gave no sign of having heard or understood the words. "Daemon," she whispered. "How could I have forgotten Daemon?"

"I must go back to Terreille. I must find him."

"No," Jaenelle said in her midnight voice. "*I'll* find him."

Tersa stopped her restless movements. "Yes," she said slowly, as if trying hard to remember something. "He would trust you. He would follow you out of the Twisted Kingdom."

Jaenelle closed her eyes.

Still holding Sylvia, Lucivar braced himself against the wall. Hell's fire, why was the room slowly spinning?

When Jaenelle opened her eyes, Lucivar stared, unable to look away. He'd never seen her eyes look like that. He hoped he'd never again see her eyes look like that. Jaenelle swept out of the room.

Leaving Sylvia to manage on her own, Lucivar raced after Jaenelle, who was striding toward the landing web at the edge of the village.

"Cat, the Hall's in the other direction."

When she didn't answer him, he tried to grab her arm. The shield around her was so cold it burned his hand.

She passed the landing web and kept walking. He fell into step beside her, not sure what to say—not sure what he *dared* say.

"Stubborn, snarly male," she muttered as tears filled her eyes. "I *told* you the chalice needed time to heal. I *told* you to go someplace safe. Why didn't you listen to me? Couldn't you obey just *once*?" She stopped walking.

Lucivar watched her grief slowly transform into rage as she turned in the direction of the Hall.

"Saetan," she said in a malevolent whisper. "You were there that night. You . . ."

Lucivar didn't try to keep up with her when she ran back to the Hall. Instead, he sent a warning to Beale on a Red spear thread. Beale, in turn, informed him that the High Lord had just arrived.

He hoped his father was prepared for this fight.

3 / Kaeleer

He felt her coming.

Too nervous to sit, Saetan leaned against the front of his blackwood desk, his hands locked on the surface in a vise grip.

He'd had two years to prepare for this, had spent countless hours trying to find the right phrases to explain the brutality that had almost destroyed her. But, somehow, he had never found the right time to tell her. Even after last night, when he realized the memories were trying to surface, he had delayed talking to her.

Now the time had come. And he still wasn't prepared.

He'd arrived home to find Beale fretting in the great hall, waiting to convey Lucivar's warning: "She remembers Daemon—and she's furious."

He felt her enter the Hall and hoped he could now find a way to help her face those memories in the daylight instead of in her dreams.

His study door blew off the hinges and shattered when it hit the opposite wall. Dark power ripped through the room, breaking the tables and tearing the couch and chairs apart.

Fear hammered at him. But he also noted that she didn't harm the irreplaceable paintings and sculpture.

Then she stepped into the room, and nothing could have prepared him for the cold rage focused directly at him.

"Damn you." Her midnight voice sounded calm. It sounded deadly.

She meant it. If the malevolence and loathing in her eyes was any indication of the depth of her rage, then he was truly damned.

"You heartless bastard."

His mind chattered frantically. He couldn't make a sound. He desperately hoped that her feelings for him would balance her fury—and knew they wouldn't, not with Daemon added to the balance.

She walked toward him, flexing her fingers, drawing part of his attention to the dagger-sharp nails he now had reason to fear.

"You used him. He was a friend, and *you used him*."

Saetan gritted his teeth. "There was no choice."

"There *was* a choice." She slashed open the chair in front of his desk. "THERE WAS A CHOICE!"

His rising temper pushed the fear aside. "To lose you," he said roughly. "To stand back and let your body die and lose *you*. I didn't consider that a choice, Lady. Neither did Daemon."

"You wouldn't have lost me if the body had died. I

would have eventually put the crystal chalice back together and—"

"You're Witch, and Witch doesn't become *cildru dyathe*. We *would* have lost you. Every part of you. He knew that."

That stopped her for a moment.

"I gave him all the strength I had. He went too deep into the abyss trying to reach you. When I tried to draw him back up, he fought me and the link between us snapped."

"He shattered his crystal chalice," Jaenelle said in a hollow voice. "He shattered his mind. I put it back together, but it was so terribly fragile. When he rose out of the abyss, anything could have damaged him. A harsh word would have been enough at that point."

"I know," Saetan said cautiously. "I felt him."

The cold rage filled her eyes again. "But you left him there, didn't you, Saetan?" she said too softly. "Briarwood's uncles had arrived at the Altar, and you left a defenseless man to face them."

"He was supposed to go through the Gate," Saetan replied hotly. "I don't know why he didn't."

"Of course you know." Her voice became a sepulchral croon. "We both know. If a timing spell wasn't put on the candles to snuff them out and close the Gate, then someone had to stay behind to close it. Naturally it was the Warlord Prince who was expected to stay."

"He may have had other reasons to stay," Saetan said carefully.

"Perhaps," she replied with equal care. "But that doesn't explain why he's in the Twisted Kingdom, does it, High Lord?" She took a step closer to him. "That doesn't explain why you left him there."

"I didn't know he was in the Twisted Kingdom until—" Saetan clamped his teeth to hold the words back.

"Until Lucivar came to Kaeleer," Jaenelle finished for him. She waved a hand dismissively before he could speak. "Lucivar was in the salt mines of Pruul. I know there was nothing he could do. But you."

Saetan spaced out the words. "Getting you back was the

first requirement. I gave my strength to that task. Daemon would have understood that, would have demanded it.''

"I came back two years ago, and there's nothing draining your strength now." Pain and betrayal filled her eyes. "But you didn't even try to reach him, did you?"

"Yes, I tried! DAMN YOU, I TRIED!" He sagged against the desk. "Stop acting like a petty little bitch. He may be your friend, but he's also my *son*. Do you really think I wouldn't try to help him?" The bitter failure filled him again. "I was so close, witch-child. So close. But he was just out of reach. And he didn't trust me. If he would have tried a little, I would have had him. I could have shown him the way out of the Twisted Kingdom. But he didn't trust me."

The silence stretched.

"I'm going to get him back," Jaenelle said quietly.

Saetan straightened up. "You can't go back to Terreille."

"Don't tell me what I can or can't do," Jaenelle snarled.

"Listen to me, Jaenelle," he said urgently. "You can't go back to Terreille. As soon as she realized you were there, Dorothea would do everything she could to contain you or destroy you. And you're still not of age. Your Chaillot relatives could try to regain custody."

"I'll take that chance. I'm not leaving him to suffer." She turned to leave the room.

Saetan took a deep breath and let it out slowly. "Since I'm his father, I can reach him without needing physical contact."

"But he doesn't trust you."

"I can help you, Jaenelle."

She turned back to look at him, and he saw a stranger.

"I don't want your help, High Lord," she said quietly.

Then she walked away from him, and he knew she was doing a great deal more than simply walking out of a room.

Everything has a price.

Lucivar found her in the gardens a couple of hours later, sitting on a stone bench with her hands pressed between her knees hard enough to bruise. Straddling the bench, he sat as close as he could without touching her. "Cat?" he said softly, afraid that even sound would shatter her. "Talk to me. Please."

"I—" She shuddered.

"You remember."

"I remember." She let out a laugh full of knife-sharp edges. "I remember all of it. Marjane, Dannie, Rose. Briarwood. Greer. All of it." She glanced at him. "You've known about Briarwood. And Greer."

Lucivar brushed a lock of hair away from his face. Maybe he should get it cut short, the way Eyrien warriors usually wore it. "Sometimes when you have bad dreams you talk in your sleep."

"So you've both known. And said nothing."

"What could we have said, Cat?" Lucivar asked slowly. "If we had forced someone else to remember something that emotionally scarring, you would have thrown a fit—as well as a few pieces of furniture."

Jaenelle's lips curved in a ghost of a smile. "True." Her smile faded. "Do you know the worst thing about it? I forgot him. Daemon was a friend, and I forgot him. That Winsol, before I was . . . he gave me a silver bracelet. I don't know what happened to it. I had a picture of him. I don't know what happened to that either. And then he gave everything he had to help me, and when it was done, everyone walked away from him as if he didn't matter."

"If you had remembered the rape when you first came back, would you have stayed? Or would you have fled from your body again?"

"I don't know."

"Then if forgetting Daemon was the price that had to be paid in order to keep those memories at bay until you were strong enough to face them. . . . He would say it was a fair price."

"It's very easy to make statements about what Daemon would say since he's not here to deny them, isn't it?" Tears filled her eyes.

"You're forgetting something, little witch," Lucivar said

sharply. "He's my brother, and he's a Warlord Prince. I've known him longer and far better than you."

Jaenelle shifted on the bench. "I don't blame you for what happened to him. The High Lord—"

"If you're going to demand that the High Lord shoulder the blame for Daemon being in the Twisted Kingdom, then you're going to have to shovel some of that blame onto me as well."

She twisted around to face him, her eyes chilly.

Lucivar took a deep breath. "He came to get me out of Pruul. He wanted me to go with him. And I refused to go because I thought he had killed you, that he was the one who had raped you."

"Daemon?"

Lucivar swore viciously. "Sometimes you can be incredibly naive. You have no idea what Daemon is capable of doing when he goes cold."

"You really believed that?"

He braced his head in his hands. "There was so much blood, so much pain. I couldn't get past the grief to think clearly enough to doubt what I'd been told. And when I accused him, he didn't deny it."

Jaenelle looked thoughtful. "He seduced me. Well, seduced Witch. When we were in the abyss."

"He what?" Lucivar asked with deadly calm.

"Don't get snarly," Jaenelle snapped. "It was a trick to make me heal the body. He didn't really want me. Her. He didn't . . ." Her voice trailed away. She waited a minute before continuing. "He said he'd been waiting for Witch all his life. That he'd been born to be her lover. But then he didn't want to be her lover."

"Hell's fire, Cat," Lucivar exploded. "You were a twelve-year-old who had recently been raped. What did you expect him to do?"

"I wasn't twelve in the abyss."

Lucivar narrowed his eyes, wondering what she meant by that.

"He lied to me," she said in a small voice.

"No, he didn't. He meant exactly what he said. If you had been eighteen and had offered him the Consort's ring, you would have found that out quick enough." Lucivar stared at the blurry garden. He cleared his throat. "Saetan loves you, Cat. And you love him. He did what he had to do to save his Queen. He did what any Warlord Prince would do. If you can't forgive him, how will you ever be able to forgive me?"

"Oh, Lucivar." Sobbing, Jaenelle threw her arms around him.

Lucivar held her, petted her, took aching comfort from the way she held him tight. His silent tears wet her hair. His tears were for her, whose soul wounds had been reopened; for himself, because he may have lost something precious so soon after it was found; for Saetan, who may have lost even more; and for Daemon. Most of all, for Daemon.

It was almost twilight when Jaenelle gently pulled away from him. "There's someone I need to talk to. I'll be back later."

Worried, Lucivar studied her slumped shoulders and pale face. "Where—" Caution warred with instinct. He floundered.

Jaenelle's lips held a shadow of an understanding smile. "I'm not going anywhere dangerous. I'll still be in Kaeleer. And no, Prince Yaslana, this isn't risky. I'm just going to see a friend."

He let her go, unable to do anything else.

Saetan stared at nothing, holding the pain at bay, holding the memories at bay. If he released his hold and they flooded in . . . he wasn't sure he would survive them, wasn't sure he would even try.

"Saetan?" Jaenelle hovered near the open study doorway.

"Lady." Protocol. The courtesies given and granted when a Warlord Prince addressed a Queen of equal or darker rank. He'd lost the privilege of addressing her any other way, of being anything more.

When she entered the room, he walked around the desk. He couldn't sit while she was standing, and he couldn't offer her a seat since the rest of the furniture in his study had been destroyed and he hadn't allowed Beale to clear up the mess.

Jaenelle approached hesitantly, her lower lip caught between her teeth, her hands twining restlessly. She didn't look at him.

"I talked to Lorn." Her voice quivered. She blinked rapidly. "He agreed with you that I shouldn't go to Terreille—except the Keep. We decided that I would create a shadow of myself that can interact with people so that I can search for Daemon while my body remains safe at the Keep. I'll only be able to search three days out of every month because of the physical drain the shadow will place on me, but I know someone I think will help me look for him."

"You must do what you think best," he said carefully.

She looked at him, her beautiful, ancient, haunted eyes full of tears. "S-Saetan?"

Still so young for all her strength and wisdom.

He opened his arms, opened his heart.

She clung to him, trembling violently.

She was the most painful, most glorious dance of his life.

"Saetan, I—"

He pressed a finger against her lips. "No, witch-child," he said with gentle regret. "Forgiveness doesn't work that way. You may want to forgive me, but you can't do it yet. Forgiving someone can take weeks, months, years. Sometimes it takes a lifetime. Until Daemon is whole again, all we can do is try to be kind to one another, and understanding, and take each day as it comes." He held her close, savoring the feeling, not knowing when, or if, he'd ever hold her like this again. "Come along, witch-child. It's almost dawn. You need to rest now."

He led her to her bedroom but didn't enter. Safe in his own room, he felt the loneliness already pressing down on him.

He curled up on his bed, unable to stop the tears he'd held back throughout the long, terrible night. It would take time. Weeks, months, maybe years. He knew it would take time.

But, please, sweet Darkness, please don't let it take a lifetime.

4 / Terreille

Surreal walked down the neglected street toward the market square, hoping her icy expression would offset her vulnerable physical state. She shouldn't have used that witch's brew to suppress last month's moontime, but the Hayllian guards Kartane SaDiablo had sent after her had been breathing down her neck then and she hadn't felt safe enough to risk being defenseless during the days when her body couldn't tolerate the use of her power beyond basic Craft.

Damn all Blood males to the bowels of Hell. When a witch's body made her vulnerable for a few days, it also made every Blood male a potential enemy. And right now she had enough enemies to worry about.

Well, she'd pick up a few things at the market and then hole up in her rooms with a couple of thick novels and wait it out.

Stifled, frightened cries came from the alley up ahead.

Calling in a long-bladed knife, Surreal slipped to the edge of the alley and peeked around the corner.

Four large, surly, Hayllian men. And one girl who was barely more than a child. Two of the men stood back, watching, as one of their comrades held the girl and the other's hands yanked her clothes aside.

Damn, damn, damn. It was a trap. There was no other reason for Hayllians to be in this part of the Realm, especially in this part of a dying city. She should just slip back to her rooms. If she was careful, they might not find her. There would be other Hayllians waiting around the places where she might purchase a ticket for a Web Coach, so that was out. And riding the Winds without the protection of a Coach might not be suicidal right now, but it would feel damn close.

But there was that girl. If she didn't intervene, that child was going to end up under those four brutes. Even if someone "rescued" her afterward, she'd be passed from man to man until the constant use or the brutality of one of them killed her.

Taking a deep breath, Surreal rushed into the alley.

An upward slash opened one man from armpit to collarbone. She swung her arm, just missing the girl's face, and managed to get in a shallow slash across the other's chest while she tried to pull the girl away.

Then the other two men joined the fight.

Diving under a fist that would have pulped one side of her head, Surreal rolled, sprang up, took two running steps and, because no one tried to stop her from going deeper into the alley, spun around.

A dead end behind her, and the Hayllians blocking the only way out.

Surreal looked at the girl, wanting to express her regret.

Smiling greedily as one of the unwounded men dropped a small bag of coins into her hands, the girl pulled her clothes together and hurried out of the alley.

Mercenary little bitch.

Surreal tried hard to remember the other girls she'd helped over the past five years, but remembering them didn't diminish the overwhelming sense of betrayal. Well, she'd come full circle. She'd come up from living in stinking alleys. Now she'd die in one, because she wasn't about to let Kartane SaDiablo truss her up and hand her over as a present to the High Priestess of Hayll.

The men stepped forward, smiling viciously.

"Let her go."

The quiet, eerie, midnight voice came from behind her.

Surreal watched the men, watched surprise, uneasiness, and fear harden into a look that always meant pain for a woman.

"Let her go," the voice said again.

"Go to Hell," the largest Hayllian said, stepping forward.

A mist rose up behind the men, forming a wall across the alley.

"Just slit the bitch's throat and be done with it," the man with the shoulder wound said.

"Can't have any fun and games with the half-breed, so the other will have to learn some manners," the largest man said.

Thick mist suddenly filled the alley. Eyes, like burning red gems, appeared, and something let out a wet-sounding snarl.

Surreal screamed breathlessly as a hand clamped on her left arm.

"Come with me," said that terrifyingly familiar midnight voice.

The mist swirled, too thick to see the person guiding her through it as easily as if it were clear water.

More snarls. Then high-pitched, desperate screams.

"W-what—" Surreal stammered.

"Hell Hounds."

To the right of her, something hit the ground with a wet plop.

Surreal tried hard to swallow, tried hard not to breathe.

The next step took them out of the mist and back to the welcome sight of the neglected street.

"Are you staying around here?" the voice asked.

Surreal finally looked at her companion and felt a stab of disappointment immediately followed by a sense of relief. The woman was her height, and the body in the form-fitting black jumpsuit, though slender, definitely didn't belong to the child she remembered. But the long hair was golden, and the eyes were hidden behind dark glasses.

Surreal tried to pull away. "I'm grateful you got my ass out of that alley, but my mother told me not to tell strangers where I live."

"We're not strangers, and I'm sure that's not all Titian told you."

Surreal tried again to pull away. The hand on her arm clamped down harder. Finally realizing she still held a weapon in her other hand, Surreal swung the knife, bringing it down hard on the woman's wrist.

The knife went through as if there was nothing there and vanished.

"What are you?" Surreal gasped.

"An illusion that's called a shadow."

"Who are you?"

"Briarwood is the pretty poison. There is no cure for Briarwood." The woman smiled coldly. "Does that answer your question?"

Surreal studied the woman, trying to find some trace of

the child she remembered. After a minute, she said, "You really are Jaenelle, aren't you? Or some part of her?"

Jaenelle smiled, but there was no humor in it. "I really am." A pause. Then, "We need to talk, Surreal. Privately."

Oh, yes, they needed to talk. "I have to go to the market first."

The hand with the dagger-sharp, black-tinted nails tightened for a moment before releasing her. "All right."

Surreal hesitated. Snarls and crunching noises came out of the mist behind them. "Don't you have to finish the kill?"

"I don't think that'll be a problem," Jaenelle said dryly. "Piles of Hound shit aren't much of a threat to anyone."

Surreal paled.

Jaenelle's lips tightened. "I apologize," she said after a minute. "We all have facets to our personalities. This has brought out the nastier ones in mine. No one will enter the alley and nothing will leave. The Harpies will arrive soon and take care of things."

Surreal led the way to the market square, where she bought folded breads filled with chicken and vegetables from one vendor, small beef pies from another, and fresh fruit from a third.

"I'll make you a healing brew," Jaenelle said when they finally returned to Surreal's rooms.

Still wondering why Jaenelle had sought her out, Surreal nodded before retreating into the bathroom to get cleaned up. When she returned, there was a covered plate on the small kitchen table and a steaming cup filled with a witch's brew.

Settling into a chair, Surreal sipped the brew and felt the pain in her abdomen gradually dull. "How did you find me?" she asked.

For the first time, there was amusement in Jaenelle's smile. "Well, sugar, since you're the only Gray Jewel in the entire Realm of Terreille, you're not that hard to find."

"I didn't know someone could be traced that way."

"Whoever is hunting you can't use that method. It requires wearing a Jewel equal or darker than yours."

"Why did you find me?" Surreal asked quietly.

"I need your help. I want to find Daemon."

Surreal stared at the cup. "Whatever he did at Cassandra's Altar that night was done to help you. Hasn't he suffered enough?"

"Too much."

There was sorrow and regret in Jaenelle's voice. The eyes would have told her more. "Do you have to wear those damn dark glasses?" Surreal asked sharply.

Jaenelle hesitated. "You might find my eyes disturbing."

"I'll take the chance."

Jaenelle raised the glasses.

Those eyes belonged to someone who had experienced the most twisted nightmares of the soul and had survived.

Surreal swallowed hard. "I see what you mean."

Jaenelle replaced the glasses. "I can bring him out of the Twisted Kingdom, but I need to make the link through his body."

If only Jaenelle had come a few months ago.

"I don't know where he is," Surreal said.

"But you can look for him. I can stay in this form only three days out of the month. He's running out of time, Surreal. If he isn't shown the road back soon, there won't be anything left of him."

Surreal closed her eyes. *Shit.*

Jaenelle poured the rest of the brew into Surreal's cup. "Even a Gray-Jeweled witch's moontime shouldn't give her this much pain."

Surreal shifted. Winced. "I suppressed last month's time." She wrapped her hands around the cup. "Daemon lived with me for a little while. Until a few months ago."

"What happened a few months ago?"

"Kartane SaDiablo happened," Surreal said viciously. Then she smiled. "Your spell or web or whatever it was you spun around Briarwood's uncles did a good job on him. You wouldn't even recognize the bastard." She paused. "Robert Benedict is dead, by the way."

"How unfortunate," Jaenelle murmured, her voice dripping venom. "And dear Dr. Carvay?"

"Alive, more or less. Not for much longer from what I've heard."

"Tell me about Kartane . . . and Daemon."

"Last spring, Daemon showed up at the flat where I was living. Our paths have crossed a few times since—" Surreal faltered.

"Since the night at Cassandra's Altar."

"Yes. He's like Tersa used to be. Show up, stay a couple of days, and vanish again. This time he stayed. Then Kartane showed up." Surreal drained her cup. "Apparently he's been hunting for Daemon for some time, but, unlike Dorothea, he seems to have a better idea of where to look. He started demanding that Daemon help him get free of this terrible spell someone had put on him. As if he'd never done anything to deserve it. When it became apparent that Daemon was lost in the Twisted Kingdom and, therefore, useless, Kartane looked at me—and noticed my ears. At the same moment he realized I was Titian's child—and his—Daemon exploded and threw him out.

"I guess he figured that bringing Sadi to Dorothea wouldn't buy him enough help, but bringing Dorothea his only possible offspring would be a solid bargaining chip. And a female offspring who could continue the bloodline would provide strong incentive—even if she was a half-breed.

"Daemon insisted that we leave immediately because Kartane would return after dark with guards. And he did.

"Before Daemon and I caught the Wind and headed out, we had agreed on a city in another Territory. He was right behind me, riding close. And then he wasn't there anymore. I haven't seen him since."

"And you've been running since then."

"Yeah." She felt so tired. She wanted to lose herself in a book, in sleep. Too much of a risk now. The rest of the Hayllian guards would start wondering about those four men, would start looking soon.

"Eat your food, Surreal."

Surreal bit into the folded bread and finally wondered why she hadn't tested that brew—and wondered why she didn't care.

Jaenelle checked the bedroom, then studied the worn

sofa in the living area. "Do you want to tuck up in bed or curl up here?"

"Can't," Surreal mumbled, annoyed because she was going to cry.

"Yes, you can." Taking comforters and pillows from the bedroom, Jaenelle turned the sofa into an inviting nest. "I can stay two more days. No one will disturb you while I'm here."

"I'll help you search," Surreal said, snuggling into the sofa.

"I know." Jaenelle smiled dryly. "You're Titian's daughter. You wouldn't do anything else."

"Don't know if I like being that predictable," Surreal grumbled.

Jaenelle made another cup of the healing brew, gave Surreal first choice of two new novels, and settled into a chair.

Surreal drank her brew, read the first page of the novel twice, and gave up. Looking at Jaenelle, questions buzzed inside her head.

She didn't want to hear the answers to any of them.

For now, it was enough that, once they found Daemon, Jaenelle would bring him out of the Twisted Kingdom.

For now, it was enough to feel safe.

PART IV

CHAPTER
THIRTEEN

1 / Kaeleer

"Spring is the season of romance," Hekatah said, watching her companion. "And she's eighteen now. Old enough to enjoy a husband."

"True." Lord Jorval traced little circles on the scarred table. "But selecting the *right* husband is important."

"All he needs to be is young, handsome, and virile—and capable of obeying orders," Hekatah snapped. "The husband will merely be the sexual bait that will lure her away from that monster. Or do you want to live under the High Lord's thumb, once his 'daughter' sets up her court and begins her reign?"

Jorval looked stubborn. "A husband could be much more than sexual bait. A mature man could guide his Queen wife, help her to make the right decisions, keep unhealthy influences away from her."

Frustrated to the point of screaming, Hekatah sat back and curled her hands around the wooden arms of the chair so that she wouldn't reach across the table and rip half that fool's face off.

Hell's fire, she missed Greer. He had understood subtlety. He had understood the sensible precaution of using intermediaries whenever possible to avoid being in the direct line of fire. As a member of the Dark Council, Jorval was extremely useful in keeping the Council's dislike and distrust of Saetan quietly simmering. But he lusted for Jaenelle Angelline and entertained fantasies of nightly

bouts of masterful sex which made the pale bitch pliant
and submissive to his every whim, in and out of the bed.
Which was fine, but the fool couldn't seem to see past the
sweaty sheets to consider what might be waiting to have a
little chat with him.

She was fairly sure that Saetan would grit his teeth and
endure an unwelcome male his Queen was besotted with.
He was too well trained and too committed to the old ways
of the Blood to do otherwise. But the Eyrien half-breed. . . .
He wouldn't think twice about tearing his Lady out of her
lover's arms—or tearing off her lover's arms—and keeping
her isolated until she was clearheaded again.

And she doubted either of them could be convinced that
Jaenelle was panting and moaning for someone who looked
like Lord Jorval.

"He must be young," Hekatah insisted. "A pretty boy
with enough experience between the sheets to be convincing, and charming enough for her family to believe, however doubtfully, that she's wildly in love."

Jorval sulked.

Tightening her hold on her temper a little more, Hekatah
altered her voice to sound hesitant. "There are reasons for
caution, Jorval. Perhaps you remember a colleague of
mine." She curled her hands until they looked like
twisted claws.

Jorval abandoned his sulk. "I remember him. He was
most helpful. I'd hoped he would return." When Hekatah
said nothing, he took an unsteady breath. "What happened
to him?"

"The High Lord happened to him," Hekatah replied.
"He made the mistake of drawing attention to himself. No
one has seen him since."

"I see."

Yes, finally, he *was* beginning to see.

Hekatah leaned forward and stroked Jorval's hand.
"Sometimes the duties and responsibilities of power require sacrifices, Lord Jorval." When he didn't protest,
she hid a triumphant smile. "Now, if you were to arrange
a marriage for Jaenelle Angelline with the son of a man

you felt comfortable working with—a handsome, controllable son—"

"How would that help me?" Jorval demanded.

Hekatah stifled her irritation. "The father would advise the son on the policies and changes that should be implemented in Kaeleer—changes that, at Jaenelle's insistence, would be accepted. A great many decisions are made during pillow talk, as I'm sure you know."

"And how would that help me?" Jorval demanded again.

"Just as the son follows the advice of the father, so the father follows the advice of his friend—who just happens to be the only source for the tonic that keeps the Lady so hungry for the son's attentions that she'll agree to anything."

"Ah." Jorval stroked his chin. "Aahhh."

"And if, for some reason, the High Lord or some other member of the family"—the flicker of fear in Jorval's eyes told her he'd already had a close brush with Lucivar Yaslana's temper—"should react badly, well, finding another hot, handsome boy would be easy enough, but finding strong, intelligent men to guide the Realm . . ." Hekatah spread her hands and shrugged.

Jorval considered her words for several minutes. Hekatah waited patiently. As much as he might want the hot sexual fantasy, Jorval wanted power—or the illusion of power—much more.

"Lady Angelline will be coming to Little Terreille in two weeks. And I do have a . . . friend . . . with a suitable offspring. However, getting Lady Angelline to agree to the marriage . . ."

Hekatah called in a small bottle and set it on the table. "Lady Angelline is well-known for her compassion and her healing abilities. If, by some terrible accident, a child were injured, I'm sure she could be prevailed upon to do the healing. If the injuries were life-threatening, the power expended for a full healing would leave her physically and mentally exhausted. Then, if someone she trusted were to offer her a relaxing glass of wine, she would probably be too tired to test it. The wedding would, regrettably, have to be a small, quiet affair that would take place shortly afterward. Between the fatigue and this brew mixed with the wine, she would be compliant enough to say what she was told to say and sign what she was told to sign.

"The young couple would stay at the wedding feast for a short time before retreating to their room to consummate the marriage."

Jorval's nostrils flared. "I see."

Hekatah called in a second bottle. "The proper dose of this aphrodisiac, slipped into her wine during the wedding toast, will make her hungry for her new husband."

Jorval licked his lips.

"The next morning, the second dose must be given. This is very important because her hunger must be strong enough to override the High Lord's desire for an interview with her husband. By the time she's ready to release the boy from his conjugal duties, the High Lord won't be able to deny or object to the attachment without looking like a tyrant or a jealous fool." Hekatah paused, not pleased with the way Jorval was eyeing those bottles. "And the wise man guiding this affair will never be suspected—unless he calls attention to himself."

With visible effort, Jorval put his fantasies aside. He carefully vanished the bottles. "I'll be in touch."

"There's no need," Hekatah said a little too quickly. "Knowing I could help is enough. I'll let you know where, and when, to pick up the next supply of the aphrodisiac."

Jorval bowed and left.

Hekatah sat back, exhausted. Jorval was ignorant of, or chose to ignore, the common courtesies. He'd brought no refreshment and had offered none. Probably thought he was too important. And he was, damn him. Right now he was too important to her plans for her to insist on the amenities. However, once the little bitch was sufficiently cut off from Saetan, she would be able to eliminate Jorval.

Two weeks. That would give her enough time to complete the rest of her plan and set the trap that would, with luck, get rid of a half-breed Eyrien Warlord Prince as well.

2 / Kaeleer

Something felt wrong.

Lucivar set the armload of wood into the box by the kitchen hearth.

Very wrong.

Straightening up, he made a sweeping psychic probe of the area, using Luthvian's house as the center point.

Nothing. But the feeling didn't go away.

Preoccupied with the nagging uneasiness, he didn't move when Roxie entered the kitchen, didn't really notice the light in her eyes or the way her walk changed as she came toward him.

He'd spent the past two days doing chores for Luthvian while dodging Roxie's amorous advances. Two days was about all he and Luthvian could manage together, and they only managed that because she was busy with her students most of the day, and he left right after dinner to spend the night in a mountain clearing.

"You're so strong," Roxie said, running her hands over his chest.

Not again. Not again.

Normally he wouldn't have allowed a woman to touch him like that. Normally he would have considered that tone of voice an invitation to an intimate introduction to his fist.

So why was he afraid? Why were his nerves buzzing?

Sever it this time. Break the link for good. No. Can't. Won't be able to reach him if . . .

Roxie's arms wound around Lucivar's neck. She rubbed her breasts against his chest. "I haven't had a Warlord Prince yet."

Where was the fear coming from?

You can't have this body. This body is promised to him.

Roxie pressed against him. She playfully nipped his neck. He set his hands on her hips, holding her still while he concentrated on finding the source of that wasp-angry buzzing.

No. Not again.

It was coming from the Ring of Honor Jaenelle had given him. The buzzing, the fear, the cold rage building under the fear. Those weren't his feelings washing through him, but hers.

Hell's fire, Mother Night, and may the Darkness be merciful. Hers.

"I see you've changed your tune," Luthvian said tartly as she entered the kitchen.

Cold, cold rage. If it wasn't banked quickly . . .

"I have to go," Lucivar said absently. He felt the pull of arms around his neck and automatically shoved the body away from him.

Luthvian started swearing.

Ignoring her, he turned toward the door and wondered for a moment why Roxie was lying in a heap on the kitchen floor.

"You have to service me!" Roxie shouted, pushing herself into a sitting position. "You got me aroused. You have to service me."

Spinning around, Lucivar snapped a leg off a kitchen chair and tossed it into Roxie's lap. "Use that." He headed out the door.

I won't allow this. I will not submit to this.

"Lucivar!"

Snarling, he tried to shake off Luthvian's hand. "I have to go. Cat's in trouble."

Luthvian's hand tightened. "You're sure, aren't you? You sense her well enough that you're sure."

"Yes!" He didn't want to hit her. He didn't want to hurt her. But if she didn't let him go . . .

The hand on his arm trembled. "You'll send word to me? You'll let me know if . . . if she needs help?"

Lucivar gave Luthvian a hard, steady look. She might be jealous of the way the men in the family were drawn to Jaenelle, but she cared. He kissed her cheek roughly. "I'll send word."

Luthvian stepped back. "You spent all those years training to be a warrior, so go make yourself useful."

No.

Lucivar sped along the Ebon-gray Web, squeezing out all the speed he could, knowing it was already too late.

I won't let you.

Whatever happened, he'd take care of her afterward. Sweet Darkness, please let there be an afterward. He pushed harder.

No feelings from the Ring. No buzzing. Nothing at all except . . .

Noooooo!

. . . the rage. Mother Night, the rage!

Lucivar thrust his way through the sick-faced crowd, homing in on the spot where Jaenelle's unleashed power was concentrated. A middle-aged Warlord stood on one side of the hallway, babbling at a grim-looking Mephis. The aftertaste of power swirled behind a door on the opposite side.

Lucivar swung toward the door.

"Lucivar, no!"

Ignoring Mephis's command, Lucivar snapped the Gray lock his demon-dead elder brother had placed on the door.

"Lucivar, don't go in there!"

Lucivar threw the door open, stepped inside the room, and froze.

In front of him, a finger lay on the carpet, its gold ring partially melted into the flesh, the Jewel shattered to a fine powder.

It was the largest—and the only identifiable piece—of what must have been a full-grown man. The rest was splattered all over the room.

The buzzing in his head warned him to take a normal breath before he passed out. If he took a normal breath while standing in this room, he'd heave for a week.

But there was something wrong about the room, and he wasn't leaving until he figured it out.

When he did, Lucivar's temper rose to the killing edge.

One male body. One demolished bed. The rest of the furniture, although ruined by bone fragments and blood, was untouched.

Lucivar backed out of the room and turned toward the man who had been babbling at Mephis. "What did you do to her?" he asked too calmly.

"To *her*?" The Warlord pointed a shaking hand toward

the room. "Look what that bitch did to my son. She's mad. Mad! She—"

Roaring an Eyrien war cry, Lucivar slammed the Warlord against the wall. "WHAT DID YOU DO TO HER?"

The Warlord squealed. No one tried to help him.

"Lucivar." Mephis held up a handful of papers. "It appears Jaenelle got married this afternoon to Lord—"

Lucivar snarled. "She wouldn't marry willingly without the family present." He bared his teeth at the Warlord. "Would she?"

"T-they were in l-love," the Warlord stammered. "A whirlwind r-romance. She didn't want you to know until it was done."

"Someone didn't," Lucivar agreed. Smiling, he called in the Eyrien war blade and held it up where the Warlord could see it. "Do you want your face?" he asked mildly.

"Lucivar," Mephis warned.

"Stay out of this, Mephis," Lucivar snapped, his barely restrained fury freezing everyone in the hallway.

Think. She'd been afraid, and very little frightened Jaenelle. She'd been afraid, but also angry enough to consider breaking the link between spirit and body, determined enough to abandon the husk rather than submit. Think. If this was Terreille . . .

"What did you give her?" When the Warlord didn't answer, Lucivar set the edge of the war blade against the man's cheek. The skin sliced cleanly. The blood ran.

"A m-mild brew. To calm her down. She was afraid. Afraid of all of them. Especially y-you."

A stupid thing to say to a man holding a weapon large enough and sharp enough to cut through bone.

They had drugged her. Something strong enough to scramble her wits while still leaving her capable of signing the marriage contract. That still didn't explain that room.

"Afterward," Lucivar crooned. "What did you give her to prepare her for the marriage bed?" When the Warlord just stared at him, he shifted the war blade, cut a little deeper this time. "Where are the bottles?"

Panting, the Warlord waved a hand toward a nearby door.

Mephis went into the room, then returned with two small bottles.

Lucivar vanished the war blade, took one bottle, and flicked the top off. Probed the drops in the bottom. If he'd been given a drink with this in it, he wouldn't have touched it. Under normal circumstances, Jaenelle wouldn't have either.

He vanished that bottle, took the other one that was still half filled with a dark powder, and swore viciously. He knew—how well he knew!—what a large dose of *safframate* would do to someone of his build and weight. He could imagine the agony it would produce in Jaenelle.

He held up the bottle. "You gave her this? Then you're responsible for what's in that room."

The Warlord shook his head violently. "It's harmless. Harmless! Added to a glass of wine, it's just a variety of the Night of Fire brew. Always use a Night of Fire brew on the wedding night."

Lucivar bared his teeth in a smile. "Since it's harmless, you won't mind drinking the other dose. Mephis, get him a glass of wine."

Sweat popped out on the Warlord's forehead.

Mephis disappeared for a minute, then returned with the wine.

After pouring almost all of the dark powder into the wine, Lucivar handed the bottle to Mephis and took the wineglass. His other hand closed around the Warlord's throat. "Now, you can drink this, or I can tear your throat out. Your choice."

"W-want a hearing before the Dark Council," the Warlord whimpered.

"That's certainly within your rights," Mephis agreed quietly. He looked at Lucivar. "Are you going to tear his throat out or shall I?"

Lucivar laughed maliciously. "Wouldn't do him much good to go to the Council then, would it?" His fingers dug into the Warlord's throat.

"D-drink."

"I knew you'd be reasonable," Lucivar crooned. He loosened his hold enough to let the Warlord swallow the wine.

"Now." He threw the Warlord into the room where Mephis had found the bottles. "In order to give the Dark Council an accurate accounting, I think you should enjoy the same experience you intended for Lady Angelline." After sealing the room with an Ebon-gray shield and adding a timing spell, he turned to a man hovering nearby. "The shield will vanish in twenty-four hours."

This time he didn't have to shove his way through the crowd. They pressed against the walls to let him pass.

Mephis caught up with him before he got out of the manor house. Probing the area, he walked into the nearest empty room—someone's study. He found it grimly appropriate, even if it wasn't Saetan's.

Mephis locked the door. "That was quite a show you put on."

"The show's just started." Lucivar prowled the room. "I didn't see you trying to stop me."

"We can't afford to be publicly divided. Besides, there wasn't any point in trying to stop you. You outrank me, and I doubt you'd let brotherly feelings get in your way."

"You got that right."

Mephis swore. "Do you realize the trouble we're going to have with the Dark Council over this? We're not above the Law, Lucivar."

Lucivar stopped in front of Mephis. "You play by your rules, and I'll play be mine."

"She signed a marriage contract."

"Not willingly."

"You don't know that. And twenty witnesses say otherwise."

"I wear her Ring. I can *feel* her, Mephis." Lucivar's voice shook. "She was ready to break the link rather than submit to being mounted."

Mephis said nothing for a full minute. "Jaenelle has problems with physical intimacy. You know that."

Lucivar slammed his fist into the door. "Damn you! Are you so blind or have your balls dried up so much you'll submit to anything rather than have someone bleat about the SaDiablo family misusing their power? Well, I'm not blind and there's nothing wrong with my balls. She's my

Queen—mine!—and rules or not, Laws or not, Dark Council or not, if someone makes her suffer, I will pay them
back in kind."

They stared at each other, Lucivar breathing hard,
Mephis unmoving.

Finally, Mephis slumped against the door. "We can't go
through this again, Lucivar. We can't go through the fear
of losing her again."

"Where is she?"

"Father took her to the Keep—with strict orders for the
rest of the family to stay away."

Lucivar pushed Mephis aside. "Well, we all know how
well I follow orders, don't we?"

3 / Kaeleer

Saetan looked like a man who had barely survived a
battlefield.

Which wasn't far from the truth, Lucivar thought as he
quietly closed the door of Jaenelle's sitting room at the
Keep.

"My instructions were explicit, Lucivar."

The voice had no strength. The face looked gray and
strained.

Lucivar pointed casually to the Birthright Red Jewels
Saetan wore. "You're not going to be able to toss me out
wearing those."

Saetan didn't call in the Black.

Lucivar guessed, correctly, that getting Jaenelle to the
Keep in her present physical and emotional condition had
drained the Black.

Saetan limped to a chair, swearing softly. He tried to
lift a decanter of yarbarah from the side table. His hand
shook violently.

Crossing the room, Lucivar took the decanter, filled a
glass, and warmed the blood wine. "Do you need fresh
blood?" he asked quietly.

Saetan stared at him coldly.

Even after all these centuries, Luthvian's accusations

were still deep wounds barely scabbed over. Guardians needed fresh blood from time to time to maintain their strength. At first, Lucivar had tried to understand Saetan's anger at being offered blood hot from the vein, tried not to feel insulted that the High Lord would accept that gift from anyone but him. Now he felt annoyed that someone else's words still hung between them. He wasn't a child. If the son willingly offered the gift, why couldn't the father graciously accept it?

Saetan looked away. "Thank you, but no."

Lucivar pressed the wineglass into Saetan's hand. "Drink this."

"I want you away from here, Lucivar."

Lucivar poured a large glass of brandy for himself, booted a footstool over to Saetan's chair, and sat down. "When I walk away from here, I'm taking her with me."

"You can't," Saetan snapped. "She's . . ." He raked his fingers through his hair. "I don't think she's sane."

"Not surprising since they dosed her with *safframate*."

Saetan glared at him. "Don't be an ass. *Safframate* doesn't do that to a person."

"How would you know? You've never been dosed with it." Lucivar struggled to keep the bitterness out of his voice. This wasn't the time to worry old hurts.

"I've used *safframate*."

Lucivar narrowed his eyes and studied his father. "Explain."

Saetan drained his glass. "*Safframate* is a sexual stimulant that's used to prolong stamina, prolong one's ability to give pleasure. The seeds are the size of a snapdragon seed. You add one or two crushed seeds to a glass of wine."

"One or two seeds." Lucivar snorted. "High Lord, in Terreille they crush it into a powder and use it by the spoonful."

"That's madness! If you gave someone that much—" Saetan stared at the closed door that led into Jaenelle's bedroom.

"Exactly," Lucivar said softly. "Pleasure very quickly becomes pain. The body becomes so stimulated, so sensitive that contact with anything hurts. The sex drive obliterates everything else, but that much *safframate* also blocks the ability to achieve orgasm so there's no relief, just driving need and sensitivity that's constantly increased by the stimulation."

"Mother Night," Saetan whispered, slumping in his chair.

"But if, for whatever reason, a person doesn't submit to being used until the drug wears off . . . well, the encounter can turn violent."

Saetan blinked back tears. "You were used like that, weren't you?"

"Yes. But not often. Most witches didn't think riding my cock was worth having my temper in the bed with it. And most of the ones who tried didn't walk away intact if they walked away at all. I had my own definition of violent passion."

"And Daemon?"

"He had his own way of dealing with it." Lucivar shuddered. "They didn't call him the Sadist for nothing."

Saetan reached for the yarbarah. His hand still shook, but not as badly as before. "What do you suggest we do for Jaenelle?"

"She doesn't deserve to endure this alone, and she'll never agree to sex for whatever small relief it might give her. So that leaves violence." Lucivar drained his brandy glass. "I'm taking her into Askavi. I'll keep us away from the villages. That way, if anything goes wrong, no one else will get caught in the backlash."

Saetan lowered his glass. "What about you?"

"I promised myself I'd take care of her. That's what I'm going to do."

Not giving himself any more time to think, Lucivar set his glass on the table and crossed the room. He paused at the door, not sure how to approach a witch strong enough to tear his mind apart with a thought. Then he shrugged and opened the door, trusting instinct.

The bedroom felt heavy with the growing psychic storm. He stepped into the room and braced himself.

Jaenelle paced frantically, her hands gripping her upper arms tight enough to bruise. She glanced at him and bared her teeth. Her eyes held revulsion and no recognition. "Get out."

Relief swept through him. Every second she resisted the desire to attack a male increased his chances of surviving the next few days.

"Pack a bag," Lucivar said. "Casual clothes. A warm jacket for evenings. Walking boots."

"I'm not going anywhere," Jaenelle snarled.

"We're going hunting."

"No. Get out."

Lucivar braced his hands on his hips. "You can pack a bag or not, but we're going hunting. Now."

"I don't want to go anywhere with you."

He heard the desperation and fear in her voice. Desperation because she didn't want to leave the safety of this room. Fear because he was pushing her and, cornered, she might strike back and hurt him.

It gave him hope.

"You can leave this room on your own two feet or over my shoulder. Your choice, Cat."

She grabbed a pillow and shredded it, swearing viciously in several languages. When his only response was to step toward her, she scrambled away from him, putting the bed between them.

He wondered if she saw the irony of it.

"You're running out of time, Cat," he said softly.

She grabbed another pillow and threw it at him. "Bastard!"

"Prick," he corrected. He started around the bed.

She ran for the dressing room door.

He got there ahead of her, his spread wings making him look huge.

She backed away from him.

Saetan stepped into the bedroom. "Go with him, witch-child."

Trapped between father and brother, she stood there, shaking.

"We'll get away from everyone," Lucivar coaxed. "Just the two of us. Lots of fresh air and open ground."

The thoughts flashed through her eyes, over her face. Open ground. Room to maneuver. Room to run. Open ground, where she wouldn't be trapped in a room with all this maleness pulling at her, choking her.

"You won't touch me." Not a question or a demand. A plea.

"I won't touch you," Lucivar promised.

Jaenelle's shoulders slumped. "All right. I'll pack."

He folded his wings and stepped aside so that she could slip into the dressing room. The defeat in her voice made him want to weep.

Saetan joined him. "Be careful, Lucivar," he said quietly.

Lucivar nodded. He already felt tired. "It'll be better in the open, out on the land."

"Experience?"

"Yeah. We'll stop at the cabin first to pick up the sleeping bags and other gear. Ask Smoke to join us. I think she'll be able to tolerate him. And if anything goes wrong, he can send word."

Saetan didn't need to ask what could go wrong. They both knew what a Black-Jeweled Black Widow Queen could do to a man.

Saetan ran his hands over Lucivar's shoulders. He kissed his son's cheek. "May the Darkness embrace you," he said hoarsely, turning away. Lucivar pulled Saetan into a hard hug.

"Be careful, Lucivar. I don't want anything to happen to you now that you're finally here. And I *don't* want you with me in Hell."

Lucivar leaned back and smiled his lazy, arrogant smile. "I promise to stay out of trouble, Father."

Saetan snorted. "You mean it as much now as you did when you were little," he said dryly.

"Maybe even less."

Left alone while Jaenelle finished packing, Lucivar wondered if he was doing the right thing. He already mourned the game they would hunt, the animals who would die so savagely. If the four-legged bloodletting wasn't enough, she would turn on him. He expected her to. When she did, Saetan wouldn't find his son waiting for him in the Dark Realm. There wouldn't be anything left of him to wait.

4 / Kaeleer

"The Dark Council is quite distressed over the whole matter." Lord Magstrom shifted uneasily in his chair.

Saetan held his temper through sheer force of will. The man sitting on the other side of his blackwood desk had done nothing to deserve his rage. "The Council isn't alone in its distress."

"Yes, of course. But for Lady Angelline to . . ." Magstrom faltered.

"Among the Blood, rape is punishable by execution. At least it is in the rest of Kaeleer," Saetan said too softly.

"It's punishable by execution in Little Terreille as well," Magstrom replied stiffly.

"Then the little bastard got what he deserved."

"But . . . they were newly married," Magstrom protested.

"Even if that were true, which I doubt despite the damn signatures, a marriage contract doesn't excuse rape. Drugging a woman so that she's incapable of refusing doesn't mean she's agreed to anything. I'd say Jaenelle expressed her refusal quite eloquently, wouldn't you?" Saetan steepled his fingers and leaned back in his chair. "I've analyzed the two 'harmless substances' Jaenelle was given. Being a Black Widow, I have the training to reproduce them. If you choose to insist they had nothing to do with Jaenelle's behavior, why don't I make up another batch? We can test them on your granddaughter. She's Jaenelle's age."

Clutching the arms of the chair, Lord Magstrom said nothing.

Saetan rounded the desk and poured two glasses of brandy. Handing one to Lord Magstrom, he rested his hip on the corner of his desk. "Relax. I wouldn't do that to a child. Besides," he added quietly, "I may lose two of my children within the next few days. I wouldn't wish that on another man."

"Two?"

Saetan looked away from the concern and sympathy in Magstrom's eyes. "The first brew they gave Jaenelle inhibits will. She would have said what she'd been told to say, done what she'd been told to do. Unfortunately, that particular brew also has the side effect of magnifying emotional distress. A large dose of *safframate* and a forced sexual encounter were just the kind of stimulants that would have pushed her to the killing edge. And she'll remain on the killing edge until the drugs totally wear off."

Magstrom sipped his brandy. "Will she recover?"

"I don't know. If the Darkness is merciful, she will." Saetan clenched his teeth. "Lucivar took her to Askavi to spend some time with the land, away from people."

"Does he know about these violent tendencies?"

"He knows."

Magstrom hesitated. "You don't expect him to return, do you?"

"No. Neither does he. And I don't know what that will do to her."

"I like him," Magstrom said. "He has a rough kind of charm."

"Yes, he does." Saetan drained his glass, fighting not to give in to grief before there was a need to. He tightened his control. "No matter what the outcome, Jaenelle will no longer visit Little Terreille without a full escort of my choosing."

Magstrom pushed himself out of the chair and carefully set his glass on the desk. "I think that's for the best. I hope Prince Yaslana will be among them."

Saetan held on until Lord Magstrom left the Hall. Then he threw the brandy glasses against the wall. It didn't make him feel better. The broken glass reminded him too much of a shattered crystal chalice and two sons who had paid dearly because he was their father.

He sank to his knees. He'd already wept for one son. He wouldn't grieve for the other. Not yet. He wouldn't grieve for that foolish, arrogant Eyrien prick, that charming, temperamental pain in the ass.

Ah, Lucivar.

5 / Kaeleer

"Damn it, Cat, I told you to wait." Lucivar threw an Ebongray shield across the game trail, half-wincing in anticipation of her running into it face first.

She stopped inches away from the shield and spun

around, her glazed eyes searching for a spot in the thick undergrowth that she could push her way through.

"Stay away from me," she panted.

Lucivar held up the waterskin. "You ripped up your arm on the thorns back there. Let me pour some water over the cuts to clean them."

Looking down at her bare arm, she seemed surprised at the blood flowing freely from half a dozen deep scratches.

Lucivar gritted his teeth and waited. She'd stripped down to a sleeveless undershirt that offered her skin no protection in rough country, but right now sharp pain didn't hurt as much as the constant rub of cloth against oversensitive skin.

"Come on, Cat," he coaxed. "Just stick your arm out so that I can pour some water over it."

She cautiously held out her arm, her body angled away from him. Stepping only as close as necessary, he poured water over the scratches, washing away the blood and, he hoped, most of the dirt.

"Have a sip of water," he said, offering the waterskin. If he could coax her into taking a drink, maybe he could coax her into standing still for five minutes—something she hadn't done since he'd brought them to this part of Ebon Rih.

"Stay away from me." Her voice came out low and harsh. Desperate.

He shifted slightly, still offering the water.

"Stay away from me." She whirled and ran through the Ebon-gray shield as if it weren't there.

He took a long drink and sighed. He would get her through this, somehow. But after the past two days of unrelenting movement, he wasn't sure how much more either of them could take.

Lucivar leaned against a tree, finding a little comfort in the rhythmic *whack whack whack* coming from the clearing. At least destroying the abandoned shack with a sledgehammer gave Jaenelle an outlet for sexual rage and burning energy. Even more important, it was an outlet that would keep her in one place for a little while.

Hell's fire, he was tired. The Masters of the Eyrien hunting camps couldn't match Jaenelle's ability to set a grueling pace. Even Smoke, with that tireless, ground-eating trot, was struggling. Of course, unlike one drug-driven witch, wolves liked to do things like eat and sleep, two items now high on Lucivar's list of sensual pleasures.

He called in his sleeping bag, unrolled it, and used Craft to fix it in the air high enough so that his wings wouldn't drag the ground. Pushing the top of the sleeping bag against the tree trunk, he sat down with a groan he didn't try to stifle.

Lucivar?

Lucivar looked around until he spotted Smoke peering at him from behind a tree. "It's all right. The Lady's tearing up a shack."

Smoke whined and hid behind the tree.

He puzzled over the wolf's distress, then hastily sent a mental picture of the broken-down structure.

Cabin made by stupid humans. Smoke sneezed.

Lucivar smothered a laugh. He couldn't argue with Smoke's conclusion. The wolf's reference points for a "proper human den" included the Hall, the cottages in Halaway, the family's other country houses, and Jaenelle's cabin. So it made sense that Smoke would see the shack as a den made by an inept human.

As knowledge of the kindred's reemergence spread, the human Blood had divided into two camps arguing over the intelligence and Craft abilities of the nonhuman Blood. It had amused and dismayed the few humans who had the opportunity to work with the wild kindred to discover that they had similar prejudices about humans. Humans were divided into two groups: their humans and other humans. Their humans were the Lady's humans—intelligent, well trained, and willing to learn the ways of others without insisting their way was best. The other humans were dangerous, stupid, cruel, and—as far as the feline Blood were concerned—prey. Both the Arcerian cats and the kindred tigers had a "word" for humans that roughly translated as "stupid meat."

Lucivar had argued once that since humans were dangerous and could hunt with weapons as well as Craft, they shouldn't be considered stupid. Smoke had pointed out that the tusked wild pigs were dangerous, too. They were still stupid.

Reassured that the Lady wasn't attacking anything with four feet, Smoke disappeared for a moment, returning with a dead rabbit. *Eat.*

"Have you eaten?" When Smoke didn't answer, Lucivar called in the food pack and large flask Draca had given him before he and Jaenelle left the Keep. He'd almost refused the food, thinking there would be plenty of fresh meat, thinking there would be time to build a fire and cook it. "You keep the rabbit," he said, digging into the pack. "I don't like raw meat."

Smoke cocked his head. *Fire?*

Lucivar shook his head, refusing to think about fires and sleep. He pulled a beef sandwich out of the pack and held it up.

Lucivar eat. Smoke settled down to his rabbit dinner.

Lucivar sipped from the flask of whiskey and slowly ate his sandwich, his attention partly focused on the sound of breaking wood.

This trip hadn't gone as he'd expected. He'd brought Jaenelle out here so that she could release the savage, drug-induced needs on nonhuman prey. He'd come with her to give her the target that would enrage, and satisfy, the bloodlust the most—a human male.

She'd refused to hunt, refused to buy herself a little relief at the cost of another living creature. Including him.

But she'd had no mercy for her own body. She had treated it like an enemy worthy of nothing but her contempt, an enemy that had betrayed her by leaving her vulnerable to someone's sadistic game.

Lucivar?

Lucivar shook his head, automatically probing for the source of Smoke's anxiety. A few birds chattering. A squirrel scrambling through the branches overhead. The usual wood sounds. *Only* the usual sounds.

His heart pounded as he and Smoke ran to the little clearing.

The shack was now a pile of broken timbers. A few feet away, Jaenelle sat on the ground, spraddle-legged, her hands still gripping the sledgehammer's handle while the head rested between her feet.

Approaching cautiously, Lucivar squatted beside her. "Cat?"

Tears flowed down her face. Blood dribbled down her chin from the bite in her lower lip. She gulped air and shuddered. "I'm so tired, Lucivar. But it grabs me and . . ."

Her muscles tightened until her body shook from the tension. Her back arched. The cords in her neck stood out. She sucked air through clenched teeth. The sledgehammer's handle snapped in her hands.

Lucivar waited, not daring to touch her while her muscles were tight enough to snap. It didn't last more than a couple of minutes. It felt like hours. When it finally passed, her body sagged and she began crying so hard he thought it would tear him apart.

She didn't fight him when he put his arms around her, so he held her, rocked her, and let her cry herself out.

He felt the sexual tension rising as soon as she stopped crying, but he held on. If he was reading the intensity correctly, she was over the worst of it now.

After several minutes, she relaxed enough to rest her head on his shoulder. "Lucivar?"

"Mmm?"

"I'm hungry."

His heart sang. "Then I'll feed you."

Fire?

Jaenelle's head snapped up. She stared at the wolf standing at the edge of the clearing. "Why does he want to build a fire?"

"Damned if I know why he wants one. But if we did build one, I could make some laced coffee."

Jaenelle pondered this for a while. "You make good laced coffee."

Taking that for a "yes," Lucivar led Jaenelle to the other side of the clearing while Smoke started searching the debris for pieces of wood big enough to use for fuel.

Lucivar called in the food pack, flask, and sleeping bag

he'd left by the creek. Jaenelle wandered from one side of the clearing to the other, nibbling the sandwich he'd given her. He kept an eye on her as he built the fire, called in the rest of their gear, and made camp. She seemed restless but not uncontrollably driven, which was good since they were losing the light and the day's warmth.

By the time he had the whisky-laced coffee ready, Jaenelle was tucked in her sleeping bag, shivering, eagerly reaching for the cup he handed her. He didn't suggest that she put on another layer of clothes. As long as she focused on the fire being the source of warmth, she'd be reluctant to wander away from it until morning.

He was rummaging through the food pack, looking for something else he could offer her to eat, when he heard a delicate snore.

After more than two days of unrelenting movement, Jaenelle slept.

Lucivar closed her sleeping bag and added a warming spell to keep her comfortable as the temperature dropped throughout the night. He pulled the coffeepot away from the heat and added more wood to the fire. Then he pulled off his boots and settled into his sleeping bag.

He should put a protective shield around the camp. He doubted a four-footed predator would want what was left in the food pack enough to challenge the combined scents of human and wolf, but they were on the northern border of Ebon Rih and uncomfortably close to Jhinka territory. The last thing Jaenelle needed right now was being jolted awake by a Jhinka hunting party's surprise attack.

Lucivar was sound asleep before he finished the thought.

6 / Hell

Resigned to the intrusion, Saetan settled back in one of the chairs by the fire and poured two glasses of yarbarah. He'd decided to spend some time in his private study beneath the Hall because he hadn't wanted to deal with any more frightened, clamoring minds—not after the past twenty-four hours. But Black-Jeweled Warlord Prince or not, High

Lord or not, a man didn't refuse a Dea al Mon Queen when she asked for an audience—especially when she was also a demon-dead Harpy.

"What can I do for you, Titian?" he asked politely, handing her a glass of the warmed blood wine.

Titian accepted the glass and sipped delicately, her large blue eyes never looking away from his gold ones. "You've made the citizens of Hell very nervous. This is the first time, in all the centuries you've been the High Lord, that you've purged the Dark Realm."

"I rule Hell. I can do as I please here," Saetan said mildly. Even a fool could have heard the warning under the mild tone.

Titian hooked her long, fine, silver hair behind her pointed ear and chose to ignore the warning. "Do as you please or do what you must? It didn't escape the notice of the observant that the Dark Priestess's followers were the only ones consumed in this purge."

"Really?" He sounded politely interested. In truth, he felt relieved the connection had been made. Not only would the rest of the demon-dead relax once they realized his choice of who had been hurried to the final death was based on a specific allegiance, anyone Hekatah approached in the future would think long and hard about the cost of such allegiance. "Since you've no personal concern, why are you here?"

"You missed a few. I thought you should know."

Saetan quickly masked his distaste and dismay. Titian always saw too much. "You'll give me the names." It wasn't a question.

Titian smiled. "There's no need. The Harpies took care of them for you." She hesitated for a moment. "What about the Dark Priestess?"

Clenching his teeth, Saetan stared at the fire. "I couldn't find her. Hekatah's very good at playing least-in-sight."

"If you had, would you have hurried her return to the Darkness? Would you have sent her to the final death?"

Saetan flung his glass into the fireplace and instantly regretted it as the fire sizzled and the smell of hot blood filled the room.

He'd been asking himself that question since he'd made the decision to eliminate all the support Hekatah had among the demon-dead. If he had found her, could he have coldly drained her strength until she faded into the Darkness? Or would he have hesitated, as he'd done so many times before, because centuries of dislike and distrust couldn't erase the simple fact that she'd given him two of his sons. Three if he counted . . . but he didn't, couldn't count that child, just as he'd never allowed himself to consider who had held the knife.

He jerked when Titian brushed her hand over his.

"Here." She handed him another glass of warmed yarbarah. Sitting back, she traced the rim of her own glass with one finger. "You don't like killing women, do you?"

Saetan gulped the blood wine. "No, I don't."

"I thought so. You were much cleaner, much kinder with them than you were with the males."

"Perhaps by your standards." By his own standards, he'd been more than sufficiently brutal. He shrugged. "We are our mothers' sons."

"A reasonable assumption." She sounded solemn. She looked amused.

Saetan twitched his shoulders, unable to shake the feeling that she'd just dropped a noose over his head. "It's a pet theory of mine about why there's no male rank equal to a Queen."

"Because males are their mothers' sons?"

"Because, long ago, only females were Blood."

Titian curled up in her chair. "How intriguing."

Saetan studied her warily. Titian had the same look Jaenelle always had when she'd successfully cornered him and was quite willing to wait until he finished squirming and told her what she wanted to know.

"It's just something Andulvar and I used to argue about on long winter nights," he grumbled, refilling their glasses.

"It may not be winter but, in Hell, the nights are always long."

"You know the story about the dragons who first ruled the Realms?"

Titian shrugged, indicating that it didn't matter if she knew or not. She'd settled in to hear a story.

Saetan raised his glass in a salute and smiled grudgingly. Jeweled males might be trained as defenders of their territories, but no male could beat a Queen when it came to tactical strategy.

"Long ago," he began, "when the Realms were young, there lived a race of dragons. Powerful, brilliant, and magical, they ruled all the lands and all the creatures in them. But after hundreds of generations, there came a day when they realized their race would be no more, and rather than have their knowledge and their gifts die with them, they chose to give them to the other creatures so that they could continue the Craft and care for the Realms.

"One by one, the dragons sought their lairs and embraced the forever night, becoming part of the Darkness. When only the Queen and her Prince, Lorn, were left, the Queen bid her Consort farewell. As she flew through the Realms, her scales sprinkled down, and whatever creature her scales touched, whether it walked on two legs or four or danced in the air on wings, whatever creature a scale touched became blood of her blood—still part of the race it came from, but also Other, remade to become caretaker and ruler. When the last scale fell from her, she vanished. Some stories say her body was transformed into some other shape, though it still contained a dragon's soul. Others say her body faded and she returned to the Darkness."

Saetan swirled the yarbarah in his glass. "I've read all the old stories—some from the original text. What's always intrigued me is that, no matter what race the story came from, the Queen is never named. In all the stories, Lorn is mentioned by name, repeatedly, but not her. The omission seems deliberate. I've always wondered why."

"And the Prince of Dragons?" Titian asked. "What happened to him?"

"According to the legends, Lorn still exists, and he contains all the knowledge of the Blood."

Titian looked thoughtful. "When Jaenelle turned fifteen and Draca said that Lorn had decided Jaenelle would live with you at the Hall, I had thought she was just saying that to block Cassandra's objections."

"No, she meant it. He and Jaenelle have been friends for years. He gifted her with her Jewels."

Titian opened and closed her mouth without making a sound.

Her stunned expression pleased him.

"Have you seen him?"

"No," Saetan replied sourly. "*I've* not been granted an audience."

"Oh, dear," Titian said with no sympathy whatsoever. "What does the legend have to do with the Blood once being all female, and why didn't we keep it that way?"

"You would have liked that, wouldn't you?"

She smiled.

"All right, my theory is this. Since the Queen's scales gifted the Craft to other races, and since like calls to like, it seems reasonable that only the females were able to absorb the magic. They became bonded to the land, drawn by their own body rhythms to the ebb and flow of the natural world. They became the Blood."

"Which would have lasted one generation," Titian pointed out.

"Not all men are stupid." When she looked doubtful, Saetan let out an exasperated sigh. The only thing more pointless than arguing with a Harpy about the value of males was trying to teach a rock to sing. He would have better luck with the rock. "For theory's sake, let's say we're talking about the Dea al Mon."

"Ah." Titian settled back, content. "*Our* males *are* intelligent."

"I'm sure they're relieved you think so," Saetan said dryly. "So, upon discovering that some of the women in their Territory suddenly had magical powers and skills . . ."

"The best young warriors would offer themselves as mates and protectors," Titian said promptly.

Saetan raised an eyebrow. Since landens, the non-Blood of each race, tended to be so wary of the Blood and their Craft, that wasn't quite the way he'd always pictured it, but he found it interesting that a Dea al Mon witch would make that assumption. He'd have to ask Chaosti and Gabrielle at some point. "And from those unions, children were born. The girls, because of gender, received the full gift."

"But the boys were half-Blood with little or no Craft." Titian held out her glass. Saetan refilled it.

"Witches don't bear many children," Saetan continued after refilling his own glass. "Depending on the ratio of sons to daughters, it could have taken several more generations before males bred true. Through all that time, the power would have been in the distaff gender, each generation learning from the one before and becoming stronger. The first Queens probably appeared long before the first Warlord, let alone a male stronger than that. By then, the idea that males served and protected females would have been ingrained. In the end, what you have is the Blood society where Warlords are equal in status to witches, Princes are equal to Priestesses and Healers, and Black Widows only have to defer to Warlord Princes and Queens. And Warlord Princes, who are considered a law unto themselves, are a step above the other castes and a step—a long step—beneath the Queens."

"When caste is added to each individual's social rank and Jewel rank, it makes an intriguing dance." Titian set her glass on the table. "An interesting theory, High Lord."

"An interesting diversion, Lady Titian. Why did you do it? Why did you offer me your company tonight?"

Titian smoothed her forest-green tunic. "You are kin of my kin. It seemed . . . fitting . . . to offer you comfort tonight since Jaenelle could not. Good night, High Lord."

Long after she'd gone, Saetan sat quietly, watching the logs in the fireplace break and settle. He roused himself enough to pour and warm one last glass of yarbarah, content now with the solitude and silence.

He didn't dispute her theory of why males came to serve, but it wasn't his. It wasn't just the magic that had drawn the males. It was the inner radiance housed within those female bodies, a luminescence that some men had craved as much as they might have craved a light they could see glowing in a window when they were standing out in the cold. They had craved that light as much as they had craved being sheathed in the sweet darkness of a woman's body, if not more.

Males had become Blood because they'd been drawn to both.

And, as he knew all too well, they still were.

7 / Kaeleer

Lucivar lay on his back in the young grass, his hands behind his head, his wings spread to dry after the quick dip in the spring-fed pool. Jaenelle was still splashing around in the cold water, washing the sweat and dirt out of her long hair.

He closed his eyes and groaned contentedly as the sun slowly warmed and loosened tight muscles.

Yesterday, he'd awakened just before dawn to find Jaenelle busily rummaging through the food pack. They'd managed a hasty meal before the physical tension produced by the drugs forced her to move.

It wasn't the unrelenting drive of the previous days, and as the day wore on, physical tension gave way to emotional storms. Anger would flood her suddenly, then turn to tears. He gave her space while she raged and swore. He held her while she cried. When the storm passed, she'd be fine for a little while. They would walk at an easy pace, stopping to pick wild berries or rest near a stream. Then the cycle would start over, each time with a little less intensity.

This morning, he and Smoke had brought down a small deer. He'd kept enough meat to fill the small, cold-spelled food box he'd brought with him and had sent Smoke back to the Keep with the rest. If Saetan wasn't at the Keep, Smoke would go on to the Hall to let the High Lord know that the worst had passed and they would spend a few more days in Askavi before coming home.

Home. He'd lived in Kaeleer for a year now, and the way witches treated males in the Shadow Realm still bewildered him sometimes.

One day he'd walked in on a discussion Chaosti, Aaron, and Khardeen were having about how the Ring of Honor worn by males in a Queen's First Circle differed from the

Restraining Ring Terreillean males were required to wear until they proved themselves trustworthy. He told them about the Ring of Obedience that was used in Terreille.

They didn't believe him. Oh, intellectually they understood what he said, but they had never known the saturating, day-to-day fear Terreillean males lived with, so they didn't, *couldn't*, believe him.

Wondering if the boys simply weren't old enough to have firsthand experience in the ways a witch kept her males leashed, he had asked Sylvia, Halaway's Queen, how a Queen controlled a male who didn't want to serve in her court.

She'd gaped at him a moment before blurting out, "Who'd want one?"

A few months ago, while in Nharkhava running an errand for the High Lord, he'd been invited to tea by three elderly Ladies who had praised his physique with such good-natured delight that he couldn't feel insulted. Feeling comfortable with them, he had asked if they'd heard anything about the Warlord Prince who had recently killed a Queen.

They reluctantly admitted that the story was true. A Queen who had acquired a taste for cruelty had been unable to form a court because she couldn't convince twelve males to serve her willingly. So she decided to *force* males into service by using that Ring of Obedience device. She had collected eleven lighter-Jeweled Warlords and was looking for the twelfth male when the Warlord Prince confronted her. *He* was looking for a younger cousin who had disappeared the month before. When she tried to force him to submit, he killed her.

What happened to the Warlord Prince?

It took them a moment to understand the question.

Nothing happened to the Warlord Prince. After all, he did exactly what he was supposed to do. Granted, they all wished he had simply restrained that horrible woman and handed her over to Nharkhava's Queen for punishment, but one has to expect this sort of thing when a Warlord Prince is provoked enough to rise to the killing edge.

Lucivar had spent the rest of that day in a tavern, unsure

if he felt amused or terrified by the Ladies' attitude. He thought about the beatings, the whippings, the times he'd screamed in agony when pain was sent through the Ring of Obedience. He thought of what he'd done to earn that pain. He sat in that tavern and laughed until he cried when he finally realized he would never be able to reconcile the differences between Terreille and Kaeleer.

In Kaeleer, service was an intricate dance, the lead constantly changing between the genders. Witches nurtured and protected male strength and pride. Males, in turn, protected and respected the gentler, but somehow deeper, feminine strength.

Males weren't slaves or pets or tools to be used without regard to feelings. They were valuable, and valued, partners.

That, Lucivar had decided that day, was the leash the Queens used in Kaeleer—control so gentle and sweet a man had no reason to fight against it and every reason to fiercely protect it.

Loyalty, on both sides. Respect, on both sides. Honor, on both sides. Pride, on both sides.

This was the place he now proudly called home.

"Lucivar."

Lucivar shot to his feet, cursing silently. Considering the tension he felt in her, he was lucky she hadn't taken off without him.

"Something's wrong," she said in her midnight voice.

He immediately probed the area. "Where? I don't sense anything."

"Not right here. To the east."

The only thing east of them was a landen village under the protection of Agio, the Blood village at the northern end of Ebon Rih.

"There's something wrong there, but it's elusive," Jaenelle said, her eyes narrowed as she stared eastward. "And it feels *twisted* somehow, like a snare filled with poison bait. But it slips away from me every time I try to focus on it." She snarled, frustrated. "Maybe the drugs are messing up my ability to sense things."

He thought about the Queen who had ensnared eleven young men before being killed. "Or maybe you're just the wrong gender for the bait." Keeping his inner barriers tightly shielded, he sent a delicate psychic probe eastward. A minute later, swearing viciously, he snapped the link and clung to Jaenelle, letting her clean, dark strength wash away the foulness he'd brushed against.

He pressed his forehead against hers. "It's bad, Cat. A lot of desperation and pain surrounded by . . ." He searched for some way to describe what he'd felt.

Carrion.

Shuddering, he wondered why the word came to mind.

He could fly over the village and take a quick look. If the landens were fighting off a Jhinka raiding party, he was strong enough to give them whatever help they needed. If it was one of those spring fevers that sometimes ran through a village, it would be better to know that before sending a message to Agio since the Healers would be needed.

His main concern was finding a safe—

"Don't even think it, Lucivar," Jaenelle warned softly. "I'm going with you."

Lucivar eyed her, trying to judge just how far he could push her this time. "You know, the Ring of Honor you had made for me won't stop me the way the Restraining Ring would have."

She muttered an Eyrien curse that was quite explicit.

He smiled grimly. That pretty much answered the question of how far he could push. He looked toward the east. "All right, you're going with me. But we'll do this my way, Cat."

Jaenelle nodded. "You're the one with fighting experience. But . . ." She pressed her right palm against the Ebon-gray Jewel resting on his chest. "Spread your wings."

As he opened his wings to their full span, he felt a hot-cold tingle from the Ring of Honor.

She stepped back, satisfied. "This shield is braided into the protective shield already contained in the Ring. You could drain your Jewels to the breaking point, and it will still hold around you. It's fixed about a foot out from your body and will mesh with mine so we can stay tight without endangering each other. But make sure you keep clear of anything else you don't want to damage."

Having made regular circuits to all the villages in Ebon Rih, Lucivar knew the landen village and surrounding land fairly well. Plenty of low hills and woodland within striking distance of the village—perfect hiding places for a Jhinka raiding party.

The Jhinka were a fierce, winged people made up of patriarchal clans loosely joined together by a dozen tribal chiefs. Like the Eyriens, they were native to Askavi, but they were smaller and had a fraction of the life span of the long-lived Eyriens. The two races had hated each other for as long as either of them could remember.

While Eyriens had the advantage of Craft, the Jhinka had the advantage of numbers. Once drained of his psychic power and the reserves in the Jewels, an Eyrien warrior was as vulnerable as any other man when fighting against overwhelming odds. So, accepting the slaughter required to bring down an enemy, the Jhinka had always been willing to meet an Eyrien in battle.

With two exceptions. One walked among the dead, the other among the living. Both wore Ebon-gray Jewels.

"All right," Lucivar said. "We'll run on this White radial thread until we're past the village, then drop from the Winds and come in fast from the other side. If this is a Jhinka raid, I'll handle it. If it's something else . . ."

She just looked at him.

He cleared his throat. "Come on, Cat. Let's give whoever is messing with our valley a reason to regret it."

8 / Kaeleer

Dropping from the White Wind, Lucivar and Jaenelle glided toward the peaceful-looking village still a mile away.

You said we'd go in fast, Jaenelle said on a psychic thread.

I also said we'd do this my way, Lucivar replied sharply.

There's pain and need down there, Lucivar.

There was also the foulness that now eluded him. It was still there. Had to be. That he could no longer sense it, would never have sensed it if he'd simply come to check on the village, made him uneasy. He would have stumbled into whatever trap was waiting down there.

He felt the predator wake in her at the same moment she began a hawk-dive, dropping toward the village at full speed. Swearing, he folded his wings and dove after her just as hundreds of Jhinka appeared out of nowhere, screeching their battle cries as they tried to surround him and pull him down.

Using Craft to enhance his speed, Lucivar drove through the Jhinka swarm, relishing the screams when they hit his protective shield. Roaring an Eyrien war cry, he unleashed the power in his Ebon-gray Jewels in short, controlled bursts.

Jhinka bodies exploded into a bloody mist full of severed limbs.

He burst through the bottom of the swarm, coming out of his dive a wing-length from the ground. *Cat!*

Come down the main street, but hurry. The tunnel won't hold for long. Avoid the side streets. They're . . . fouled. There's a shielded building at the other end of the village.

Flying low, Lucivar swung toward the main street, hit the village boundary at top speed, and swore every curse he knew as his shield brushed against the psychic witch storm engulfing the deceptively peaceful-looking village. The shield sizzled like drops of cold water flicked into a hot pan. All the ensnaring psychic threads flared as if they were physical threads made out of lightning.

Pushing hard, he flew through the already contracting tunnel Jaenelle had created as she passed through the witch storm and finally caught up with her a block away from the shielded building. A fast psychic probe showed him the parameters of the domed, oval-shaped shield that protected a two-story stone building and ten yards of ground all around it.

Four men ran toward the edge of the shield, waving their arms and shouting, "Go back! Get away from here!"

Behind the men, thousands of Jhinka rose from the low hills beyond the village, filling the sky until they blotted out the sun.

Jaenelle passed through the building's shield as easily as if it were a thin layer of water. Distracted by the men and the approaching Jhinka, Lucivar felt like he was passing through a wall of warm taffy.

As soon as they were inside the building's shield, Lucivar landed next to the four men. The protective shield Jaenelle had created for him contracted to a skintight sheath, produced a mild tingle in the Ring of Honor, then vanished completely.

"How many wounded?" Jaenelle snapped.

Lord Randahl, the Agio Warlord who was Lady Erika's Master of the Guard, replied reluctantly, "Last count, about three hundred, Lady."

"How many Healers?"

"The village had two physicians and a wisewoman who could do a bit of herb healing. All dead."

Knowing better than to interrupt when Jaenelle focused on healing, Lucivar waited until she ran into the building before snapping out his own demands. "Who's holding the shield?"

"Adler is," Randahl said, jerking a thumb toward a young, haggard-faced Warlord.

Lucivar glanced toward the low hills. The Jhinka would descend on them at any moment. "Can you push your shield out another inch or two all around?" he asked Adler. "I'll put an Ebon-gray shield behind it. Then you can drop your shield and rest."

The young Warlord nodded wearily and closed his eyes.

Seconds after Lucivar put up his shield, the Jhinka attacked. They slammed against the invisible barrier, their bodies piling up five and six deep as they clawed at the shield. Some of the Jhinka, pressed between the shield and the rest of the swarm, were smothered or crushed by the mass of writhing bodies. Dead, hate-filled eyes stared at the five men below.

"Hell's fire," Randahl muttered. "Even during the worst attacks, they didn't come in like *this*."

Lucivar studied the middle-aged Warlord for a moment before returning his attention to the Jhinka. *Maybe they hadn't trapped what they'd wanted until now.*

He could feel the pressure of all those bodies piling up on the shield, could feel the Ebon-gray Jewels release drop after drop of his reserve strength. While all the Jewels provided a reservoir for the psychic power, the darker the Jewel, the deeper the reservoir. As the second darkest Jewel, the Ebon-gray provided a cache of power deep enough that, if he didn't need to use them for anything beyond maintaining the shield against physical attacks, he could hold the Jhinka off for a week before he felt the strain. Someone would come looking for them before that. All he needed to do was wait.

But there was that witch storm to consider. He felt certain someone had created this trap especially for him. He'd have to check with Randahl, but he suspected the first Jhinka attack hadn't given them time to get in supplies. And Jaenelle needed other Healers to assist with the wounded. The Darkness knew she had the psychic reserves to do all the healing, but her body wouldn't hold up under that kind of demand, especially after the drugs and the physical strain of the past few days.

Besides, no one had ever accused him of having a passive temper.

Lucivar vanished his Ebon-gray ring and called in his Birthright Red. The Ebon-gray around his neck would feed the shield. The Red . . .

"Tell your men to stay tight to the building," Lucivar said quietly to Randahl. "It's time to even up the odds a bit."

Smiling his lazy, arrogant smile, he raised his right hand and triggered the spell he'd spent years perfecting. Seven thin psychic "wires" shot out of the Red Jewel in his ring. Keeping his arm straight, he made leisurely sweeps back and forth, always careful that he didn't stray too close to the building. Back and forth. Up and down.

Jhinka blood ran down the shield. Jhinka bodies slithered

and slid as the ones who could see the danger tried to push themselves out of the pile before that sweeping arm returned.

Satisfied with the panicked scramble on that side of the shield, he walked around the building, his hand always aimed at the shield.

And the Jhinka died.

He was starting a third circuit when the Jhinka who were still trying to pile onto the shield finally caught the panic of the ones trying to get away from it. Chittering and screeching, they rose off the shield and headed for the low hills.

Lucivar drew the psychic "wires" back into his ring, ended the spell, and slowly lowered his arm.

Randahl, Adler, and the two Warlords Lucivar hadn't been introduced to yet stared, sick-faced, at the blood running down the shield, at the pieces of bodies sliding to the ground.

"Mother Night," Randahl whispered. "Mother Night."

They wouldn't look at him. Or rather, whenever their glances brushed in his direction, he saw the worried speculation that they might have something locked inside with them that was far more dangerous and deadly than the enemy waiting outside.

Which was true.

"I'm going to check on the Lady," Lucivar said abruptly.

Being a Master of the Guard, Randahl would try to act normally once he had a few minutes to steady himself. If nothing else, the man would fall back on the Protocol for dealing with a Warlord Prince. But the others . . .

Everything has a price.

Lucivar approached the front of the building and gave himself a moment to steady his own feelings. If other Blood couldn't deal with a Warlord Prince on the killing edge, wounded landens most certainly couldn't. And right now, hysteria could trigger a vicious desire for bloodletting. A male coming away from the killing edge needed someone, preferably female, to help him stabilize. That was one of the many slender threads that bound the Blood. The witches, during their vulnerable times, needed that aggressive male strength, and the males needed, sometimes desperately, the shelter and comfort they found in a woman's gentle strength.

He needed Jaenelle.

Lucivar smiled bitterly as he entered the building. Right now, everyone needed Jaenelle. He hoped—sweet Darkness, how he hoped!—being near her would be enough.

The community hall held various-sized rooms where the villagers could gather for dances or meetings. At least, he assumed that's what it was for. He'd never had much contact with landens. As he scanned the largest room, aching for Jaenelle's familiar presence, he felt the pain and fear of the wounded landens sitting against the walls or lying on the floor. The pain he could handle. The fear, which spiked in the ones who noticed him, undermined his shaky self-control.

Lucivar started to turn away when he noticed the young man lying on a narrow mattress near the door. Under normal circumstances, he might have assumed the man was another landen, but he'd seen too many men in similar circumstances not to recognize a weak psychic scent.

Dropping to one knee, Lucivar carefully lifted the side of the doubled-over sheet that covered the body from neck to feet. His eyes shifted from the wounds to the still, pain-tight face and back again. He swore silently. The gut wounds were bad. Men had died from less. They weren't beyond Jaenelle's healing skill, but he wondered if she could rebuild the parts that were no longer there.

Lowering the sheet, Lucivar left the room, his curses becoming louder and more vicious as he searched for some empty room where he could try to leash a temper spiraling out of control.

Randahl hadn't said any of his men had been wounded. And why was the boy—no, man; anyone with those kinds of battle wounds didn't deserve to be called a boy—kept apart from the others, tucked against a shadowed wall where he might easily go unnoticed?

Catching the warmth of a feminine psychic scent, Lucivar threw open a door and stepped inside the kitchen before he realized, too late, the woman trying to pump water one-handed wasn't Jaenelle.

She spun around when the door crashed against the wall, throwing her left arm up as if to stop an attacker.

Lucivar hated her. Hated her for not being Jaenelle. Hated her for the fear in her eyes that was pushing him toward blind rage. Hated her for being young and pretty. And most of all, hated her because he knew that, at any second now, she would bolt and he would be on her, hurting her, even killing her before he could stop himself.

Then she swallowed hard, and said in a quiet, quivering voice, "I'm trying to boil some water to make teas for the wounded, but the pump's stiff and I can't work it with one hand. Would you help me?"

A knot of tension eased inside him. Here, at least, was a landen female who knew how to deal with Blood males. Asking for help was always the easiest way to redirect one of them toward service.

As Lucivar came forward, she stepped aside, trembling. His temper started to climb again until he noticed the bandaged right arm she held over her stomach, her hand tucked between her dress and apron.

Not fear then, but fatigue and blood loss.

He placed a chair close enough for her to supervise, but far enough away so that he wouldn't keep brushing against her. "Sit down."

Once she was seated, he pumped water and set the filled pots on the wood-burning stove. He noticed the bags of herbs laid out on the wooden table next to the double sink and looked at her curiously. "Lord Randahl said the wise-woman died along with your two physicians."

Her eyes filled with tears as she nodded. "My grandmother. She said I had the gift and was teaching me."

Lucivar leaned against the table, puzzled. Landen minds were too weak to give off a psychic scent, but hers did. "Where did you learn how to handle Blood males?"

Her eyes widened with anxiety. "I wasn't trying to control you!"

"I said handle, not control. There's a difference."

"I—I just did what the Lady said to do."

The tension inside him loosened another notch. "What's your name?"

"Mari." She hesitated. "You're Prince Yaslana, aren't you?"

"Does that bother you?" Lucivar asked in a colorless voice. To his surprise, Mari smiled shyly.

"Oh, no. The Lady said we could trust you."

The words warmed him like a lover's caress. But, having caught the slight emphasis in her tone, he wondered whom the landens in the village couldn't trust. His gold eyes narrowed as he studied her. "You have some Blood in your background, don't you?"

Mari paled a little and wouldn't look at him. "My great-grandmother was half-Blood. S-some people say I'm a throwback to her."

"From my point of view, that's no bad thing." Her naked relief was too much for him, so he began inspecting the bags of herbs. She'd be too quick to think she was the cause of his anger, so he fiddled with the bags until he had his feelings leashed again.

In his experience, half-Blood children were seldom welcomed or accepted by either society. The Blood didn't want them because they didn't have enough power to expend on all the basic things the Blood used Craft for and, therefore, could never be more than base servants. The landens didn't want them because they had too much power, and that kind of ability, untrained and free of any moral code, had produced more than its share of petty tyrants who had used magic and fear to rule a village that wouldn't accept them otherwise.

The water reached a boil.

"Sit down," Lucivar snapped when Mari started to rise. "You can tell me from there what you want blended. Besides," he added with a smile to take the sting out of the snap, "I've blended simple healing brews for a harder task-mistress than you."

Looking properly sympathetic and murmuring agreement that the Lady could be a bit snarly about mixing up healing brews, Mari pointed out the herbs she intended to use and told him the blends she wanted.

"Do you see much of the Lady?" Lucivar asked as he pulled the pots off the stove and set them on stone trivets arranged at one end of the table. Despite Jaenelle's continued refusal to set up a formal court, her opinions were heeded throughout most of Kaeleer.

"She comes by for an afternoon every couple of weeks. She and Gran and I talk about healing Craft while her friends teach Khevin."

"Who's—" He bit off the question. He'd thought the young man's psychic scent was so weak because of the seriousness of the wounds. But it was strong for a half-Blood. "Which friends are teaching him?"

"Lord Khardeen and Prince Aaron."

Khary and Aaron were good choices if you were going to teach basic Craft to a half-Blood youth. Which didn't excuse Jaenelle from not asking *him* to participate. Lucivar carefully lowered the herb-filled gauze pouches into the pots of water. "They're both strongly grounded in basic Craft." Then, feeling spiteful, he added, "Unlike the Lady, who still can't manage to call in her own shoes."

Mari's prim sniff caught him by surprise. "I don't see why you all make such a fuss about it. If I had a friend who could do all those wonderful bits of magic, *I* wouldn't begrudge fetching her shoes."

Annoyed, Lucivar grumbled under his breath as he rattled through the cupboards searching for the cups. Damn woman certainly *was* a throwback. If nothing else, she had a witch's disposition.

He shut up when he saw how pale Mari had become. A little ashamed, he ladled out a cup of one of the healing brews and stood over her while she drank it.

"I saw Khevin when I came in," Lucivar said quietly. "I saw the wounds. Why didn't Khary and Aaron teach him how to shield?"

Mari looked up, surprised. "They did. Khevin's the one who shielded the community hall when the Jhinka started to attack."

"I think you'd better explain that," Lucivar said slowly, feeling as if she'd just punched the air out of him. A strong half-Blood might have enough power to create a personal shield for a few minutes, but he shouldn't have been able to create and hold a shield large enough to protect a building. Of course, Jaenelle had uncanny instincts when it came to recognizing strength that had been blocked in some way.

Mari, looking puzzled, confirmed that. "Khevin met the Lady one day when she came to visit Gran and me. She just looked at him for a long minute and then said he was too strong not to be properly trained in the Craft. When she came the next time, she brought Lord Khardeen and Prince Aaron. Creating a shield was the first thing they taught him."

Mari's hand started to tremble. The cup tipped.

Lucivar used Craft to steady the cup so that the hot liquid wouldn't spill on her.

"They were the first friends Khevin's ever had." Her eyes pleaded with him to understand. Then she blushed and looked down. "Male friends, I mean. They didn't laugh at him or call him names like some of the young Warlords from Agio do."

"What about the older Warlords?" Lucivar asked, careful to keep the anger out of his voice.

Mari shrugged. "They seemed embarrassed if they saw him when they came to check on the village. They didn't want to know he existed. They didn't want to see me around either," she added bitterly. "But with Lord Khardeen and Prince Aaron. . . . When the lesson was over, they would stay a little while to have a glass of ale and just talk. They told him about the Blood's code of honor and the rules Blood males are supposed to live by. Sometimes it made me wonder if the Blood in Agio had ever heard of those rules."

If they hadn't, they were going to. "The shield," he prompted.

"All of a sudden, the sky was filled with Jhinka screaming like they do. Khevin told me to come to the community hall. We . . . the Lady says that sometimes a link is formed when people like us are . . . close."

Lucivar glanced at her left hand. No marriage ring. Lovers then. At least Khevin had known, and given, that pleasure.

"I was at this end of the village, delivering some of Gran's herb medicines. The adults wouldn't listen to me, so I just grabbed a little girl who was playing outside and yelled at the other children to come with me. I—I think I *made* some of them come with me.

"When we got to the community building, Khevin had a shield around it. He was sweating. It looked like it was hurting him."

Lucivar was sure that it had.

"He said he'd tried to send a message to Agio on a psychic thread, but he wasn't sure anyone would hear it. Then he told me someone had to stay inside the shield in order to reach through it to bring another person in. He brought me through just as one of the Jhinka flew at us. The Jhinka hit the shield so hard it knocked him out. Khevin got his ax—he'd been chopping wood when the attack started. He went through the shield and k-killed the Jhinka. By then all the men in the village were in the streets, fighting. Khevin stayed outside to protect the children while I pulled them through the shield.

"By then the Jhinka were all around us. A lot of the women who tried to reach the building didn't make it, or were badly wounded by the time I pulled them through the shield. Gran . . . Gran was almost within reach when one of the Jhinka swooped down and. . . . He laughed. He looked at me and he laughed while he killed her."

Lucivar refilled the cup and put a warming spell on the pots while Mari groped in her apron pocket for a handkerchief.

She sipped the herbal tea, saying nothing for a minute. "Khevin couldn't keep fighting and hold the shield, too. Even I could see that. He had a-arrows in his legs. He couldn't move very fast. They caught him before he could go through the shield and did that to him. Then Lord Randahl and the others came and started fighting.

"Two of the Warlords were shielding the wounded, leading them here, while the other two kept killing and killing.

"Khevin's shield started to fail. I was afraid the Warlords would put up another one that I couldn't get through, and Khevin would be left outside. As I reached out and grabbed

him, a Jhinka saw me and slashed my arm. I pulled Khevin
through just before the Warlords slipped inside and put up
another shield."

Mari sipped her tea. "Lord Adler started swearing because they couldn't break through the witch storm around
the village to send a message to Agio. But Lord Randahl
just kept looking at Khevin.

"Then he and Lord Adler picked Khevin up l-like he
was finally worth something. They took the mattress and
sheets from the caretaker's bed and did what they could to
make him comfortable." Mari stared at the cup, tears running down her face. "That's it."

Lucivar took the empty cup, wanting to offer her some
comfort but not sure if she could accept it from a Warlord
Prince. Maybe from someone like Aaron, who was the
same age, but from him?

"Mari?"

Relief washed through him when Jaenelle walked into
the kitchen.

"Let's see your arm," Jaenelle said, gently loosening the
bandage and ignoring Mari's stammered pleas to take care
of Khevin. "First your arm. I need you whole so you can
help me with the others. We're going to need some mild—
ah, you've already prepared some."

While Jaenelle healed the deep knife wound that had
opened Mari's arm from elbow to wrist, Lucivar ladled out
cups of the healing teas and put a warming spell on each
cup. After a bit of cupboard hunting, he found two large
metal serving trays. Full, they'd be too heavy for Mari—
especially since Jaenelle had just warned her that the kind
of fast healing she was going to have to do wasn't going to
hold up under strain—but the young Warlords out there
could do the heavy hauling and lifting now that he was
maintaining the shield.

Jaenelle solved the problem by putting a float spell on
both trays so that they hovered waist high. Mari didn't need
to lift, just steer.

With Lucivar and Mari guiding the trays, the three of
them went to the large room. Jaenelle ignored the clamor

that began as soon as the villagers saw her and went to the
shadowed wall where Khevin lay.

Mari hesitated, biting her lip, obviously torn between her
desire to go to her lover and her duties as assistant Healer.
Lucivar gave her shoulder a quick, encouraging squeeze
before he joined Jaenelle. He didn't know what help he
could give her, but he'd do whatever he could.

As Jaenelle started to lift the sheet, Khevin's eyes
opened. With effort, he grabbed her hand.

She stared at the young man, her eyes blank. It was as
if she had gone so deep within herself that the windows of
the soul could no longer reveal the person who lived within.

"Do you fear me?" she asked in a midnight whisper.

"No, Lady." Khevin licked his dry lips. "But it's a Warlord's privilege to protect his people. Take care of them
first."

Lucivar tried to reach her with a psychic thread, but
Jaenelle had shut him out. *Please, Cat. Let him have his
pride.*

She reached under the sheet. Khevin moaned a wordless protest.

"I'll do as you ask because you asked," she said, "but
I'm going to tie in some of the threads from the healing
web I've built *now* so that you'll stay with me." She
smoothed the sheet and rested one long-nailed finger at the
base of his throat. "And I warn you, Khevin, you had better
stay with me."

Khevin smiled at her and closed his eyes.

Cupping her elbow, Lucivar led Jaenelle into the hallway.
"Since they won't be needed for the shield, I'll send the
younger Warlords in to help with the fetching and
carrying."

"Adler, yes. Not the other two."

The ice in her voice chilled him. He'd never heard any
Queen condemn a man so thoroughly.

"Very well," he said respectfully. "I can—"

"Keep this place safe, Yaslana."

He felt the quiver, swiftly leashed, and locked his emotions up tight. Hell's fire, even if the drugs were out of her

system enough for her to do the healings, her emotions weren't stable. And she knew it.

"Cat . . ."

"I'll hold. You don't have to watch your back because of that."

He grinned. "Actually, it's when you're hissing and spitting that you're the most useful when it comes to guarding my back."

Her sapphire eyes warmed a little. "I'll remind you of that."

Lucivar headed for the outside door. He'd have to keep an eye on her to make sure she drank some water and had a bite to eat every couple of hours. He'd slip a word to Mari. It was always easier to get Jaenelle to eat if someone else was eating, too.

As he turned back, he felt the impact of bodies against the shield and heard the warning shouts from the Warlords outside.

He'd talk to Mari later. The Jhinka had returned.

9 / Kaeleer

Lucivar leaned against the covered well and gratefully took the mug of coffee Randahl handed to him. It tasted rough and muddy. He didn't care. At that moment, he would have drunk piss as long as it was hot.

The Jhinka had attacked throughout the night—sometimes small parties striking the shield and then fleeing, sometimes a couple hundred battering at the shield while he sliced them apart. There had been no sleep, no rest. Just the steadily increasing fatigue and physical drain of channeling the power stored in the Jewels as well as the steady drain of that power—a more rapid drain than he had anticipated. Randahl and the other Warlords had exhausted their reserves by the time he and Jaenelle had arrived yesterday, so he was now their only protection and most of their fighting ability.

Because the shield hadn't extended more than a couple of inches below the ground, he'd discovered, almost too late, that the Jhinka had been using the piles of bodies for cover while they dug under the shield. So now the shield went down five feet before turning inward and running underground until it reached the building's foundation.

While they were fighting the Jhinka who'd gotten under the south side of the shield, Lucivar had responded to instinct and raced to the north side of the building, reaching the corner just as one of the Jhinka ran toward the well. The earthenware jar the Jhinka carried had contained enough concentrated poison to destroy their only water supply. So the well now had a separate shield around it.

As soon as the attack on the well had been thwarted and the shield extended, the witch storm had re-formed over the building. No longer spread out to cover the whole village and hide the destruction, it had become a tight mass of tangled psychic threads, an invisible cloud full of psychic lightning that sizzled every time it brushed the shield.

The extra shielding and the constant reinforcement against another's Craft were doing what the Jhinka alone couldn't do—draining him to the breaking point. It would take another day. Maybe two. After that, weak spots would appear in the shield—spots the witch storm could penetrate to entangle already exhausted minds, spots the Jhinka could break through to attack already exhausted bodies.

He'd briefly toyed with the idea of insisting that Jaenelle return to the Keep for help. He'd dismissed the idea just as quickly. Until the healings were done, nothing and no one would convince her to leave. If he admitted the shield might fail, more than likely she would throw a Black shield around the building, straining a body already overtaxed by the large healing web she'd created to strengthen all the wounded until she could get to them. Totally focused on the healing, she wouldn't give a second thought to driving her body beyond its limits. And he already knew what she would say if he argued with her about the damage she was doing to herself: everything has a price.

So he'd held his tongue and his temper, determined to hold out until someone from Agio or the Keep came looking for them.

Now, in the chill, early dawn, he couldn't find enough

energy to produce any body heat, so he wrapped his cold hands around the warm mug.

Randahl sipped his coffee in silence, his back turned toward the village. He was a fair-skinned Rihlander with faded blue eyes and thinning, cinnamon hair. His body had a middle-years thickness but the muscles were still solid, and he had more stamina than the three younger Warlords put together.

"The women who can are helping out in the kitchen," Randahl said after a few minutes. "They were pleased to get the venison and other supplies you brought with you. They're using most of the meat to make broth for the seriously wounded, but they said they'd make a stew with the rest. You should have seen the sour looks they gave Mari when she insisted that we get the first bowls. Hell's fire, they even whined about giving us this sludge to drink, and me standing right there." He shook his head in disgust. "Damn landens. It's gotten to the point where the little ones run, screaming, whenever we walk into a village. They go around making signs against evil behind our backs, but they squeal loud enough when they need help."

Lucivar sipped his quickly cooling coffee. "If you feel that way about landens, why did you come to help when the Jhinka attacked?"

"Not for *them*. To protect the land. Won't have that Jhinka filth in Ebon Rih. We came to protect the land— and to get those two out." Randahl's shoulders sagged. "Hell's fire, Yaslana. Who would have thought the boy could build a shield like that?"

"No one in Agio, obviously." Before Randahl could snap a reply, Lucivar continued harshly, "If Mari and Khevin matter to you, why didn't you let them live in Agio instead of leaving them here to be sneered at and slighted?"

Randahl's face flushed a dull red. "And what would an Ebon-gray Warlord Prince know about being sneered at or slighted?"

Lucivar didn't know whether he made the decision because he no longer cared what people knew about him or because he wasn't sure he and Randahl would survive. "I grew up in Terreille, not Kaeleer. I was too young to remember my father when I was taken from him, so I grew up being told, and believing, that I was a half-breed bastard, unwanted and unclaimed. You don't know what it's like to be a bastard in an Eyrien hunting camp. Sneered at?" Lucivar laughed bitterly. "The favorite taunt was 'your father was a Jhinka.' Do you have any idea what that means to an Eyrien? That you were sired by a male from a hated race and that your mother must have accepted the mount willingly since she carried you full term and birthed you? Oh, I think I know how someone like Khevin feels."

Randahl cleared his throat. "It shames me to say it, but it wasn't any easier for him in Agio. Lady Erika tried to make a place for him in her court. Felt she owed it to him because her ex-Consort had sired the boy. But he wasn't happy, and Mari and her grandmother were here. So he came back."

And had endured ostracism from the landens and taunts from the young Blood males—which explained why the two Warlords now using Craft to move the Jhinka bodies away from the shield were being kept as far away from Jaenelle as possible.

Lucivar finally answered the question he saw in Randahl's eyes. "Two of Lady Angelline's friends were training Khevin."

Randahl rubbed the back of his neck. "Should have thought to ask her ourselves. She has a way about her."

Lucivar smiled wearily. "That she does." And she might also have some idea of where the young couple might relocate. If they survived.

For a moment, he allowed himself to believe they would survive.

Then the Jhinka returned.

10 / Kaeleer

Randahl shaded his eyes against the late afternoon sun and studied the low hills that were black with waiting Jhinka. "They must have called up all the clans from all the tribes," he said hoarsely. Then he sagged against the back of the community hall. "Mother Night, Yaslana, there must be five thousand of them out there."

"More like six." Lucivar widened his stance. It was the only way his tired, trembling legs would keep him upright.

Six thousand more than the hundreds he'd already killed during the past few days and that witch storm still raging around them, feeding on the shield to maintain its strength and draining him in the process. Six thousand more and no way to catch the Winds because that storm made it impossible to detect those psychic roadways.

They could shield and they could fight, but they couldn't send out a call for help and they couldn't escape. The food had run out yesterday. The well dried up that morning. And there were still six thousand Jhinka waiting for the sun to sink a little farther behind the low western hills before they attacked.

"We're not going to make it, are we?" Randahl said.

"No," Lucivar replied softly. "We're not going to make it."

In the past three days, he'd drained both Ebon-gray Jewels as well as his Red ring. The Red Jewel around his neck was now the only power reserve they had, and that wasn't going to hold much beyond the first attack. Randahl and the other three had exhausted their Jewels before he and Jaenelle had arrived. There hadn't been enough food or rest to bring any of them back up to strength.

No, the males weren't going to make it. But Jaenelle had to. She was too valuable a Queen to lose in a trap that, he was convinced, had been set to destroy him.

Satisfied that he'd lined up every argument that Protocol gave him to make this demand, Lucivar said, "Ask the Lady to join me here."

No fool, Randahl understood why the request was being made now.

Alone for a moment, Lucivar rolled his neck and stretched his shoulders, trying to ease the tense, tired muscles.

It is easier to kill than to heal. It is easier to destroy than to preserve. It is easier to tear down than to build. Those who feed on destructive emotions and ambitions and deny the responsibilities that are the price of wielding power can bring down everything you care for and would protect. Be on guard, always.

Saetan's words. Saetan's warning to the young Warlords and Warlord Princes who gathered at the Hall.

But Saetan had never mentioned the last part of that warning: sometimes it was kinder to destroy.

He wasn't strong enough to give Jaenelle a swift, clean death. But even at full strength, Randahl and the other Warlords wore lighter-rank Jewels, and landens had no inner defense against the Blood. Once Jaenelle and Mari were away from here, once the Jhinka started their final attack, he would make a fast descent, pull up every drop of power he had left, and unleash that force. The landens would die instantly, their minds burned away. Randahl and the others might survive for a few seconds longer, but not long enough for the Jhinka to reach them.

And the Jhinka . . . they, too, would die. Some of them. A lot of them. But not all of them. He would be left, alone, when the survivors tore him apart. He would make sure of it. He'd fought Jhinka in Terreille. He'd seen what they did to captives. When it came to cruelty, they were an ingenious people. But then, so were many of the Blood.

Lucivar turned as movement caught his eye.

Jaenelle stood a few feet away, her eyes fixed on the Jhinka.

She wore nothing but the Black Jewel around her neck

He could understand why. Even her underclothes wouldn't have fit. All the muscle, all the feminine curves she'd gained over the past year were gone. Having no other source of fuel, her body had consumed itself in its struggle to be the receptacle for the power within. Bones pressed against pale, damp, blood-streaked skin. He could count her ribs, could see her hipbones move as she shifted her feet. Her golden hair was dark and stiff with the blood that must have been on her hands when she ran her fingers through it.

Despite that, or perhaps because of it, her face was strangely compelling. Her youth had been consumed in the healing fire, leaving her with a timeless, ageless beauty that suited her ancient, haunted sapphire eyes. It looked like an exquisite mask that would never again be touched by living concerns.

Then the mask shattered. Her grief and rage flooded through him, sending him careening against the building.

Lucivar grabbed the corner and hung on with a desperation rapidly being consumed by overwhelming fear.

The world spun with sick speed, spun in tighter and tighter spirals, dragging at his mind, threatening to tear him away from any sane anchor. Faster and faster. Deeper and deeper.

Spirals. Saetan had told him something about spirals, but he couldn't see, couldn't breathe, couldn't think.

His shield broke, its energy sucked down into the spiral. The witch storm got pulled in, too, its psychic threads snapping as it tried to remain anchored around the building.

Faster and faster, deeper and deeper, and then the dark power rose out of the abyss, roaring past him with a speed that froze his mind.

Lucivar jerked away from the building and staggered toward Jaenelle. Down. He had to get her down on the ground, had to—

Pop.

Pop pop.

Pop pop pop pop pop.

"MOTHER NIGHT!" Adler screamed, pointing toward the hills.

Lucivar wrenched a muscle in his neck as he snapped his head toward the sound of Jhinka bodies exploding.

Another surge of dark power flashed through what was left of the witch storm's psychic threads. They flared, blackened, disappeared.

He thought he heard a faint scream.

Pop pop pop.

Pop pop.

Pop.

It took her thirty seconds to destroy six thousand Jhinka.

She didn't look at anyone. She just turned around and started walking slowly, stiffly toward the other end of the village.

Lucivar tried to tell her to wait for him, but his voice wouldn't work. He tried to get to his feet, not sure how he'd ended up on his knees, but his legs felt like jelly.

He finally remembered what Saetan had told him about spirals.

He didn't fear her but, Hell's fire, he wanted to know what had set her off so that he had some idea of how to deal with her.

Hands pulled at his arm.

Randahl, looking gray-skinned and sick, helped him get to his feet.

They were both panting from the effort it took to reach the building and brace themselves against the stone wall.

Randahl rubbed his eyes. His mouth trembled. "The boy died," he said hoarsely. "She'd just finished healing the last landen. Hell's fire, Yaslana, she healed all three hundred of them. Three hundred in three days. She was swaying on her feet. Mari was telling her she had to sit down, had to rest. She shook her head and stumbled over to where Khevin was lying, and . . . and he just smiled at her and died. Gone. Completely gone. Not even a whisper of him left."

Lucivar closed his eyes. He'd think about the dead later. There were still things that needed to be done for the living. "Are you strong enough to send a message to Agio?"

Randahl shook his head. "None of us are strong enough to ride the Winds right now, but we're overdue by a day, so someone ought to be out on the roads searching for us."

"When your people arrive, I want Mari escorted to the Hall."

"We can look after her," Randahl replied sharply.

But would Mari want to be looked after by the Blood in Agio?

"Escort her to the Hall," Lucivar said. "She needs time to grieve, and she needs a place where her heart can start to heal. There are some at the Hall who can help her with that."

Randahl looked unhappy. "You think the Dhemlan Blood will be kinder to her than we were?"

Lucivar shrugged. "I wasn't thinking of the Dhemlan Blood. I was thinking of the kindred."

Having gotten Randahl's agreement, Lucivar stopped in-

side the community hall long enough to see Mari and tell
her she would be going to the Hall. She clung to him for
a few minutes, crying fiercely.

He held her, giving what comfort he could.

When two of the landen women, casting defiant looks at
the rest, offered to look after Mari, he let her go, sincerely
hoping he'd never have to deal with landens again.

He found Jaenelle a few steps outside the village boundary,
curled up into a tight ball, making desperate little sounds.

He dropped to his knees and cradled her in his arms.

"I didn't want to kill," she wailed. "That's not what the
Craft is for. That's not what *my* Craft is for."

"I know, Cat," Lucivar murmured. "I know."

"I could have put a shield around them, holding them in
until we got help from Agio. That's what I meant to do,
but the rage just boiled out of me when Khevin . . . I could
feel their minds, could feel them wanting to hurt. I couldn't
stop the anger. I couldn't *stop* it."

"It's the drugs, Cat. The damn things can scramble your
emotions for a long time, especially in a situation like this."

"I don't like killing. I'd rather be hurt than hurt someone else."

He didn't argue with her. He was too exhausted and her
emotions were too raw. Nor did he point out that she'd
reacted to a friend's pain and death. What she couldn't, or
wouldn't, do for her own sake she would do for someone
she cared for.

"Lucivar?" Jaenelle said plaintively. "I want a bath."

That was just one of the things he wanted. "Let's go
home, Cat."

11 / Terreille

Dorothea SaDiablo sank into a chair and stared at her unexpected guest. "Here? You want to stay *here*?" Had the
bitch looked into a mirror lately? How was she supposed
to explain a desiccated walking corpse that looked like it
had just crawled out of an old grave?

"Not here in your precious court," Hekatah replied, her

fleshless lips curling in a snarl. "And I'm not asking for your permission. I'm *telling* you that I'm staying in Hayll and require accommodations."

Telling. Always telling. Always reminding her that she never would have become the High Priestess of Hayll without Hekatah's guidance and subtle backing, without Hekatah pointing out the rivals who had too much potential and would thwart her dream of being a High Priestess who was so strong even the Queens yielded to her.

Well, she *was* the High Priestess of Hayll, and after centuries of twisting and savaging males who, in turn, did their own share of savaging, there were no dark-Jeweled Queens left in Terreille. There were no Queens, no Black Widows, no other Priestesses equal to her Red Jewel. In some of the smaller, more stubborn Territories, there were no Jeweled Blood at all. Within another five years, she would succeed where Hekatah had failed—she would be *the* High Priestess of Terreille, feared and revered by the entire Realm.

And when that day came, she would have something very special planned for her mentor and adviser.

Dorothea settled back in her chair and suppressed a smile. Still, the bag of bones might have a use. Sadi was still out there somewhere, playing his elusive, teasing game. Although she hadn't felt his presence in quite some time, every time she opened a door, she expected to find him on the other side waiting for her. But if a Red-Jeweled Black Widow High Priestess was staying at the country lodge she kept for more vigorous and imaginative evenings, and if he happened to become aware of a witch living there quietly . . . well, her psychic scent permeated the place and he might not take the time to distinguish between the scent of the place and the occupant's psychic scent. It would be a shame to lose the building, but she really didn't think there would be anything left of it by the time he was done.

Of course, there wouldn't be anything left of Hekatah either.

Dorothea tucked a loose strand of black hair back into the simple coil around her head. "I realize you weren' asking my permission, Sister," she purred. "When have you ever *asked* me for anything?"

"Remember who you speak to," Hekatah hissed.

"I never forget," Dorothea replied sweetly. "I have a lodge in the country, about an hour's carriage ride from Draega. I use it for discreet entertaining. You're welcome to stay there as long as you please. The staff is very well-trained, so I do ask that you not make a meal out of them. I'll supply you with plenty of young feasts." Frowning at a fingernail, she called in a nail file and smoothed an edge, studied the result, and smoothed again. Finally satisfied, she vanished the nail file and smiled at Hekatah. "Of course, if my accommodations aren't to your liking, you can always return to Hell."

Greedy, ungrateful bitch.

Hekatah opaqued another mirror. Even that little bit of Craft was almost too much.

This wasn't the way she'd planned to return to Hayll, hidden away like some doddering, drooling relative dispatched to some out-of-the-way property with no one but hard-faced servants for company.

Of course, once some of her strength returned . . .

Hekatah shook her head. The amusements would have to come later.

She considered ringing for a servant to come and put another log on the fire, then dismissed the idea and added the wood herself. Curling up into an old, stuffed chair, she stared at the wood being embraced and consumed by the flames.

Consumed just like all her pretty plans.

First the fiasco with the girl. If that was the best Jorval could do, she was going to have to rethink his usefulness.

Then the Eyrien managed to escape her trap and destroy all those lovely Jhinka that she'd cultivated so carefully. And the backlash of power that had come through her witch storm had done *this* to her.

And last, but far from least, was that gutter son of a whore's purge of the Dark Realm. There was no safe haven in Hell now, and no one, *no one* to serve her.

So, for now, she had to accept Dorothea's sneering hospitality, had to accept handouts instead of the tribute that was her due.

No matter. Unlike Dorothea, who was too busy trying to grab power and gobble up Territories, she had taken a good long look at the two living Realms.

Let Dorothea have the crumbling ruins of Terreille.

She was going to have Kaeleer.

CHAPTER
FOURTEEN

1 / Kaeleer

Saetan braced his hand against the stone wall, momentarily unbalanced by the double blast of anger that shook the Keep.

"Mother Night," he muttered. "*Now* what are they squabbling about?" Mentally reaching out to Lucivar, he met a psychic wall of fury.

He ran.

As he neared the corridor that led to Jaenelle's suite of rooms, he slowed to a walk, pressing one hand against his side and swearing silently because he didn't have enough breath to roar. Wouldn't have mattered anyway, he thought sourly. Whatever was provoking his children's tempers certainly wasn't affecting their lungs.

"Get out of my way, Lucivar!"

"When the sun shines in Hell!"

"Damn your wings, you've no right to interfere."

"I serve you. That gives me the right to challenge anything and anyone that threatens your well-being. And that includes you!"

"If you serve me, then obey me. GET OUT OF MY WAY!"

"The First Law is not obedience—"

"Don't you dare start quoting Blood Laws to me."

"—and even if it was, I still wouldn't stand here and let you do this. It's suicidal!"

Saetan rounded the corner, shot up the short flight of stairs, and stumbled on the top step.

In the dimly lit corridor, Lucivar looked like something out of the night-tales landens told their children: dark, spread wings blending into the darkness beyond, teeth bared, gold eyes blazing with battle-fire. Even the blood dripping from the shallow knife slash in his left upper arm made him look more like something other than a living man.

In contrast, Jaenelle looked painfully real. The short black nightgown revealed too much of the body sacrificed to the power that had burned within her while she'd done the healing in the landen village a week ago. If cared for, the flesh wouldn't suffer that way, not even when it was the instrument of the Black Jewels.

Seeing the results of her careless attitude toward her body, seeing the hand that held the Eyrien hunting knife shake because she was too weak to hold a blade that, a month ago, she had handled easily, he gave in to the anger rising within him. "Lady," he said sharply.

Jaenelle spun to face him, weaving a little as she struggled to stay on her feet. Her eyes blazed with battle-fire, too.

"Daemon's been found."

Saetan crossed his arms, leaned against the wall, and ignored the challenge in her voice. "So you intend to channel your strength through an already weakened body, create the shadow you've been using to search Terreille, send it to wherever his body is, travel through the Twisted Kingdom until you find him, and then lead him back."

"Yes," she said too softly. "That's exactly what I'm going to do."

Lucivar slammed the side of his fist against the wall. "It's too much. You haven't even begun to recover from the healings you did. Let this friend of yours keep him for a couple of weeks."

"You can't 'keep' someone who's lost in the Twisted Kingdom," Jaenelle snapped. "They don't see or live in the tangible world the way everyone else does. If something spooks him and he slips away from her, it could be weeks even months before she finds him again. By then it may be too late. *He's running out of time.*"

"So have her bring him to the Keep in Terreille," Lucivar argued. "We can hold him there until you're strong enough to do the healing."

"He's insane, not broken. He still wears the Black. If someone tried to 'hold' you, what sort of memories would that stir up?"

"She's right, Lucivar," Saetan said calmly. "If he thinks this friend is leading him into a trap, no matter what her real intentions, what little trust he has in her will shatter, and that will be the last time she finds him. At least, while there's anything worth finding."

Lucivar thumped the wall with his fist. He kept thumping the wall while he swore, long and low. Finally, he rubbed the side of his hand against the other palm. "Then I'll go back to Terreille and get him."

"Why should he trust you?" Jaenelle said bitterly.

Pain flared in Lucivar's eyes.

Saetan felt Jaenelle's inner barriers open just a crack. He didn't stop to think. At the moment when she was torn between anger at and distress for Lucivar, he swept in and out of that crack, tasting the emotional undercurrents.

So their little witch thought she could force them to yield. Thought she had an emotional weapon they wouldn't challenge.

She was right. She did.

But now, so did he.

"Let her go, Lucivar," Saetan crooned, his voice a purring, soft thunder. Still leaning against the wall with his arms crossed, he tilted his upper body in a mocking bow. "The Lady has us by the balls, and she knows it."

He felt bitterly pleased to see the wariness in Jaenelle's eyes.

She looked quickly at both of them. "You're not going to stop me?"

"No, we're not going to stop you." Saetan smiled malevolently. "Unless, of course, you don't agree to pay the price for our submission. If you refuse, the only way you'll walk out of here is by destroying both of us."

Such a neat trap. Such sweet bait.

He confused her, had finally managed to unnerve her.

She was about to find out how neatly he could spin her into a web.

"What's your price?" Jaenelle asked reluctantly.

One casual, flicking glance took in everything from her head to her feet. "Your body."

She dropped the knife.

It probably would have cut off a couple of toes if Lucivar hadn't vanished it in midair.

"Your body, my Lady," Saetan crooned. "The body you treat with such contempt. Since you obviously don't want it, I'll take it in trust for the one who already has a claim to it."

Jaenelle stared at him, her eyes wide and blank. "You want me to leave this body? L-like I did before?"

"Leave?" His voice sounded silky and dangerous. "No, you don't have to leave. I'm sure the claimant would be perfectly willing to give you a permanent loan. But it would be a loan, you understand, and you would be expected to give the body the same kind of care you'd give any object lent to you by a friend."

She studied him for a long time. "And if I don't take care of it? What will you do?"

Saetan pushed away from the wall.

Jaenelle flinched, but her eyes never left his.

"Nothing," he said too softly. "I won't fight with you. I won't use physical strength or Craft to force you. I'll do nothing except keep a record of the transgressions. I'll never ask you for an explanation, and I'll never explain for you. *You* can try to justify abusing part of what Daemon paid for with dear coin."

Jaenelle's face turned dead-white. Saetan caught her as she swayed and held her against his chest.

"Heartless bastard," she whispered.

"Perhaps," he replied. "So what is your answer, Lady?"

Jaenelle! You promised!

Jaenelle jumped out of his arms, back-pedaled to try to keep her balance, and ended up with her back smacking against the wall.

Saetan studied Jaenelle's guilty expression and began to feel maliciously cheerful. Noting that Lucivar had come up on her blind side, he turned his attention toward the annoyed, half-grown Sceltie and the silent, but equally annoyed, Arcerian kitten who now weighed as much as Lucivar and still had five more years to grow.

"What did the Lady promise?" he asked Ladvarian.

You promised to eat and sleep and read books and take easy walkies until you healed, Ladvarian said accusingly, staring at Jaenelle.

"I am," Jaenelle stammered. "I did."

You've been playing with Lucivar.

Lucivar stepped away from the wall so that they could see his left arm. "She was playing rough, too."

Ladvarian and Kaelas snarled at Jaenelle.

"This is different," Jaenelle snapped. "This is important. And I wasn't playing with Lucivar. I was fighting with him."

"Yes," Lucivar agreed mournfully. "And all because I thought she should be resting instead of pushing herself until she collapsed."

Ladvarian and Kaelas snarled louder.

For shame, Lady, Saetan said, using a Black thread to keep the conversation private. *Breaking a promise to your little Brothers. Care to agree to my terms now, or shall we all snarl a bit longer?*

Her venomous look was not only an answer but a good indication of how often she lost these kinds of "discussions" once Ladvarian and, therefore, Kaelas made up their furry little minds about something.

"My Brothers." Saetan tipped his head courteously toward Ladvarian and Kaelas. "The Lady would never break a promise without good reason. Despite the risks to her own well-being, she has pledged herself to a delicate task, one that cannot be delayed. Since this promise was made before the one she made to you, we must yield to the Lady's wishes. As she said, this is important."

What's more important than the Lady? Ladvarian demanded.

Saetan didn't answer.

Jaenelle squirmed. "My . . . mate . . . is trapped in the

Twisted Kingdom. If I don't show him the way out, he'll be destroyed."

Mate? Ladvarian's ears perked up. His white-tipped tail waved once, twice. He looked at Saetan. *Jaenelle has a mate?*

Interesting that the Sceltie looked to him for confirmation. Something to keep in mind in the future.

"Yes," Saetan said. "Jaenelle has a mate."

"She won't have if she's delayed much longer," Jaenelle warned.

They all politely stepped aside and watched her painfully slow journey down the corridor.

Saetan had no doubt that she would use Craft to float her body as soon as she was out of their sight, which would put more strain on her physically but would also speed her journey to the Dark Altar that stood within Ebon Askavi. And except for being carried, that was the only way she was going to reach the Gate that would take her to the Keep in Terreille.

After Ladvarian and Kaelas had trotted off to tell Draca about the Lady's mate, Saetan turned to Lucivar. "Come into the healing workroom. I'll take care of that arm."

Lucivar shrugged. "It's not bleeding anymore."

"Boyo, I know the Eyrien drill as well as you do. Wounds are cleansed and healed." *And I want to talk to you in a shielded room away from furry ears.*

"Do you think she'll make it?" Lucivar asked a few minutes later as he watched Saetan clean the shallow knife wound.

"She has the strength, the knowledge, and the desire. She'll bring him out of the Twisted Kingdom."

It wasn't what Lucivar meant, and they both knew it.

"Why didn't you stop her? Why are you letting her risk herself?"

Saetan bent his head, avoiding Lucivar's eyes. "Because she loves him. Because he really *is* her mate."

Lucivar was silent for a minute. Then he sighed. "He always said he'd been born to be Witch's lover. Looks like he was right."

2 / Terreille

Surreal watched Daemon prowl the center of the overgrown maze and wondered how much longer she would be able to keep him here.

He didn't trust her. She couldn't trust him.

She'd found him about a mile from the ruins of SaDiablo Hall, weeping silently as he watched a house burn to the ground. She didn't ask about the burning house, or about the twenty freshly butchered Hayllian guards, or why he kept whispering Tersa's name over and over.

She'd taken his hand, caught the Winds, and brought him here. Whoever had owned this estate had either abandoned it by choice or had been forced out or killed when Dhemlan Terreille had finally caved in to Hayll's domination. Now Hayllian guards used the manor house as a barracks for the troops who were teaching the Dhemlan people about the penalties of disobedience.

Daemon had watched passively while she'd used illusion spells to fill in the gaps in the hedges that would lead to the center of the maze. He'd said nothing when she created a double Gray shield around their hiding place.

His passive obedience had melted away when she called in the small web Jaenelle had given her and placed four drops of blood in its center to awaken it, turning it into a signal and a beacon.

He'd started prowling after that, started smiling that cold, familiar, brutal smile while she waited. And waited. And waited.

"Why don't you call your friends, Little Assassin?" Daemon said as he glided past the place where she sat with her knees up and her back against the hedge. "Don't you want to earn your pay?"

"There's no pay, Daemon. We're waiting for a friend."

"Of course we are," he said too softly as he made another circuit around the center of the maze. Then he stopped and looked at her, his gold eyes filled with a glazed, cold fire. "She liked you. She asked me to help you. Do you remember that?"

"Who, Daemon?" Surreal asked quietly.

"Tersa." His voice broke. "They burned the house Tersa had lived in with her little boy. She had a son, did you know that?"

Hell's fire, Mother Night, and may the Darkness be merciful. "No, I didn't know that."

Daemon nodded. "But that bitch Dorothea took him from her, and she went far, far away. And then that bitch put a Ring of Obedience on the little boy and trained him to be a pleasure slave. Took him into her bed and . . ." Daemon shuddered. "You're blood of her blood."

Surreal scrambled to her feet. "Daemon. I'm not like Dorothea. I don't acknowledge her as kin."

Daemon bared his teeth. "Liar," he snarled. He took a step toward her, his right thumb flicking the ragged ring-finger nail. "Silky, court-trained liar." Another step. "Butchering whore."

As he raised his right hand, Surreal saw a tiny, glistening drop fall from the needlelike nail under the regular nail.

She dove to his left, calling in her stiletto as she fell.

He was on her before she hit the ground.

She screamed when he broke her right wrist. She screamed again when he clamped his left hand over both of her wrists, grinding bones.

"Daemon," she said, breathless and panicked as his right hand closed around her throat.

"Daemon."

Surreal gulped back a sob of relief at the sound of that familiar midnight voice.

Hope and horror filled Daemon's eyes as he slowly raised his head. "Please," he whispered. "I never meant. . . . *Please.*" He threw his head back, let out a heart-shattering cry, and collapsed.

Using Craft, Surreal rolled him off her and sat up, cradling her broken wrist. Dizzy and nauseous, she closed her eyes as she felt Jaenelle approach. "I realize arriving a few seconds sooner would have made a less dramatic entrance, but I would've appreciated it more."

"Let me see your wrist."

Surreal looked up and gasped. "Hell's fire, what happened to you?"

During the other times when Jaenelle's "shadow" had joined Surreal to search for Daemon, it had been impossible to guess she wasn't a living woman unless you tried to touch her. No one would mistake this transparent, wasted creature for something that walked the living Realms. But the sapphire eyes were still filled with their ancient fire, and the Black Jewels still glowed with untapped strength.

Jaenelle shook her head and wrapped her hands around Surreal's wrist. A flash of numbing cold was followed by a steadily growing warmth. Surreal felt the bones shift and set.

Jaenelle's transparent hands pulsed, fading and returning again and again. For a moment, she faded completely, her Black Jewels suspended as if waiting for her return.

When she reappeared, her eyes were filled with pain and she panted as if she couldn't draw a full breath.

"Collapsing," Jaenelle gasped. "Not now. Not *yet.*" Her transparent body convulsed. "Surreal, I can't finish the healing. The bones are set, but . . ." A tooled, leather wristband hovered in the air. Jaenelle slipped it over Surreal's wrist and snapped it shut. "That will help support it until it heals."

Surreal's left forefinger traced the stag head set in a circle of flowering vines—the same stag that was a symbol for Titian's kin, the Dea al Mon.

Before she could ask Jaenelle about the wristband, something heavy hit the ground nearby. A man cursed softly.

"Mother Night, the guards heard us." Using her left arm for leverage, Surreal got to her feet. "Let's get him out of here and—"

"I can't leave here, Surreal," Jaenelle said quietly. "I have to do what I came here to do . . . while I still can."

The Black Jewels flared, and Surreal felt a shivering, liquid darkness flow into the maze.

Jaenelle tried to smile. "They won't find their way through the maze. Not *this* maze, anyway." Then she looked sadly at Daemon's gaunt, bruised body and gently brushed the long, dirty, tangled black hair off his forehead. "Ah, Daemon. I had gotten used to thinking of my body as a weapon that was used against me. I'd forgotten that it's also a gift. If it's not too late, I'll do better. I promise."

Jaenelle placed her transparent hands on either side of Daemon's head. She closed her eyes. The Black Jewel glowed.

Listening to the Hayllian guards thrashing around somewhere in the maze, Surreal sank to the ground and settled down to wait.

Daemon.

The island slowly sank into the sea of blood. He curled up in the center of the pulpy ground while the word sharks circled, waiting for him.

Daemon.

Hadn't they all been waiting for the end of this torment? Hadn't they all been waiting for the debt to be paid in full? Now she was calling him, calling for his complete surrender.

Move your ass, Sadi!

He rolled to his hands and knees and stared at the golden-maned, sapphire-eyed woman who stood on a blood-drenched shore that hadn't existed a minute ago. A tiny spiral horn rose from the center of her forehead. Her long gown looked as if it were made from black cobwebs and didn't quite hide her delicate hooves.

The pleasure of seeing her made him giddy. Her mood made him cautious. He carefully sat back on his heels. *You're annoyed with me.*

Let me put it this way, Jaenelle replied sweetly. *If you go under and I have to pull you out, I'm going to be pissed.*

Daemon shook his head slowly and tsked. *Such language.*

With precise enunciation, she spoke a phrase in the Old Tongue.

His jaw dropped. He choked on a laugh.

That, Prince Sadi, is language.

You are my instrument.

Words lie. Blood doesn't.

Butchering whore.

He swayed, steadied himself, rose carefully to his feet. *Have you come to call in the debt, Lady?*

He didn't understand the sorrow in her eyes.

I'm here because of a debt, she said, her voice filled with pain. She slowly raised her hands.

Between the shore and the sinking island, the sea churned, churned, churned. Waves lifted and froze into waist-high walls. Between them, the sea solidified, becoming a bridge made of blood.

Come, Daemon.

His hands lightly brushed the crests of the red, frozen waves. He stepped onto the bridge.

The word sharks circled, tore off chunks of the island, tried to slice away the bridge beneath his feet.

You are my instrument.

Jaenelle called in a bow, nocked an arrow, and took aim. The arrow sang through the air. The word shark thrashed as it withered and sank.

Words lie. Blood doesn't.

Another arrow sang a death song.

Butchering who—

The island and the last word shark sank together.

Jaenelle vanished the bow, turned away from the sea, and walked into the twisted, shattered-crystal landscape.

Her voice reached him, faint and fading. *Come, Daemon.*

Daemon rushed across the bridge, hit the shore running, and then swore in frustration as he searched for some sign of where she'd gone.

He caught her psychic scent before he noticed the glittering trail. It was like a ribbon of star-sprinkled night sky that led him through the twisted landscape to where she perched on a rock far above him.

She looked down at him, smiling with exasperated amusement. *Stubborn, snarly male.*

Stubbornness is a much-maligned quality, he panted as he climbed toward her.

Her silvery, velvet-coated laugh filled the land.

Then he finally got a good look at her. He sank to his knees. *I owe you a debt, Lady.*

She shook her head. *The debt is mine, not yours.*

I failed you, he said bitterly, looking at her wasted body.

No, Daemon, Jaenelle replied softly. *I failed *you.* You asked me to heal the crystal chalice and return to the living world. And I did. But I don't think I ever forgave my body for being the instrument that was used to try to destroy me, and I became its cruelest torturer. For that I'm sorry because you treasured that part of me.*

*No, I treasured *all* of you. I love you, Witch. I always will. You're everything I'd dreamed you would be.*

She smiled at him. *And I—* She shuddered, pressed her hand against her chest. *Come. There's little time left.*

She fled through the rocks, out of sight before he could move.

He hurried after her, following the glittering trail, gasping as he felt a crushing weight descend on him.

Daemon. Her voice came back to him, faint and pain-filled. *If the body is going to survive, I can't stay any longer.*

He fought against the weight. *Jaenelle!*

You have to take this in slow stages. Rest there now. Rest, Daemon. I'll mark the trail for you. Please follow it. I'll be waiting for you at the end.

JAENELLE!

A wordless whisper. His name spoken like a caress. Then silence.

Time meant nothing as he lay there, curled in a ball, fighting to hang on to the glittering trail that led upward while everything beneath him pulled at him, trying to drag him back down.

He held on fiercely to the memory of her voice, to her promise that she would be waiting.

Later—much later—the pulling eased, the crushing weight lessened.

The glittering trail, the star-sprinkled ribbon still led upward.

Daemon climbed.

Surreal watched the sky lighten and listened to the guards shouting and cursing as the maze sizzled from the explosions of power against power. Throughout the long night, the guards had pounded their way toward the center of the maze as Jaenelle's shields broke piece by piece. If the screams were any indication, it had cost the guards dearly to break as much of her shields as they had.

There was some satisfaction in that, but Surreal also knew what the surviving guards would do to whomever they found in the maze.

"Surreal? What's happening?"

For a moment, Surreal couldn't say anything. Jaenelle's eyes looked dead-dull, the inner fire burned to ash. Her Black Jewels looked as if she'd drained most of the reserve power in them.

Surreal knelt beside Daemon. Except for the rise and fall of his chest, he hadn't stirred since he collapsed. "The guards are breaking through the shield," she said, trying to sound calm. "I don't think we have much time left."

Jaenelle nodded. "Then you and Daemon have to leave. The Green Wind runs over the edge of the garden. Can you reach it?"

Surreal hesitated. "With all the power that's been unleashed in this area, I'm not sure."

"Let me see your Gray ring."

She held out her right hand.

Jaenelle brushed her Black ring against Surreal's Gray.

Surreal felt a psychic thread shoot out of the rings as they made contact, felt the Green Web pull at her.

"There," Jaenelle gasped. "As soon as you launch yourself, the thread will reel you into the Green Web. Take the beacon web with you. Destroy it completely as soon as you can."

Daemon stirred, moaned softly.

"What about you?" Surreal asked.

Jaenelle shook her head. "It doesn't matter. I won't be coming back. I'll hold the guards long enough to give you a head start."

Jaenelle opened Daemon's tattered shirt. Taking Surreal's right hand, she pricked the middle finger and pressed it against Daemon's chest while she murmured words in a language Surreal didn't know.

"This binding spell will keep him with you until he's out of the Twisted Kingdom." Jaenelle faded, came back. "One last thing."

Surreal took the gold coin that hovered in the air. On one side was an elaborate S. On the other side were the words "Dhemlan Kaeleer."

"That's a mark of safe passage," Jaenelle said, straining to get the words out. "If you ever come to Kaeleer, show it to whomever you first meet and tell them you're expected at the Hall in Dhemlan. It guarantees you a safe escort."

Surreal vanished the coin and the small beacon web.

Daemon rolled onto his side and opened his eyes.

Jaenelle floated backward until she faded into the hedge.
Go quickly, Surreal. May the Darkness embrace you.

Swearing quietly, Surreal tugged Daemon to his feet. He stared at her with simpleminded bewilderment. She pulled his left arm over her shoulders and winced as she tightened her right arm around his waist.

Taking a deep breath, she let the psychic thread reel them through the Darkness until she caught the Green Wind and headed north.

The hiding place was ready and waiting.

Before the night when she'd drunkenly broken the warm friendship that had existed between them, Daemon had told her about two people: Lord Marcus, the man of business who took care of Daemon's very discreet investments, and Manny.

Shortly after Jaenelle had contacted her, she'd gone to see Lord Marcus about finding a hiding place and had discovered that one already existed—a small island that was owned by "a reclusive invalid Warlord" who lived with a handful of servants.

Daemon owned the island. Everyone who lived there had been physically or emotionally maimed by Dorothea SaDiablo. It was a sheltered place where they could rebuild some semblance of a life.

She hadn't dared go to the island while she was still hunting for Daemon because she'd been afraid of leading Kartane SaDiablo there. Now she and Daemon could both drop out of sight, and the fictitious invalid Warlord and his newly acquired companion would become a reality.

But first there was one fast stop to make, one question to ask. She hoped beyond words that Manny would say "yes."

Surreal . . .

Surreal tried to strengthen the distaff thread. *Jaenelle?*

Surreal . . . g . . . Keep . . . o . . .

Surreal tightened the leash on her emotions as the distaff thread snapped. She'd do her best to keep Daemon safe.

Because she owed him. Because what was left of Jaenelle cared.

Not allowing herself to think about what was happening in the center of the maze, Surreal flew on.

3 / Kaeleer

Ladvarian's frantic barking and Lucivar's shouted "Father!" snapped Saetan out of his worried brooding. Propelling himself out of a chair in Jaenelle's sitting room at the Keep, he rushed to the door leading into her bedroom, then clung to the frame, paralyzed for a moment by the sight of the ravaged body Lucivar held in his arms.

"Mother Night," he muttered as he grabbed Kaelas by the scruff of the neck and pulled the snarling young cat off the bed. Throwing back the bedcovers, he placed a warming spell on the sheets. "Put her down."

Lucivar hesitated.

"Put her down," he snapped, unnerved by the tears in Lucivar's eyes. As soon as Lucivar gently laid Jaenelle on the bed, Saetan knelt beside her. Laying one hand lightly against her chest, he used a delicate psychic tendril to sense and catalog the injuries.

Lungs collapsing, arteries and veins collapsing, heart erratic and weak. The rest of the inner organs on the verge of failing. Bones as fragile as eggshells.

Jaenelle, Saetan called. Sweet Darkness, had she severed the link between body and spirit? *Witch-child!*

Saetan? Jaenelle's voice sounded faint and far away. *I made a mess of it, didn't I?*

He fought to remain calm. She had the knowledge and the Craft to perform the healing. If he could keep her connected with her body, they might have a chance to save her. *You could say that.*

Did Ladvarian bring the healing web from the Keep in Terreille?

"Ladvarian!" He instantly regretted shouting because the Sceltie just cowered and whined, too upset to remember how to speak to him. *Stay calm, SaDiablo. Temper is destructive in any healing room, but it could be fatal in this one.* "The Lady is asking about the healing web," he said quietly. "Did you bring it?"

Kaelas planted his front paws on either side of the small dog's body and gave his friend an encouraging lick.

After another nudge from Kaelas, Ladvarian said, *Web?* He stood up, still safely sheltered by the cat's body. *Web. I brought the web.*

A small wooden frame appeared between Ladvarian and the bed.

To Saetan's eye, the healing web attached to the frame looked too simple to help a body as damaged as Jaenelle's. Then he noticed the single thread of spidersilk that went from the web to the Black-Jeweled ring attached to the frame's base.

Three drops of blood on the ring will waken the healing web, Jaenelle said.

Saetan looked at Lucivar, who stood near the bed as if waiting for a fatal blow. He hesitated—and swore silently because he still felt the sting of old accusations even though he wasn't asking for himself. "She needs three drops of blood on the ring. I don't dare give her mine. I'm not sure what a Guardian's blood will do to her."

Rage flashed in Lucivar's eyes, and Saetan knew his son had understood why he'd hesitated to ask.

"Damn you to the bowels of Hell," Lucivar said as he pulled a small knife out of the sheath in his boot. "You *didn't* take my blood when I was a child, so stop apologizing for something you didn't do." He jabbed a finger and let three drops of blood fall on the Black-Jeweled ring.

Saetan held his breath until the web started glowing.

Lucivar sheathed the knife. "I'm going to fetch Luthvian."

Saetan nodded. Not that Lucivar had waited for his agreement before stepping through the glass door that led to Jaenelle's private garden and launching himself skyward.

Jaenelle's body twitched. Through the psychic tendril, Saetan could feel the Craft in the web washing through her, stabilizing her. He glanced at the web and tried to block out any feelings of despair. One-third of the threads were already darkened, used up.

I didn't expect it to be this bad, Jaenelle said apologetically.

Luthvian will be here soon.

Good. With her help, I can transfer the power my body can't hold now into the web to use for the healing.

He felt her fade. *Jaenelle!*

I found him, Saetan. I marked a trail for him to follow. And I . . . I told Surreal to take him to the Keep, but I'm not sure she heard me.

Don't think about it now, witch-child. Concentrate on healing.

She drifted into a light sleep.

By the time Luthvian arrived at the Keep, two-thirds of Jaenelle's simple healing web was used up, and he wondered if there would be enough time to create another one before the last thread darkened.

He couldn't stay and watch. As soon as Luthvian regained enough of her composure to begin, he retreated to the sitting room, taking Ladvarian and Kaelas with him. He didn't ask where Lucivar was. He simply felt grateful that they wouldn't rub against each other's fraying tempers for a little while.

He paced until his leg ached. He embraced the physical discomfort like a sweet lover. Far better to focus on that than the heart-bruises that might be waiting for him.

Because he wasn't sure if he could stand another bedside vigil.

Because he didn't know if she'd succeeded enough to make her suffering worth it.

4 / The Twisted Kingdom

He learned as he climbed.

She had left small resting places next to the glittering trail: violets nestled against a boulder; sweet, clean water trickling down stone to a quiet pool that soothed the spirit; a patch of thick, green grass large enough to stretch out on; a plump, brown bunny watching him while it stuffed its face with clover; a cheerful fire that melted the first layer of ice around his heart.

At first, he'd tried to ignore the resting places. He learned he could pass one, maybe two, while he fought against the weight that made each step more difficult. If he tried to pass a third, he found the trail blocked. Instinct always warned him that if he stepped off the glittering trail to go around the obstruction, he might never find his way back. So he'd backtrack and rest until he absorbed the weight and found it comfortable to go on.

He slowly realized the weight had a name: body. This confused him for a while. Didn't he already have a body? He walked, he breathed, he heard, he saw. He felt tired. He felt pain. This other body felt different, heavy, solid. He wasn't sure he liked absorbing its essence into himself— or, perhaps, having it absorb him.

But the body was part of the same delicate web as the violets, the water, the sky, and the fire—reminders of a place beyond the shattered landscape—so he resigned himself to becoming reacquainted with it.

After a while, each resting place held an intangible gift, too: a Craft puzzle piece, one small aspect of a spell. Gradually the pieces began to make a whole and he learned the basics of the Black Widows' Craft, learned how to build simple webs, learned how to be what he was.

So he rested and treasured her little gifts and puzzles.

And he climbed to where she had promised to be waiting.

PART V

CHAPTER
FIFTEEN

1 / Kaeleer

"The first part of our plan is coming along nicely," Hekatah said. "Little Terreille is, at last, justly represented in the Dark Council."

Lord Jorval smiled tightly. Since slightly more than half of the Council members now came from Little Terreille, he could agree that the Territory that had always felt wary of the rest of the Shadow Realm was, at last, "justly" represented. "With all the injuries and illnesses that have caused members to resign in the past two years, the Blood in Little Terreille were the only ones willing to accept such a heavy responsibility for the good of the Realm." He sighed, but his eyes glittered with malicious approval. "We've been accused of favoritism because so many voices come from the same Territory, but when the other men and women who were judged worthy of the task refused to accept, what were we to do? The Council seats must be filled."

"So they must," Hekatah agreed. "And since so many of those new members, who owe their current rise in status to your supporting their appointment to the Council, wouldn't want to find themselves distressed because they didn't heed your wisdom when it came time to vote, it's time to implement the second part of our plan."

"And that is?" Jorval wished she would take off that deep-hooded cloak. It wasn't as if he hadn't seen her before. And why had she chosen to meet in a seedy little inn in Goth's slums?

"To broaden Little Terreille's influence in the Shadow Realm. You're going to have to convince the Council to be more lenient in their immigration requirements. There are plenty of Blood aristos here already. You need to let in the lesser Blood—workers, craftsmen, farmers, hearth-witches, servants, lighter-Jeweled warriors. Stop deciding who can come in by whether or not they can pay the bribes."

"If the Terreillean Queens and the aristo males want servants, let them use the landens," Jorval said in a sulky voice. The bribes, as she well knew, had become an important source of income for a number of Blood aristos in Goth, Little Terreille's capital.

"Landens are demon fodder," Hekatah snapped. "Landens have no magic. Landens have no Craft. Landens are about as useful as Jhin—" She paused. She tugged her hood forward. "Accept Terreillean landens for immigration, too. Promise them privileges and a settlement after service. But bring in the lesser Terreillean Blood as well."

Jorval spread his hands. "And what are we supposed to do with all these immigrants? At the twice-yearly immigration fairs, the other Territories altogether only take a couple dozen people, if that. The courts in Little Terreille are already swelled and there are complaints about the Terreillean aristos always whining about serving in the lower Circles and not having land to rule like they expected. And none of the ones already here have fulfilled their immigration requirement."

"They will have land to rule. They'll establish small, new territories on behalf of the Queens they're serving. That will increase the influence the Queens in Little Terreille have in Kaeleer as well as providing them with an additional source of income. Some of that land is obscenely rich in precious metals and precious gems. In a few years, Little Terreille's Queens will be the strongest force in the Realm, and the other Territories will have to submit to their dominance."

"What land?" Jorval said, failing to hide his exasperation.

"The unclaimed land, of course," Hekatah replied sharply. She called in a map of Kaeleer, unrolled it, and used Craft to keep it flat. One bony finger brushed against large areas of the map.

"That's not unclaimed land," Jorval protested. "Those are closed Territories. The so-called kindred Territories."

"*Exactly*, Lord Jorval," Hekatah said, tapping the map. "The *so-called kindred* Territories."

Jorval looked at the map and sat up straighter. "But the kindred are supposed to be Blood. Aren't they?"

"Are they?" Hekatah countered with venomous sweetness. "What about the human Territories, like Dharo and Nharkhava and Scelt? Their Queens might file a protest on the kindred's behalf."

"They can't. Their lands aren't being interfered with. By Blood Law, Territory Queens *can't* interfere outside their own borders."

"The High Lord . . ."

Hekatah waved a hand dismissively. "He has always lived by a strict code of honor. He'll viciously defend his own Territory, but he won't step one toe outside of it. If anything, he'll stand *against* those other Territories if they step outside the Law."

Jorval rubbed his lower lip. "So the Queens of Little Terreille would eventually rule all of Kaeleer."

"And those Queens would be consolidated under one wise, experienced individual who would be able to guide them properly."

Jorval preened.

"Not you, idiot," Hekatah hissed. "A male can't rule a Territory."

"The High Lord does!"

The silence went on so long Jorval began to sweat.

"Don't forget who he is or what he is, Lord Jorval. Don't forget about his particular code of honor. You're the wrong gender. If *you* tried to stand against him, he would tear you apart. *I* will rule Kaeleer." Her voice sweetened. "You will be my Steward, and as my trusted right hand and most valued adviser, you will be so influential there won't be a woman in the Realm who would dare refuse you."

Heat filled Jorval's groin as he thought of Jaenelle Angelline.

The map rolled up with a snap, startling him.

"I think we've postponed the amenities long enough, don't you?" Hekatah pushed back the cloak's hood.

Jorval let out a faint scream. Leaping up, he knocked over his chair, then tripped over it when he turned to get away from the table.

As Hekatah slowly walked around the table, Jorval scrambled to his feet. He kept backing away until he ended up pressed against the wall.

"Just a sip," Hekatah said as she unbuttoned his shirt. "Just a taste. And maybe next time you'll remember to provide refreshments."

Jorval felt his bowels turn to water.

She'd changed in the last two years. Before, she'd looked like an attractive woman past her prime. Now she looked like someone had squeezed all the juice out of her flesh. And the liberally applied perfume didn't mask the smell of decay.

"There's one other very important reason why *I'm* going to rule Kaeleer," Hekatah murmured as her lips brushed his throat. "Something you shouldn't forget."

"Yes, P-Priestess?" Jorval clenched his hands.

"With me ruling, the Realm of Terreille will support our efforts."

"It will?" Jorval said faintly, trying to take shallow breaths.

"I guarantee it," Hekatah replied just before her teeth sank into his throat.

2 / Kaeleer

The new two-wheeled buggy rolled smartly down the middle of the wide dirt road that ran northeast out of the village of Maghre.

Saetan tried—again—to tell Daffodil that he should keep the buggy on the right-hand side of the road. And Daffodil replied—again—that if he did that, Yaslana and Sundancer wouldn't be able to trot alongside. He would move over if another wagon came down the road. He knew how to pull a buggy. The High Lord worried too much.

Sitting beside him, Jaenelle glanced at his clenched hands and smiled with sympathetic amusement. "Being the passenger when you're used to having control isn't an easy adjustment to make. Khary thinks kindred-drawn conveyances should have a set of reins attached to the front of the buggy to give the passenger something to hold on to, just to feel more secure."

"Sedatives would be more helpful," Saetan growled. He forced his hands open and pressed them firmly on his thighs, ignoring Lucivar's low chuckle and trying hard not to resent the reins attached to the headstall Sundancer wore.

Much to the humans' chagrin, the kindred had insisted that reins be kept as part of the riding equipment because humans needed something to hold on to when kindred ran and jumped. Fortunately, after the initial shock three years ago when the Scelt people had learned how many Blood races inhabited their island, the humans there had enthusiastically embraced their kindred Brothers and Sisters.

"Aren't we stopping at Morghann and Khary's house?" Jaenelle asked, clapping a hand on top of her head to keep the wide-brimmed straw hat from blowing away.

"They wanted to show us something and said they'd meet us," Lucivar replied. "Sundancer and I will go on ahead and see if they're waiting." He and the Warlord Prince stallion took off cross-country.

Daffodil made a wistful sound but kept trotting down the road. A few minutes later, he turned off the main road and trotted smartly down a long, tree-lined drive.

Jaenelle's eyes lit up. "We're going to see Duana's country house? Oh, it's such a lovely place. Khary mentioned that someone had taken a lease on it and was fixing it up a bit."

Saetan breathed a sigh of relief. Trust Khary to know just how much to say to pique her interest and still not give it away.

It had taken her six months to heal after she went into the Twisted Kingdom to save Daemon two years ago. She had remained at the Keep for the first two months, too ill to be moved. After he and Lucivar brought her back to the Hall, it had taken her another four months to get her physical strength back. During that time, her friends had once again taken up residence at the Hall, resigning from the courts they were serving in so that they could be with her. She had welcomed the coven's presence but had shied away from the boys seeing her—the first show of feminine vanity she had ever displayed.

Bewildered by her refusal to see them, they had settled in to care from a distance and had channeled their energy into looking after the coven. During that time, under his watchful but blind eye, some friendships had bloomed into love: Morghann and Khardeen, Gabrielle and Chaosti, Grezande and Elan, Kalush and Aaron. He'd watched the girls and had wondered if Jaenelle's eyes would ever shine like that for a man. Even if that man was Daemon Sadi.

When Daemon and Surreal didn't show up at the Terreille Keep, he had tried to locate them. After a few weeks, he stopped because there were indications that he wasn't the only one looking for them, and he had decided that failure was preferable to leading an enemy to a vulnerable man. Besides, Surreal was Titian's daughter. Wherever she had chosen to go to ground, she had hidden her tracks well.

And there was another reason he didn't want to stir things up. Hekatah had never returned to the Dark Realm. He suspected she was well hidden in Hayll. As long as she stayed there, she and Dorothea could rot together, but she would also latch on to any sign of his renewed interest in Terreille and hunt down the cause.

"Lucivar and Sundancer made better time than we did," Jaenelle noted as they pulled up in front of the well-proportioned sandstone manor house.

Daffodil snorted.

"No," Saetan said sternly as he helped Jaenelle out of the buggy. "Buggies *do not* go over fences."

"Especially when the human riding in it doesn't know he's responsible for getting his half over," Jaenelle murmured. She shook out the folds of her sapphire skirt and straightened the matching jacket, too busy to look him in the eye.

Which was just as well.

Jaenelle looked up at the manor house and sighed. "I hope the new tenants will give this place the love it deserves. Oh, I know Duana's busy and prefers living in her country house near Tuathal, but this land needs to be sung awake. The gardens here could be so lovely."

Acknowledging Lucivar's pleased smile, Saetan pulled a flat, rectangular box out of his pocket and handed it to Jaenelle. "Happy birthday, witch-child. From the whole family."

Jaenelle accepted the box but didn't open it. "If it's from the whole family, shouldn't I wait until we're back home to open it?"

Saetan shook his head. "We agreed you should open that here."

Jaenelle opened the box and frowned at the large brass key.

Letting out an exasperated growl, Lucivar turned her around until she was facing the front of the house. "It fits the front door."

Jaenelle's eyes widened. "Mine?" She looked at the front door, then at the key, then back to the front door. "Mine?"

"Well, the family purchased a ten-year lease on the house and land," Saetan replied, smiling. "Duana said that, short of tearing the house down, you could do whatever you wanted with the place."

Jaenelle gave both of them a choke-hold hug and raced to the door. It flew open before she reached it.

"SURPRISE!"

Smiling at her stunned expression, Saetan pushed her into the house at the same time Khary and Morghann pulled her forward into the crowd.

His throat tightened as he watched Jaenelle being passed from friend to friend for a birthday hug. Astar and Sceron, from Centauran. Zylona and Jonah, from Pandar. Grezande and Elan, from Tigrelan. Little Katrine, from Philan. Gabrielle and Chaosti, from Dea al Mon. Karla and Morton, from Glacia. Morghann and Khary, from Scelt. Sabrina and Aaron, from Dharo. Kalush, from Nharkhava. Ladvarian and Kaelas. Had the Shadow Realm ever seen a gathering such as this?

The years when the coven and the male circle had gathered at the Hall had passed so swiftly, and the youngsters were no longer children to be cared for, but adults to be met on equal ground. All the boys had made the Offering to the Darkness, and all of them wore dark Jewels. If the strong friendship between Khary, Aaron, and Chaosti survived the demands of young adulthood and serving in different courts, they would be a formidable, influential triangle of strength in the coming years. And the girls were almost ready to make the Offering. When they did . . . ah, the power!

And then there was Jaenelle. What would become of the lovely, gifted daughter of his soul when she made the Offering?

He tried to shake off his mood before she felt it. But today was a bittersweet day for him, which was why the family had celebrated her birthday—together, privately—a couple of days ago.

A roll of thunder silenced the chatter.

"There now," Karla said with a wicked smile. "Let Uncle Saetan give Jaenelle the grand tour while we finish setting out the food. This might be the only chance we'll get to play in the kitchen."

The girls scampered off to the back of the house.

"I think we'd better help them," Khary said, leading the young men, who hustled off to save the house and edibles.

Lucivar promised to be back, muttering something about unhitching Daffodil before the horse tried to do it himself.

"Duana said that any furniture you don't want to use can be tucked in the attics," Saetan said after he and Jaenelle explored downstairs.

Jaenelle nodded absently as they headed upstairs. "I've seen some grand pieces that would be perfect for this place. There was a—" Open-mouthed, she stood in the bedroom doorway and stared at the canopied bed, dresser, tables, and chests.

"The horde downstairs bought this for you. I gather you

had admired something similar often enough that they figured you would like it."

Jaenelle stepped into the room and ran her hand over the dresser's silky maple wood. "It's wonderful. All of it's wonderful. But, why?"

Saetan swallowed hard. "You're twenty years old today."

Jaenelle raised her right hand and fluffed her hair. "I know that."

"My legal guardianship ends today."

They stared at each other for a long moment.

"What does that mean?" she asked quietly.

"Exactly that. My *legal* guardianship ends today." He saw her relax as she assimilated the distinction. "You're a young woman now, witch-child, and should have a place of your own. You've always loved Scelt. We thought it would be helpful to have a home base on this side of the Realm as well as the other." When she still didn't say anything, his heart started pounding. "The Hall will always be your home. We'll always be your family—as long as you want us."

"As long as I want you." Her eyes changed.

It took everything he had in him not to sink to his knees and beg Witch to forgive him.

Jaenelle turned away from him, hugging herself as if she were cold. "I said some cruel things that day."

Saetan took a deep breath. "I did use him. He was my instrument. And even knowing what I know, if I had the choice to make again, I would do it again. A Warlord Prince is expendable. A good Queen is not. And, in truth, if we had done nothing and you hadn't survived, I don't think Daemon would have either. I know I wouldn't have."

Jaenelle opened her arms.

He stepped into them and held her tight. "I don't think you've ever realized how strong, how necessary the bond is between Warlord Princes and Queens. We need you to stay whole. That's why we serve. That's why *all* Blood males serve."

"But it's always seemed so unfair that a Queen can lay claim to a man and control every aspect of his life if she chooses to without him having any say in the matter."

Saetan laughed. "Who says a man has no choice? Haven't you ever noticed how many men who are invited to serve in a court decline the privilege? No, perhaps you haven't. You've had too many other things occupying your time, and that sort of thing is done very quietly." He paused and shook his head, smiling. "Let me tell you an open secret, my darling little witch. You *don't* choose us. *We* choose *you*."

Jaenelle thought about this and growled, "Lucivar's never going to give that damn Ring back, is he?"

Saetan chuckled softly. "You could try to get it back, but I don't think you'd win." He rubbed his cheek against her hair. "I think he'll serve you for the rest of his life, regardless of whether or not he's actually with you."

"Like you and Uncle Andulvar, with Cassandra."

He closed his eyes. "No, not like me and Andulvar."

She pulled back far enough to study his face. "I see. A bond as strong as family."

"Stronger."

Jaenelle hugged him and sighed. "Maybe we should find Lucivar a wife. That way he would have someone else to pester besides me."

Saetan choked. "How unkind of you to dump Lucivar on some unsuspecting Sister."

"But it would keep him busy."

"Consider for a moment the possible consequence of that busyness."

She did. "A houseful of little Lucivars," she said faintly.

They both groaned.

"All right," Jaenelle grumbled. "I'll think of something else."

"You two get lost up here?"

They jumped. Lucivar smiled at them from the doorway.

"Papa was just explaining that I'm stuck with you forever."

"And it only took you three years to figure that out." Lucivar's arrogant smile widened. "You don't deserve the warning, but while you've been up here busily, but futilely, rearranging my life, Ladvarian's been downstairs busily rearranging yours. The exact quote was 'We can raise and train the puppies here.' "

"Who's we?" Jaenelle squeaked. "What puppies? *Whose* puppies?"

Lucivar stepped aside as Jaenelle flew out of the room, muttering.

Saetan found the doorway blocked by a strong, well-muscled arm.

"You wouldn't have helped her do something that silly, would you?" Lucivar asked.

Saetan leaned against the doorway and shook his head. "If the right woman comes into your life, you won't let her go. I'm the last man who would tell you to compromise. Marry someone you can love and accept as she is, Lucivar. Marry someone who will love and accept you. Don't settle for less."

Lucivar lowered his arm. "Do you think the right man will come into Cat's life?"

"He'll come. If the Darkness is kind, he'll come."

3 / The Twisted Kingdom

He stood at the edge of the resting place for a long time, studying the details, absorbing the message and the warning. Unlike the other resting places she'd provided for him, this one disturbed him.

It was an altar, a slab of black stone laid over two others. At its center was a crystal chalice that once had been shattered. Even from where he stood, his eyes could trace every fracture line, could see where the pieces had been carefully fitted back together. There were sharp-edged chips around the rim where small pieces had been lost, chips that could cut a man badly. Inside the chalice, lightning and black mist performed a slow, swirling dance. Fitted around the chalice's stem was a gold ring with a faceted ruby. A man's ring.

A Consort's ring.

He finally stepped closer.

If he read the message correctly, she had healed but was soul-scarred and not completely whole. By claiming the

Consort's ring, he would have the privilege of savoring what the chalice held, but the sharp edges could wound any man who tried.

However, a careful man . . .

Yes, he decided as he studied the sharp-edged chips, a careful man who knew those edges existed and was willing to risk the wounds would be able to drink from that cup.

Satisfied, he returned to the trail and continued climbing.

4 / Kaeleer

Saetan fell out of bed in his haste to find out why Lucivar was roaring so early in the morning.

A part of his mind insisted that he couldn't go charging out of the room wearing nothing but his skin, so he grabbed the trousers he'd dropped over a chair when the birthday party finally wound down but didn't stop to put them on. He wrenched his arm when he tried to open the door that had swollen from last night's rain. Swearing, he gripped the doorknob and, using Craft, tore the door off its hinges.

By then the hallway was stuffed with bodies in various stages of dress. He tried to push past Karla and got a sharp elbow in the belly.

"What in the name of Hell is going on here?" he yelled.

No one bothered to answer him because, at that moment, Lucivar stepped out of Jaenelle's bedroom and roared, "CAT!"

Apparently Lucivar didn't have any inhibitions about standing stark naked in front of a group of young men and women. Of course, a man in his prime with that kind of build had no reason to feel inhibited.

And no one in their right mind would tease a man who vibrated with such intense fury.

"Where are Ladvarian and Kaelas?" Lucivar demanded.

"More to the point," Saetan said, pulling on his trousers, "where's Jaenelle?" He looked pointedly at the Ring of Honor that circled Lucivar's organ. "You can feel her through that, can't you?"

Lucivar quivered with the effort to stay in control. "I can

feel her, but I can't *find* her." His fist hammered down on a small table and split it in half. "Damn her, I'm going to whack her ass for this!"

"Who are you to dare say that?" Chaosti snarled, pushing to the front of the group, his Gray Jewel glowing with his gathering power.

Lucivar bared his teeth. "I'm the Warlord Prince who serves her, the warrior sworn to protect her. *But I can't protect her if I don't know where she is.* Her moon's blood started last night. Do I need to remind you how vulnerable a witch is during those days? Now she's upset—I can feel that much—and her only protection is two half-trained males *because she didn't tell me where she was going.*"

"That's enough," Saetan said sharply. "Leash the anger. NOW!" While he waited, he called in his shoes and stuffed his feet into them. Then he froze Chaosti and Lucivar with a look.

When no one moved, he stepped away from the group and pressed his back against the wall for support. He took a few deep breaths to calm his own temper, closed his eyes, and descended to the Black.

While it was true that witches couldn't channel Jeweled strength during their moon time without pain, that wouldn't stop Jaenelle.

Using himself as a center point, he cautiously pushed his Black-Jeweled strength outward in ever-widening circles, looking for some sense of her that would at least give him an idea of where she was. The circles widened farther and farther, beyond the village of Maghre, beyond the isle of Scelt, until . . .

Kaetien!

He felt fear and horror braiding with anger growing into rage.

Black rage. Spiraling rage. Cold rage.

He started to pull back to escape the psychic storm that was about to explode over Sceval. He strengthened his inner barriers, knowing that it wouldn't help much. Her rage would flood in under his barriers, where he had no protection from it. He just hoped he had enough time to warn the others.

KAETIEN!

As she unleashed the strength of her Black Jewels, Jaenelle's anguished scream filled his head and paralyzed him. A rush of dark power smashed against him, tossing him around like a tidal wave tosses driftwood, at the same time a psychic shield snapped up around Sceval.

Then, nothing.

He floated just beyond that shield, scared but oddly comforted—like being safely indoors while a violent storm raged outside.

He must have gotten caught between the conflicting uses of Black power when Jaenelle put up the shield to contain the storm. Clever little witch. And all that psychic lightning had a terrifying kind of beauty. He wouldn't mind just floating here for a while, but he had the nagging feeling there was something he should do.

High Lord.

Damn troublesome voice. How was he supposed to think when . . .

Father.

Father. Father. Hell's fire, Lucivar!

Up. He had to go up, out of the Black. Had to get his head clear enough to tell Lucivar. . . . Which way was up?

Someone grabbed him and dragged him out of the abyss. He sputtered and snarled. Did him as much good as a puppy snarling when it was picked up by the scruff.

The next thing he knew, something was pressed against his lips and blood was filling his mouth.

"Swallow it or I'll knock your damn teeth down your throat."

Ah, yes. Lucivar. Both of him.

His eyes finally focused. He pushed Lucivar's wrist away from his mouth. "Enough." He tried to get to his feet, which wasn't easy with Lucivar holding him down on one side and Chaosti holding him down on the other. "Is everyone all right?"

Karla bent over him. "*We're* fine. *You're* the one who fainted."

"I didn't faint. I got caught . . ." He started struggling. "Let me up. If the storm's over, we have to get to Sceval."

"Cat's there?" Lucivar asked, hauling him to his feet.

"Yes." Remembering Jaenelle's anguished scream, Saetan shuddered. "You and I have to get there as soon as possible."

Karla poked a sharp-nailed finger into his bare chest. "*We* have to get there as soon as possible."

Before he could argue, they'd all disappeared into their rooms.

"If we move, we can get there ahead of the rest of them," Lucivar said quietly as they entered Saetan's bedroom. He called in his own clothes and hurriedly dressed. "Are you strong enough for this?"

Saetan pulled on a shirt. "I'm ready. Let's go."

"Are you strong enough for this?"

Saetan brushed past Lucivar without answering. How could a man answer that question when he didn't know what was waiting for him?

"Mother Night," Saetan whispered. "Mother Night."

He and Lucivar stood on a flat-topped hill that was one of Sceval's official landing places, the gently rolling land spread out below them. Large meadows provided good grazing. Stands of trees provided shade on summer afternoons. Creeks veined the land with clean water.

He had stood on this hill a handful of times in the past five years, looking down on the unicorns while the stallions kept careful watch over the grazing mares and the foals playing tag.

Now he looked down on a slaughter.

Turning to the north, Lucivar shook his head and swore softly. "This wasn't a few bastards who had come for a horn to take home as a hunting trophy, this was a war."

Saetan blinked away tears. Of all the Blood, of all the kindred races, the unicorns had always been his favorite. They had been the stars in the Darkness, the living examples of power and strength blended with gentleness and beauty. "When the others arrive, we'll split up to look for survivors."

The unicorns attacked at the same moment the coven and the male circle appeared on the hill.

"Shield!" Saetan and Lucivar shouted. They threw Black and Ebon-gray shields around the whole group while the other males formed a protective circle around the coven.

The eight unicorn stallions veered off before they hit the shields head-on, but the power they were channeling through their horns and hooves created blinding-bright sparks as they scraped across the invisible barriers.

"Wait!" Saetan shouted, the thunder in his voice barely competing with the stallions' screams and trumpeted challenges. "We're friends! We're here to help you!"

You are not friends, said an older stallion with a broken horn. *You are humans!*

"We're friends," Saetan insisted.

YOU ARE NOT FRIENDS! the unicorns screamed. *YOU ARE HUMANS!*

Sceron took a step forward. "The Centauran people have never fought with our unicorn Brothers and Sisters. We do not wish to fight now."

You come to kill. First you call us Brothers and then you come to kill. No more. NO MORE. This time, we kill!

Karla stuck her head over Saetan's shoulder. "Damn your hooves and horns, we're *Healers.* Let us take care of the injured!"

The unicorns hesitated for a moment, then shook their heads and charged the shields again.

"I don't recognize any of them," Lucivar said, "and they're too blood-crazed to listen."

Saetan watched the stallions charge the shields over and over again. He sympathized with their rage, fully understood their hatred. But he couldn't walk away until they were calm enough to listen because more would die if they weren't cared for soon.

And because Jaenelle was among those bodies, somewhere.

Then the unicorns stopped attacking. They circled the group, snorting and pawing the ground, their horns lowered for another charge.

"Thank the Darkness," Khary muttered as a young stallion slowly climbed up the hill, favoring his left foreleg.

Relieved, the girls began murmuring about healing teams.

Watching the young stallion approach, Saetan wished he could share their confidence, but out of all of Kaetien's offspring, Mistral had always been the most wary of humans—and the most dangerous. Necessary traits for a young male who everyone anticipated would be the next Warlord Prince of Sceval, but damned uncomfortable for the man on the receiving end of that distrust.

"Mistral." Saetan stepped forward, raising his empty hands. "You've known all of us since you were a foal. Let us help."

I have known you, Mistral said reluctantly.

That sounds ominous, Lucivar said on an Ebon-gray spear thread.

If this goes wrong, get everyone else out of here, Saetan replied. *I'll hold the shield.*

We still have to find Cat.

Get them out, Yaslana.

Yes, High Lord.

Saetan took another step forward. "Mistral, I swear to you by the Jewels that I wear and by my love for the Lady that we mean no harm."

Whatever Mistral thought about a human male laying claim to the Lady was lost when Ladvarian's light tenor pounded into their heads.

High Lord? High Lord! We have some little ones shielded, but they're scared and won't listen. They keep running into the shield. Jaenelle is crying and won't listen either. High Lord?

Saetan held his breath. Which would prove stronger—Mistral's loyalty to his own kind or his love for and belief in Jaenelle?

Mistral looked toward the north. After a long moment, he snorted. *The little Brother believes in you. We will trust. For now.*

Desperately wanting to sit down and not daring to show any sign of weakness, Saetan cautiously lowered the Black shield.

A moment later, Lucivar dropped the Ebon-gray.

They divided into groups. Khary and Morghann went to help Ladvarian and Kaelas with the foals. Lucivar and Karla headed north from the landing place with Karla as primary Healer, Lucivar as secondary, and the rest of their team scouting for the wounded and providing assistance. Saetan, Gabrielle, and their team headed south.

It hurt to look at the mares' hacked-up bodies. It hurt even worse to see a young colt lying dead over his dam, his forelegs sliced off. There were some he could save. There were many more where all he could do was take away the pain to ease the journey back to the Darkness.

Hours passed as he searched for the foals that might be hidden under their dams. He found yearlings hidden in shallow dips in the land, dips that held a power unlike any he'd ever felt before. He didn't trespass into those places. The young unicorns watched him with terrified eyes as he carefully circled around them looking for wounds. It came to him slowly as he stepped around torn human bodies that any of the unicorns who had reached these places had, at worst, minor cuts or scratches.

He continued to work, ignoring the headache the sun gave him, ignoring the aching muscles and growing fatigue.

His emotions numbed as a defense against the slaughter.

But they weren't numb enough when he found Jaenelle and Kaetien.

"There, my fine Lady," Lucivar said, running one hand down the mare's neck. "It'll feel sore for a few days, but it will heal well."

The mare's colt snorted and pawed the ground until Lucivar gave them a few carrot chunks and a sugar lump.

When the mare and her colt moved off, he helped himself to a long drink of water and half of a cheese sandwich while he waited for the next unicorn to gather the courage to be touched by a human.

May the Darkness bless Khary's equine-loving heart. After a rapid look at the carnage, Khary and Aaron had gone back to Maghre. They'd returned with Daffodil and Sundancer pulling carts loaded with healing supplies, food for the humans, changes of clothes, blankets, and Khary's "bribes"—carrots and sugar lumps.

Seeing Daffodil and Sundancer working confidently with the humans had acted as a balm on the unicorns' fear. The words "I serve the Lady" had produced an even stronger response. On the strength of those words, most of the unicorns had let him touch them and heal what he could.

Taking the last bite of his sandwich, he watched a yearling colt cautiously approach him, its skin twitching as the flies buzzed around the shoulder wound protected by a fading shield.

Lucivar spread his arms, showing empty hands. "I serve—"

The yearling bolted as Sceron's war cry shattered the uneasy truce and Kaelas roared in challenge.

Calling in his Eyrien war blade, Lucivar launched himself skyward.

As he sped toward the man running for the landing place, he coldly ticked off each little scene as it flashed under him: Morghann, Kalush, and Ladvarian herding the foals into the trees; Kaelas pulling a man down and tearing him open; Astar pivoting on her hindquarters as she nocked an arrow in a Centauran bow; Morton shielding Karla and the unicorn she was healing; Khary, Aaron, and Sceron protecting each others' backs as they unleashed the strength of their Jewels in short, controlled bursts that ripped the invading humans apart.

Focusing on his chosen prey, Lucivar unleashed a burst of Ebon-gray power just as the man reached the bottom of the hill.

The man fell, both legs neatly broken, his Yellow Jewel drained.

Lucivar landed at the same moment the old stallion with the broken horn charged the downed man. *Wait!* he yelled as he threw a tight Red shield over the man.

The stallion screamed in rage and pivoted to face Lucivar.

Wait, Lucivar said again. *First I want answers. Then you can pound him.*

The stallion snorted but stopped pawing the ground.

Keeping a watchful eye on the stallion, Lucivar dropped the shield. Applying a foot to a shoulder, he rolled the man over onto his back. "This is a closed Territory," he said harshly. "Why are you here?"

"I don't have to answer to the likes of you."

Brave words for a man with two broken legs. Stupid, but brave.

Using the Eyrien war blade, Lucivar pointed to the man's right knee and looked at the stallion. "Once. Right there."

The stallion reared and happily obliged.

"Shall we try this again?" Lucivar asked mildly once the man stopped screaming. "The other knee or a hand next? Your choice."

"You've no right to do this. When this is reported—"

Lucivar laughed. "Reported to whom? And for what? You're an invader waging war on the rightful inhabitants of this island. Who's going to care what happens to you?"

"The Dark Council, that's who." Sweat beaded the man's forehead as Lucivar fingered the war blade. "You've no claim to this land."

"Neither do you," Lucivar said coldly.

"We've a claim, you bat-winged bastard. My Queen and five others were given this island as their new territory. We came here first to settle the territory boundaries and take care of any problems."

"Like the race that's ruled this land for thousands of years? Yes, I can see how that might be a problem."

"No one rules here. This is unclaimed land."

"This is the unicorns' Territory," Lucivar said fiercely.

"I hurt," the man whined. "I need a Healer."

"They're all busy. Let's get back to something more interesting. The Dark Council has no right to hand out land, and they have no right to replace an established race who already has a claim."

"Show me the signed land grant. My Queen has one, properly signed and sealed."

Lucivar gritted his teeth. "The unicorns rule here."

The man rolled his head back and forth. "Animals have no rights to the land. Only human claims are considered legitimate. Anything that lives here now lives by the Queens' sufferance."

"They're kindred," Lucivar said, his voice roughened by feelings he didn't want to name. "They're Blood."

"Animals. Just animals. Get rid of the rogues, the rest might be useful." The man whimpered. "Hurt. Need a Healer."

Lucivar took a step back. Took another. Oh, yes. Wouldn't the Terreillean bitch-Queens just love to ride around on unicorns? It wouldn't bother them in the least that the animals' spirits would have to be broken before they could do it. Wouldn't bother them at all.

Three glorious years of living in Kaeleer couldn't cleanse the 1,700 years he'd lived in Terreille. He tried very hard to put the past aside, but there were nights when he woke up shaking. He could control his mind for the most part, but his body still remembered all too well what a Ring of Obedience felt like and what it could do.

Swallowing hard, Lucivar licked his dry lips and looked at the old stallion. "Start with the arms and legs. It'll take longer for him to die that way."

Vanishing his war blade, he turned and walked away, ignoring the sound of hooves smashing bone, ignoring the screams.

Saetan stumbled over a severed arm and finally admitted he had to stop. Jaenelle's blood-tonic allowed him to tolerate, and enjoy, some daylight, but he still needed to rest during the hours when the sun was strongest. As the morning gave way to afternoon, he'd worked in the shade as much as possible, but that hadn't been enough to counteract the drain strong sunlight caused in a Guardian's body, and he couldn't take the strain of doing so much healing for so many hours.

He had to stop.

Except he couldn't until he found Jaenelle.

He'd tried everything he could think of to locate her. Nothing had worked. All Ladvarian could tell him was she was here and she was crying, but neither Ladvarian nor Kaelas could give him the barest direction of where to search. When he finally got Mistral to understand his concern, the stallion said, "Her grief will not let us find her."

Saetan rubbed his eyes and hoped his fatigue-fogged brain kept working long enough to get him to the camp Chaosti and Elan had set up. He was too tired, too drained. He was starting to see things.

Like the unicorn Queen standing in front of him, who looked like she was made of moonlight and mist, with dark eyes as old as the land.

It took him a minute to realize he could see through her. "You're—"

Gone, said the caressing, feminine voice. *Gone long and long ago. And never gone. Come, High Lord. My Sister needs her sire now.*

Saetan followed her until they reached a circle of low, evenly spaced stones. In the center, a great stone horn rose up from the land. An old, deep power filled the circle.

"I can't go there," Saetan said. "This is a sacred place."

An honored place, she replied. *They are nearby. She grieves for what she could not save. You must make her see what she did save.*

The mare stepped into the circle. As she approached the great stone horn, she faded until she disappeared, but he still had the feeling that dark eyes as old as the land watched him.

The air shimmered on his right. A veil he hadn't known was there vanished. He walked toward the spot. And he found them.

The bastards had butchered Kaetien. They had cut off his legs, his tail, his genitals. They had sliced open his belly.

They had cut off his horn.

They had cut off his head.

But Kaetien's dark eyes still held a fiery intelligence.

Saetan's stomach rolled.

Kaetien was demon-dead in that mutilated body.

Jaenelle sat next to the stallion, leaning against the open belly. Tears trickled from her staring eyes. Her white-knuckled hands were wrapped around Kaetien's horn.

Saetan sank to his knees beside her. "Witch-child?" he whispered.

Recognition came slowly. "Papa? P-Papa?" She threw herself into his arms. The quiet tears became hysterical weeping. Kaetien's horn scraped his back as she clung to him.

"Oh, witch-child." While he and the others had been searching for survivors, she'd been sitting there all day, locked in her pain.

"May the Darkness be merciful," said a voice behind him.

Saetan looked over his shoulder, feeling every muscle as he turned his head. Lucivar. Living strength that could do what he could not.

Lucivar stared at Kaetien's head and shook himself.

Saetan listened to the swift conversations taking place on spear threads, but he was too tired to make sense out of them.

Lucivar dropped to one knee, took a handful of Jaenelle's blood-matted hair, and gently pulled her head away from Saetan's shoulder. "Come on, Cat. You'll feel better once you've had a sip of this." He pressed a large silver flask against her mouth.

She choked and sputtered when the liquid went down her throat.

"This time swallow it," Lucivar said. "This stuff does less harm to your stomach than it does to your lungs."

"This stuff will melt your teeth," Jaenelle wheezed.

"What did you give her?" Saetan demanded when she suddenly sagged in his arms.

"A healthy dose of Khary's home brew. Hey!"

Saetan found himself braced against Lucivar's chest. He concentrated on breathing for a minute. "Lucivar. You asked if I was strong enough for this. I'm not."

A strong, warm hand stroked his head. "Hang on. Sundancer's coming. We'll get you to the camp. The girls will take care of Cat. A few minutes more and you can rest."

Rest. Yes, he needed rest. The headache that was threatening to tear his skull apart was gaining in intensity with every breath.

Someone took Jaenelle out of his arms. Someone half

carried him to where Sundancer waited. Strong hands kept him on the stallion's back.

The next thing he knew, he was sitting in the camp wrapped in blankets with Karla kneeling beside him, urging him to drink the witch's brew she'd made for him.

After drinking a second cup, he submitted to being pushed, plumped, and rearranged in a sleeping bag. He snarled a bit at being fussed over until Karla tartly asked how he expected them to get Jaenelle to rest when he was setting such a bad example?

Not having an answer for that, he surrendered to the brew-dulled headache and slept.

Lucivar sipped laced coffee and watched Gabrielle and Morghann lead Jaenelle to a sleeping bag. She stopped, ignoring their coaxing to lie down and rest. Her eyes lost their dull, half-dazed look as her attention focused on Mistral hovering at the edge of the camp, still favoring his wounded left foreleg.

Lucivar felt very thankful that the cold, dangerous fire in her eyes wasn't directed at him.

"Why hasn't that leg been tended?" Jaenelle asked in her midnight voice as she stared at the young stallion.

Mistral snorted and fidgeted. He obviously didn't want to admit he hadn't allowed anyone to touch him.

Lucivar didn't blame him.

"You know how males get," Gabrielle said soothingly. " 'I'm fine, I'm fine, tend the others first.' We were just about to take care of him when you and Uncle Saetan came in."

"I see," Jaenelle said softly, her eyes still pinning Mistral to the ground. "I thought, perhaps, because they were human, you were insulting my Sisters by refusing to let them heal you."

"Nonsense," Morghann said. "Now, come on, set a good example."

Once they got her tucked in, they descended on Mistral.

It would be all right, Lucivar thought dully. It had to be all right. The unicorns and the other kindred wouldn't lose all their trust in humans and retreat again behind the veils of power that had closed them off from the rest of Kaeleer. Cat would see to that. And Saetan . . .

Hell's fire. Until today, he hadn't given much thought to the differences between a Guardian and the living. At the Hall, those differences seemed so subtle.

He hadn't realized strong sun would cause so much pain, hadn't fully appreciated how many years the High Lord had walked the Realms. Oh, he *knew* how old Saetan was, but today was the first time his father had seemed *old*.

Of course, the rest of them were feeling pretty beaten physically and emotionally, so it wasn't much of a yardstick to measure by.

Khary squatted beside him and splashed some of the home brew into the already heavily laced coffee. "There's something bothering our four-footed Brothers," he said quietly. "Something more than that." He waved a hand at the still, white bodies lying within sight.

The unicorns hadn't cared what happened to the human bodies—except to insist that the intruders not remain in their land—but they had been vehement about not moving the dead unicorns. The Lady would sing them to the land, they had said.

Whatever that meant.

But as the wounded mares and foals had been led to this side of the landing hill, the surviving stallions had become more and more upset.

"Ladvarian might know," Lucivar said, sipping his coffee. He sent out a quiet summons. A few minutes later, the Sceltie trotted wearily into the camp.

Moonshadow's missing, Ladvarian said when Lucivar asked him. *Starcloud was getting old. Moonshadow was going to be the next Queen. She wears an Opal Jewel. One of the mares said she saw humans throw ropes and nets around Moonshadow, but she didn't see where they went.*

Lucivar closed his eyes. From what he could tell, all of the Blood males who had invaded Sceval had worn lighter Jewels, but enough of them with spelled nets and ropes could control an Opal-Jeweled Queen. Were the spelled nets preventing her from calling to the others, or had she been taken off the island altogether?

"I'll be back before twilight," he said, handing the cup to Khary.

"Watch your back," Khary said softly. "Just in case."

Lucivar flew north. As he flew, he kept sending the same message: He served the Lady. The Lady was at a camp near the landing hill. Healers were with the Lady.

He saw a few small herds of unicorns, who ran for the trees as best they could as soon as they sensed him.

He saw a lot of still, white bodies.

He saw even more exploded human corpses, and thanked the Darkness that Jaenelle had somehow kept her rage confined to this island.

And he wondered about the pockets of power he kept sensing as he flew over woods and clearings. Some were faint; others much stronger. He was turning away from an especially strong one that was in the trees to his left when something grabbed him. Something angry and desperate.

Using his Birthright Red, he broke the contact, but it took effort.

You serve the Lady, said a harsh male voice.

Lucivar hovered, breathing hard. *I serve the Lady,* he agreed cautiously. *Do you need help?*

She needs help.

Landing, he allowed the power to guide him through the trees until he reached its source. In a hollow, a mare lay tangled in nets and ropes, breathing hard and sweating.

"Ah, sweetheart," Lucivar said softly.

While most of the unicorns were some shade of white, there were a few rare dappled grays. This mare was a pale pewter with a white mane and tail. An Opal Jewel hung from a silver ring around her horn.

She was not only a Queen, she was also a Black Widow. The only combination that was rarer was the Queen/Black Widow/Healer. He'd never heard of a witch like that when he'd lived in Terreille. In Kaeleer, there were only three— Karla, Gabrielle, and Jaenelle.

Standing very still, Lucivar slowly spread his dark, membranous wings. He'd heard enough disparaging remarks about "human bats" in his life to recognize the advantage his wings might give him now. Wings, like hooves and fur, were usually part of the kindred's domain.

"Lady Moonshadow," he said, keeping his voice low and soothing, "I am Prince Lucivar Yaslana. I serve the Lady. I'd like to help you."

She didn't reply, but the panic in her eyes gradually receded.

He walked toward her, gritting his teeth as the male power surrounding her swelled, then ebbed.

"Easy, sweetheart," he said, crouching beside her. "Easy."

Her panic spiked when his hand touched her withers.

Lucivar swore silently as he cut the nets and ropes. They'd tried to break her, tried to shatter her inner web. The only difference between what the Terreillean bastards had tried to do to her and what they usually did to human witches was physical rape. Maybe that's why they hadn't succeeded before Jaenelle had unleashed the Black. They hadn't been able to use their best weapon.

"There now," Lucivar said as he tossed the last of the ropes away. "Come on, sweetheart. On your feet. Easy now."

Step by step, he coaxed her out of the trees and into the clearing. Her fear increased with every step she took away from that power-filled hollow. He needed to get her to the camp before her fear finished what those bastards had started. A radial line from the Rose Wind was close enough to catch, and he could certainly guide and shield her for the short trip, but how to convince her to trust him that much?

"Mistral's going to be very glad to see you," he said casually.

Mistral? Her head swung around. He dodged the horn before it impaled him. *He is well?*

"He's at the camp with the Lady. If we ride the Rose Wind, we'll get there before twilight."

Pain and sorrow filled her thoughts. *The lost ones must be sung to the land at twilight.*

Lucivar suppressed a shiver. Suddenly he very much wanted to be back in the camp. "Shall we go, Lady?"

* * *

Everyone had returned to the camp, physically weary and heartsore.

Everyone except Lucivar.

As he drank the restorative brew Karla had made for him, Saetan tried not to worry. Lucivar could take care of himself; he was a strong, fit, well-trained warrior; he knew his limitations, especially after extending himself so much today; he wouldn't do anything foolish like try to take on a gang of Blood-Jeweled males alone just because he was pissed about the kindred deaths.

And tomorrow the sun would rise in the west.

"He's fine," Jaenelle said quietly as she settled next to him on one of the logs the boys had dragged from somewhere to provide seats around the fire. Tucking the spell-warmed blanket around herself, she smiled ruefully. "The Ring's *supposed* to let me monitor *his* spikes of temper. I hadn't realized I'd messed up somewhere when I created it until Karla, Morghann, Grezande, *and* Gabrielle bitched about my setting a bad precedent since all the boyos want a Ring that works like that." Her voice took on a hint of whine. "I always thought it was just extraordinary intuition that he always showed up whenever I felt grumpy. *He* certainly never hinted it was anything more than that."

"He's not an idiot, witch-child," Saetan replied, sipping his brew to hide his smile.

"That's debatable. But why did he have to go and tell the others?"

He understood why the Queens were annoyed. The foundation of any official court was twelve males and a Queen. Through the Ring of Honor, a Queen could monitor every nuance of a male's life. But because the Queens respected the privacy of the males who served them and because no woman in her right mind would want to keep track of the emotional currents of that many men, they usually adjusted their monitoring to block out everything but things like fear, rage, and pain—the kinds of feelings that indicated the wearer needed help.

Each man, however, only had to keep track of one Queen.

He'd have to talk to Lucivar about the self-imposed limits of that kind of monitoring. He'd be interested in where his son drew the line.

"Speaking of the pain in the ass who's not an idiot," Jaenelle said, pointing to the two figures walking slowly toward the camp.

Mistral bugled wildly. *Moonshadow! Moonshadow!*

He took off at a gallop. At least, he tried to.

As Mistral leaped forward, Gabrielle jumped up from her seat on the other log, reached out, closed her hand as if she'd grabbed something, and jerked her hand up.

Mistral hung in the air, his legs flailing.

Gabrielle's arm shook from the effort of holding that much weight suspended, even if she was using Craft. Watching her, Saetan decided he and Chaosti needed to have a chat very soon. A witch who could pull a trick like that after an exhausting day of healing was a Lady who needed careful handling.

"If you gallop on that leg, I'll knock you silly," Gabrielle said.

It's Moonshadow!

"I don't care if it's the Queen of the unicorns or your mate," Gabrielle replied hotly. "You're not galloping on that leg!"

"Actually," Jaenelle said with a dry smile, "she's both."

"Well, Hell's fire." Gabrielle set Mistral down but didn't let go.

"Gabrielle," Chaosti said in that coaxing tone of voice Saetan labeled male-soothing-female-temper. "She's his mate. He's been worried. I wouldn't want to wait if it were you. Let him go."

Gabrielle glared at Chaosti.

"He'll walk," Chaosti said. "Won't you, Mistral?"

Mistral wasn't about to turn down allies, even if they did have only two legs. *I'll walk.*

Reluctantly, Gabrielle released him.

Mistral plodded toward Moonshadow, his head down like a small boy who's been scolded and hasn't yet gotten away from the scolder's watchful eyes.

"Now see what you did," Khary said. "You made his horn wilt."

"I'll bet your horn wilts too when you're scolded," Karla said with a wicked smile.

Before Khary could reply, Jaenelle set her cup down and said quietly, "It's time."

Everyone became subdued as she walked into the trees.

"Do you know what's supposed to happen?" Lucivar asked Saetan when he reached the camp and sat down next to his father.

Saetan shook his head. Like everyone else in the camp, he couldn't take his eyes off the mare. "Mother Night, she's beautiful."

"She's also a Black Widow Queen," Lucivar said dryly, watching Mistral escort his Lady. "Well, if someone's going to get kicked for fussing, better him than me."

Saetan laughed softly. "By the way, your sister has something she wants to discuss with you." When he didn't get a response, he looked at his son. "Lucivar?"

Lucivar's mouth hung open, his eyes fixed on the trees to Saetan's left—the trees Jaenelle had walked into a few minutes before.

He turned . . . and forgot how to breathe.

She wore a long, flowing dress made of delicate black spidersilk. Strands of cobwebs dripped from the tight sleeves. Beginning just above her breasts, the dress became an open web framing her chest and shoulders. Black Jewel chips sparkled with dark fire at the end of each thread.

Black-Jeweled rings decorated both hands. Around her neck was a Black Jewel centered in a web made of delicate gold and silver strands.

It was a gown made for Jaenelle the Witch. Erotic. Romantic. Terrifying. He could feel the latent power in every thread of that gown. And he knew then who had created it: the Arachnians. The Weavers of Dreams.

Saying nothing, Jaenelle picked up Kaetien's horn and glided toward open ground, the gown's small train flowing out behind her.

Saetan wanted to remind her that it was her moon time, that she shouldn't be channeling her power through her body right now. But he remembered that, behind the human mask, Witch had a tiny spiral horn in the center of her forehead, so he said nothing.

She spent several minutes walking around, looking at the ground as if she wanted a particular site.

Finally satisfied, she faced the north. Raising Kaetien's horn to the sky, she sang one keening note. She lowered her hands, pointed the horn at the ground, and sang another note. Then she swept her arms upward and began to sing in the Old Tongue.

Witchsong.

Saetan felt it in his bones, felt it in his blood.

A ghostly web of power formed under her bare feet and swiftly spread across the land. Spread and spread and spread.

Her song changed, became a dirge filled with sorrow and celebration. Her voice became the wind, the water, the grass, the trees. Circling. Spiraling.

The still, white bodies of the dead unicorns began to glow. Mesmerized, Saetan wondered if, viewed from above, the glowing bodies would look like stars that had come to rest on sacred ground.

Perhaps they were. Perhaps they had.

The song changed again until it became a blend of the other two. Ending and beginning. From the land and back to the land.

The unicorn bodies melted into the earth.

Kindred didn't come to the Dark Realm. Now he knew why. Just as he knew why humans would never easily settle in kindred Territories without the kindred's welcome. Just as he knew what had created those pockets of power he'd avoided so carefully.

Kindred never left their Territories, they became part of it. What strength was left in each of them became bound with the land.

The ghostly web of power faded.

Jaenelle's voice and the last of the daylight faded.

No one moved. No one spoke.

Coming back to himself, Saetan realized Lucivar's arm was around his shoulders.

"Damn," Lucivar whispered, brushing away tears.

"The living myth," Saetan whispered. "Dreams made flesh." His throat tightened. He closed his eyes.

He felt Lucivar leave him and reach for something.

Opening his eyes, he watched Lucivar support Jaenelle into the camp. Her face was tight with pain and exhaustion, but there was peace in her sapphire eyes.

The coven gathered around her and led her into the trees.

Talking quietly, the boys stirred the pots of stew, sliced bread and cheese, gathered bowls and plates for the evening meal.

Beyond the firelight, the unicorns settled down for the night.

Khary and Aaron took bowls of stew and water out to where Ladvarian and Kaelas were keeping watch over the foals.

When the girls returned, Jaenelle was dressed in trousers and a long, heavy sweater. She gave Lucivar a halfhearted snarl when he wrapped her in a spell-warmed blanket and settled her on the log next to Saetan, but she didn't grumble about the food he brought.

They all talked quietly as they ate. Small talk and gentle teasing. Nothing about what they'd done today or what still waited for them tomorrow. Despite their best efforts, they'd covered a very small part of Sceval, and only Jaenelle knew how many unicorns lived there.

Only Jaenelle knew how many had been sung back to the land.

"Saetan?" Jaenelle said, resting her head against his shoulder.

He kissed her forehead. "Witch-child?" She didn't respond for so long he thought she'd dozed off.

"When does the Dark Council next meet?"

5 / Kaeleer

Lord Magstrom tried to keep his mind on the petitioner standing in the circle, but she had the same complaints as the seven petitioners before her, and he doubted the twenty petitioners after her would have anything different to say to the Dark Council.

He had thought that, when he became Third Tribune, his opinions might carry a little more weight. He had hoped his position would help quell the continued, whispered insinuations about the SaDiablo family.

That none of the Territory Queens outside of Little Terreille believed there was any truth in those whispers should have told the Council something. That the Dark Council's judgments had been respected and trusted by all of the Blood races for all the years the High Lord and Andulvar Yaslana had served in the Council should have told them even more—especially since it was no longer true.

Lord Jorval was First Tribune now, and it was disturbing how easily he shaped other Council members' opinions.

And now this.

"How can I settle the territory granted to me when my men are being slaughtered before they even set up camp?" the Queen petitioner demanded. "The Council has to do something!"

"The wilderness is always dangerous, Lady," Lord Jorval said smoothly. "You were warned to take extra precautions."

"Precautions!" The Queen quivered in outrage. "You said these beasts, these so-called kindred had a bit of magic."

"They do."

"That wasn't just a bit of magic they were using. That was Craft!"

"No, no. Only the human races are Blood, and only the Blood has the power to use Craft." Lord Jorval looked soulfully at the Council members seated on either side of the large chamber. "But, perhaps, since we know so little about them, we were not fully aware of the extent of this animal magic. It may be that the only way our Terreillean Brothers and Sisters will be able to secure the land granted to them is if the Kaeleer Queens they're serving are willing to send in their own warriors to clear out these infestations."

And every Queen who sent assistance would expect a higher percentage of the profit from the conquered land, Magstrom thought sourly. He was about to antagonize the rest of the Council—again—by reminding the members that the Dark Council had been formed to act as arbitrators to prevent wars, not to provoke them. Before he could speak, a midnight voice filled the Council chamber.

"Infestations?" Jaenelle Angelline strode toward the Tribunal's bench and stopped just outside the petitioner's circle, flanked by the High Lord and Lucivar Yaslana. "Those infestations you speak of, Lord Jorval, are kindred. They are Blood. They have every right to defend themselves and their land against an invading force."

"We're not invading!" the petitioning Queen snapped. "We went in to settle the unclaimed land that was granted to us by the Dark Council."

"It's not unclaimed," Jaenelle snarled. "It's kindred Territories."

"Ladies." Lord Jorval had to raise his voice to be heard over the muttering of Council members and petitioners. "Ladies!" When the Council and the petitioners subsided, Lord Jorval smiled at Jaenelle. "Lady Angelline, while it's always a pleasure to see you, I must ask that you not disrupt a Council meeting. If there is something you wish to bring before the Council, you must wait until the petitioners who have already requested an audience have been heard."

"If all the petitioners have the same complaint, I can save the Council a great deal of time," Jaenelle replied coldly. "Kindred Territories are not unclaimed land. The Blood have ruled there for thousands of years. The Blood still rule there."

"While it pains me to disagree," Lord Jorval said gently, "there are no Blood in these 'kindred territories.' The Council has studied this matter most diligently and has reached the conclusion that, while these animals may be thought of as 'magical cousins,' they are not Blood. One must be human to be Blood. And this Council was formed to deal with the Blood's concerns, the Blood's rights."

"Then what are the centaurs? What are the satyrs? Half-human with half rights?"

No one answered.

"I see," Jaenelle said too softly.

Lord Magstrom's mouth felt parched. His tongue felt shriveled. Did no one else remember what had happened the last time Jaenelle Angelline had stood before the Council?

"Once the Blood are established in these Territories, they will look after the kindred. Any disagreements can then be brought to the Council by the human representatives for those Territories."

"You're saying that the kindred require a human representative before they're entitled to any consideration or any rights?"

"Precisely," Lord Jorval said, smiling.

"In that case, *I* am the kindred's human representative."

Lord Magstrom suddenly felt as if a trap had been sprung. Lord Jorval was still smiling, still looked benign, but Magstrom had worked with him enough to recognize the subtle, underlying cruelty in the man.

"Unfortunately, that isn't possible," Lord Jorval said. "This Lady's claim may be under dispute"—he nodded at the petitioning Queen—"but you have no claim whatsoever. You don't rule these Territories. Your rights are not being infringed upon. And since neither you nor yours are affected by this, you have no justifiable complaint. I must ask you now to leave the Council chambers."

Lord Magstrom shuddered at the blankness in Jaenelle's eyes. He sighed with relief when she walked out of the Council chamber, followed by the High Lord and Prince Yaslana.

"Now, Lady," Lord Jorval said with a weary smile, "let's see what we can do about your *rightful* petition."

"Bastards," Lucivar snarled as they walked toward the landing web.

Saetan slipped an arm around Jaenelle's shoulders. Lucivar's open anger didn't worry him. Jaenelle's silent withdrawal did.

"Don't fret about it, Cat," Lucivar continued. "We'll find a way around those bastards and keep the kindred protected."

"I'm not sure there *is* a legitimate way around the Council's decision," Saetan said carefully.

"And you've never stepped outside the Law? You've never overruled a bad decision by using strength and temper?"

Saetan clenched his teeth. In trying to explain why the family had difficulties with the Dark Council, someone must have told Lucivar why the Council made him Jaenelle's guardian. "No, I'm not saying that."

"Are you saying kindred aren't important enough to fight for because they're animals?"

Saetan stopped walking. Jaenelle drifted a little farther down the flagstone walk, away from them.

"No, I'm not saying that, either," Saetan replied, struggling to keep his voice down. "We have to find an answer that fits the Council's new rules or this will escalate into a war that tears the Realm apart."

"So we sacrifice the nonhuman Blood to save Kaeleer?" Smiling bitterly, Lucivar opened his wings. "What am I, High Lord? By the Council's reckoning of who is human and who is not, what am I?"

Saetan took a step back. It could have been Andulvar standing there. It *had* been Andulvar standing there all those years ago. *When honor and the Law no longer stand on the same side of the line, how do we choose, SaDiablo?*

Saetan rubbed his hands over his face. *Ah, Hekatah, you spin your schemes well. Just like the last time.* "We'll find a legitimate way to protect the kindred and their land."

"You said there wasn't a legitimate way."

"Yes, there is," Jaenelle said softly as she joined them. She leaned against Saetan. "Yes, there is."

Alarmed by how pale she looked, Saetan held her against him, stroking her hair as he probed gently. Nothing physically wrong except the fatigue brought on by overwork and the emotional stress of tallying the kindred deaths. "Witch-child?"

Jaenelle shuddered. "I never wanted this. But it's the only way to help them."

"What's the only way, witch-child?" Saetan crooned.

Trembling, she stepped away from him. The haunted look in her eyes would stay with him forever.

"I'm going to make the Offering to the Darkness and set up my court."

CHAPTER
SIXTEEN

1 / Kaeleer

Banard sat in the private showroom at the back of his shop, sipping tea while he waited for the Lady.

He was a gifted craftsman, an artist who worked with precious metals, precious and semiprecious stones, and the Blood Jewels. A Blood male who wore no Jewel himself, he handled them with a delicacy and respect that made him a favorite with the Jeweled Blood in Amdarh. He always said, "I handle a Jewel as if I were handling someone's heart," and he meant it.

Among his clients were the Queen of Amdarh and her Consort, Prince Mephis SaDiablo, Prince Lucivar Yaslana, the High Lord and, his favorite, Lady Jaenelle Angelline.

Which was why he was sitting here long after the shops had closed for the day. As he'd told his wife, when the Lady asked for a favor, why, that was almost like serving her, wasn't it?

He nearly spilled his tea when he looked up from his musings and saw the shadowy figure standing in the doorway of the private showroom. His shop had strong guard spells and protection spells—gifts from his darker-Jeweled clients. No one should have been able to get this far without triggering the alarms.

"My apologies, Banard," said the feminine, midnight voice. "I didn't mean to startle you."

"Not at all, Lady," Banard lied as he increased the illumination of the candle-lights around the velvet-covered display table. "My mind was wandering." He turned to smile at her, but when he saw what she held in her hands, he broke out in a cold sweat.

"There's something I'd like you to make for me, if you can," Jaenelle said, stepping into the small room.

Banard gulped. She had changed since he'd last seen her a few months ago. It was more than the Widow's weeds she was wearing. It was as if the fire that had always burned within her was now closer to the surface, illuminating and shadowing. He could feel the dark power swirling around her—brutal strength offset by a worrisome fragility.

"This is what I'd like you to make," Jaenelle said.

A piece of paper appeared on the display table.

Banard studied the sketch for several minutes, wondering what he could say, wondering how to refuse gracefully, wondering why she, of all people, would have the thing she held in her hands.

As if understanding his silence and reluctance, Jaenelle caressed the spiraled horn. "His name was Kaetien," she said softly. "He was the Warlord Prince of the unicorns. He was butchered a few days ago, along with hundreds of his people, when humans came in to claim Sceval as their territory." Tears filled her eyes. "I've known him since I was a little girl. He was the first friend I made in Kaeleer, and one of the best. He gifted me with his horn. For remembrance. As a reminder."

Banard studied the sketch again. "If I may make one or two suggestions, Lady?"

"That's why I came to you," Jaenelle said with a trembling smile.

Using a thin, charcoal pencil, Banard altered the sketch. At the end of an hour of fine-tuning, they were both satisfied.

Alone again, Banard made another cup of tea and sat for a while, studying the sketch and staring at the horn he couldn't yet bring himself to touch.

What she wanted made would be a fitting tribute for a beloved friend. And it would be an appropriate tool for such a Queen.

2 / Kaeleer

Saetan paced the length of the sitting room Draca had reserved for them at the Keep. Reserved? Confined them to was closer to the truth.

Lucivar abandoned his chair and stretched his back and shoulders. "Why is it that your pacing isn't supposed to annoy me, but when I start pacing I get chucked into the garden?" he asked dryly.

"Because I'm older and I outrank you," Saetan snarled. He pivoted and paced to the other side of the room.

From sunset to sunrise. That's how long it took to make the Offering to the Darkness. It didn't matter if a person came away from the Offering wearing a White Jewel or a Black, that's how long it took. From sunset to sunrise.

Jaenelle had been gone three full days.

He had remained calm when the first dawn had passed into late morning because he could still remember how shaky he'd felt after making the Offering, how he'd remained in the altar room of the Sanctuary for hours while he adjusted to the feel of the Black Jewels.

But when the sun began to set again, he'd gone to the Dark Altar in the Keep to find out what had happened to her. Draca had forbidden him entrance, sharply reminding him of the consequences of interrupting an Offering. So he'd returned to the sitting room to wait.

When midnight came and went, he'd tried to reach the Dark Altar again and had found all the corridors blocked by a shield even the Black couldn't penetrate. Desperate, he'd sent an urgent message to Cassandra, hoping she would be able to break through Draca's resistance. But Cassandra hadn't responded, and he'd cursed this evidence of her further withdrawal.

She was tired. He understood that. He came from a long-lived race and had already gone several lifetimes beyond the norm. Cassandra had lived hundreds, had watched the people she'd come from decline, fade, and finally be absorbed into younger, emerging races. When she had ruled, she had been respected, revered.

But Jaenelle was loved.

So Cassandra hadn't responded. Tersa had.

"Something's wrong," Saetan snarled as he passed the couch and low table Tersa hunched over while she arranged puzzle pieces into shapes that had meaning only for her. "It doesn't take this long."

Tersa poked a puzzle piece into place and pushed her tangled black hair away from her face. "It takes as long as it takes."

"An Offering is made between sunset and sunrise."

Tersa tilted her head, considering. "That was true for the Prince of the Darkness. But for the Queen?" She shrugged.

Cold whispered up Saetan's spine. What would Jaenelle be like when she was the Queen of the Darkness?

He crouched opposite Tersa, the table between them. She paid no more attention to him than she did to Lucivar's silent approach.

"Tersa," Saetan said quietly, trying to catch her attention. "Do you know something, see something?"

Tersa's eyes glazed. "A voice in the Darkness. A howling, full of joy and pain, rage and celebration. The time is coming when the debts will be paid." Her eyes cleared. "Leash your fear, High Lord," she said with some asperity. "It will do her more harm now than anything else. Leash it, or lose her."

Saetan's hand closed over her wrist. "I'm not afraid *of* her, I'm afraid *for* her."

Tersa shook her head. "She will be too tired to sense the difference. She will only sense the fear. Choose, High Lord, and live with what you choose." She looked at the closed door. "She is coming."

Saetan tried to rise too quickly and winced. He'd overworked his bad leg again. Tugging down the sleeves of his tunic jacket and smoothing back his hair, he wished, futilely, that he'd bathed and changed into fresh clothes. He also wished, futilely, that his heart would stop pounding so hard.

Then the door opened and Jaenelle stood on the threshold.

In the seconds before rational thought fled, his mind registered her hesitation, her uncertainty. It also registered the amount of jewelry she was wearing.

Lorn had gifted her with thirteen uncut Black Jewels. An uncut Jewel was large enough to be made into a pendant and a ring, as well as providing smaller chips that could be used for a variety of purposes. If he was estimating correctly, she'd taken the equivalent of six of those thirteen Jewels in with her when she made the Offering. Six Black Jewels that, somehow, had been transformed into more than Black.

Into Ebony.

No wonder it had taken her so long to make the descent to her full strength. He couldn't begin to estimate the power at her disposal now. Since the day he'd met her, he'd known it would come to this. She was traveling roads now the rest of them couldn't even imagine.

What would it do to her?

His choice.

The thought shocked him with its clarity. It freed him to act.

Stepping forward, he offered his right hand.

Wild-shy, Jaenelle slipped into the room, hesitated a moment, then placed her hand in his.

He pulled her into arms, burying his face against her neck. "I've been worried sick about you," he growled softly.

Jaenelle stroked his back. "Why?" She sounded genuinely puzzled. "You've made the Offering. You know—"

"It doesn't usually take three days!"

"Three days!" She jerked back, stumbling into Lucivar, who had come up behind her. "Three *days*?"

"Do we have to observe Protocol from now on?" Lucivar asked.

"Don't be daft," Jaenelle snapped.

Grinning, Lucivar immediately wrapped his left arm around her, pinning her arms to her sides and holding her tight against his chest. "In that case, I propose dunking her in the nearest fountain."

"You can't do that!" Jaenelle sputtered, squirming.

"Why not?" Lucivar sounded mildly curious.

The reason she gave was inventive but anatomically impossible.

Since laughing wouldn't be diplomatic, even if it was prompted by the relief that wearing Ebony Jewels hadn't changed her, Saetan clenched his teeth and stayed silent.

Tersa, however, finally stirred herself and joined them. Shaking her head, she gave Jaenelle a poke in the shoulder. "There's no use wailing about it. You've taken up the responsibilities of a Queen now, and part of your duties is taking care of the males who belong to you."

"Fine," Jaenelle snarled. "When do I get to pound him?"

Tersa tsked. "They're males. They're allowed to fuss and pet." Then she smiled and patted Jaenelle's cheek. "Warlord Princes especially need physical contact with their Queen."

"Oh," Jaenelle said sourly. "Well, that's just fine then."

Tersa stretched out on the couch.

"All right, grumpy little cat, you have a choice," Lucivar said.

"Not one of your choices," Jaenelle groaned, sagging against him.

"Does either of those choices include food and sleep?" Saetan asked.

"And a bath?" Jaenelle added, wrinkling her nose.

"One does," Lucivar said, releasing her.

"Then I don't want to know what the other one is." Jaenelle rubbed her back. "Your belt buckle bites."

"So do you."

Saetan rubbed his temples. "Enough, children."

Amazingly, they both stopped. Gold and sapphire eyes studied him for a moment before they left the room, arms about each other's waists.

"You did well, Saetan," Tersa said quietly.

Picking up a blanket draped over a chair, Saetan tucked it around Tersa and smoothed back her hair. "I had help," he replied, then laughed softly when she batted at his hand. "Males are allowed to fuss and pet, remember?"

"I'm not a Queen."

Saetan watched her until she fell asleep. "No, but you are a very gifted, very extraordinary Lady."

3 / Kaeleer

Telling himself he wasn't nervous, despite the pounding heart and sweaty palms, Saetan entered the large stone chamber that Draca had indicated was the place where the invited guests were to wait until they were summoned to the Dark Throne. Except for the blackwood pillars that contained the candle-lights and a few long tables against the walls that held assorted beverages, the room was bare of furniture.

Which was just as well since threading their way through seating designed for humans would have made the kindred more tense than they already were, and some species—like the small dragons from the Fyreborn Islands—needed a generous amount of space. Saetan noticed, with growing uneasiness, that *all* the kindred, not just the ones who had had little or no contact with people, weren't mingling with the human Blood, even though most of the humans present were friends—or had been before the slaughters. That they were in this closed, confined space at all said a great deal for their devotion to Jaenelle.

That was one worry. Ebon Rih was the Keep's Territory in Kaeleer—Jaenelle's Territory now. Ruling Ebon Rih wouldn't help the kindred or keep the human invaders out of their Territories. Traditionally, the Queen of Ebon Askavi had considerable influence in all the Realms, but would that influence and the innate caution within the Blood not to antagonize a mature dark power be enough? Would any of the fools in Kaeleer's Dark Council even recognize who they were challenging?

Another worry was who was going to make up Jaenelle's court. He'd always assumed that the coven and Jaenelle's male friends would form the First Circle. It wasn't unprecedented for Queens to serve in a stronger Queen's court since District Queens served Province Queens who, in their turn, served the Territory Queen. That was the web of power that kept a Territory united.

But Queens who ruled a Territory didn't serve in other courts. They were the final law of their land and yielded to no one.

In the past week, while Jaenelle rested after making the Offering, her coven, Queens all, had also made the Offering. And every one of them had been chosen as the new Queen of their respective Territories, the former Queens stepping aside and accepting positions in the newly formed courts.

The boys, too, had come to power. Chaosti was now the Warlord Prince of Dea al Mon and Gabrielle's Consort. Khardeen, Morghann's Consort, was the ruling Warlord of Maghre, his home village. After accepting Kalush's Consort ring, Aaron had become the Warlord Prince of Tajrana, the capital of Nharkhava. Sceron and Elan were the Warlord Princes of Centauran and Tigrelan, serving in the First Circles of Astar's and Grezande's courts. Jonah now served as First Escort for his sister, Zylona, and Morton served as First Escort for his cousin Karla.

As feminine voices drifted down the corridor behind him, Saetan headed for the table where Lucivar, Aaron, Khary, and Chaosti were gathered. Geoffrey and Andulvar nodded in greeting but didn't break away from their conversation with Mephis and Prothvar. Sceron, Elan, Morton, and Jonah were talking to a diminutive Warlord Prince Saetan hadn't seen before. Little Katrine's First Escort or Consort?

"The tailor did an excellent job," Saetan told Lucivar, accepting the glass of warmed yarbarah.

"Uh-huh." The reply sounded sour, but after a moment Lucivar shook his head and laughed. He put his hand over his heart. "I represent a challenge worthy of good Lord Aldric who, as he happily informed me while he was sticking pins everywhere, had never designed formal attire that had to accommodate wings."

"Well, now that he has your measurements—" Saetan began.

"Oh, no." Lucivar shook his head, wearing an expression Saetan recognized all too well from his own dealings with good Lord Aldric. " 'Each fabric has a character of its own, Prince Yaslana,' " Lucivar said, mimicking the tailor's mournful voice. " 'We must learn how each one will flow around these marvelous additions to your physique.' "

Khary, Aaron, and Chaosti coughed in unison.

"Maybe he just wants to stroke your wings," Karla said as she joined them. She slid her hand over Saetan's shoulder and leaned against his back, her sharp chin digging into his other shoulder. "They *are* impressive. Is it true that the length of your"—her ice-blue eyes flicked to Lucivar's groin—"is in direct proportion to your wings?"

Lucivar made a very crude sexual gesture.

"Touchy, isn't he? But not touchable? Ah, well. Kiss kiss."

"Stuff yourself, Karla," Lucivar said, baring his teeth in a smile.

Karla laughed. "It's so good to be back among the surly. A few days ago I said 'kiss kiss' and everyone tried to." She shuddered dramatically, then ruffled Saetan's hair, cheerfully ignoring the accompanying snarl. "You know what, Uncle Saetan?"

"What?" Saetan replied warily, sipping his yarbarah.

Karla's wicked smile bloomed. "Since you're the Warlord Prince of Dhemlan and rule that Territory, and I'm the Queen of Glacia and rule *that* Territory, now whenever Dhemlan has to deal with Glacia, you get to deal with me."

Saetan choked.

"Appalling thought, isn't it, that you're going to have to deal with all the things you taught me."

"Mother Night," Saetan gasped as Karla plucked the glass out of his hand and thumped his back.

"What'd you do to Uncle Saetan?" Morghann asked, accepting a glass of wine from Khary.

"Just reminded him that we're now the Queens he has to deal with."

"How unfair, Karla," Kalush said, joining them. "You should have eased into it instead of springing it on him."

"How?" Karla frowned. "Besides, he knew it already. Didn't you?"

Saetan retrieved his glass and drained it to avoid answering. After all the hours he, Geoffrey, Andulvar, and Mephis had spent chewing over the implications of having this particular group of Queens coming into power at this time, none of them had thought of the obvious—that he was going to have to deal with them as Territory Queens.

A gong sounded throughout the Keep. Once. Twice. Thrice. Then, after a pause, a fourth time.

Four times for the four sides of a Blood triangle, the fourth side being what was held within the other three. Like the three males—Steward, Master of the Guard, and Consort—who formed a strong, intimate triangle around a Queen.

At the back of the room, huge double doors opened outward, revealing a dark emptiness.

Paying no attention to the hesitant stirring around him, Saetan set his glass aside, smoothed his hair, and straightened his new clothes. Since Protocol dictated that processions went from light Jewels to dark, first all the males and then the females, he would be at the end of the male line.

So he didn't realize no one had moved and that everyone was looking at him until Lucivar poked him.

"Protocol dictates—" he began.

"Screw Protocol," Karla replied succinctly. "*You* go first."

When everyone nodded agreement, he slowly walked toward the double doors. Lucivar and Andulvar fell into step on either side of him. Mephis, Geoffrey, and Prothvar followed them.

"What's in there?" Lucivar asked quietly.

"I don't know," Saetan replied. "I've never been in this part of the Keep before." He glanced back at Geoffrey, who shook his head.

They reached the doors and stopped. The lights from the room behind them revealed the first handful of wide, descending steps.

We'll all break our necks trying to go down without lights.

The thought was barely completed when little sparkles embedded in the dark stone began to glow, growing brighter and brighter.

Like swirls of stars, Saetan thought, his breath catching. Like the poem Geoffrey quoted to him years ago, about the great dragons who had created the Blood. *They spiral down into ebony, catching the stars with their tails.*

Ebony had once been the poetic term for the Darkness. Saetan froze, his foot suspended over the first step.

Was it still?

"Something wrong?" Lucivar whispered.

Saetan shook his head and slowly descended, grateful for the solid Eyrien strength on either side of him.

When he reached the bottom step, a second set of double doors swung inward. The midnight-black chamber slowly lightened, the dark giving way to the dawn. The light gradually spread from their end of the chamber to the other. But he noticed, as he moved forward, that it didn't illuminate the ceiling. At thrice his height, the light gave way to twilight, which, in its turn, yielded once again to the dark.

The back wall began to lighten from either side. Filling the wall, as high as the light reached, was a highly detailed bas-relief. A dreamscape, a nightscape, shapes rising up from and dissolving into others. Kindred shapes. Human shapes. Blending. Entwined. Fierce and beautiful. Ugly and gentle.

The light finally reached the center of the back wall and the Dark Throne. Three wide steps ran around the dais on three sides. On the dais itself was a simple blackwood chair with a high, carved back. Its simplicity said that the power that ruled here had no need for ornamentation or ostentation—especially when it was protected on the right-hand side by a huge dragon head coming out of the stone.

"Mother Night," Andulvar said in a hushed voice. "She created a sculpture of Lorn's head."

"Hell's fire," Lucivar whispered. "Where'd she find so many uncut Jewels to make the scales?"

Trembling, Saetan shook his head, unable to speak. Maybe Andulvar couldn't see the darkness beyond the lit bas-relief from where he stood, a darkness that suggested another large chamber beyond this one. Maybe he couldn't see the iridescent fire in the dragon's scales. Maybe he'd forgotten the sound of that ancient, powerful voice. Maybe . . .

Eyelids slowly opened. Midnight eyes pinned them where they stood.

Geoffrey clutched Saetan's arm, his fingers digging in

hard enough to hurt. "Mother Night, Saetan," Geoffrey said, his breathing ragged. "The Keep is his lair. He's been here all the time."

He hadn't expected Lorn to be so big. If the body was in proportion to the head . . .

Dragon scales. The Jewels were dragon scales somehow transformed into hard, translucent stones. Had there been dragons who matched the specific colors of the Jewels or had they all been that iridescent silver-gold, changing color to match the strength of the recipient?

Saetan gingerly touched the Black Jewel around his neck. His Birthright Red and the Black had been uncut Jewels. Were there two missing scales somewhere along the great body that must lie in the next chamber that would have matched his uncut Jewels?

Then he finally understood why there had been a hint of maleness in the uncut Jewels Jaenelle had been gifted with.

Lorn. The great Prince of the Dragons. The Guardian of the Keep.

Needing to get his mind focused on something other than the power that ancient body must contain, Saetan turned to Geoffrey. "His Queen. What was the name of his Queen?"

"Draca," said a sibilant voice behind them.

They turned and stared at the Keep's Seneschal.

Her lips curled in a tiny smile. "Her name wass Draca."

Looking into her eyes, Saetan wondered what subtle spell had been lifted that allowed him to see what he should have guessed long before. Her age, her strength, the uneasiness so many felt in her presence. Which made him think of something else. "Does Jaenelle know?"

Draca made a sound that might have been a laugh. "Sshe hass alwayss known, High Lord."

Saetan grimaced, then gave in as gracefully as he could. Even if he'd thought to ask, he doubted he'd have gotten an answer. Jaenelle was very good at keeping her own counsel.

"Are they relatives of yours?" Lucivar asked, indicating the Fyreborn dragons who were staring at Lorn.

"You are all relativess," Draca replied, looking pointedly at Lucivar's Ebon-gray Jewel. "We created the Blood. All the Blood. Therefore, you are all dragonss under the sskin."

Saetan glanced at the kindred who were edging closer. "You, of course, would know." He saw amusement in Draca's eyes.

"It iss not I who ssayss sso, High Lord. *Jaenelle* ssayss sso." Draca looked past them to the Dark Throne.

As one, they turned.

Dressed in that cobwebby black gown and wearing Ebon Jewels, Jaenelle sat serenely in the blackwood chair. Her long golden hair was brushed away from the face that finally revealed its unique beauty.

"The time has come for me to take up my duties as the Queen of Ebon Askavi," Jaenelle said. Her voice wasn't loud, but it carried throughout the chamber. "The time has come for me to choose my court."

A breathless tension filled the chamber.

Saetan concentrated on breathing slowly, steadily. For days he'd been telling himself that court service was for the young and vigorous, that he'd never intended to serve formally, that the unspoken service he performed was enough, that he had experienced serving in the Dark Court at Ebon Askavi when he'd been Cassandra's Consort.

Except he hadn't, because, in a way he couldn't put into words, it hadn't really been the Dark Court. Not like this one.

And he suddenly understood why Cassandra had withdrawn from them.

This was the court he had waited to serve in. *This* was the court he'd always craved. He wanted to serve the daughter of his soul, who had finally come into her dark, glorious power.

Witch. The living myth. Dreams made flesh.

This had been *his* dream.

And Lucivar's, he realized, seeing the fire in his son's eyes. Yes, Lucivar would have craved a Queen who could meet his strength.

Jaenelle's voice pulled him back. "Prince Chaosti, will you serve in the First Circle?"

Gracefully, Chaosti knelt on one knee, a fisted hand over his heart. "I will serve."

Saetan frowned. How was Chaosti going to serve in Jaenelle's First Circle when he'd already accepted service in Gabrielle's First Circle?

"Prince Kaelas, will you serve in the First Circle?"

I will serve.

He became more and more puzzled as Jaenelle called out name after name. Mephis, Prothvar, Aaron, Khardeen, Sceron, Jonah, Morton, Elan. Ladvarian, Mistral, Smoke, Sundancer.

And then he, Andulvar, and Lucivar were the only males left standing, and everything in him waited for her next words.

"Lady Karla, will you serve in the First Circle?"

"I will serve."

Shock ripped through Saetan, quickly followed by pain so intense he didn't think it would be possible to survive it. She hadn't forgiven him. At least, not enough.

"Lady Moonshadow, will you serve in the First Circle?"

I will serve.

He swallowed hard. He couldn't react, *wouldn't* let the others see the hurt. But if she was going to allow Mephis and Prothvar to serve, why not Andulvar? Why not Lucivar, who already served her?

He barely heard the other names being called out. Gabrielle, Morghann, Kalush, Grezande, Sabrina, Zylona, Katrine, Astar, Ash. On and on until all the witches had accepted a place in the court.

Draca and Geoffrey couldn't formally serve because they served the Keep itself. If there was comfort knowing that, it was a bitter brew.

He could feel Lucivar trembling beside him.

After a moment's silence, Jaenelle rose and walked down the three steps. Her eyes narrowed as she looked at him. He felt her exasperation as she lightly brushed against the first of his inner barriers.

She pushed up her left sleeve and made a small cut in her wrist.

Blood welled and ran.

"Prince Lucivar Yaslana, will you serve as First Escort and Warlord Prince of Ebon Rih?"

Lucivar stared at her for a heartbeat or two, then slowly approached her. "I will serve." He sank to his knees, held her left hand with his right, and placed his mouth over the wound.

Absolute surrender. Lifetime surrender. By accepting her blood, Lucivar surrendered every aspect of his being for all time. She would rule him, body and soul, mind and Jewels.

It wasn't long—it was a lifetime—before Lucivar lifted his mouth, rose, and stepped to one side, looking dazed.

Not surprising, Saetan thought. From where he stood, he could smell the heat, the strength that flowed in her veins.

"Prince Andulvar Yaslana, will you serve as Master of the Guard?"

"I will serve," Andulvar said, approaching her and sinking to his knees to accept the lifeblood.

When Andulvar stepped aside, Jaenelle looked at Saetan. "Prince Saetan Daemon SaDiablo, will you serve as Steward of the Dark Court?"

Saetan approached slowly, searching her eyes for some clue that would tell him which answer she truly wanted. Since he couldn't ask the question aloud, he reached hesitantly for her mind. *Are you sure?*

Of course I'm sure, she replied tartly. *There are times, Saetan, when you're an idiot. The only reason I waited was so that the three of you would know what you were getting into before you agreed.*

*In that case . . . * He sank to his knees. "I will serve."

Just before his mouth closed over the wound, just before his tongue had the first taste of her blood at its mature strength, Jaenelle added, *Besides, who else is going to be willing to referee squabbles?*

Giving her a sharp look, he took the blood. Night sky, deep earth, the song of the tides, the nurturing darkness of a woman's body. And fire. He tasted all of it, savored it as it washed through him, burned through him, branded him as hers.

He lifted his mouth and brushed a finger over the wound,

using healing Craft to seal it and stop the flow of blood.
It needs to be healed properly.

Soon. She withdrew her hand and returned to the
Dark Throne.

No, he decided as he got to his feet and heard everyone
else rising, this wasn't a good time for a display of male
stubbornness. Besides, the ceremony would be over shortly.

Notice anything odd about this court? Lucivar asked
him as tension filled the chamber again.

Surprised by the question, Saetan looked at all the solemn, determined faces. *Odd? No. They're the same . . . *

It finally struck him. He'd thought of it, discussed it, and
then had been so hurt when Jaenelle passed over him that
he had failed to see it. The coven had joined the First
Circle, and they shouldn't have because they were Territory Queens . . .

Karla stepped forward. "My Queen. May I speak?"

"You may speak, my Sister," Jaenelle replied solemnly.

. . . and Territory Queens served no one.

Contained fire lit Karla's ice-blue eyes as she said trium-
phantly, "Glacia yields to Ebon Askavi!"

Saetan choked on his heart. Mother Night! Karla was
making Jaenelle the ruling power of the Territory *she* was
supposed to rule.

Gabrielle stepped forward. "Dea al Mon yields to
Ebon Askavi!"

"Scelt yields to Ebon Askavi!" Morghann shouted.

"Nharkhava!" "Dharo!" "Tigrelan!" "Centauran!"

Sceval! *Arceria!* *The Fyreborn Islands!*

Someone nudged his back, breaking his stunned silence.
"Dhemlan yields to Ebon Askavi!"

He jumped when Andulvar roared, "Askavi yields to
Ebon Askavi!"

The shouted names of the Territories that now stood in
the shadow of Ebon Askavi finally stopped echoing through
the chamber. Then a small voice drifted into their minds.

Arachna yields to the Lady of the Black Mountain.

"Mother Night," Saetan whispered, and wondered if the
Weavers of Dreams were spinning their tangled webs across
the chamber's ceiling.

"I accept," Jaenelle said quietly.

Lucivar briefly squeezed Saetan's shoulder in amused sympathy. "Should I wish the Steward of this court my congratulations or condolences?" he said quietly.

"Mother Night." Saetan staggered back a step. Hands grabbed his arms, keeping him upright.

Lucivar laughed softly as he slipped around Saetan. He climbed the steps to the Throne and extended his right hand. Jaenelle rose and placed her left hand over his right. A wide aisle opened up as the new court stepped aside to allow the First Escort to lead his Queen from the chamber.

Starting to follow, Saetan felt something hold him back. Waving Andulvar and the others on, he felt his throat tighten as the kindred shyly blended in with the humans, once more offering their trust.

The chamber emptied, Draca and Geoffrey being the last to leave.

No longer having an excuse, Saetan turned toward Lorn. As they stared at one another, he felt gentle sadness pressing down on him, a sadness all the more terrible because it was cloaked in understanding. He knew then why Lorn had remained apart. He had experienced that kind of sadness, too, when petitioners had stood before him, terrified of the Prince of the Darkness, the High Lord of Hell. He knew how it felt to crave affection and companionship and have it denied because of what he was.

Fingering his Black Jewel, he said, "Thank you."

You have made good usse of my gift. You have sserved well.

Saetan thought of all he'd done in his life. All the mistakes, the regrets. All the blood spilled. "Have I?" he asked quietly, more to himself than Lorn.

You have honored the Darknesss. You have resspected the wayss of the Blood. You have alwayss undersstood what the Blood were meant to be—caretakerss and guardianss. You have ussed teeth and clawss when teeth and clawss were needed. You have protected your young. The Darknesss hass ssung to you, and you have followed roadss few but the Dragonss have walked. You have undersstood the Blood'ss heart, the Blood'ss ssoul. You have sserved well.

Saetan took a deep breath. His throat felt too tight to make an answer. "Thank you," he said hoarsely.

There was a long pause. *Ass sshe iss the daughter of your ssoul, you are the sson of mine.*

Saetan clutched the Jewel around his neck. Did Lorn have any idea what those words meant to him?

It didn't matter. What mattered was it formed a bond between them, a bridge he could cross. He would finally be able to talk to the keeper of all the Blood's Craft knowledge. Maybe he'd even find out how Jae—

"If I'm the daughter of Saetan's soul and he's the son of yours, does that make you my grandfather?" Jaenelle asked, joining them.

No, Lorn replied promptly.

"Why not?"

Hot, dusty-dry air hit them with enough force to push them back a couple of steps.

"I suppose that's an answer," Jaenelle grumped. She shook her arms to untangle all the cobwebby strands. "Although I don't see why you're getting all snorty about one little granddaughter."

"And the wide assortment of grandnieces and nephews that come with her," Saetan muttered under his breath.

Jaenelle gave him a sharp look and her wrists a last shake. "Well, at least you've finally met. You should've invited him sooner," she added, giving Lorn an I-told-you-so look.

He wass not ready. He wass too young.

Saetan would have protested but Jaenelle beat him to it.

"I was much younger when you invited me," Jaenelle said.

Saetan pressed an arm against his stomach and tried very hard to keep his expression neutral. But the emotional flavor of baffled male he was picking up from Lorn was making it very difficult.

I did not invite you, Jaenelle, Lorn said slowly.

"Yes, you did. Sort of. Well, not as blatantly as Saetan did—"

Saetan clamped his teeth together and made a funny, fizzy noise.

"—but I heard you, so I answered." She smiled at both of them.

Being smiled at like that was a good reason for a man to panic.

Before he had time to, Jaenelle rapidly headed for the stairs, muttering something about having to be there for the toast, and Lucivar had a very strong hand clamped on his shoulder.

"If great-grandpapa is finished with you," Lucivar said with a feral smile, "I'd like you to come upstairs and lean hard on Karla because, Queen of Glacia or not, if she makes one more of those smart-ass remarks about wingspans, I'm going to drop her into a deep mountain lake."

"Lucivar, this is a dignified occasion," Saetan said at the same time Lorn said, *I am not your great-grandpapa.*

"No, you're not," Lucivar agreed. "But since no one was quite sure how many generations separate them from you— and it's different for each race or species—it was decided to condense all the generations into one 'great.' As for this being a dignified occasion, it was. As for the party that's waiting for Saetan to make the opening toast, I suspect it's going to be a lot of things and none of them are going to be remotely close to dignified." Lucivar looked at them and let out a pitying sigh. "You're both old enough to know better. And you've both known Jaenelle long enough to know better."

Saetan found himself being steered toward the doors at the other end of the chamber.

"Come on, be a good papa and let great-grandpapa dragon get some rest before all the little dragons pile on top of him."

Reaching the stairs, Saetan thought that the inner doors to the chamber closed just a little too quickly.

We will talk, Lorn said softly. *There iss much to talk about.*

Yes, there was, Saetan thought as he entered the upper chamber, accepted a glass of yarbarah, and looked at the animated, laughing faces that now ruled Kaeleer.

He wondered what Lorn thought about the many-strand web Jaenelle had woven over Kaeleer, the web that had called so many races out of the mist they'd hidden in for thousands of years.

And he wondered what the Dark Council was going to think.

4 / Kaeleer

Lord Magstrom rubbed his forehead and wished, violently, that this session of the Dark Council would end soon. Lord Jorval, the First Tribune, had been making soothing noises and deftly evading making firm promises since the first petitioner had stepped into the circle. They all wanted the same thing: assurance that the males sent into the kindred lands that had been granted as human territories wouldn't be slaughtered by these "Hell-spawned animals."

The Council couldn't give such assurances.

The stories told by the few survivors who returned from those first attempts to secure the land had roused a great anger in the people of Little Terreille and demands for retaliation. The piles of mutilated corpses—some partially eaten—that clogged the main street of Goth a few days later when all the males who had gone into kindred lands were mysteriously returned had chilled that anger into furious impotence.

Everyone wanted something done to make these unclaimed lands safe for human occupation. No one wanted to face what was already living in those "unclaimed" lands.

"I assure you, Lady," Lord Jorval said to the strident petitioner, "we're doing everything possible to rectify the situation."

"When I came here, I was promised land to rule and males who knew how to serve properly," the Terreillean Queen replied angrily.

Lord Magstrom wondered if anyone else had noticed that the majority of Kaeleer-born males, even with the enticement of serving in the First or Second Circle of a Terreillean Queen's court, resigned with bitter animosity after a

few weeks of service. Terreillean males pleaded to serve
Kaeleer-born Queens, willing to serve in the Thirteenth
Circle as a menial servant if that's all that was available.
Over the past three years, he'd had a few tearfully beg him
to approach minor Queens outside of Little Terreille and
see if there was any way they could serve in a Territory
like Dharo or Nharkhava. They would do anything, they'd
told him. Anything.

For some of the younger ones he thought might be acceptable to those Territory Queens, he'd written respectful
letters pointing out the men's skills and their pledged willingness to adapt to the ways of the Shadow Realm. Some
had been accepted into service. At each turn of the season,
he received brief letters from each of those young men,
and all of them expressed their relief and delight in their
new life.

But the pleas were getting more desperate as more and
more Terreilleans flooded into Little Terreille. And with
every plea, with every story he heard about Terreille, he
worried more and more about his youngest granddaughter.
Even in his small village incidents had already occurred,
and it was no longer wise for a woman to travel after dusk
without a strong escort. Was that how it had begun in Terreille, with fear and distrust spiraling deeper and deeper
until there was no way to stop it?

"Your request has been noted," Lord Jorval said, making
a gesture that indicated dismissal. "Will the next—"

The doors at the end of the chamber blew open with a
force that sent them crashing into the walls.

Jaenelle Angelline glided into the Council chamber, once
again standing outside the petitioner's circle, once again
flanked by the High Lord and Prince Lucivar Yaslana.
Along the edges of her black, cobwebby gown's low neckline were dozens of Black Jewel chips glittering with dark
fire. Around her neck was a Black—Black?—Jewel set in
a necklace that looked like a spider's web made of delicate
gold and silver strands. In her hands . . .

Lord Magstrom's hands shook.

She held a scepter. The lower half was made of gold and
silver and had two Black-looking Jewels inset above the

hand-hold. The upper half of the scepter was a spiraled horn.

Fingers pointed at the horn. Murmurs filled the chamber.

"Lady Angelline, I must protest your interrupting—" Jorval began.

"I have something to say to this Council," Jaenelle said coldly, her voice carrying over the others. "It will not take long."

The murmurs grew louder, more forceful.

"Why is *she* allowed to have a unicorn's horn?" the dismissed Terreillean Queen shouted. "*I* wasn't allowed to have one as compensation for my men being killed."

There was no expression on the High Lord's face as he looked at the Terreillean Queen. Lucivar, however, didn't try to hide his loathing.

"Silence." Jaenelle didn't raise her voice, but the undisguised malevolence in it hushed everyone. She looked at the Terreillean Queen and spoke five words.

Lord Magstrom knew enough of the Old Tongue to recognize the language but not enough to understand. Something about remembering?

Jaenelle caressed the horn, stroking it from base to tip and back down. "His name was Kaetien," she said in her midnight voice. "This horn was a gift, freely given."

"Lady Angelline," Jorval said, pounding on the Tribunal's bench as he tried to regain order.

From the seats closest to the Tribunal's bench, Lord Magstrom heard harsh voices talking about *some* people who thought they could ignore the authority of the *Council.*

Jaenelle swung the scepter in an arc, holding it for a moment when the horn pointed at the floor before swinging it up until it pointed at the chamber ceiling.

A cold wind whipped through the chamber. Thunder shook the building. Lightning came down from the ceiling and entered the unicorn's horn.

Dark power filled the chamber. Unyielding, unforgiving power.

When the thunder finally stopped, when the wind finally died, the shaking members of the Dark Council climbed back into their seats.

Jaenelle Angelline stood calmly, quietly, the scepter once again held in both hands. The unicorn's horn was unmarked, but Magstrom could see the flashes of lightning now held within those Black-but-not-Black Jewels, could feel the power waiting to be unleashed.

"Hear me," Jaenelle said, "because I will say this only once. I have made the Offering to the Darkness. I am now the Queen of Ebon Askavi." She pointed the scepter at the Tribunal's bench.

Lord Magstrom shook. The horn was pointing straight at him. He held his breath, waiting for the strike. Instead, a rolled parchment tied with a blood-red ribbon appeared in front of him.

"That is a list of the Territories that yielded to Ebon Askavi. They now stand in the shadow of the Keep. They are mine. Anyone who tries to settle in my Territory without my consent will be dealt with. Anyone who harms any of my people will be executed. There will be no excuses and no exceptions. I will say it simply so that the members of this Council and the intruders who thought to take land they had no right to claim can never say they misunderstood." Jaenelle's lips curled into a snarl. "STAY OUT OF MY TERRITORY!"

The words rang through the chamber, echoing and reechoing.

Her sapphire eyes, eyes that didn't look quite human, held the Tribunal for a long moment. Then she turned and glided out of the Council chamber, followed by the High Lord and Prince Yaslana.

Magstrom's hands shook so hard it took him four tries to untie the blood-red ribbon. He unrolled the parchment, ignoring the fact that he should have given it to Jorval as First Tribune.

Name after name after name after name. Some he'd heard of as stories his grandmother used to tell him. Some he'd heard of as "unclaimed land." Some he'd never heard of at all.

Name after name after name.

At the bottom of the parchment, above Jaenelle's signature and black-wax seal, was a map of Kaeleer, the Territories that now stood in the shadow of the Keep shaded in.

Except for Little Terreille and the island that had been granted to the Dark Council centuries ago, the Shadow Realm now belonged to Jaenelle Angelline.

Magstrom looked at the graceful, calligraphic signature. She had stood before the Council twice as a maid, and twice they had ignored the warnings of what she would become. Now they had to deal with a Queen who would not tolerate mistakes.

He shuddered and looked at the seal. In the center was a mountain. Overlaying the mountain was a unicorn's horn. Around the edge of the seal were five words in the Old Tongue.

A small piece of folded paper suddenly appeared on top of the seal. Magstrom grabbed it at the same moment Jorval pulled the parchment out of his hands. While Jorval and the Second Tribune read the list to the rest of the Council, their voices quivering more and more as they realized what it meant, Magstrom unfolded the paper, keeping it hidden.

A masculine hand had written the same five words that were on the seal. Below them was the translation.

For remembrance. As a reminder.

Magstrom looked up.

The High Lord stood just outside the open chamber doors.

Magstrom nodded slightly and vanished the paper, relieved no one had noticed that Saetan had remained behind to give him that message.

He would take the warning to heart and send a message home tonight. His two older granddaughters had made happy marriages outside of Little Terreille. He'd tell Arnora, his youngest granddaughter, to go to one of her sisters' homes immediately. Once she was there, surely there would be some way of persuading the new Queen of Dharo or Nharkhava to permit her to stay.

Half-listening to the Council's indignant, frightened babbling, Magstrom felt a flicker of hope for Arnora's future.

He didn't know the new Queens, but he knew someone who did.

After all the whispers, after all the stories, he thought it was fitting irony that the one person he could go to who would sympathize with his concerns and assist him was the High Lord of Hell.

5 / Kaeleer

"I never wanted to rule," Jaenelle said as she and Saetan strolled through the Keep's moonlit gardens. "I never wanted power over anyone's life but my own."

Saetan slipped an arm around her waist. "I know. That's why you're the perfect Queen to rule Kaeleer." When she looked puzzled, he laughed softly. "You're the one person who can weave all the separate strands into a unified web while still encouraging every strand to remain distinct. If you promise not to snarl at me, I'll tell you a secret."

"What? Okay, okay. I promise not to snarl."

"You've been ruling Kaeleer unofficially for years now, and you're probably the only person who hasn't realized it."

Jaenelle snarled, then muttered, "Sorry."

Saetan laughed. "Forgiven. But knowing that should be some comfort. I doubt there's going to be much difference between the official Dark Court and the unofficial one that was formed the first summer the coven and the boyos descended on the Hall and made it a second home."

Jaenelle brushed her hair away from her face. "Well, if that's true, then you *really* were an idiot not to have realized you would become the Steward since you've been the unofficial Steward for at least as long as I've been the unofficial Queen."

Since there was no good way to respond to that, he didn't.

"Saetan . . ." Jaenelle nibbled her lower lip. "You don't think they'll start acting differently now, do you? It's never made a difference before, but . . . the coven and the boyos aren't going to start acting subservient, are they?"

Saetan raised an eyebrow. "I'm surprised any of you know the word, let alone what it means." He hugged her. "I wouldn't worry about it. I think Lucivar's about as subservient as he's going to get."

Jaenelle leaned against him and groaned. Then she perked up a bit. "Well, that's one good thing about forming the court. At least I found something for him to do that'll keep him from being underfoot and badgering me all the time."

Saetan started to reply, then thought better of it. She was entitled to a few illusions—especially since they wouldn't last long.

Jaenelle yawned. "I'm going in. I'm telling the bedtime story tonight." She kissed his cheek. "Good night, Papa."

"Good night, witch-child." He waited until she'd gone inside before heading for the far end of the garden.

"The waif turned in early?" Andulvar asked, falling into step.

"She's doing the bedtime story and howl-along," Saetan replied.

"She'll be a good Queen, SaDiablo."

"The best we've ever had." They walked in silence for a couple of minutes. "The bitch has gone to ground again?"

Andulvar nodded. "Plenty of indications that she's got her hooks firmly into the Dark Council, but no sign of her. Hekatah was always good at staying out of the nastiness once she got it started. It still surprises me that she managed to get herself killed in the last war between the Realms." He rubbed the back of his neck and sighed. "It must be biting Hekatah's ass that the waif's got the kind of power over a Realm that she's always wanted."

"Yes, it must be. So stay sharp, all right?"

"We should warn all the boyos before they return to their own Territories so they know what to look for in case she tries to come in from another direction."

"Agreed. But if the Darkness is kind, we'll have some time for these youngsters to get some ground under their feet before we have to deal with another of Hekatah's schemes."

"If the Darkness is kind." Andulvar cleared his throat.

"I know why you've wanted to wait, and I know who you've been waiting for, but, Saetan, Jaenelle's a grown woman and she's the Queen now. The triangle should be complete. She should have a Consort."

Saetan rested his arms on the top of the garden's stone wall. A soft, night wind sang through the pines beyond the garden. "She already has a Consort," he said quietly, firmly. "As First Escort, Lucivar can stand in for most of a Consort's duties and be the third side of the triangle until . . ." His voice faded.

"If ever, SaDiablo," Andulvar said with gentle roughness. "Until someone wears the Consort's ring, every ambitious buck in the Realm—and not a few of them being straight from Terreille—is going to be trying to slip into her bed for the power and prestige he'll gain by being her Consort. She needs a good man, Saetan, not a memory. She needs a strong, flesh-and-blood man who'll warm her bed at night because he cares about *her*."

Saetan stared at the land beyond the garden. "She has a Consort."

"Does she?" When Saetan didn't answer, Andulvar patted his shoulder and walked away.

Saetan stayed there a long time, listening to the night wind's song. "She has a Consort," he whispered. "Doesn't she?"

The night wind didn't answer.

6 / The Twisted Kingdom

He climbed.

The land wasn't as twisted here or as steep, but the mist-wisps that filled the hollows sometimes covered the trail, leaving him with the unsettling feeling that nothing existed below his knees.

As time passed, he realized the place felt familiar, that he had explored these roads before when he had been strong and whole. He had entered the borderland that separated sanity from the Twisted Kingdom.

The air held a dew-fresh softness. The light was gentle,

like early morning. Somewhere nearby, birds chirped and twittered the day awake, and in the distance was the sound of heavy surf.

His crystal chalice was almost intact. During the long climb, the fragments had fit into place, one by one. There were a few slivers, a few memories missing. One in particular. He couldn't remember what he had done the night Jaenelle had been brought to Cassandra's Altar.

As he passed between two large stones that stood like sentinels, one on either side of the trail, the mist rose up around him.

Ahead of him were the water, the birds, the smell of rich earth, the warmth of the sun—and her promise that she would be waiting for him.

Ahead of him was sanity.

But there was also knowledge there, pain there. He could feel it.

Daemon.

A familiar voice, but not the one he longed to hear. He sorted through his memories until he could attach a name to the voice.

Manny. Talking to someone about toast and eggs.

Daemon.

He knew that voice, too. Surreal.

A part of him ached for ordinary conversation, for simple things like toast and eggs. A part of him was very afraid.

He took a step backward . . . and felt a door gently close behind him.

The stone sentinels had become a high, solid wall.

He leaned against it, trembling.

No way back.

Daemon.

Gathering up his shredded courage, he walked toward the voices, toward the promise.

Walked out of the Twisted Kingdom.

Queen of the Darkness concludes the story
of Saetan, Daemon, Lucivar, and Jaenelle.

The *New York Times* bestselling Black Jewels Series

by Anne Bishop

"Darkly mesmerizing...fascinatingly different."
—*Locus*

This is the story of the heir to a dark throne, a magic more powerful than that of the High Lord of Hell, and an ancient prophecy. These books tell of a ruthless game of politics and intrigue, magic and betrayal, love and sacrifice, destiny and fulfillment.

Daughter of the Blood
Heir to the Shadows
Queen of the Darkness
The Invisible Ring
Dreams Made Flesh
Tangled Webs
The Shadow Queen
Shalador's Lady

R420

THE TIR ALAINN TRILOGY

by

Anne Bishop

The Pillars of the World, **Book I:**
"Bishop only adds luster to her reputation for
fine fantasy." —*Booklist*

Shadows and Light, **Book II:**
"Plenty of thrills, faerie magic, human nastiness, and
romance." —*Locus*

The House of Gaian, **Book III:**
"A vivid fantasy world....Beautiful." —*BookBrowser*